# LINDA LAEL MILLER

HOLIDAY IN STONE CREEK

D0003499

HQN™

ISBN-13: 978-0-373-77606-1

HOLIDAY IN STONE CREEK

Copyright © 2011 by Harlequin Books S.A.

The publisher acknowledges the copyright holder of the individual works as follows:

A STONE CREEK CHRISTMAS
Copyright © 2008 by Linda Lael Miller

AT HOME IN STONE CREEK
Copyright © 2009 by Linda Lael Miller

PLEASE RECYCLE
THIS PRODUCT IS RECYCLABLE

Recycling programs
for this product may
not exist in your area.

Also available from
# LINDA LAEL MILLER
### and HQN Books

### The McKettricks of Texas

*McKettricks of Texas: Tate*
*McKettricks of Texas: Garrett*
*McKettricks of Texas: Austin*
*A Lawman's Christmas*

### The McKettricks series

*McKettrick's Choice*
*McKettrick's Luck*
*McKettrick's Pride*
*McKettrick's Heart*
*A McKettrick Christmas*

### The Montana Creeds series

*Logan*
*Dylan*
*Tyler*
*A Creed Country Christmas*

### The Mojo Sheepshanks series

*Deadly Gamble*
*Deadly Deceptions*

### The Stone Creek series

*The Man from Stone Creek*
*A Wanted Man*
*The Rustler*
*The Bridegroom*

### The Creed Cowboys

*A Creed in Stone Creek*
*Creed's Honor*
*The Creed Legacy*

# CONTENTS

# A STONE CREEK CHRISTMAS

For Sandi Howlett, dog foster mom, with love. Thank you.

# CHAPTER ONE

SOMETIMES, ESPECIALLY in the dark of night, when pure exhaustion sank Olivia O'Ballivan, DVM, into deep and stuporous sleep, she heard them calling—the finned, the feathered, the four-legged.

Horses, wild or tame, dogs beloved and dogs lost, far from home, cats abandoned alongside country roads because they'd become a problem for someone, or left behind when an elderly owner died.

The neglected, the abused, the unwanted, the lonely.

Invariably, the message was the same: *Help me.*

Even when Olivia tried to ignore the pleas, telling herself she was only *dreaming,* she invariably sprang to full wakefulness as though she'd been catapulted from the bottom of a canyon. It didn't matter how many eighteen-hour days she'd worked, between making stops at farms and ranches all over the county, putting in her time at the veterinary clinic in Stone Creek, overseeing the plans for the new, state-of-the-art shelter her famous big brother, Brad, a country musician, was building with the proceeds from a movie he'd starred in.

Tonight it was a reindeer.

Olivia sat blinking in her tousled bed, trying to catch her breath. Shoved both hands through her short dark hair. Her current foster dog, Ginger, woke up, too, stretching, yawning.

*A reindeer?*

"O'Ballivan," she told herself, flinging off the covers to sit up on the edge of the mattress, "you've really gone around the bend this time."

But the silent cry persisted, plaintive and confused.

Olivia only sometimes heard actual words when the animals spoke, though Ginger was articulate—generally, it was more of an unformed concept made up of strong emotion and often images, somehow coalescing into an intuitive imperative. But she could see the reindeer clearly in her mind's eye, standing on a frozen roadway, bewildered.

She recognized the adjoining driveway as her own. A long way down, next to the tilted mailbox on the main road. The poor creature wasn't hurt—just lost. Hungry and thirsty, too—and terribly afraid. Easy prey for hungry wolves and coyotes.

"There are no reindeer in Arizona," Olivia told Ginger, who looked skeptical as she hauled her arthritic yellow Lab/golden retriever self up off her comfy bed in the corner of Olivia's cluttered bedroom. "Absolutely, positively, no doubt about it, there *are no reindeer in Arizona.*"

*"Whatever,"* Ginger replied with another yawn, already heading for the door as Olivia pulled sweatpants on over her boxer pajama bottoms. She tugged a hoodie, left over from one of her brother's preretirement concert tours, over her head and jammed her feet into the totally unglamorous work boots she wore to wade through pastures and barns.

Olivia lived in a small rental house in the country, though once the shelter was finished, she'd be moving into a spacious apartment upstairs, living in town. She drove an old gray Suburban that had belonged to her late grandfather, called Big John by everyone who knew him, and did not aspire to anything fancier. She had not exactly been feathering her nest since she'd graduated from veterinary school.

Her twin sisters, Ashley and Melissa, were constantly after her to 'get her act together,' find herself a man, have a family. Both of them were single, with no glimmer of honeymoon cottages and white picket fences on the horizon, so in Olivia's opinion, they didn't have a lot of room to talk. It was just that she was a few years older than they were, that was all.

Anyway, it wasn't as if she didn't want those things— she did—but between her practice and the "Dr. Dolittle routine," as Brad referred to her admittedly weird animal-communication skills, there simply weren't enough hours in the day to do it all.

Since the rental house was old, the garage was detached. Olivia and Ginger made their way through a deep, powdery field of snow. The Suburban was no spiffy rig—most of the time it was splattered with muddy slush and worse—but it always ran, in any kind of weather. And it would go practically anywhere.

"Try getting to a stranded reindeer in that sporty little red number Melissa drives," Olivia told Ginger as she shoved up the garage door. "Or that silly hybrid of Ashley's."

*"I wouldn't mind taking a spin in the sports car,"* Ginger replied, plodding gamely up the special wooden steps Olivia dragged over to the passenger side of the Suburban. Ginger was getting older, after all, and her joints gave her problems, especially since her "accident." Certain concessions had to be made.

"Fat chance," Olivia said, pushing back the steps once Ginger was settled in the shotgun seat, then closing the car door. Moments later she was sliding in on the driver's side, shoving the key into the ignition, cranking up the geriatric engine. "You know how Melissa is about dog hair. You might tear a hole in her fancy leather upholstery with one of those Fu-Manchu toenails of yours."

*"She likes dogs,"* Ginger insisted with a magnanimous lift of her head. *"It's just that she thinks she's allergic."* Ginger always believed the best of everyone in particular and humanity in general, even though she'd been ditched alongside a highway, with two of her legs fractured, after her first owner's vengeful boyfriend had tossed her out of a moving car. Olivia had come along a few minutes later, homing in on the mystical distress call bouncing between her head and her heart, and rushed Ginger to the clinic, where she'd had multiple surgeries and a long, difficult recovery.

Olivia flipped on the windshield wipers, but she still squinted to see through the huge, swirling flakes. "My sister," she said, "is a hypochondriac."

*"It's just that Melissa hasn't met the right dog yet,"* Ginger maintained. *"Or the right man."*

"Don't start about men," Olivia retorted, peering out, looking for the reindeer.

*"He's out there, you know,"* Ginger remarked, panting as she gazed out at the snowy night.

"The reindeer or the man?"

*"Both,"* Ginger said with a dog smile.

"What am I going to do with a reindeer?"

*"You'll think of something,"* Ginger replied. *"It's almost Christmas. Maybe there's an APB from the North*

*Pole. I'd check Santa's website if I had opposable thumbs."*

"Funny," Olivia said, not the least bit amused. "If you had opposable thumbs, you'd order things off infomercials just because you like the UPS man so much. We'd be inundated with get-rich-quick real estate courses, herbal weight loss programs and stuff to whiten our teeth." The ever-present ache between her shoulder blades knotted itself up tighter as she scanned the darkness on either side of the narrow driveway. Christmas. One more thing she didn't have the time for, let alone the requisite enthusiasm, but Brad and his new wife, Meg, would put up a big tree right after Thanksgiving, hunt her down and shanghai her if she didn't show up for the family festival at Stone Creek Ranch, especially since Mac had come along six months before, and this was Baby's First Christmas. And because Carly, Meg's teenage sister, was spending the semester in Italy, as part of a special program for gifted students, and both Brad and Meg missed her to distraction. Ashley would throw her annual open house at the bed-and-breakfast, and Melissa would probably decide she was allergic to mistletoe and holly and develop convincing symptoms.

Olivia would go, of course. To Brad and Meg's because she loved them, and *adored* Mac. To Ashley's open house because she loved her kid sister, too, and could mostly forgive her for being Martha Stewart incarnate. Damn, she'd even pick up nasal spray and chicken soup for Melissa, though she drew the line at actually cooking.

*"There's Blitzen,"* Ginger said, adding a cheerful yip.

Sure enough, the reindeer loomed in the snow-speckled cones of gold from the headlights.

Olivia put on the brakes, shifted the engine into neutral. "You stay here," she said, pushing open the door.

*"Like I'm going outside in* this *weather,"* Ginger said with a sniff.

Slowly Olivia approached the reindeer. The creature was small, definitely a miniature breed, with eyes big and dark and luminous in the light from the truck, and it stood motionless.

*"Lost,"* it told her, not having Ginger's extensive vocabulary. If she ever found a loving home for that dog, she'd miss the long conversations, even though they had very different political views.

The deer had antlers, which meant it was male.

"Hey, buddy," she said. "Where did you come from?"

*"Lost,"* the reindeer repeated. Either he was dazed or not particularly bright. Like humans, animals were unique beings, some of them Einsteins, most of them ordinary joes.

"Are you hurt?" she asked, to be certain. Her intuition was rarely wrong where such things were concerned, but there was always the off chance.

Nothing.

She approached, slowly and carefully. Ran skillful hands over pertinent parts of the animal. No blood, no obvious breaks, though sprains and hairline fractures were a possibility. No identifying tags or notched ears.

The reindeer stood still for the examination, which might have meant he was tame, though Olivia couldn't be certain of that. Nearly every animal she encountered, wild or otherwise, allowed her within touching distance. Once, with help from Brad and Jesse McKettrick, she'd treated a wounded stallion who'd never been shod, fitted with a halter, or ridden.

"You're gonna be okay now," she told the little deer. It *did* look as though it ought to be hitched to Santa's sleigh. There was a silvery cast to its coat, its antlers were delicately etched and it was petite—barely bigger than Ginger.

She cocked a thumb toward the truck. "Can you follow me to my place, or shall I put you in the back?" she asked.

The reindeer ducked its head. Shy, then. And weary.

"But you've already traveled a long way, haven't you?" Olivia went on.

She opened the back of the Suburban, pulled out the sturdy ramp she always carried for Ginger and other four-legged passengers no longer nimble enough to make the jump.

The deer hesitated, probably catching Ginger's scent.

"Not to worry," Olivia said. "Ginger's a lamb. Hop aboard there, Blitzen."

*"His name is Rodney,"* Ginger announced. She'd turned, forefeet on the console, to watch them over the backseat.

"On Dasher, on Dancer, on Prancer or—Rodney," Olivia said, gesturing, but giving the animal plenty of room.

Rodney raised his head at the sound of his name, seemed to perk up a little. Then he pranced right up the ramp, into the back of the Suburban, and lay down on a bed of old feed sacks with a heavy reindeer snort.

Olivia closed the back doors of the rig as quietly as she could, so Rodney wouldn't be startled.

"How did you know his name?" Olivia asked once she was back in the driver's seat. "All I'm getting from him is 'Lost.'"

*"He told me,"* Ginger said. *"He's not ready to go into a lot of detail about his past. There's a touch of amnesia, too. Brought on by the emotional trauma of losing his way."*

"Have you been watching soap operas again, while I'm away working? *Dr. Phil? Oprah?*"

*"Only when you forget and leave the TV on when you go out. I don't have opposable thumbs, remember?"*

Olivia shoved the recalcitrant transmission into reverse, backed into a natural turnaround and headed back up the driveway toward the house. She supposed she should have taken Rodney to the clinic for X-rays, or over to the homeplace, where there was a barn, but it was the middle of the night, after all.

If she went to the clinic, all the boarders would wake up, barking and meowing fit to wake the whole town. If she went to Stone Creek Ranch, she'd probably wake the baby, and both Brad and Meg were sleep deprived as it was.

So Rodney would have to spend what remained of the night on the enclosed porch. She'd make him a bed with some of the old blankets she kept on hand, give him water, see if he wouldn't nosh on a few of Ginger's kibbles. In the morning she'd attend to him properly. Take him to town for those X-rays and a few blood tests, haul him to Brad's if he was well enough to travel, fix him up with a stall of his own. Get him some deer chow from the feed and grain.

Rodney drank a whole bowl of water once Olivia had coaxed him up the steps and through the outer door onto the enclosed porch. He kept a watchful eye on Ginger, though she didn't growl or make any sudden moves, the way some dogs would have done.

Instead, Ginger gazed up at Olivia, her soulful eyes glowing with practical compassion. *"I'd better sleep out here with Rodney,"* she said. *"He's still pretty scared. The washing machine has him a little spooked."*

This was a great concession on Ginger's part, for she loved her wide, fluffy bed. Ashley had made it for her, out of the softest fleece she could find, and even monogrammed the thing. Olivia smiled at the image of her blond, curvaceous sister seated at her beloved sewing machine, whirring away.

"You're a good dog," she said, her eyes burning a little as she bent to pat Ginger's head.

Ginger sighed. Another day, another noble sacrifice, the sound seemed to say.

Olivia went into her bedroom and got Ginger's bed. Put it on the floor for her. Carried the water bowl back to the kitchen for a refill.

When she returned to the porch the second time, Rodney was lying on the cherished dog bed, and Ginger was on the pile of old blankets.

"Ginger, your bed—?"

Ginger yawned yet again, rested her muzzle on her forelegs and rolled her eyes upward. *"Everybody needs a soft place to land,"* she said sleepily. *"Even reindeer."*

THE PONY WAS NOT a happy camper.

Tanner Quinn leaned against the stall door. He'd just bought Starcross Ranch, and Butterpie, his daughter's pet, had arrived that day, trucked in by a horse-delivery outfit hired by his sister, Tessa, along with his own palomino gelding, Shiloh.

Shiloh was settling in just fine. Butterpie was having a harder time of it.

Tanner sighed, shifted his hat to the back of his head. He probably should have left Shiloh and Butterpie at his sister's place in Kentucky, where they'd had all that fabled bluegrass to run in and munch on, since the ranch wasn't going to be his permanent home, or theirs. He'd picked it up as an investment, at a fire-sale price, and would live there while he oversaw the new construction project in Stone Creek—a year at the outside.

It was the latest in a long line of houses that never had time to become homes. He came to each new place, bought a house or a condo, built something big and sleek and expensive, then moved on, leaving the property he'd temporarily occupied in the hands of some eager real-estate agent.

The new project, an animal shelter, was not his usual thing—he normally designed and erected office buildings, multimillion-dollar housing compounds for movie stars and moguls, and the occasional government-sponsored school, bridge or hospital, somewhere on foreign soil—usually hostile. Before his wife, Katherine, died five years ago, she'd traveled with him, bringing Sophie along.

But then—

Tanner shook off the memory. Thinking about the way Katherine had been killed required serious bourbon, and he'd been off the sauce for a long time. He'd never developed a drinking problem, but the warning signs had been there, and he'd decided to save Sophie—and himself—the extra grief. He'd put the cork back in the bottle and left it there for good.

It should have been him, not Kat. That was as far as he could go, sober.

He shifted his attention back to the little cream-colored pony standing forlornly in its fancy new stall. He was no vet, but he didn't have to be to diagnose the problem. The horse missed Sophie, now ensconced in a special high-security boarding school in Connecticut.

He missed her, too. More than the horse did, for sure. But she was *safe* in that high-walled and distant place—safe from the factions who'd issued periodic death threats over things he'd built. The school was like a fortress—he'd designed it himself, and his best friend, Jack McCall, a Special Forces veteran and big-time security consultant, had installed the systems. They were top-of-the-line, best available. The children and grandchildren of presidents, congressmen, Oscar winners and software inventors attended that school—it had to be kidnap-proof, and it was.

Sophie had begged him not to leave her there.

Even as Tanner reflected on that, his cell phone rang. Sophie had chosen the ring tone before their most recent parting—the theme song from *How the Grinch Stole Christmas.*

He, of course, was the Grinch.

"Tanner Quinn," he said, even though he knew this wasn't a business call. The habit was ingrained.

"I *hate* this place!" Sophie blurted without preamble. "It's like a *prison!*"

"Soph," Tanner began, on another sigh. "Your roommate sings lead for your favorite rock band of all time. How bad can it be?"

"I want to come home!"

*If only we had one,* Tanner thought. The barely palatable reality was that he and Sophie had lived like Gypsies—if not actual fugitives—since Kat's death.

"Honey, you know I won't be here long. You'd make

friends, get settled in and then it would be time to move on again."

"I want you," Sophie all but wailed. Tanner's heart caught on a beat. "I want Butterpie. I want to be a *regular kid!*"

Sophie would never be a "regular kid." She was only twelve and already taking college-level courses—another advantage of attending an elite school. The classes were small, the computers were powerful enough to guide satellites and the visiting lecturers were world-renowned scientists, historians, linguistics experts and mathematical superstars.

"Honey—"

"Why can't I live in Stoner Creek, with you and Butterpie?"

A smile tugged at one corner of Tanner's mouth. "*Stone* Creek," he said. "If there are any stoners around here, I haven't made their acquaintance yet."

Not that he'd really made *anybody's* acquaintance. He hadn't been in town more than a few days. He knew the real estate agent who'd sold him Starcross, and Brad O'Ballivan, because he'd built a palace for him once, outside Nashville, which was how he'd gotten talked into the animal-shelter contract.

Brad O'Ballivan. He'd thought the hotshot country-and-western music star would never settle down. Now he was over-the-top in love with his bride, Meg, and wanted all his friends married off, too. He probably figured if he could fall that hard for a woman out here in Noplace, U.S.A., Tanner might, too.

"Dad, please," Sophie said, sniffling now. Somehow his daughter's brave attempt to suck it up got to Tanner even more than the crying had. "Get me out of here. If

I can't come to Stone Creek, maybe I could stay with Aunt Tessa again, like I did last summer…."

Tanner took off his hat, moved along the breezeway to the barn doorway, shut off the lights. "You know your aunt is going through a rough time right now," he said quietly. *A rough time?* Tessa and her no-account husband, Paul Barker, were getting a divorce. Among other things, Barker had gotten another woman pregnant—a real blow to Tess, who'd wanted a child ever since she'd hit puberty—and now she was fighting to hold on to her home. She'd bought that horse farm with her own money, having been a successful TV actress in her teens, and poured everything she had into it—including the contents of her investment portfolio. Against Tanner's advice, she hadn't insisted on a prenup.

*We're in love,* she'd told him, starry-eyed with happiness.

Paul Barker hadn't had the proverbial pot to piss in, of course. And within a month of the wedding he'd been a signer on every account Tess had. As the marriage deteriorated, so did Tess's wealth.

Cold rage jangled along Tanner's nerves, followed the fault line in his soul. At Kat's suggestion, he'd set up a special trust fund for Tess, way back, and it was a damn good thing he had. To this day, she didn't know the money existed—he and Kat hadn't wanted Barker to tap into it—and when she did find out, her fierce Quinn pride would probably force her to refuse it.

At least if she lost the horse farm to Barker and his dream team of lawyers—more like *nightmare* team— she'd have the means to start over. The question was, would she have the *heart* to make a new beginning?

"Dad?" Sophie asked. "Are you still there?"

"I'm here," Tanner said, looking around at the night-shrouded landscape surrounding him. There must have been a foot of snow on the ground already, with more coming down. Hell, November wasn't even over yet.

"Couldn't I at least come home for Christmas?"

"Soph, we don't *have* a home, remember?"

She was sniffling again. "Sure we do," she said very softly. "Home is where you and Butterpie are."

Tanner's eyes stung all of a sudden. He told himself it was the bitterly cold weather. When he'd finally agreed to take the job, he'd thought, *Arizona.* Cacti. Sweeping desert vistas. Eighty-degree winters.

But Stone Creek was in *northern* Arizona, near Flagstaff, a place of timber and red rock—and the occasional blizzard.

It wasn't like him to overlook that kind of geographical detail, but he had. He'd signed on the dotted line because the money was good and because Brad was a good friend.

"How about if I come back there? We'll spend Christmas in New York—skate at Rockefeller Center, see the Rockettes—"

Sophie loved New York. She planned to attend college there, and then medical school, and eventually set up a practice as a neurosurgeon. No small-time goals for *his* kid, but then, the doctor gene had come from Kat, not him. Kat. As beautiful as a model and as smart as they come, she'd been a surgeon, specializing in pediatric cardiology. She'd given all that up, swearing it was only temporary, to have Sophie. To travel the world with her footloose husband…

"But then I wouldn't get to see Butterpie," Sophie protested. A raw giggle escaped her. "I don't think they'd let her stay at the Waldorf with us, even if we paid a pet deposit."

Tanner pictured the pony nibbling on the ubiquitous mongo flower arrangement in the hotel's sedate lobby, with its Cole Porter piano, dropping a few road apples on the venerable old carpets. And he grinned. "Probably not."

"Don't you want me with you, Dad?" Sophie spoke in a small voice. "Is that it? My friend Cleta says her mom won't let her come home for Christmas because she's got a new boyfriend and she doesn't want a kid throwing a wet blanket on the action."

Cleta. Who named a poor, defenseless kid Cleta?

And what kind of person put "action" before their own child, especially at Christmas?

Tanner closed his eyes, walking toward the dark house he didn't know his way around in yet, since he'd spent the first couple of nights at Brad's, waiting for the power to be turned on and the phones hooked up. Guilt stabbed through his middle. "I love you more than anything or anybody else in the world," he said gruffly, and he meant it. Practically everything he did was geared to provide for Sophie, to protect her from the nameless, faceless forces who hated him. "Trust me, there's no *action* going on around here."

"I'm going to run away, then," she said resolutely.

"Good luck," Tanner replied after sucking in a deep breath. "That school is hermetically sealed, kiddo. You know that as well as I do."

"What are you so afraid of?"

*Losing you.* The kid had no way of knowing how big, and how dangerous, the world was. She'd been just seven years old when Kat was killed, and barely remembered the long flight home from northern Africa, private bodyguards occupying the seats around them, the sealed coffin, the media blitz.

"U.S. Contractor Targeted by Insurgent Group," one headline had read. "Wife of American Businessman Killed in Possible Revenge Shooting."

"I'm not afraid of anything," Tanner lied.

"It's because of what happened to Mom," Sophie insisted. "That's what Aunt Tessa says."

"Aunt Tessa ought to mind her own business."

"If you don't come and get me, I'm breaking out of here. And there's no telling where I'll go."

Tanner had reached the old-fashioned wraparound porch. The place had a certain charm, though it needed a lot of fixing up. He could picture Sophie there all too easily, running back and forth to the barn, riding a yellow bus to school, wearing jeans instead of uniforms. Tacking up posters on her bedroom walls and holding sleepovers with ordinary friends instead of junior celebrities and other mini-jet-setters.

"Don't try it, Soph," he said, fumbling with the knob, shouldering open the heavy front door. "You're fine at Briarwood, and it's a long way between Connecticut and Arizona."

"Fine?" Sophie shot back. "This place isn't in a parallel dimension, you know. Things *happen.* Marissa Worth got ptomaine from the potato salad in the cafeteria, just last week, and had to be airlifted to Walter Reed. Allison Mooreland's appendix ruptured, and—"

"Soph," Tanner said, flipping on the lights in the entryway.

Which way was the kitchen?

His room was upstairs someplace, but where?

He hung up his hat, shrugged off his leather coat, tossed it in the direction of an ornate brass peg designed for the purpose.

Sophie didn't say a word. All the way across country, Tanner could feel her holding her breath.

"How's this? School lets out in May. You can come out here then. Spend the summer. Ride Butterpie all you want."

"I might be too big to ride her by summer," Sophie pointed out. Tanner wondered, as he often did, if his daughter wouldn't make a better lawyer than a doctor. "Thanksgiving is in three days," she went on in a rush. "Let me come home for that, and if you still don't think I'm a good kid to have around, I'll come back to Briarwood for the rest of the year and pretend I love it."

"It's not that I don't think you're a good kid, Soph." In the living room by then, Tanner paused to consult a yellowed wall calendar left behind by the ranch's previous owner. Unfortunately, it was several years out of date.

Sophie didn't answer.

"Thanksgiving is in three days?" Tanner muttered, dismayed. Living the way he did, he tended to lose track of holidays, but it figured that if Christmas was already a factor, turkey day had to be bearing down hard.

"I could still get a ticket if I flew standby," Sophie said hopefully.

Tanner closed his eyes. Let his forehead rest against the wall where a million little tack holes testified to all the calendars that had gone before this one. "That's a long way to travel for a turkey special in some greasy spoon," he said quietly. He knew the kid was probably picturing a Norman Rockwell scenario—old woman proudly presenting a golden-brown gobbler to a beaming family crowded around a table.

"Someone will invite you to Thanksgiving dinner," Sophie said, with a tone of bright, brittle bravery in her voice, "and I could just tag along."

He checked his watch, started for the kitchen. If it wasn't where he thought it was, he'd have to search until he found it, because he needed coffee. Hold the Jack Daniel's.

"You've been watching the Hallmark Channel again," he said wearily, his heart trying to scramble up his windpipe into the back of his throat. There were so many things he couldn't give Sophie—a stable home, a family, an ordinary childhood. But he *could* keep her safe, and that meant staying at Briarwood.

A long, painful pause ensued.

"You're not going to give in, are you?" Sophie asked finally, practically in a whisper.

"Are you just figuring that out, shortstop?" Tanner retorted, trying for a light tone.

She huffed out a weight-of-the-world sigh. "Okay, then," she replied, "don't say I didn't warn you."

## CHAPTER TWO

It was a pity Starcross Ranch had fallen into such a state of disrepair, Olivia thought as she steered the Suburban down the driveway to the main road, Ginger beside her in the passenger seat, Rodney in the back. The place bordered her rental to the west, and although she passed the sagging rail fences and the tilting barn every day on her way to town, that morning the sight seemed even lonelier than usual.

She braked for the stop sign, looked both ways. No cars coming, but she didn't pull out right away. The vibe hit her before she could shift out of neutral and hit the gas.

"Oh, no," she said aloud.

Ginger, busy surveying the snowy countryside, offered no comment.

"Did you hear that?" Olivia persisted.

Ginger turned to look at her. Gave a little yip. Today, evidently, she was pretending to be an ordinary dog— as if *any* dog was ordinary—incapable of intelligent conversation.

The call was coming from the ancient barn on the Starcross property.

Olivia took a moment to rest her forehead on the cold steering wheel. She'd known Brad's friend the big-time contractor was moving in, of course, and she'd seen at least one moving truck, but she hadn't known there were any animals involved.

"I could ignore this," she said to Ginger.

*"Or not,"* Ginger answered.

"Oh, hell," Olivia said. Then she signaled for a left turn—Stone Creek was in the other direction—and headed for the decrepit old gate marking the entrance to Starcross Ranch.

The gate stood wide open. No sheep or cattle then, probably, Olivia reasoned. Even greenhorns knew livestock tended to stray at every opportunity. Still, *some* kind of critter was sending out a psychic SOS from that pitiful barn.

They bumped up the rutted driveway, fishtailing a little on the slick snow and the layer of ice underneath, and Olivia tooted her horn. A spiffy new red pickup stood in front of the house, looking way too fancy for the neighborhood, but nobody appeared to see who was honking.

Muttering, Olivia brought the Suburban to a rattling stop in front of the barn, got out and shut the door hard.

"Hello?" she called.

No answer. Not from a human being, anyway.

The animal inside the barn amped up the psychic summons.

Olivia sprinted toward the barn door, glancing upward once at the sagging roof as she entered, with some trepidation. The place ought to be condemned. "Hello?" she repeated.

It took a moment for her eyes to adjust to the dimmer light, since the weather was dazzle-bright, though cold enough to crystallize her bone marrow.

*"Over here,"* said a silent voice, deep and distinctly male.

Olivia ventured deeper into the shadows. The ruins of a dozen once-sturdy stalls lined the sawdust-and-straw aisle. She found two at the very back, showing fresh-lumber signs of recent restoration efforts.

A tall palomino regarded her from the stall on the right, tossed his head as if to indicate the one opposite.

Olivia went to that stall and looked over the half gate to see a small, yellowish-white pony gazing up at her in befuddled sorrow. The horse lay forlornly in fresh wood shavings, its legs folded underneath.

Although she was technically trespassing, Olivia couldn't resist unlatching the gate and slipping inside. She crouched beside the pony, stroked its nose, patted its neck, gave its forelock an affectionate tug.

"Hey, there," she said softly. "What's all the fuss about?"

A slight shudder went through the little horse.

*"She misses Sophie,"* the palomino said, from across the aisle.

Wondering who Sophie was, Olivia examined the pony while continuing to pet her. The animal was sound, well fed and well cared for in general.

The palomino nickered loudly, and that should have been a cue, but Olivia was too focused on the pony to pay attention.

"Who are you and what the hell are you doing sneaking around in my barn?" demanded a low, no-nonsense voice.

Olivia whirled, and toppled backward into the straw. Looked up to see a dark-haired man glowering down at her from over the stall gate. His eyes matched his blue denim jacket, and his Western hat looked a little too new.

"Who's Sophie?" she asked, getting to her feet, dusting bits of straw off her jeans.

He merely folded his arms and glared. He'd asked the first question and, apparently, he intended to have the first answer. From the set of his broad shoulders, she guessed he'd wait for it until hell froze over if necessary.

Olivia relented, since she had rounds to make and a reindeer owner to track down. She summoned up her best smile and stuck out her hand. "Olivia O'Ballivan," she said. "I'm your neighbor—sort of—and…" *And I heard your pony calling out for help?* No, she couldn't say that. It was all too easy to imagine the reaction she'd get. "And since I'm a veterinarian, I always like to stop by when somebody new moves in. Offer my services."

The blue eyes sized her up, clearly found her less than statuesque. "You must deal mostly with cats and poodles," he said. "As you can see, I have horses."

Olivia felt the sexist remark like the unexpected back-snap of a rubber band, stinging and sudden. Adrenaline coursed through her, and she had to wait a few moments for it to subside. "This horse," she said when she'd regained her dignity, indicating the pony with a gesture of one hand, "is depressed."

One dark eyebrow quirked upward, and the hint of a smile played at the corner of Tanner Quinn's supple-looking mouth. That had to be who he was, since he'd said "*I* have horses," not "we" or "they." Anyhow, he didn't look like an ordinary ranch hand.

"Does she need to take happy pills?" he asked.

*"She wants Sophie,"* the palomino said, though of course Mr. Quinn didn't hear.

"Who's Sophie?" Olivia repeated calmly.

Quinn hesitated for a long moment. "My daughter," he finally said. "How do you happen to know her name?"

Olivia thought fast. "My brother must have mentioned her," she answered, heading for the stall door and hoping he'd step back so she could pass.

He didn't. Instead, he stood there like a support beam, his forearms resting on top of the door. "O'Ballivan," he mused. "You're Brad's sister? The one who'll be running the shelter when it's finished?"

"I think I just said Brad is my brother," Olivia replied, somewhat tartly. She felt strangely shaken and a little cornered, which was odd, because she wasn't claustrophobic and despite her unremarkable height of five feet three inches, she knew how to defend herself. "Now, would you mind letting me out of this stall?"

Quinn stepped back, even executed a sweeping bow.

*"You're not leaving, are you?"* the palomino fretted. *"Butterpie needs help."*

"Give me a second here," Olivia told the concerned horse. "I'll make sure Butterpie is taken care of, but it's going to take time." An awkward moment passed before she realized she'd spoken out loud, instead of using mental email.

Quinn blocked her way again, planting himself in the middle of the barn aisle, and refolded his arms. "Now," he said ominously, "I *know* I've never mentioned that pony's name to anybody in Stone Creek, including Brad."

Olivia swallowed, tried for a smile but slid right down the side of it without catching hold. "Lucky guess," she said, and started around him.

He caught hold of her arm to stop her, but let go immediately.

Olivia stared up at him. The palomino was right; she couldn't leave, no matter how foolish she might seem to Tanner Quinn. Butterpie was in trouble.

"Who are you?" Tanner insisted gruffly.

"I told you. I'm Olivia O'Ballivan."

Tanner took off his hat with one hand, shoved the other through his thick, somewhat shaggy hair. The light was better in the aisle, since there were big cracks in the roof to let in the silvery sunshine, and she saw that he needed a shave.

He gave a heavy sigh. "Could we start over, here?" he asked. "If you're who you say you are, then we're going to be working together on the shelter project. That'll be a whole lot easier if we get along."

"Butterpie misses your daughter," Olivia said. "*Severely.* Where is she?"

Tanner sighed again. "Boarding school," he answered, as though the words had been pried out of him. The denim-colored eyes were still fixed on her face.

"Oh," Olivia answered, feeling sorry for the pony *and* Sophie. "She'll be home for Thanksgiving, though, right? Your daughter, I mean?"

Tanner's jawline looked rigid, and his eyes didn't soften. "No," he said.

"No?" Olivia's spirits, already on the dip, deflated completely.

He stepped aside. Before, he'd blocked her way. Now he obviously wanted her gone, ASAP.

It was Olivia's turn with the folded arms and stubborn stance. "Then I have to explain that to the horse," she said.

Tanner blinked. "What?"

She turned, went back to Butterpie's stall, opened the door and stepped inside. *"Sophie's away at boarding school,"* she told the animal silently. *"And she can't make it home for Thanksgiving. You've got to cheer up, though. I'm sure she'll be here for Christmas."*

"What are you doing?" Tanner asked, sounding testy again.

"Telling Butterpie that Sophie will be home at Christmas and she's got to cheer up in the meantime." He'd asked the question; let him deal with the answer.

"Are you crazy?"

"Probably," Olivia said. Then, speaking aloud this time, she told Butterpie, "I have to go now. I have a lost reindeer in the back of my Suburban, and I need to do some X-rays and then get him settled in over at my brother's place until I can find his owner. But I'll be back to visit soon, I promise."

She could almost hear Tanner grinding his back teeth.

"You should stand up," Olivia told the pony. "You'll feel better on your feet."

The animal gave a snorty sigh and slowly stood.

Tanner let out a sharp breath.

Olivia patted Butterpie's neck. "Excellent," she said. "That's the spirit."

"You have a reindeer in the back of your Suburban?"

Tanner queried, keeping pace with Olivia as she left the barn.

"See for yourself," she replied, waving one hand toward the rig.

Tanner approached the vehicle, and Ginger barked a cheerful greeting as he passed the passenger-side window. He responded with a distracted wave, and Olivia decided there might be a few soft spots in his steely psyche after all.

Rubbing off dirt with one gloved hand, Tanner peered through the back windows.

"I'll be damned," he said. "It *is* a reindeer."

"Sure enough," Olivia said. Ginger was all over the inside of the rig, barking her brains out. She liked good-looking men, the silly dog. Actually, she liked *any* man. "Ginger! Sit!"

Ginger sat, but she looked like the poster dog for a homeless-pets campaign.

"Where did you get a reindeer?" Tanner asked, drawing back from the window to take a whole new look at Olivia.

Ridiculously, she wished she'd worn something remotely feminine that day, instead of her usual jeans, flannel work shirt and mud-speckled down-filled vest. Not that she actually owned anything remotely feminine.

"I found him," she said, opening the driver's door. "Last night, at the bottom of my driveway."

For the first time in their acquaintance, Tanner smiled, and the effect was seismic. His teeth were white and straight, and she'd have bet that was natural enamel, not a fancy set of veneers. "Okay," he said, stretching the word out a way. "Tell me, Dr. O'Ballivan—how does a reindeer happen to turn up in Arizona?"

"When I find out," Olivia said, climbing behind the wheel, "I'll let you know."

Before she could shut the door, he stood in the gap. Pushed his hat to the back of his head and treated her to another wicked grin. "I guess there's a ground-breaking ceremony scheduled for tomorrow morning at ten," he said. "I'll see you there."

Olivia nodded, feeling unaccountably flustered.

Ginger was practically drooling.

"Nice dog," Tanner said.

*"Be still, my heart,"* Ginger said.

"Shut up," Olivia told the dog.

Tanner drew back his head, but the grin lurked in his eyes.

Olivia blushed. "I wasn't talking to you," she told Tanner.

He looked as though he wanted to ask if she'd been taking her medications regularly. Fortunately for him, he didn't. He merely tugged at the brim of his too-new hat and stepped back.

Olivia pulled the door closed, started up the engine, ground the gearshift into first and made a wide 360 in front of the barn.

*"That* certainly went well," she told Ginger. "We're going to be in each other's hip pockets while the shelter is being built, and he thinks I'm certifiable!"

Ginger didn't answer.

Half an hour later, the X-rays were done and the blood had been drawn. Rodney was good to go.

TANNER STOOD IN THE middle of the barnyard, staring after that wreck of a Suburban and wondering what the hell had just hit him. It felt like a freight train.

His cell phone rang, breaking the spell.

He pulled it from his jacket pocket and squinted at the caller ID panel. Ms. Wiggins, the executive principal at Briarwood. She'd certainly taken her time returning his call—he'd left her a message at sunrise.

"Tanner Quinn," he said automatically.

"Hello, Mr. Quinn," Ms. Wiggins said. A former CIA agent, Janet Wiggins was attractive, if you liked the armed-and-dangerous type. Tanner didn't, particularly, but the woman had a spotless service record, and a good résumé. "I'm sorry I couldn't call sooner—meetings, you know."

"I'm worried about Sophie," he said. A cold wind blew down off the mountain looming above Stone Creek, biting into his ears, but he didn't head for the house. He just stood there in the barnyard, letting the chill go right through him.

"I gathered that from your message, Mr. Quinn," Ms. Wiggins said smoothly. She was used to dealing with fretful parents, especially the guilt-plagued ones. "The fact is, Sophie is not the only student remaining at Briarwood over the holiday season. There are several others. We're taking all the stay-behinds to New York by train to watch the Thanksgiving Day parade and dine at the Four Seasons. You would know that if you read our weekly newsletters. We send them by email every Friday afternoon."

*I just met a woman who talks to animals—and thinks they talk back.*

Tanner kept his tone even. "I read your newsletters faithfully, Ms. Wiggins," he said. "And I'm not sure I like having my daughter referred to as a 'stay-behind.'"

Ms. Wiggins trilled out a very un-CIA-like giggle.

"Oh, we don't use that term in front of the pupils, Mr. Quinn," she assured him. "Sophie is *fine.* She just tends to be a little overdramatic, that's all. In fact, I'm encouraging her to sign up for our thespian program, beginning next term—"

"You're sure she's all right?" Tanner broke in.

"She's one of our most emotionally stable students. It's just that, well, kids get a little sentimental around the holidays."

*Don't we all?* Tanner thought. He always skipped Thanksgiving and Christmas both, if he couldn't spend them with Sophie. Up until now it had been easy enough, given that he'd been out of the country last year, and the year before that. Sophie had stayed with Tessa, and he'd ordered all her gifts online.

Remembering that gave him a hollow feeling in the middle of his gut.

"I know Sophie is stable," he said patiently. "That doesn't mean she's completely okay."

Ms. Wiggins paused eloquently before answering. "Well, if you would like Sophie to come home for Thanksgiving, we'd certainly be glad to make the arrangements."

Tanner wanted to say yes. Instantly. *Book a plane. Put her on board. I don't care what it costs.* But it would only lead to another tearful parting when it came time for Sophie to return to school, and Tanner couldn't bear another one of those. Not just yet, anyway.

"It's best if Sophie stays there," he said.

"I quite agree," Ms. Wiggins replied. "Last-minute trips home can be very disruptive to a child."

"You'll let me know if there are any problems?"

"Of course I will," Ms. Wiggins assured him. If there

was just a hint of condescension in her tone, he supposed he deserved it. "We at Briarwood pride ourselves on monitoring our students' mental health as well as their academic achievement. I promise you, Sophie is not traumatized."

Tanner wished he could be half as sure of that as Ms. Wiggins sounded. A few holiday platitudes were exchanged, and the call ended. Tanner snapped his phone shut and dropped it into his coat pocket.

Then he turned back toward the barn.

Could a horse get depressed?

Nah, he decided.

But a man sure as hell could.

A SNOWMAN STOOD in the center of the yard at the homeplace when Olivia drove in, and there was one of those foldout turkeys taped to the front door. Brad came out of the barn, walking toward her, just as Meg, her sister-in-law, stepped onto the porch, smiling a welcome.

"How do you like our turkey?" she called. "We're really getting into the spirit this year." Her smile turned wistful. "It's strange, without Carly here, but she's having such a good time."

Grinning, Olivia gestured toward Brad. "He'll do," she teased.

Brad reached her, hooked an arm around her neck and gave her a big-brother half hug. "She's referring to the paper one," he told her in an exaggerated whisper.

Olivia contrived to look surprised. "Oh!" she said.

Brad laughed and released her from the choke hold. "So what brings you to Stone Creek Ranch, Doc?"

Olivia glanced around, taking in the familiar surroundings. Missing her grandfather, Big John, the way she always did when she set foot on home ground. The place had changed a lot since Brad had semiretired from his career in country music—he'd refurbished the barn, replaced the worn-out fences and built a state-of-the-art recording studio out back. At least he'd given up the concert tours, but even with Meg and fourteen-year-old Carly and the baby in the picture, Olivia still wasn't entirely convinced that he'd come home to stay.

He'd skipped out before, after all, just like their mother.

"I have a problem," she said in belated answer to his question.

Meg had gone back inside, but she and Brad remained in the yard.

"What sort of problem?" he asked, his eyes serious.

"A reindeer problem," Olivia explained. *Oh, and I got off to a fine start with your friend the contractor, too.*

Brad's brow furrowed. "A what?"

*"I need to get out of this truck,"* Ginger transmitted from the passenger seat. *"Now."*

With a slight sigh Olivia opened Ginger's door so she could hop out, sniff the snow and leave a yellow splotch. That done, she trotted off toward the barn, probably looking for Brad's dog, Willie.

"I found this reindeer," Olivia said, heading for the back of the Suburban and unveiling Rodney. "I was hoping he could stay here until we find his owner."

"What if he doesn't have an owner?" Brad asked reasonably, running a hand through his shaggy blond hair before reaching out to stroke the deer.

"He's tame," Olivia pointed out.

"Tame, but not housebroken," Brad said.

Sure enough, Rodney had dropped a few pellets on his blanket.

"I don't expect you to keep him in the house," Olivia said.

Brad laughed. Reached right in and hoisted Rodney down out of the Suburban. The deer stumbled a little, wobbly legged from riding, and looked worriedly up at Olivia.

"You'll be safe here," she told the animal. She turned back to Brad. "He can stay in the barn, can't he? I know you have some empty stalls."

"Sure," Brad said after a hesitation that would have been comical if Olivia hadn't been so concerned about Rodney. "Sure," he repeated.

Knowing he was about to ruffle her hair, the way he'd done when she was a little kid, Olivia took a step back.

"I want something in return, though," Brad continued.

"What?" Olivia asked suspiciously.

"You, at our table, on Thanksgiving," he answered. "No excuses about filling in at the clinic. Ashley and Melissa are both coming, and Meg's mother, too, along with her sister, Sierra."

The invitation didn't come as any surprise to Olivia— Meg had mentioned holding a big Thanksgiving blow-out weeks ago—but the truth was, Olivia preferred to work on holidays. That way, she didn't miss Big John so much, or wonder if their long-lost mother might come waltzing through the door, wanting to get to know the grown children she'd abandoned so many years before.

"Livie?" Brad prompted.

"Okay," she said. "I'll be here. But I'm on call over

Thanksgiving, and all the other vets have families, so
if there's an emergency—"

"Liv," Brad broke in, "*you* have a family, too."

"I meant wives, husbands, children," Olivia said, embarrassed.

"Two o'clock, you don't need to bring anything, and
wear something you haven't delivered calves in."

She glared up at him. "Can I see my nephew now,"
she asked, "or is there a dress code for that, too?"

Brad laughed. "I'll get Rudolph settled in a nice,
cozy stall while you go inside. Check the attitude at the
door—Meg wasn't kidding when she said she was in
the holiday spirit. Of course, she's working extra hard
at it this year, with Carly away."

Willie and Ginger came from behind the barn, Willie rushing to greet Olivia.

"His name is Rodney," Olivia said. "Not Rudolph."

Brad gave her a look and started for the barn, and
Rodney followed uncertainly, casting nary a backward
glance at Olivia.

Willie, probably clued in by Ginger, was careful
to give Rodney a lot of dog-free space. Olivia bent to
scratch his ears.

He'd healed up nicely since being attacked by a wolf
or coyote pack on the mountain rising above Stone
Creek Ranch. With help from Brad and Meg, Olivia
had brought him back to town for surgery and follow-
up care. He'd bonded with Brad, though, and been his
dog ever since.

With Ginger and Willie following, Olivia went into
the house.

Mac's playpen stood empty in the living room.

Olivia stepped into the nearest bathroom to wash her

hands, and when she came out, Meg was standing in the hallway, holding six-month-old Mac. He stretched his arms out to Olivia and strained toward her, and her heart melted.

She took the baby eagerly and nuzzled his neck to make him laugh. His blondish hair stood up all over his head, and his dark blue eyes were round with mischievous excitement. Giggling, he tried to bite Olivia's nose.

"He's grown!" Olivia told Meg.

"It's only been a week since you saw him last," Meg chided, but she beamed with pride.

Olivia felt a pang, looking at her. Wondered what it would be like to be that happy.

Meg, blond like her husband and son, tilted her head to one side and gave Olivia a humorously pensive once-over. "Are you okay?" she asked.

"I'm fine," Olivia said, too quickly. Mac was gravitating toward his playpen, where he had a pile of toys, and Meg took him and gently set him inside it. She turned back to Olivia.

Just then Brad blew in on a chilly November wind. Bent to pat Ginger and Willie.

"Rudolph is snug in his stall," Brad said. "Having some oats."

"Rudolph?" Meg asked, momentarily distracted.

Olivia was relieved. She and Meg were very good friends, as well as family, but Meg was half again too perceptive. She'd figured out that something was bothering Olivia, and in another moment she'd have insisted on finding out what was up. Considering that Olivia didn't know that herself, the conversation would have been pointless.

"Liv will be here for Thanksgiving," Brad told Meg, pulling his wife against his side and planting a kiss on the top of her head.

"Of course she will," Meg said, surprised that there'd ever been any question. Her gaze lingered on Olivia, and there was concern in it.

Suddenly Olivia was anxious to go.

"I have two million things to do," she said, bending over the playpen to tickle Mac, who was kicking both feet and waving his arms, before heading to the front door and beckoning for Ginger.

"We'll see you tomorrow at the ground-breaking ceremony," Meg said, smiling and giving Brad an affectionate jab with one elbow. "We're expecting a big crowd, thanks to Mr. Country Music here."

Olivia laughed at the face Brad made, but then she recalled that Tanner Quinn would be there, too, and that unsettled feeling was back again. "The ground's pretty hard, thanks to the weather," she said, to cover the momentary lapse. "Let's hope Mr. Country Music still has the muscle to drive a shovel through six inches of snow and a layer of ice."

Brad showed off a respectable biceps, Popeye-style, and everybody laughed again.

"I'll walk you to the truck," he said, when Olivia would have ducked out without further ado.

He opened the driver's door of the Suburban, and Ginger made the leap, scrabbling across to the passenger seat. Olivia looked at her in surprise, since she usually wasn't that agile, but Brad reclaimed her attention soon enough.

"Is everything okay with you, Livie?" he asked. He and the twins were the only people in the world, now that Big John was gone, who called her Livie. It seemed right, coming from her big brother or her sisters, but it also made her ache for her grandfather. He'd loved Thanksgiving even better than Christmas, saying he figured the O'Ballivans had a great deal to be grateful for.

"Everything's fine," Olivia said. "Why does everybody keep asking me if I'm okay? Meg did—now you."

"You just seem—I don't know—kind of sad."

Olivia didn't trust herself to speak, and suddenly her eyes burned with moisture.

Brad took her gently by the shoulders and kissed her on the forehead. "I miss Big John, too," he said. Then he waited while she climbed onto the running board and then the driver's seat. He shut the door and waved when she went to turn around, and when she glanced into the rearview mirror, he was still standing there with Willie, both of them staring after her.

## CHAPTER THREE

ALTHOUGH BRAD LIKED to downplay his success, especially now that he didn't go out on tour anymore, he was clearly still a very big deal. When Olivia arrived at the building site on the outskirts of Stone Creek at nine forty-five the next morning, the windswept clearing was jammed with TV news trucks and stringers from various tabloids. Of course the townspeople had turned out, too, happy that work was about to begin on the new animal shelter—and proud of their hometown boy.

Olivia's feelings about Brad's fame were mixed—he'd been away playing star when Big John needed him most, and she wasn't over that—but seeing him up there on the hastily assembled plank stage gave her a jolt of joy. She worked her way through the crowd to stand next to Meg, Ashley and Melissa, who were grouped in a little cluster up front, fussing over Mac. The baby's blue snowsuit was so bulky that he resembled the Michelin man.

Ashley turned to smile at Olivia, taking in her trim, tailored black pantsuit—a holdover from her job interview at the veterinary clinic right after she'd finished graduate school. She'd ferreted through boxes until she'd found it, gone over the outfit with a lint roller to get rid of the ubiquitous pet hair, and hoped for the best.

"I guess you couldn't quite manage a dress," Ashley said without sarcasm. She was tall and blond, clad in a long skirt, elegant boots and a colorful patchwork jacket she'd probably whipped up on her sewing machine. She was also stubbornly old-fashioned—no cell phone, no internet connection, no MP3 player—and Olivia had often thought, secretly of course, that her younger sister should have been born in the Victorian era, rather than modern times. She would have fit right into the 1890s, been completely comfortable cooking on a wood-burning stove, reading by gaslight and directing a contingent of maids in ruffly aprons and scalloped white caps.

"Best I could do on short notice," Olivia chimed in, exchanging a hello grin with Meg and giving Mac's mittened hand a little squeeze. His plump little cheek felt smooth and cold as she kissed him.

"Since when is a *year* 'short notice'?" Melissa put in, grinning. She and Ashley were fraternal twins, but except for their deep blue eyes, they bore no noticeable resemblance to each other. Melissa was small, an inch shorter than Olivia, and wore her fine chestnut-colored hair in a bob. Having left the law office where she worked to attend the ceremony, she was clad in her usual getup of high heels, pencil-straight skirt, fitted blazer and prim white blouse.

Up on stage, Brad tapped lightly on the microphone.

Everybody fell silent, as though the whole gathering had taken a single, indrawn breath all at the same time. The air was charged with excitement and civic pride and the welcome prospect of construction jobs to tide over the laid-off workers from the sawmill.

Meg's eyes shone as she gazed up at her husband. "Isn't he something?" she marveled, giving Olivia a little poke with one elbow as she shifted Mac to her other hip.

Olivia smiled but didn't reply.

"Sing!" someone shouted, somewhere in the surging throng. Any moment now, Olivia thought, they'd all be holding up disposable lights in a flickering-flame salute.

Brad shook his head. "Not today," he said.

A collective groan rose from the crowd.

Brad put up both hands to silence them.

"He'll sing," Melissa said in a loud and certain whisper. She and Ashley, being the youngest, barely knew Brad. He'd been trying to remedy that ever since he'd moved back from Nashville, but it was slow going. They admired him, they were grateful to him, but it seemed to Olivia that her sisters were still in awe of their big brother, too, and therefore a strange shyness possessed them whenever he was around.

Brad asked Olivia and Tanner to join him on stage.

Even though Olivia had expected that, she wished she didn't have to go up there. She was a behind-the-scenes kind of person, uncomfortable at the center of attention. When Tanner appeared from behind her, took her arm and hustled her toward the wooden steps, she caught her breath. Stone Creekers raised an uproarious cheer, and Olivia flushed with embarrassment, but Tanner seemed untroubled.

He wore too-new, too-expensive boots, probably custom-made, to match his too-new hat, along with jeans, a black silk shirt and a denim jacket. He seemed as at home getting up in front of all those people as Brad did—his grin dazzled, and his eyes were bright with enjoyment.

*Drugstore cowboy,* Olivia thought, but she couldn't work up any rancor. Tanner Quinn might be laying on the Western bit a little thick, but he did look good. Way, way too good for Olivia's comfort.

Brad introduced them both: Tanner as the builder, and Olivia—"You all know my kid sister, the horse doctor"—as the driving force behind the project. Without her, he said, none of this would be happening.

Never having thought of herself as a driving force behind anything in particular, Olivia grew even more flustered as Brad went on about how she'd be heading up the shelter when it opened around that time next year.

More applause followed, the good-natured, hometown kind, indulgent and laced with chuckles.

*Let this be over,* Olivia thought.

"Sing!" someone yelled. The whole audience soon took up the chant.

"Here's where we make a run for it," Tanner whispered to Olivia, and the two of them left the stage. Tanner vanished, and Olivia went back to stand with her sisters and Meg.

Brad grinned, shaking his head a little as one of his buddies handed up a guitar. "One," he said firmly. After strumming a few riffs and turning the tuning keys this way and that, he eased into "Meg's Song," a ballad he'd written for his wife.

Holding Mac and looking up at Brad with an expression of rapt delight, Meg seemed to glow from the inside. A sweet, strange alchemy made it seem as though only Brad, Meg and Mac were really *there* during those magical minutes, on that blustery day, with the snow crusting hard around everybody's feet. The rest of them

might have been hovering in an adjacent dimension,
like actors waiting to go on.

When the song ended, the audience clamored for
more, but Brad didn't give in. Photographers and reporters shoved in close as he handed off the guitar again,
descended from the stage and picked up a brand-new
shovel with a blue ribbon on the handle. The ribbon,
Olivia knew, was Ashley's handiwork; she was an expert with bows, where Olivia always got them tangled
up, fiddling with them until they were grubby.

"Are you making a comeback?" one reporter demanded.

"When will you make another movie?" someone else
wanted to know.

Still another person shoved a microphone into Brad's
face; he pushed it away with a practiced motion of one
arm. "We're here to break ground for an animal shelter," he said, and only the set of his jaw gave away the
annoyance he felt. He beckoned to Olivia, then to Tanner, after glancing around to locate him.

Then, with consummate showmanship, Brad drove
the shovel hard into the partially frozen ground. Tossed
the dirt dangerously close to one reporter's shoes.

Olivia thought of the finished structure, and what it
would mean to so many stray and unwanted dogs, cats
and other critters, and her heart soared. That was the
moment the project truly became real to her.

*It was really going to happen.*

There were more pictures taken after that, and Brad
gave several very brief interviews, carefully steering
each one away from himself and stressing the plight
of animals. When one reporter asked if it wouldn't be
better to build shelters for homeless *people,* rather than

dogs and cats, Brad responded that compassion ought to begin at the simplest level, with the helpless, voiceless ones, and grow from there.

Olivia would have hugged her big brother in that moment if she'd been able to get close enough.

"Hot cider and cookies at my place," Ashley told her and Melissa. She was already heading for her funny-looking hybrid car, gleaming bright yellow in the wintry sunshine. "We need to plan what we're taking to Brad and Meg's for Thanksgiving dinner."

"I have to get back to work," Melissa said crisply. "Cook something and I'll pay you back." With that, she made for her spiffy red sports car without so much as a backward glance.

Olivia had rounds to make herself, though none of them were emergencies, and she had some appointments at the clinic scheduled for that afternoon, but when she saw the expression of disappointment on Ashley's face, she stayed behind. "I'll change clothes at your house," she said, and got into the Suburban to follow her sister back through town. Ginger had elected to stay home that day, claiming her arthritis was bothering her, and it felt odd to be alone in the rig.

Ashley's home was a large white Victorian house on the opposite side of Stone Creek, near the little stream with the same name. There was a white picket fence and plenty of gingerbread woodwork on the façade, and an ornate but tasteful sign stood in the snowy yard, bearing the words "Mountain View Bed-and-Breakfast" in elegant golden script. "Ashley O'Ballivan, Proprietor."

In summer, the yard burgeoned with colorful flowers.

But winter had officially come to the high country, and the blooming lilacs, peonies and English roses were just a memory. The day after Thanksgiving, the Christmas lights would go up outside, as though by the waving of an unseen wand, and a huge wreath would grace the leaded-glass door, making the house look like a giant greeting card.

Olivia felt a little sad, looking at that grand house. It was the off-season, and guests would be few and far between. Ashley would rattle around in there alone like a bean in the bottom of a bucket.

She needed a husband and children.

Or at least a cat.

"Brad was spectacular, wasn't he?" Ashley asked, bustling around her big, fragrant kitchen to heat up the spiced cider and set out a plate of exquisitely decorated cookies.

Olivia, just coming out of the powder room, where she'd changed into her regulation jeans, flannel shirt and boots, helped herself to a paper bag from the de-coupaged wooden paper-bag dispenser beside the back door and stuffed the pantsuit into it. "Brad was—Brad," she said. "He loves being in the limelight."

Ashley went still and frowned, oddly defensive. "His heart's in the right place," she replied.

Olivia went to Ashley and touched her arm. She'd removed the patchwork jacket, hanging it neatly on a gleaming brass peg by the front door as they came in, and her loose-fitting beige cashmere turtleneck made Olivia feel like a thrift-store refugee by comparison.

"I wasn't criticizing Brad, Ash," she said quietly. "It's beyond generous of him to build the shelter. We need one, and we're lucky he's willing to help out."

Ashley relaxed a little and offered a tentative smile.

Looked around at her kitchen, which would have made a great set for some show on the Food Channel. "He bought this house for me, you know," she said as the cider began to simmer in its shiny pot on the stove.

Olivia nodded. "And it looks fabulous," she replied. "Like always."

"You *are* planning to show up for Thanksgiving dinner out at the ranch, aren't you?"

"Why wouldn't I?" Olivia asked, even as her stomach knotted. Who had invented holidays, anyway? Everything came to a screeching stop whenever there was a red-letter day on the calendar—everything except the need and sorrow that seemed to fill the world.

"I know you don't like family holidays," Ashley said, pouring steaming cider into a copper serving pot and then into translucent china teacups waiting in the center of the round antique table. Olivia would have dumped it straight from the kettle, and probably spilled it all over the table and floor in the process.

She just wasn't domestic. All those genes had gone to Ashley.

Her sister's eyes went big and round and serious. "Last year you made some excuse about a cow needing an appendectomy and ducked out before I could serve the pumpkin pie."

Olivia sighed. Ashley had worked hard to prepare the previous year's Thanksgiving dinner, gathering recipes for weeks ahead of time, experimenting like a chemist in search of a cure, and looked forward to hosting a houseful of congenial relatives.

"Do cows even *have* appendixes?" Ashley asked.

Olivia laughed, drew back a chair at the table and sat down. "That cider smells fabulous," she said, in order to change the subject. "And the cookies are works of art, almost too pretty to eat. Martha Stewart would be so proud."

Ashley joined her at the table, but she still looked troubled. "Why do you hate holidays, Olivia?" she persisted.

"I don't hate holidays," Olivia said. "It's just that all that sentimentality—"

"You miss Big John and Mom," Ashley broke in quietly. "Why don't you just admit it?"

"We all miss Big John," Olivia admitted. "As for Mom—well, she's been gone a long time, Ash. A *really* long time. It's not a matter of missing her, exactly."

"Don't you ever wonder where she went after she left Stone Creek, if she's happy and healthy—if she remarried and had more children?"

"I try not to," Olivia said honestly.

"You have abandonment issues," Ashley accused.

Olivia sighed and sipped from her cup of cider. The stuff was delicious, like everything her sister cooked up.

Ashley's Botticelli face brightened; she'd made another of her mercurial shifts from pensive to hopeful. "Suppose we found her?" she asked on a breath. "Mom, I mean—"

"Found her?" Olivia echoed, oddly alarmed.

"There are all these search engines online," Ashley enthused. "I was over at the library yesterday afternoon, and I searched Google for Mom's name."

*Oh. My. God,* Olivia thought, feeling the color drain out of her face.

"*You* used a computer?"

Ashley nodded. "I'm thinking of getting one. Setting up a website to bring in more business for the B and B."

Things were changing, Olivia realized. And she *hated* it when things changed. Why couldn't people leave well enough alone?

"There are more Delia O'Ballivans out there than you would ever guess," Ashley rushed on. "One of them must be Mom."

"Ash, Mom could be dead by now. Or going by a different name…"

Ashley looked offended. "You sound like Brad and Melissa. Brad just clams up whenever I ask him about Mom—he remembers her better, since he's older. 'Leave it alone' is all he ever says. And Melissa thinks she's probably a crack addict or a hooker or something." She let out a long, shaky breath. "I thought *you* missed Mom as much as I do. I really did."

Although Brad had never admitted it, Olivia suspected he knew more about their mother than he was telling. If he wanted Ashley and the rest of them to let the proverbial sleeping dogs lie, he probably had a good reason. Not that the decision was only his to make.

"I miss *having* a mother, Ash," Olivia said gently. "That's different from missing Mom specifically. She left us, remember?"

Remember? How *could* Ashley remember? She'd been a toddler when their mother boarded an afternoon bus out of Stone Creek and vanished into a world of strangers. She was clinging to memories she'd merely imagined, most likely. To a fantasy mother, the woman who should have been, but probably never was.

"Well, I want to know why," Ashley insisted, her eyes full of pain. "Maybe she regretted it. Did you ever think of that? Maybe she misses us, and wants a second chance. Maybe she expects us to reject her, so she's afraid to get in touch."

"Oh, Ash," Olivia murmured, slouching against the back of her chair. "You haven't actually made contact, have you?"

"No," Ashley said, tucking a wisp of blond hair behind her right ear when it escaped from her otherwise categorically perfect French braid, "but if I find her, I'm going to invite her to Stone Creek for Christmas. If you and Brad and Melissa want to keep your distance, that's your business."

Olivia's hand shook a little as she set her cup down, causing it to rattle in its delicate saucer. "Ashley, you have a right to see Mom if you want to," she said carefully. "But Christmas—"

"What do you care about Christmas?" Ashley asked abruptly. "You don't even put up a tree most years."

"I care about you and Melissa and Brad. If you do manage to find Mom, great. But don't you think bringing her here at Christmas, the most emotional day of the year, before anybody has a chance to get used to the idea, would be like planting a live hand grenade in the turkey?"

Ashley didn't reply, and after that the conversation was stilted, to say the least. They talked about what to contribute to the Thanksgiving shindig at Brad and Meg's place, decided on freshly baked dinner rolls for Ashley and a selection of salads from the deli for Olivia, and then Olivia left to make rounds.

Why was she so worried? she wondered, biting down hard on her lower lip as she fired up the Suburban and headed for the first farm on her list. If she was alive,

Delia had done a good job of staying under the radar all these years. She'd never written, never called, never visited. Never sent a single birthday card. And if she was dead, they'd all have to drop everything and mourn, in their various ways.

Olivia didn't feel ready to take that on.

Before, the thought of Delia usually filled her with grief and a plaintive, little-girl kind of longing. The very cadence of her heartbeat said, *Come home. Come home.*

Now, today, it just made her very, very angry. How could a woman just leave four children and a husband behind and forget the way back?

Olivia knotted one hand into a fist and bonked the side of the steering wheel once. Tears stung her eyes, and her throat felt as though someone had run a line of stitches around it with a sharp needle and then pulled them tight.

Ashley was expecting some kind of fairy-tale reunion, an *Oprah* sort of deal, full of tearful confessions and apologies and cartoon birds trailing ribbons from their chirpy beaks.

For Olivia's money, it would be more like an apocalypse.

TANNER HEARD THE RIG roll in around sunset. Smiling, he closed his newspaper, stood up from the kitchen table and wandered to the window. Watched as Olivia O'Ballivan climbed out of her Suburban, flung one defiant glance toward the house and started for the barn, the golden retriever trotting along behind her.

She'd come, he knew, to have another confab with Butterpie. The idea at once amused him and jabbed through his conscience like a spike. Sophie was on the other side of the country, homesick as hell and probably sticking pins in a daddy doll. She missed the pony, and the pony missed her, and *he* was the hard-ass who was keeping them apart.

Taking his coat and hat down from the peg next to the back door, he put them on and went outside. He was used to being alone, even liked it, but keeping company with Doc O'Ballivan, bristly though she sometimes was, would provide a welcome diversion.

He gave her time to reach Butterpie's stall, then walked into the barn.

The golden came to greet him, all wagging tail and melting brown eyes, and he bent to stroke her soft, sturdy back. "Hey, there, dog," he said.

Sure enough, Olivia was in the stall, brushing Butterpie down and talking to her in a soft, soothing voice that touched something private inside Tanner and made him want to turn on one heel and beat it back to the house.

He'd be damned if he'd do it, though.

This was *his* ranch, *his* barn. Well-intentioned as she was, *Olivia* was the trespasser here, not him.

"She's still very upset," Olivia told him without turning to look at him or slowing down with the brush.

For a second Tanner thought she was referring to Sophie, not the pony, and that got his hackles up.

Shiloh, always an easy horse to get along with, stood contentedly in his own stall, munching away on the feed Tanner had given him earlier. Butterpie, he noted, hadn't touched her supper as far as he could tell.

"Do you know anything at all about horses, Mr. Quinn?" Olivia asked.

He leaned against the stall door, the way he had the day before, and grinned. He'd practically been raised on horseback; he and Tessa had grown up on their grandmother's farm in the Texas hill country, after their folks divorced and went their separate ways, both of them too busy to bother with a couple of kids. "A few things," he said. "And I mean to call you Olivia, so you might as well return the favor and address me by my first name."

He watched as she took that in, dealt with it, decided on an approach. He'd have to wait and see what that turned out to be, but he didn't mind. It was a pleasure just watching Olivia O'Ballivan grooming a horse.

"All right, *Tanner*," she said. "This barn is a disgrace. When are you going to have the roof fixed? If it snows again, the hay will get wet and probably mold...."

He chuckled, shifted a little. He'd have a crew out there the following Monday morning to replace the roof and shore up the walls—he'd made the arrangements over a week before—but he felt no particular compunction to explain that. He was enjoying her ire too much; it made her color rise and her hair fly when she turned her head, and the faster breathing made her perfect breasts go up and down in an enticing rhythm. "What makes you so sure I'm a greenhorn?" he asked mildly, still leaning on the gate.

At last she looked straight at him, but she didn't move from Butterpie's side. "Your hat, your boots—that fancy red truck you drive. I'll bet it's customized."

Tanner grinned. Adjusted his hat. "Are you telling me real cowboys don't drive red trucks?"

"There are lots of trucks around here," she said. "Some of them are red, and some of them are new.

And *all* of them are splattered with mud or manure or both."

"Maybe I ought to put in a car wash, then," he teased. "Sounds like there's a market for one. Might be a good investment."

She softened, though not significantly, and spared him a cautious half smile, full of questions she probably wouldn't ask. "There's a good car wash in Indian Rock," she informed him. "People go there. It's only forty miles."

"Oh," he said with just a hint of mockery. "*Only* forty miles. Well, then. Guess I'd better dirty up my truck if I want to be taken seriously in these here parts. Scuff up my boots a bit, too, and maybe stomp on my hat a couple of times."

Her cheeks went a fetching shade of pink. "You are twisting what I said," she told him, brushing Butterpie again, her touch gentle but sure. "I meant..."

Tanner envied that little horse. Wished he had furry hide, so he'd need brushing, too.

"You *meant* that I'm not a real cowboy," he said. "And you could be right. I've spent a lot of time on construction sites over the last few years, or in meetings where a hat and boots wouldn't be appropriate. Instead of digging out my old gear, once I decided to take this job, I just bought new."

"I bet you don't even *have* any old gear," she challenged, but she was smiling, albeit cautiously, as though she might withdraw into a disapproving frown at any second.

He took off his hat, extended it to her. "Here," he teased. "Rub that around in the muck until it suits you."

She laughed, and the sound—well, it caused a powerful and wholly unexpected shift inside him. Scared the hell out of him and, paradoxically, made him yearn to hear it again. "That would be a little drastic," she said.

Tanner put his hat back on. "You figure me for a rhinestone cowboy," he said. "What else have you decided about me?"

She considered the question, evidently drawing up a list in her head.

Tanner was fascinated—and still pretty scared.

"Brad told me you were widowed," she said finally, after mulling for a while. "I'm sorry about that."

Tanner swallowed hard, nodded. Wondered how much detail his friend had gone into, and decided not to ask. He'd told Brad the whole grim story of Kat's death, once upon a time.

"You're probably pretty driven," Olivia went on, concentrating on the horse again. "It's obvious that you're successful—Brad wouldn't have hired you for this project if you weren't the best. And you compartmentalize."

"Compartmentalize?"

"You shut yourself off from distractions."

"Such as?"

"Your daughter," Olivia said. She didn't lack for nerve, that was for sure. "And this poor little horse. You'd like to have a dog—you like Ginger a lot—but you wouldn't adopt one because that would mean making a commitment. Not being able to drop everything and everybody and take off for the next Big Job when the mood struck you."

Tanner felt as though he'd been slapped, and it didn't help one bit that everything she'd said was true. Which didn't mean he couldn't deny it.

"I *love* Sophie," he said grimly.

She met his gaze again. "I'm sure you do. Still, you find it easy enough to—compartmentalize where she's concerned, don't you?"

"I do not," he argued. He *did* "compartmentalize"— he had to—but he sure as hell wouldn't call it easy. Every parting from Sophie was harder on him than it was on her. He was the one who always had to suck it up and be strong.

Olivia shrugged, patted the pony affectionately on the neck and set aside the brush. "I'll be back tomorrow," she told the animal. "In the meantime, think good thoughts and talk to Shiloh if you get too lonesome."

Tanner racked his brain, trying to remember if he'd told Olivia the gelding's name. He was sure it hadn't come up in their brief but tempestuous acquaintance. "How did you…?"

"He told me," Olivia said, approaching the stall door and waiting for him to step out of her way, just like before.

"Are you seriously telling me I've got Mr. Ed in my barn?" he asked, moving aside so she could pass.

She crossed to Shiloh's stall, reached up to stroke his nose when he nuzzled her and gave a companionable nicker. "You wouldn't understand," she said, with so much smug certainty that Tanner found himself wanting to prove a whole bunch of things he'd never felt the need to prove before.

"Because I compartmentalize?" Tanner gibed.

"Something like that," Olivia answered blithely. She turned from Shiloh, snapped her fingers to attract the dog's attention and started for the barn door.

"See you tomorrow, if you're here when I come by to look in on Butterpie."

Utterly confounded, Tanner stood in the doorway watching as Olivia lowered a ramp at the back of the Suburban for Ginger, waited for the dog to trot up it, and shut the doors.

Moments later she was driving off, tooting a merry "so long" on the horn.

THAT NIGHT HE DREAMED of Kat.

*She was alive again, standing in the barn at Butterpie's stall gate, watching as the pony nibbled hay at its feeder. Tall and slender, with long dark hair, Kat turned to him and smiled a welcome.*

He hated these dreams for *being* dreams, not reality. At the same time he couldn't bring himself to wake up, to leave her.

The settings were always different—their first house, their quarters in the American compound in some sandy, dangerous foreign place, even supermarket aisles and gas stations. He'd be standing at the pump, filling the vehicle *de jour,* and look up to see Kat with a hose in her hand, gassing up that old junker she'd been driving when they met.

He stood at a little distance from her, there in the barn aisle, well aware that after a few words, a few minutes at most, she'd vanish. And it would be like losing her all over again.

She smiled, but there was sadness in her eyes, in the set of her full mouth. "Hello, Tanner," she said very softly.

He couldn't speak. Couldn't move. Somehow he knew that this visit was very different from all the ones that had gone before.

She came to stand in front of him, soft as summer in

her white cotton sundress, and touched his arm as she looked up into his face.

"It's time for me to move on," she told him.

*No.*

The word swelled up inside him, but he couldn't say it.

And Kat vanished.

# CHAPTER FOUR

OLIVIA AWAKENED on the following Thursday morning feeling as though she hadn't slept at all the night before, with Ginger's cold muzzle pressed into her neck and the alarm clock buzzing insistently. She stirred, opened her eyes, slapped down the snooze button, with a muttered "Shut *up!*"

Iridescent frost embossed the window glass in intricate fans and swirls, turning it opaque, but the light got through anyway, signaling the arrival of a new day—like it or not.

*Thanksgiving,* Olivia recalled. *The official start of the holiday season.*

She groaned and yanked the covers up over her head.

Ginger let out an impatient little yip.

"I know," Olivia replied from under two quilts and a flannel sheet worn to a delectable, hard-to-leave softness. It was so warm under those covers, so cozy. Would that she could stay right there until sometime after the Second Coming. "I know you need to go outside."

Ginger yipped again, more insistently this time.

Bleary-eyed, Olivia rolled onto her side, tossed back the covers and sat up. She'd slept in gray sweats and heavy socks—less than glamorous attire, for sure, but toasty and loose.

After hitting the stop button on the clock so it wouldn't

start up again in five minutes, she stumbled out of the bedroom and down the hall toward the small kitchen at the back of the house. Passing the thermostat, she cranked it up a few degrees. As she groped her way past the coffeemaker, she jabbed blindly at yet another button to start the pot she'd set up the night before. At the door she shoved her feet into an old pair of ugly galoshes and shrugged into a heavy jacket of red-and-black-plaid wool—Big John's chore coat.

It still smelled faintly of his budget aftershave and pipe tobacco.

The weather stripping stuck when she tried to open the back door, and she muttered a four-letter word as she tugged at the knob. The instant there was a crack to pass through, Ginger shot out of that kitchen like a clown dog from a circus cannon. She banged open the screen door beyond, too, without slowing down for the enclosed porch.

"Ginger!" Olivia yelled, startled, before taking one rueful glance back at the coffeemaker. It shook and gurgled like a miniature rocket trying to lift off the counter, and it would take at least ten minutes to produce enough java to get Olivia herself off the launch pad. She needed to buy a new one—item number seventy-two on her domestic to-do list. The timer had given out weeks ago, and the handle on the carafe was loose.

And where the hell was the dog headed? Ginger *never* ran.

Olivia shook the last clinging vestiges of sleep out of her head and tromped through the porch and down the outside steps, taking care not to slip on the ice and either land on her tailbone or take a flyer into the snowbank beside the walk.

"Ginger!" she called a second time as the dog streaked halfway down the driveway, shinnied under the rail fence between Olivia's place and Tanner's and bounded out into the snowy field.

Goose-stepping it to the fence, Olivia climbed onto the lowest rail and shaded her eyes from the bright, cold sun. What was Ginger chasing? Coyotes? Wolves? Either way, that was a fight an aging golden retriever couldn't possibly win.

Olivia was about to scramble over the fence and run after the dog when she saw the palomino in the distance, and the man sitting tall in the saddle.

Tanner.

The horse moved at a smooth trot while Ginger cavorted alongside, flinging up snow, like a pup in a superchow commercial.

Olivia sighed, partly out of relief that Ginger wasn't about to tangle with the resident wildlife and partly because Tanner was clearly headed her way.

She looked down at her rumpled sweats; they were clean, but the pants had worn threadbare at the knees and there was a big bleach stain on the front of the shirt. She pulled the front of Big John's coat closed with one hand and ran the other through her uncombed hair.

Tanner's grin flashed as white as the landscape around him when he rode up close to the fence. Despite the grin, he looked pale under his tan, and there was a hollow look in his eyes. The word *haunted* came to mind.

"Mornin', ma'am," he drawled, tugging at the brim of his hat. "Just thought I'd mosey on over and say howdy."

"How very Western of you," Olivia replied with a reluctant chuckle.

Ginger, winded by the unscheduled run, was panting hard.

"What in the world got into you?" Olivia scolded the dog. "Don't you ever do that again!"

Ginger crossed the fence line and slunk toward the house.

When Olivia turned back to Tanner, she caught him looking her over.

Wise guy.

"It would be mighty neighborly of you to offer a poor wayfaring cowboy a hot cup of coffee," he said. He sat that horse as if he was part of it—a point in his favor. He might dress like a dandy, but he was no stranger to a saddle.

"Glad to oblige, mister," Olivia joked, playing along. "Unless you insist on talking like a B-movie wrangler for much longer. That could get old."

He laughed at that, rode to the rickety gate a few yards down the way, leaned to work the latch easily and joined Olivia on her side. Taking in the ramshackle shed and detached garage, he swung down out of the saddle to walk beside her, leading Shiloh by a slack rein.

"Looks to me like you don't have a whole lot of room to talk about the state of my barn," he said. His eyes were twinkling now under the brim of his hat, though he still looked wan.

It was harder going for Olivia—her legs were shorter, the galoshes didn't fit so they stuck at every step, and the snow came to her shins. "I rent this place," she said, feeling defensive. "The owner lives out of state and doesn't like to spend a nickel on repairs if he can help it. In fact, he's been threatening to sell it for years."

"Ah," Tanner said with a sage nod. "Are you just

passing through Stone Creek, Doc? I had the impression you were a lifelong resident, but maybe I was wrong."

"Except for college and veterinary school," Olivia answered, "I've lived here all my life." She looked around at the dismal rental property. "Well, not right here—"

"Hey," Tanner said, quietly gruff. "I was kidding."

She nodded, embarrassed because she'd been caught caring what he thought, and led the way through the yard toward the back door.

Tanner left Shiloh loosely tethered to the hand rail next to the porch steps.

Inside the kitchen, Olivia fed a remorseful Ginger, washed her hands at the sink and got two mugs down out of the cupboard. The coffeemaker was just flailing in for a landing, mission accomplished.

"Excuse me for a second, will you?" Olivia asked after filling mugs for herself and Tanner and giving him his. She slipped into the bedroom, closed the door, put down her coffee cup and quickly switched out the chore coat and her sweats for her best pair of jeans and the blue sweater Ashley had knitted for her as a Christmas gift. She even went so far as to splash her face with water in the tiny bathroom, give her teeth a quick brushing and run a comb through her hair.

When she returned to the kitchen, Tanner was sitting in a chair at the table, looking as if he belonged there, and Ginger stood with her head resting on his thigh while he stroked her back.

Something sparked in Tanner's weary eyes when he looked up—maybe amusement, maybe appreciation. Maybe something more complicated.

Olivia felt a wicked little thrill course through her system.

"Thanksgiving," she said without planning to, almost sighing out the word.

"You don't sound all that thankful," Tanner observed.

"Oh, I am," Olivia insisted, taking a sip from her mug.

"Me, too," Tanner said. "Mostly."

She bit her lower lip, stole a glance at the clock above the sink. It was early—two hours before she needed to check in at the clinic. So much for excusing herself to go to work.

"Mostly?" she echoed, keeping her distance.

"There are things I'd change about my life," Tanner told her. "If I could."

She drew nearer then, interested in spite of herself, and sat down, though she kept the width of the table between them. "What would you do differently?"

He sighed, and a bleak expression darkened his eyes. "I'd have kept the business smaller, for one thing," he said. The briefest flicker of pain contorted his face. "Not gone international. How about you?"

"I'd have spent more time with my grandfather," she replied after giving the question some thought. "I guess I figured he was going to be around forever."

"That was his coat you were wearing before."

"How did you guess that?"

"My grandmother had one just like it. I think they must have sold those at every farm supply store in America, back in the day."

Olivia relaxed a little. "How's Butterpie?"

Tanner sighed, met Olivia's gaze. Held it. "She's not eating," he said.

"I was afraid of that," Olivia murmured, distracted.

"I thought my grandmother was going to live forever, too," Tanner told her.

It took Olivia a moment to catch up. "She's gone, then?"

Tanner nodded. "Died on her seventy-eighth birthday, hoeing the vegetable garden. Just the way she'd have wanted to go—quick, and doing something she loved to do. Your grandfather?"

"Heart attack," Olivia said, running her palms along the thighs of her jeans. Why were they suddenly moist?

Tanner was silent for what seemed like a long time, though it was an easy silence. Then he finished his coffee and stood. "Guess I'd better not keep you," he said, crossing the room to set his cup in the sink.

Ginger's liquid eyes followed him adoringly.

"I'd like to look in on Butterpie on my way into town, if that's okay with you?" Olivia said.

One side of Tanner's fine mouth slanted slightly upward. "Would it stop you if it *wasn't* okay with me?"

She grinned. "Nope."

He chuckled at that. "I've got some things to do in town," he said. "Gotta pick up some wine for Thanksgiving dinner. So if I don't see you in my barn, we'll meet up at Brad and Meg's place later on."

Of *course* her brother and sister-in-law would have invited Tanner to join them for Thanksgiving dinner. He was a friend, and he lived alone. Still, Olivia felt blindsided. Holidays were hard enough without stirring virtual strangers into the mix. Especially *attractive* ones.

"See you then," she said, hoping her smile didn't look forced.

He nodded and left, closing the kitchen door quietly behind him. Olivia immediately went to the window to watch him mount Shiloh and ride off.

When he was out of sight, and only then, Olivia turned from the window and zeroed in on Ginger.

"What were you *thinking,* running off like that? You're not a young dog, you know."

*"I just got a little carried away, that's all,"* Ginger said without lifting her muzzle off her forelegs. Her eyes looked soulful. *"Are you wearing that getup to Thanksgiving dinner?"*

Olivia looked down at her jeans and sweater. "What's wrong with my outfit?" she asked.

*"Touchy, touchy. I was just asking a simple question."*

"These jeans are almost new, and Ashley made the sweater. I look perfectly fine."

*"Whatever you say."*

"Well, what do *you* think I should wear, O fashionista dog?"

*"The sweater's fine,"* Ginger observed. *"But I'd switch out the jeans for a skirt. You* do *have a skirt, don't you?"*

"Yes, I have a skirt. I also have rounds to make before dinner, so I'm changing into my work clothes right now."

Ginger sighed an it's-no-use kind of sigh. *"Paris Hilton you ain't,"* she said, and drifted off to sleep.

Olivia returned to her bedroom, put on her normal grubbies, suitable for barns and pastures, then located her tan faux-suede skirt, rolled it up like a towel and stuffed it into a gym bag. Knee boots and the blue sweater went in next, along with the one pair of panty hose she owned. They had runs in them, but the skirt was long and the boots were high, so it wouldn't matter.

When she got back to the kitchen, Ginger was stretching herself.

"You're coming with me today, aren't you?" Olivia asked.

Ginger eyed the gym bag and sighed again. *"As far as next door, anyway,"* she answered. *"I think Butterpie could use some company."*

"What about Thanksgiving?"

*"Bring me a plate,"* Ginger replied.

Oddly disappointed that Ginger didn't want to spend the holiday with her, Olivia went outside to fire up the Suburban and scrape off the windshield. After she'd lowered the ramp in the back of the rig, she went back to the house for Ginger.

"You're all right, aren't you?" Olivia asked as Ginger walked slowly up the ramp.

*"I'm not used to running through snow up to my chest,"* the dog told her. *"That's all."*

Still troubled, Olivia stowed the ramp and shut the doors on the Suburban. Ginger curled up on Rodney's blanket and closed her eyes.

When they arrived at Tanner's place, his truck was parked in the driveway, but he didn't come out of the house, and Olivia didn't knock on the front door. She repeated the ramp routine, and then she and Ginger headed into the barn.

Shiloh was back in his stall, brushed down and munching on hay.

Olivia paused to greet him, then opened the door to Butterpie's stall so she and Ginger could go in.

Butterpie stood with her head hanging low, but perked up slightly when she saw the dog.

"You've got to eat," Olivia told the pony.

Butterpie tossed her head from side to side, as though in refusal.

Ginger settled herself in a corner of the roomy stall, on a pile of fresh wood shavings, and gave another big sigh. *"Just go make your rounds,"* she said to Olivia. *"I'll get her to take a few bites after you're gone."*

Olivia felt bereft at the prospect of leaving Ginger and the pony. She found an old pan, filled it with water at the spigot outside, returned to set it down on the stall floor. "This is weird," she said to Ginger. "What's Tanner going to think if he finds you in Butterpie's stall?"

*"That you're crazy,"* Ginger answered. *"No real change in his opinion."*

"Very funny," Olivia said, not laughing. Or even smiling. "You're sure you'll be all right? I could come back and pick you up before I head for Stone Creek Ranch."

Ginger shut her eyes and gave an eloquent snore.

After that, there was no point in talking to her.

Olivia gave Butterpie a quick but thorough examination and left.

TANNER BOUGHT A HALF CASE of the best wine he could find—Stone Creek had only one supermarket, and the liquor store was closed. He should have lied, he thought as he stood at the checkout counter, paying for his purchases. Told Brad he had plans for Thanksgiving.

He was going to feel like an outsider, passing a whole afternoon and part of an evening with somebody else's family.

Better that, though, he supposed, than eating alone in the town's single sit-down restaurant, remembering Thanksgivings of old and missing Kat and Sophie.

Kat.

"Is that good?" the clerk asked.

Distracted, Tanner didn't know what the woman was talking about at first. Then she pointed to the wine. She was very young and very pretty, and she didn't seem to mind working on Thanksgiving when practically everybody else in the western hemisphere was bellying up to a turkey feast someplace.

"I don't know," Tanner said in belated answer to her cordial question. He'd been something of a wine aficionado once, but since he didn't indulge anymore, he'd sort of lost the knack. "I go by the labels, and the price."

The clerk nodded as if what he'd said made a lick of sense, and wished him a happy Thanksgiving.

He wished her the same, picked up the wine box, the six bottles rattling a little inside it, and made for the door.

The dream came back to him, full force, as he was setting the wine on the passenger seat of his truck.

Kat, standing in the aisle of the barn, in that white summer dress, telling him she wouldn't be back.

It was no good telling himself he'd only been dreaming in the first place. He'd held on to those night visits—they'd gotten him through a lot of emotional white water. It had been Kat who'd said he ought to watch his drinking. Kat who'd advised him to accept the Stone Creek job and oversee it himself instead of sending in somebody else.

Kat who'd insisted the newspapers were wrong; she hadn't been a target—she'd been caught in the cross fire of somebody else's fight. Sophie, she'd sworn, was in no danger.

She'd faded before his eyes like so much thin smoke a couple of nights before. The wrench in his gut had been powerful enough to wake up him up. The dream had stayed with him, though, which was the same as having it over and over again. Last night he'd been unable to sleep at all. He'd paced the dark empty house for a while, then, unable to bear it any longer, he'd gone out to the barn, saddled Shiloh and taken a moonlight ride.

For a while he'd tried to outride what he was feeling—not loss, not sorrow, but a sense of letting go. Of somehow being set free.

He'd *loved* Kat, more than his own life. Why should her going on to wherever dead people went have given him a sense of liberation, even exaltation, rather than sorrow?

The guilt was almost overwhelming. As long as he'd mourned her, she'd seemed closer somehow. Now the worst was over. There had been some kind of profound shift, and he hadn't regained his footing.

They'd been out for hours, he and Shiloh, when he was crossing the field between his place and Olivia's and that dog of hers came racing toward him. He'd have gone home, put Shiloh up with some extra grain for his trouble, taken a shower and fallen into bed if it hadn't been for Ginger and the sight of Olivia standing on the bottom rail of the fence.

She'd been wearing sweats and silly rubber boots and an old man's coat, and for all that, she'd managed to look sexy. He'd finagled an invitation for coffee—hell, he'd flat out invited *himself*—and thought about taking her to bed the whole time he was there.

Not that he would have made a move on Doc. It was way too soon, and she'd probably have conked him over the head with the nearest heavy object, but he'd been tempted, just the same.

Tempted as he'd never been, since Kat.

At home he left the wine in the truck and headed for the barn.

Shiloh was asleep, standing up, the way horses do. When Tanner looked over the stall door at Butterpie, though, his eyes started to sting. Butterpie was lying in the wood shavings, and Olivia's dog was cuddled up right alongside her, as though keeping some kind of a vigil.

"I'll be damned," Tanner muttered. He'd grown up in the country, and he'd known horses to have nonequine companions—cows, cats, dogs and even pygmy goats. But he'd never seen anything quite like this.

He figured he probably should take Ginger home— Olivia might be looking for her—but he couldn't quite bring himself to part the two animals.

"You hungry, girl?" he asked Ginger, thinking what a fine thing it would be to have a dog. The problem was, he moved around too much—job to job, country to country. If he couldn't raise his own daughter, how could he hope to take good care of a mutt?

Ginger made a low sound in her throat and looked up at him with those melty eyes of hers. He made a quick trip into the house for a hunk of cube steak and a bowl of water, and set them both down where she could reach them.

She drank thirstily of the water, nibbled at the steak.

Tanner patted her head. He'd seen her jump into Olivia's Suburban the day before, so she still had some zip in her, despite the gray hairs around her muzzle, but she hadn't gotten over that stall door by herself. Olivia must have left her here, to look after the pony.

When he spotted an old grain pan in the corner, over-turned, he knew that was what had happened. She must have found the pan in the junk around the barn, filled it with water and left it so the dog could drink. Then one of the animals, most likely Butterpie, had stepped on the thing and spilled the contents.

He was pondering that sequence of events when his cell phone rang.

Sophie.

"This parade bites," she said without any preamble. "It's cold, and Mary Susan Parker keeps sneezing on me and we're not allowed to get into the minibar in our hotel suite! Ms. Wiggins took the keys away."

Tanner chuckled. "Hello and happy Thanksgiving to you, too, sweetheart," he said, so glad to hear her voice that his eyes started stinging again.

"It's not like we want to drink *booze* or anything," Sophie complained. "But we can't even help ourselves to a soda or a candy bar!"

"Horrible," Tanner commiserated.

An annoyed silence crackled from Sophie's end.

"Butterpie has a new friend," Tanner said, to get the conversation going again. In a way, talking to Sophie made him miss her more, but at the same time he wanted to keep her on the line as long as possible. "A dog named Ginger."

He'd caught Sophie's interest that time. "Really? Is it your dog?"

It was telling, Tanner thought, that Sophie had said "your dog" instead of "our dog." "No. Ginger lives next door. She's just here for a visit."

"I'm lonely, Dad," Sophie said, sounding much younger than her twelve years. She was almost shouting to be heard over a brass band belting out "Santa Claus Is Coming to Town." "Are you lonely, too?"

"Yes," he replied. "But there are worse things than being lonely, Soph."

"Right now I can't think of any. Are you going to be all alone all day?"

Crouching now, Tanner busied himself scratching Ginger's ears. "No. A friend invited me to dinner."

Sophie sighed with apparent relief. "Good. I was afraid you'd nuke one of those frozen TV dinners or something and eat it while you watched some football game. And that would be *pathetic*."

"Far be it from me to be pathetic," Tanner said, but a lump had formed in his throat and his voice came out sounding hoarse. "Anything but that."

"What friend?" Sophie persisted. "What friend are you having dinner with, I mean?"

"Nobody you know."

"A woman?" Was that *hope* he heard in his daughter's voice? "Have you met someone, Dad?"

Damn. It *was* hope. The kid probably fantasized that he'd remarry one day, and she could come home from boarding school for good, and they'd all live happily ever after, with a dog and two cars parked in the same garage every night, like a normal family.

That was never going to happen.

Ginger looked up at him in adoring sympathy when he rubbed his eyes, tired to the bone. His sleepless night was finally catching up with him—or that was what he told himself.

"No," he said. "I haven't met anybody, Soph." Olivia's face filled his mind. "Well, I've met somebody, but I haven't *met* them, if you know what I mean."

Sophie, being Sophie, *did* know what he meant. Exactly.

"But you're dating!"

"No," Tanner said quickly. Bumming a cup of coffee in a woman's kitchen didn't constitute a date, and neither did sitting at the same table with her on Thanksgiving Day. "No. We're just—just friends."

"Oh." Major disappointment. "This whole thing bites!"

"So you said," Tanner replied gently, wanting to soothe his daughter but not having the first clue how to go about it. "Maybe it's your mind-set. Since today's Thanksgiving, why not give gratitude a shot?"

She hung up on him.

He thought about calling her right back, but decided to do it later, after she'd had a little time to calm down, regain her perspective. She was a lucky kid, spending the holiday in New York, watching the famous parade in person, staying in a fancy hotel suite with her friends from school.

"Women," he told Ginger.

She gave a low whine and laid her muzzle on his arm.

He stayed in the barn a while, then went into the house, took a shower, shaved and crashed, asleep before his head hit the pillow.

And Kat did not come to him.

OLIVIA HAD STOPPED BY Tanner's barn on the way to Stone Creek Ranch, hoping to persuade Ginger to take a break from horsesitting, but she wouldn't budge.

Arriving at the homeplace, she checked on Rodney, who seemed content in his stall, then, gym bag in hand, she slipped inside the small bath off the tack room and grabbed a quick, chilly shower. She shimmied into those wretched panty hose, donned the skirt and the blue sweater and the boots, and even applied a little mascara and lip gloss for good measure.

Never let it be said that she'd come to a family dinner looking like a—*veterinarian.*

And the fact that Tanner Quinn was going to be at this shindig had absolutely *nothing* to do with her decision to spruce up.

Starting up the front steps, she had a sudden, poignant memory of Big John standing on that porch, waiting for her to come home from a high school date with Jesse McKettrick. After the dance all the kids had gone to the swimming hole on the Triple M, and splashed and partied until nearly dawn.

Big John had been furious, his face like a thundercloud, his voice dangerously quiet.

He'd given Jesse what-for for keeping his granddaughter out all night, and grounded Olivia for a month.

She'd been outraged, she recalled, smiling sadly. Tearfully informed her angry grandfather that *nothing had happened* between her and Jesse, which was true, if you didn't count necking. Now, of course, she'd have given almost anything to see that temperamental old man again, even if he *was* shaking his finger at her and telling her that in his day, young ladies knew how to behave themselves.

Lord, how she missed him, missed his rants. *Especially* the rants, because they'd been proof positive that he cared what happened to her.

The door opened just then, and Brad stepped out onto the porch, causing the paper turkey to flutter on its hook behind him.

"Ashley's going to kill me," Olivia said. "I forgot to pick up salads at the deli."

Brad laughed. "There's so much food in there, she'll never know the difference. Now, come on in before we both freeze to death."

Olivia hesitated. Swallowed. Watched as Brad's smile faded.

"What is it?" he asked, coming down the steps.

"Ashley's looking for Mom," she said. She hadn't planned to bring that up that day. It just popped out.

*"What?"*

"She's probably going to announce it at dinner or something," Olivia rushed on. "Is it just me, or do you think this is a bad idea, too?"

"It's a very bad idea," Brad said.

"You know something about Mom, don't you? Something you're keeping from the rest of us." It was a shot in the dark, a wild guess, but it struck the bull's-eye, dead center. She knew that by the grim expression on Brad's famous face.

"I know enough," he replied.

"I shouldn't have brought it up, but I was thinking about Big John, and that led to thinking about Mom, and I remembered what Ashley told me, so—"

"It's okay," Brad said, trying to smile. "Maybe she won't bring it up."

Olivia doubted they could be that lucky. Ashley was an O'Ballivan through and through, and when she got on a kick about something, she had to ride it out to the bitter end. "I could talk to her..."

Brad shook his head, pulled her inside the house. It was too hot and too crowded and too loud, but Olivia was determined to make the best of the situation, for her family's sake, if not her own.

Big John would have wanted it that way.

She hunted until she found Mac, sitting up in his playpen, and lifted him into her arms. "It smells pretty good in here, big guy," she told him. There was a fragrant fire crackling on the hearth, and Meg had lit some scented candles, and delicious aromas wafted from the direction of the kitchen.

Out of the corner of her eye Olivia spotted Tanner Quinn standing near Brad's baby grand piano, dressed up in a black suit, holding a bottle of water in one hand and trying hard to look as though he was enjoying himself.

Seeing his discomfort took Olivia's mind off her own. Still carrying Mac, she started toward him.

A cell phone went off before she could speak to him—*How the Grinch Stole Christmas*—and Tanner immediately reached into his pocket. Flipped open the phone.

As Olivia watched, she saw the color drain out of his face.

The water bottle slipped, and he caught it before it fell, though barely.

"What's wrong?" Olivia asked.

Mac, perfectly happy a moment before that, threw back his head and wailed for all he was worth.

"My daughter," Tanner said, standing stock-still. "She's gone."

## CHAPTER FIVE

THIS WAS THE CALL Tanner had feared since the day Kat died. Sophie, gone missing—or worse. Now that it had actually happened, he seemed to be frozen where he stood, fighting a crazy compulsion to run in all directions at once.

Olivia handed off the baby to Brad, who'd appeared at her side instantly, and touched Tanner's arm. "What do you mean, she's gone?"

Before he could answer, the cell ran through its little ditty again.

He didn't bother checking the caller ID panel. "Sophie?"

"Jack McCall," his old friend said. "We found Sophie, buddy. She's okay, if a little—make that a lot—disgruntled."

Relief washed over Tanner like a tidal wave, making him sway on his feet. "She's really all right?" Jack had been there for Tanner when Kat was killed, and if there was a blow coming, he might try to soften it.

Olivia stood looking up at him, waiting, her hand still resting lightly on his arm, fingers squeezing gently.

"She's *fine,*" Jack said easily. "Like I said, she's not real happy about being nabbed, though."

"Where was she?" Tanner had to feel around inside

his muddled brain for the question, thrust it out with force.

"Grand Central," Jack answered. "She sneaked away from the school group while they were making their way through the crowds after the parade. Fortunately, one of my guys spotted her right away, and tailed her to the station. She was buying a train ticket west."

Coming home. Sophie had been trying to come home.

Brad pulled out the piano bench, and Tanner sat down heavily, tossing his friend a grateful glance.

"Question of the hour," Jack went on. "What do we do now? She swears she'll run away again if we take her back to school, and I believe her. The kid is serious, Tanner."

Tanner let out a long sigh. He felt sick, light-headed, imagining all the things that could have happened to Sophie. And very, very glad when Olivia sat down on the bench beside him, her shoulder touching his. "Can you bring her here?" he asked. "To Stone Creek?"

"I'll come with her as far as Phoenix," Jack said. "I'll have my people there bring her the rest of the way by helicopter. The jet's due in L.A. by six o'clock Pacific time, and it's a government job, high-security south-of-the-border stuff, so I can't get out of the gig."

Tanner glanced sidelong at Olivia. She took his hand and clasped it. "I appreciate this, Jack," he said into the phone, his voice hoarse with emotion. "Send Sophie home."

Olivia smiled at that. Brad let out a sigh, grinned and went back to playing host at a family Thanksgiving dinner, taking his son with him. Folks started milling toward the food, laid out buffet-style in the dining room.

"Ten-four, old buddy," Jack said. "Maybe I'll stop in out there and say hello on my way back from Señoritaville. Book me a room somewhere, will you? I could do with a few months of R & R."

A few minutes before, Tanner couldn't have imagined laughing, ever again. But he did then. "That would be good," he said, choking up again. "Your being here, I mean. I'll ask around, find you a place to stay."

"Adios, amigo," Jack told him, and rang off.

"Sophie's okay?" Olivia asked softly.

"Until I get my hands on her, she is," Tanner answered.

"Stay right here," Olivia said, rising and taking off for the dining room beyond.

A short time later she was back, carrying two plates. "You need to eat," she informed Tanner.

And that was how they shared Thanksgiving dinner, sitting on Brad O'Ballivan's piano bench, with the living room all to themselves and blessedly quiet. Tanner was surprised to discover that he wasn't just hungry, he was ravenous.

"Feeling better?" Olivia asked when he was finished.

"Yeah," he answered. "But I don't think I'm up to socializing all afternoon."

"Me, either," Olivia confessed. She'd only picked at her food.

"Is there a sick cow somewhere?" Tanner asked, indulging in a slight grin. After the shock Sophie had given him, he was still pretty shaken up. "That would probably serve as an excuse for getting the heck out of here."

"They're all ridiculously healthy today," Olivia said.

Tanner chuckled. "Sorry to hear that," he teased.

She laughed, but the amusement didn't quite get as far as her eyes. Tanner wondered why the holiday made her so uncomfortable, but he didn't figure he knew her well enough to ask. He knew why *he* didn't like them—because the loss of his wife and grandmother stood out in sharp relief against all that merriment. And maybe that was Olivia's reason, too.

"I *am* pretty concerned about Butterpie," she said, as if inspired. "What do you say we steal one of the fifty-eight pumpkin pies lining Meg's kitchen counter and head back to your barn?"

Maybe it was the release of tension. Maybe it was because Olivia looked and smelled so damn good—almost as good as she had that morning, out by the fence and then later on, in her kitchen. Either way, the place he wanted to take her wasn't his barn.

"Okay," he said. "But if you're caught pie-napping, I'll deny being in cahoots with you."

Again that laugh, soft and musical and utterly feminine. It rang in Tanner's brain, then lodged itself square in the center of his heart. "Fair enough," she said.

She took their plates and left again, making for the kitchen.

Tanner found Brad standing by the sideboard in the big dining room, affably directing traffic between the food and the long table, where there was a lot of happy talk and dish clattering going on.

"Everything okay, buddy?" Brad asked, watching Tanner's face.

"I got a little scare," Tanner answered, shoving a hand through his hair. He knew a number of famous people, and not one of them was as down-home and levelheaded as Brad O'Ballivan. He was a man who had more than enough of everything, and knew it, and lived a comparatively simple life. "Just the same, I need a little alone time."

Brad nodded. Caught sight of Olivia coming out of the kitchen with the purloined pie and small plastic container, stopping to speak to Meg as she passed the crowded table. His gaze swung right back to Tanner. "Alone time, huh?" he asked.

"It's not what you think," Tanner felt compelled to say, feeling some heat rise in his neck.

Brad arched an eyebrow. Regarded him thoughtfully. "You're a good friend," he said. "But I love my sister. Keep that in mind, all right?"

Tanner nodded, liking Brad even more than before. Look out for the womenfolk—it was the cowboy way. "I'll keep it in mind," he replied.

He and Olivia left Stone Creek Ranch at the same time, he in his too-clean red truck, she in that scruffy old Suburban. The drive to Starcross took about fifteen minutes, and Olivia was out of her rig and headed into the barn before he'd parked his pickup.

Butterpie was on her feet, Ginger rising from a stretch when Tanner caught up to Olivia in front of the stall door. Olivia opened the plastic container, revealing leftover turkey.

"Tell Butterpie Sophie's coming home," he said, without intending to say any such thing.

Olivia smiled, inside the stall now, letting Ginger scarf up cold turkey from the container. "I already did," she replied. "That's why Butterpie is up. She could use a little exercise, so let's turn her out in the corral for a while."

Tanner nodded, found a halter and slipped it over Butterpie's head. Led her outside and over to the corral gate, and turned her loose.

Olivia and Ginger stood beside him, watching as the pony looked around, as if baffled to find herself outside in the last blaze of afternoon sunlight and the heretofore pristine snow. The dog barked a couple of times, as if to encourage Butterpie.

Tanner shook his head. Ridiculous, he thought. Dogs didn't *encourage* horses.

He recalled finding Ginger huddled close to Butterpie in the stall earlier in the day. Or *did* they?

Butterpie just stood there for a while, then nuzzled through the snow for some grass.

Whether the little horse had cheered up or not, *he* certainly had. Butterpie hadn't eaten anything since she'd arrived at Starcross Ranch, and now she was ready to graze. He went back into the barn and came out with a flake of hay, tossed it into the corral.

Butterpie nosed it around a bit and began to nibble.

Olivia watched for a few moments, then turned to Tanner and took smug note of the hay stuck to the front of his best suit. "You might be a real cowboy after all," she mused, and that simple statement, much to Tanner's amazement, pleased him almost as much as knowing Sophie was safe with his best friend, Jack McCall.

"Thanks," he said, resting his arms on the top rail of the corral fence and watching Butterpie eat.

When the pony came to the gate, clearly ready to return to the barn, Tanner led her back to her stall and got her settled in. Olivia and Ginger followed, waiting nearby.

"So what happened with Sophie?" Olivia asked when Tanner came out of the stall.

"I'll explain it over coffee and pie," he said, holding his figurative breath for her answer. If Olivia decided to go home, or make rounds or something, he was going to be seriously disappointed.

"This place used to be wonderful," Olivia said, minutes later, when they were in his kitchen, with the coffee brewing and the pie sitting on the table between them.

Tanner wished he'd taken down the old calendar, spackled the holes in the wall from the tacks that had held up its predecessors. Replaced the flooring and all the appliances, and maybe the cupboards, too. The house still looked abandoned, he realized, even with him living in it.

What did *that* mean?

"I'll fix it up," he said. "Sell it before I move on." It was what he always did. Buy a house, keep a careful emotional distance from it, refurbish it and put it on the market, always at a profit.

Something flickered in Olivia's eyes. Seeing that *he'd* seen, she looked away, though not quickly enough.

"Did you know the previous owner well?" he asked, to get her talking again. The sound of her voice soothed him, and right then he needed soothing.

"Of course," she said, turning the little tub of whipped cream, stolen along with the pie and the leftovers for Ginger, in an idle circle on the tabletop. "Clarence was one of Big John's best friends. He was widowed sometime in the mid-nineties—Clarence, I mean—and after that he just lost interest in Starcross."

She paused, sighed, a small frown creasing the skin between her eyebrows. "He got rid of the livestock, cow by cow, horse by horse. He stopped doing just about everything." Another break came then. "It's the name, I think."

"The name?"

"Of the ranch," Olivia clarified. "Starcross. It's—sad."

Tanner found himself grinning a little. "What would you call it, Doc?" he asked. The coffee was finished, and he got up to find some cups and pour a dose for both of them.

She considered his question as if there were really a name change in the offing. "Something, well, *happier,*" she said as he set the coffee down in front of her, realized they'd need plates and forks for the pie and went back to the cupboards to rustle some up. "More positive and cheerful, I guess, like The Lucky Horseshoe, or The Diamond Spur. Something like that."

Tanner had no intention of giving the ranch a new name—why go to all the trouble when he'd be leaving in a year at the longest?—but he enjoyed listening to Olivia, watching each new expression cross her face. The effect was fascinating.

And oh, that face.

The body under it was pretty spectacular, too.

Tanner shifted uncomfortably in his chair.

"Don't you think those names are a little pretentious?" he asked, cutting into the pie.

"Corny, maybe," Olivia admitted, smiling softly. "But not pretentious."

He served her a piece of pie, then cut one for himself. Watched with amusement and a strange new tenderness as she spooned on the prepackaged whipped cream. She looked pink around the neck, perhaps a little discomforted because he was staring.

He averted his eyes, but a moment later he was looking again. He couldn't seem to help it.

"You took the first chance you could get to bolt out of that Thanksgiving shindig at your brother's place," he said carefully. "Why is that, Doc?"

"Why do you keep calling me 'Doc'?" She *was* nervous, then. Maybe she sensed that Tanner wanted to kiss her senseless and then take her upstairs to his bed.

"Because you're a doctor?"

"I have a name."

"A very beautiful name."

She grinned, and some of the tension eased, which might or might not have been a good thing. "Get a shovel," she said. "It's getting deep in here."

He laughed, pushed away his pie.

"I should go now," she said, but she looked and sounded uncertain.

*Hallelujah,* Tanner thought. She was tempted, at least.

"Or you could stay," he suggested casually.

She gnawed at her lower lip. "Is it just me?" she asked bluntly. "Or are there sexual vibes bouncing off the walls?"

"There are definitely vibes," he confirmed.

"We haven't even kissed."

"That would be easy to remedy."

"And we've only known each other a few days."

"We're both adults, Olivia."

"I can't just—just go to bed with you, just because I—"

"Just because you want to?"

Challenge flared in her eyes, and she straightened her shoulders. "Who says I want to?"

"Do you?"

"Yes," she said, after a very long time. Then, quickly, "But that doesn't mean I will."

"Of course it doesn't."

"People ought to say no to themselves once in a while," she went on, apparently grasping at moral straws. "This society is way too into instant gratification."

"I promise you," Tanner said drily, "it won't be instant."

Color flooded her face, and he could see her pulse beating hard at the base of her throat.

"When was the last time you made love?" he asked when she didn't say anything. Nor, to his satisfaction, did she jump to her feet and bolt for the door.

Tanner's hopes were rising, and so was something else.

"That's a pretty personal question," she said, sounding miffed. She even went so far as to glance over at the dog, sleeping the sleep of the innocent on the rug in front of the stove.

"I'll tell if you will."

"It's been a while," she admitted loftily. "And maybe I don't *want* to know who you've had sex with and how recently. Did that ever occur to you?"

"A while as in six months to a year, or never?"

"I'm not a virgin, if that's what you're trying to find out."

"Good," he said.

"I'm leaving," she said. But she didn't get up from

her chair. She didn't call the dog, or even put down her fork, though she wasn't taking in much pie.

"You're free to do that."

"Of course I am."

"*Or* we could go upstairs, right now."

She swallowed visibly, and her wonderful eyes widened.

Hot damn, she was actually considering it.

Letting herself go. Doing something totally irresponsible, just for the hell of it. Tanner went hard, and he was glad she couldn't see through the tabletop.

"No strings attached?" she asked.

"No strings," Tanner promised, though he felt a little catch inside, saying the words. He wondered at his reaction, but not for long.

He was a man, after all, sitting across a table from one of the loveliest, most confusing women he'd ever met.

"I suppose we're just going to obsess until we do it," Olivia said. Damn, but she was full of surprises. He'd expected her to be talking herself *out* of going to bed with him, not *into* it.

"Probably," Tanner said, very seriously.

"Get it out of the way."

"Out of our systems," Tanner agreed, wanting to keep the ball rolling. Watching for the right time to make his move and all the time asking himself what the hell he was doing.

He stood up.

She stood up. And probably noticed his erection.

Would she run for it after all?

Tanner waited.

She waited.

"Can I kiss you?" he asked finally. "We could decide after that."

"Good idea," Olivia said, but her pulse was still fluttering visibly, at her temple now as well as her throat, and her breathing was quick and shallow, raising and lowering her breasts under that soft blue sweater.

She didn't move, so it fell to Tanner to step in close, take her face in his hands and kiss her, very gently at first, then with tongue.

WHAT WAS SHE *DOING?* Olivia fretted, even as she stood on tiptoe so Tanner could kiss her more deeply. Sure, it had been a while since she'd had sex—ten months, to be exact, with the last man she'd dated—but it wasn't as if she were *hot to trot* or anything like that.

This...*this* was like storm chasing—venturing too close to a tornado and getting sucked in by the whirlwind. She felt both helpless and all-powerful, standing there in Tanner Quinn's dreary kitchen—helpless because she'd known even before they left Stone Creek Ranch that this would happen, and all-powerful because *damn it,* she wanted it, too.

She wanted hot, sticky, wet *sex.* And she knew Tanner could give it to her.

They kissed until her knees felt weak, and she sagged against Tanner.

Then he lifted her into his arms. "You're sure about this, Doc?"

She swallowed, nodded. "I'm sure."

Ginger raised her head, lowered it again and went back to sleep.

His room was spacious and relatively clean, though he probably hadn't made the bed since he'd moved in.

Olivia noted these things with a detached part of her brain, but her elemental, primitive side wanted to rip off her clothes as if they were on fire.

Tanner undressed her slowly, kissing her bare shoulder when he unveiled it, then her upper breast. When he tongued her right nipple, then her left, she gasped and arched her back, wanting more.

He stopped long enough to shed his suit coat and toss aside his tie.

Olivia handled the buttons and buckle and finally the zipper.

And they were both naked.

He kissed her again, eased her down on the side of the bed, knelt on the floor to kiss her belly and her thighs. "Where's the whipped cream when you need it?" he teased, his voice a low rumble against her flesh.

"Oh, God," Olivia said, because she knew what he was going to do, and because she wanted so much for him to do it.

He burrowed through the nest of curls at the apex of her thighs, found her with his mouth, suckled, gently at first, then greedily.

He made a low sound to let her know he was enjoying her, but she barely heard it over the pounding of her heart and the creaking of the bed springs as her hips rose and fell in the ancient dance.

He slid his hands under her, raised her high off the bed and feasted on her in earnest. The first orgasm broke soon after that, shattering and sudden, and so long that Olivia felt as though she were being tossed about on the head of a fiery geyser.

Just when she thought she couldn't bear the pleasure for another moment—or live without it—he allowed her to descend. She marveled at his skill even as she bounced between one smaller, softer climax after another.

At last she landed, sated and dazed, and let out a croony sigh.

She heard the drawer on the bedside stand open and close.

"Still sure?" Tanner asked, shifting his body to reach for what he needed.

She nodded. Gave another sigh. "Oh, very sure," she said.

He turned her on the bed, slipped a pillow under her head and kissed her lightly. She clasped her hands behind his head and pulled him closer, kissed him back.

This part was for him, she thought magnanimously. She'd had her multiclimax—now it was time to be generous, let Tanner enjoy the satisfaction he'd earned.

Oh, God, had he earned it.

Except that when he eased inside her, she was instantly aroused, every cell in her body screaming with need. She couldn't do it; she couldn't come like that a second time without disintegrating—could she?

She was well into the climb, though, and there was no going back.

They shared the next orgasm, and the one after that.

And then they slept.

It was dark in the room when Olivia awakened, panic-stricken, to a strange whuff-whuff-whuff sound permeating the roof of that old house. Tanner was nowhere to be seen.

She flew out of bed, scrambled into her clothes, except for the panty hose, which she tossed into the trash—what *was* that deafening noise?—and dashed down the back stairs into the kitchen. Ginger, on her feet and barking, paused to give her a knowing glance.

"Shut up," Olivia said, hurrying to the window.

Tanner was out there, standing in what appeared to be a floodlight, looking up. Then the helicopter landed, right there in the yard.

Olivia rubbed her eyes hard, but when she looked again, the copter was still there, black and ominous against the snow. The blades slowed and then a young girl got out of the bird, stood still. Tanner stooped as he went toward the child, put an arm around her shoulders and steered her away, toward the house.

He paused when the copter lifted off again, waved.

Sophie had arrived, Olivia realized. And in grand style, too.

"Do I look like I've just had sex?" she asked Ginger in a frantic whisper.

*"I wouldn't know what you look like when you've just had sex,"* Ginger answered. *"I'm a dog, remember?"*


"BEFORE YOU START yelling at me," Sophie said, looking up at Tanner with Kat's eyes, "can I just say hello to Butterpie?"

Tanner, torn between wishing he believed in spanking kids and a need to hold his daughter safe and close and tight, shoved his hands into the pockets of his leather jacket. "The barn's this way," he said, though it was plainly visible, and started walking.

Sophie shivered as she hurried along beside him. "We could," she said breathlessly, "just dispense with the yelling entirely and go on from there."

"Fat chance," Tanner told her.

"I'm in trouble, huh?"

"What do you think?" Tanner retorted, trying to sound stern. In truth, he was so glad to see Sophie, he hardly trusted himself to talk.

He should have woken Olivia when he got the call from Jack's pilot, he thought. Warned her of Sophie's impending arrival.

As if she could have missed hearing that helicopter.

"I think," Sophie said with the certainty of youth, "I'm really happy to be here, and if you yell at me, I can take it."

Tanner suppressed a chuckle. This was no time to be a pal. "You could have been kidnapped," he said. "The list of things that might have happened to you—"

"*Might* have," Sophie pointed out sagely. "That's the key phrase, Dad. Nothing *did* happen, except one of Uncle Jack's guys collared me at Grand Central. *That* was a tense moment, not to mention embarrassing."

Having made that statement, Sophie dashed ahead of him and into the barn, calling Butterpie's name.

By the time he flipped on the overhead lights, she was already in the stall, hugging the pony's neck.

Butterpie whinnied with what sounded like joy.

And Olivia appeared at Tanner's elbow. "We'll be going now," she said quietly, watching the reunion with a sweet smile. "Ginger and I."

"Wait," Tanner said when she would have turned away. "I want you to meet Sophie."

"This is your time, and Sophie's," Olivia said, standing on tiptoe to kiss his cheek. "Tomorrow, maybe."

It was a simple kiss, nothing compared to the ones they'd shared upstairs in his bedroom. Just the same, Tanner felt as though he'd stepped on a live wire. His skeleton was probably showing, like in a cartoon.

"Maybe you feel like explaining what I'm doing here at this hour," she reasoned, with a touch of humor lingering on her mouth, "but I don't."

Reluctantly Tanner nodded.

Ginger and Olivia left, without Sophie ever noticing them.

AT HOME, OLIVIA showered, donned a ragged chenille bathrobe and listened to her voice mail, just in case there was an emergency somewhere. She'd already checked her cell phone, but you never knew.

The only message was from Ashley. "Where *were* you?" her younger sister demanded. "Today was *Thanksgiving!*"

Olivia sighed, waited out the diatribe, then hit the bullet and pressed the eight key twice to connect with Ashley.

"Mountain View Bed-and-Breakfast," Ashley answered tersely. She already knew who was calling, then. Hence the tone.

"Any openings?" Olivia asked, hoping to introduce a light note.

Ashley wasn't biting. She repeated her voice mail message, almost verbatim, ending with another "Where were you?"

"There was an emergency," Olivia said. What else could she say? *I was in bed with Tanner Quinn and I had myself a hell of a fine time, thank you very much.*

Suspicion, tempered by the knowledge that emergencies were a way of life with Olivia. "What kind of emergency?"

Olivia sighed. "You don't want to know," she said. It was true, after all. Ashley was a normal, healthy woman, but that didn't mean she'd want a blow-by-blow description—so to speak—of what she and Tanner had done in his bed.

"Another cow appendectomy?" Ashley asked, half sarcastic, half uncertain.

"A clandestine operation," she said, remembering the black helicopter. *That* would give the local conspiracy theorists something to chew on for a while, if they'd seen it.

"Really? There was an operation?"

Tanner was certainly an operator, Olivia thought, so she said yes.

"And here I thought you were probably having sex with that contractor Brad hired to build the shelter," Ashley said with an exasperated little sigh.

Olivia swallowed a giggle. Spoke seriously. "Ashley O'Ballivan, why would you think a thing like that?"

"Because I saw you leave with him," Ashley answered. Her tone turned huffy again. "I wanted to tell Brad and Melissa that I've decided to look for Mom," she complained. "And I couldn't do it without you there."

Olivia sobered. "Pretty heavy stuff, when Brad and Meg had a houseful of guests, wouldn't you say?"

Ashley went quiet again.

"Ash?" Olivia prompted. "Are you still there?"

"I'm here."

"So why the sudden silence?"

Another pause. A long one that gave Olivia plenty of time to worry. Then, finally, the bomb dropped. "I think I've already found her."

# CHAPTER SIX

"THIS PLACE," SOPHIE SAID, looking around at the ranch-house kitchen the next morning, "needs a woman's touch. Or maybe a crack decorating crew from HGTV or DIY."

Tanner, still half-asleep, stood at the counter pouring badly needed coffee. Between Sophie's great adventure and all that sex with Olivia, he felt disoriented, out of step with his normal world. "You watch HGTV and DIY?" he asked after taking a sip of java to steady himself.

"Doesn't everybody?" Sophie countered. "I've been thinking of flipping houses when I grow up." She looked so much like her mother, with her long, shiny hair and expressive eyes. Right now those eyes held a mixture of trepidation, exuberance and sturdy common sense.

"Trust me," Tanner said, treading carefully, finding his way over uncertain ground, because they weren't really talking about real estate and he knew it. "Flipping houses is harder than a thirty-minute TV show makes it seem."

"You should know," Sophie agreed airily, taking in the pitiful kitchen again. "You'll manage to turn this one over for a big profit, though, just like all the others."

Tanner dragged a chair back from the table and sort

of fell into it. "Sit down, Soph," he said. "We've got more important things to discuss than the lineup on your favorite TV channels."

Sophie crossed the room dramatically and dropped into a chair of her own. She'd had the pajamas she was wearing now stashed in her backpack, which showed she'd been planning to ditch the school group in New York, probably before she left Briarwood. Now she was playing it cool.

Tanner thought of Ms. Wiggins's plans to steer her into the thespian program at school, and stifled a grimace. His sister, Tessa, had been a show-business kid, discovered when she did some catalog modeling in Dallas at the age of eight. She'd done commercials, guest roles and finally joined a long-running hit TV series. As far as he was concerned, that had been the wrong road. It was as though Tessa—wonderful, smart, beautiful Tessa—had peaked at twenty-one, and been on a downhill slide ever since.

"You're mad because I ran away," Sophie said, sitting up very straight, like a witness taking the stand. She seemed to think good posture might sway the judge to decide in her favor. In any case, she was still acting.

"Mad as hell," Tanner agreed. "That was a stupid, dangerous thing to do, and don't think you're going to get away with it just because I'm so glad to see you."

The small face brightened. "*Are* you glad to see me, Dad?"

"Sophie, of course I am. I'm your father. I miss you a lot when we're apart."

She sighed and shut off the drama switch. Or at least dimmed it a little. "Most of the time," she said, "I feel like one of those cardboard statues."

Tanner frowned, confused. "Run that by me again?"

"You know, those life-size depictions you see in the video store sometimes? Johnny Depp, dressed up like Captain Jack, or Kevin Costner like Wyatt Earp, or something like that?"

Tanner nodded, but he was still pretty confounded. There was nothing two-dimensional about Sophie—she was 3-D all the way.

But did she know that?

"It's as if I'm made of cardboard as far as you're concerned," she went on thoughtfully. "When I'm around, great. When I'm not, you just tuck me away in a closet to gather dust until you want to get me out again."

Tanner's gut clenched, hard. And his throat went tight. "Soph—"

"I know you don't really think of me that way, Dad," his daughter broke in, imparting her woman-child wisdom. "But it *feels* as if you do. That's all I'm saying."

"And I'm saying I don't want you to feel that way, Soph. Ever. All I'm doing is trying to keep you safe."

"I'd rather be happy."

Another whammy. Tanner got up, emptied his cup at the sink and nonsensically filled it up again. Stood with his back to the counter, leaning a little, watching his daughter and wondering if all twelve-year-olds were as complicated as she was.

"You'll understand when you're older," he ventured.

"I understand *now*," Sophie pressed, and she looked completely convinced. "You're the bravest man I know—you were Special Forces in the military, with Uncle Jack—but you're scared, too. You're scared I'll get hurt because of what happened to Mom."

"You can't possibly remember that very well."

Benevolent contempt. "I was *seven,* Dad. Not two." She paused, and her eyes darkened with pain. "It was awful. I kept thinking, *This can't be real, my mom can't be gone,* but she was."

Tanner went to his daughter, laid a hand on top of her head, too choked up to speak.

Sophie twisted slightly in the chair, so she could look up at him. "Here's the thing, Dad. Bad things happen to people. Good people, like you and me and Mom. You have to cry a lot, and feel really bad, because you can't help it, it hurts so much. But then you've got to go on. Mom wouldn't want us living apart like we do. I *know* she wouldn't."

He thought of the last dream-visit from Kat, and once again felt a cautious sense of peace rather than the grief he kept expecting to hit him. He also recalled the way he'd abandoned himself in Olivia's arms the day before, in his bed, and a stab of guilt pricked his conscience, small and needle sharp.

"Your mother," he said firmly, "would want what's best for you. And that's getting a first-rate education in a place where you can't be hurt."

"Get real, Dad," Sophie scoffed. "I could get hurt *anywhere,* including Briarwood."

Regrettably, that was true, but it was a whole lot less likely in a place he'd designed himself. The school was a fortress.

Or was it, as Sophie had said more than once, a prison?

You had to take the good with the bad, he decided.

"You're going back to Briarwood, kiddo," he said.

Sophie's face fell. "I could be a big help around here," she told him.

The desperation in her voice bruised him on the inside, but he had to stand firm. The stakes were too high.

"Can't I just stay until New Year's?" she pleaded.

Tanner sighed. "Okay," he said. "New Year's. Then you *have to go back*."

"What about Butterpie?" Sophie asked, always one to press an advantage, however small. "Admit it. She hasn't been doing very well without me."

"She can go with you," Tanner said, deciding the matter as the words came out of his mouth. "It's time Briarwood had a stable, anyway. Ms. Wiggins has been hinting for donations for the last year."

"I guess that's better than a kick in the pants," Sophie said philosophically. Where did she *get* this stuff?

In spite of himself, Tanner laughed. "It's my best offer, shorty," he said. "Take it or leave it."

"I'll take it," Sophie said, being nobody's fool. "But that doesn't mean I won't try to change your mind in the meantime."

Tanner opened the refrigerator door, ferreted around for the makings of a simple breakfast. If he hadn't been so busy rolling around in the sack with Olivia yesterday afternoon, he thought, he'd have gone to the grocery store. Stocked up on kid food.

Whatever that was.

"Try all you want," he said. "My mind is made up. Go get dressed while I throw together an omelet."

"Yes, sir!" Sophie teased, standing and executing a pretty passable salute. She raced up the back stairs, presumably to rummage through her backpack, the one piece of luggage she'd brought along, for clothes. Tanner simultaneously cracked eggs and juggled the cordless phone to call Tessa.

His sister answered on the third ring, and she sounded disconsolate but game. "Hello, Tanner," she said.

No matter how she felt, Tessa always tried to be a good sport and carry on. It was a trait they shared, actually, a direct dispensation from their unsinkable grandmother, Lottie Quinn.

"Hey," he responded, whipping the eggs with a fork, since he hadn't bothered to ship his kitchen gear to Stone Creek and there was no whisk. He was going to have to go shopping, he realized, for groceries, for household stuff and for all the things Sophie would need.

*Shopping,* on the busiest day of the retail year.

The thought did not appeal.

"How's Sophie?" Tessa asked, with such immediacy that for a moment Tanner thought she knew about the Great Escape. Then he realized that Tessa worried about the kid as much as he did. She disapproved of Briarwood, referring to him as an "absentee father," which never failed to get under his hide and nettle like a thorn. But she worried.

"She's here for Christmas," he said, as though he'd planned things to turn out that way. They'd need a tree, too, and lights, he reflected with half his mind, and all sorts of those hangy gewgaws to festoon the branches. Things were getting out of hand, fast, now that Hurricane Sophie had made landfall. "Why don't you join us?"

"Nobody to watch the horses," Tessa replied.

"You okay?" Tanner asked, knowing she wasn't and wishing there was one damned thing he could do about it besides wait and hope she'd tell him if she needed help. There were probably plenty of people to look after Tessa's beloved horses—most of her friends were equine fanatics, after all—but she didn't like to ask for a hand.

Another joint inheritance from Lottie Quinn.

"Getting divorced is a bummer any time of year," she said. "Over the holidays it's a *mega*bummer. Everywhere I turn, I hear "Have Yourself a Merry Little Christmas," or something equally depressing."

Tanner turned on the gas under a skillet and dobbed in some butter, recalling the first Christmas after Kat's death. He'd left Sophie with Tessa, checked in to a hotel and gone on a bourbon binge.

Not one of his finer moments.

When he'd sobered up, he'd sworn off the bottle and stuck to it.

"Look, Tess," he said gruffly. "Call one of those horse transport outfits and send the hay-burners out here. I've got a barn." Yeah, one that was falling down around his ears, he thought, but he owned a construction company. He could call in the crew early, the one he'd scheduled for Monday, pay them overtime for working the holiday weekend. "This is a big house, so there's plenty of room. And Sophie says the place needs a woman's touch."

Tess was quiet. "Feeling sorry for your kid sister, huh?"

"A little," Tanner said. "You're going through a tough time, and I hate that. But maybe getting away for a while would do you some good. Besides, I could use the help."

She laughed, and though it was a mere echo of the old, rich sound, it was still better than the brave resignation he'd heard in Tessa's voice up till then. "Sophie's still a handful, then."

"Sophie," Tanner said, "is a typhoon, followed by a tidal wave, followed by—"

"You haven't met anybody yet?"

Tanner wasn't going anywhere near that one—not yet, anyway. Sure, he'd gone to bed with one very pretty veterinarian, but they'd both agreed on the no-strings rule. "You never know what might happen," he said, too heartily, hedging.

Another pause, this one thoughtful. "I can't really afford to travel right now, Tanner. Especially not with six horses."

The eggs sizzled in the pan. Since he'd forgotten to put in chopped onions—did he even *have* an onion?— he decided he and Sophie would be having scrambled eggs for breakfast, instead of an omelet. "I can make a transfer from my account to yours, on my laptop," he said. "And I'm going to do that, Tess, whether you agree to come out to Arizona or not."

"It's hard being here," Tessa confessed bleakly. That was when he knew she was wavering. "The fight is wearing me out. Lawyers are coming out of the woodwork. I'm not even sure I want this place anymore." A short silence. Tanner knew Tess was grappling with that formidable pride of hers. "I could really bring the horses?"

"Sure," he said. "I'll make the arrangements."

"I'd rather handle that myself," Tessa said. He could tell she was trying not to cry. Once they were off the phone, she'd let the tears come. All by herself in that big Kentucky farmhouse that wasn't a home anymore. "Thanks, Tanner. As brothers go, you're not half-bad."

He chuckled. "Thanks." He was about to offer to line up one of Jack McCall's jets to bring her west, but he decided that would be pushing it. Tessa was nothing if not self-reliant, and she might balk at coming to Stone Creek at all if he didn't let her make at least some of the decisions.

Sophie clattered into the kitchen, wearing yesterday's jeans, funky boots with fake fur around the tops and a heavy cable-knit sweater. Her face shone from scrubbing, and she'd pulled her hair back in a ponytail.

"Talk to Hurricane Sophie for a minute, will you?" he asked, to give his sister a chance to collect herself. "I'm about to burn the eggs."

"Aunt Tessa?" Sophie crowed into the phone. "I'm at Dad's new place, and it's way awesome, even if it is a wreck. The wallpaper's peeling in my room, and my ceiling sags…"

Tanner rolled his eyes and set about rescuing breakfast.

"*Serious* shopping is required," Sophie went on, after listening to Tess for a few seconds. Or, more properly, waiting for her aunt to shut up so she could talk again. "But first I want to ride Butterpie. Dad's going to let me take her back to school—"

Tanner tuned out the conversation, making toast and a mental grocery list at the same time.

"When will you get here?" Sophie asked excitedly.

Tanner tuned back in. He'd forgotten to ask that question while he was on the phone with Tessa.

"You'll get here when you get here," Sophie repeated after a few beats, smiling. "Before Christmas, though, right?" Catching Tanner's eye, Sophie nodded. "Keep us updated…I love you, too…I'll tell him—bye."

Tanner lobbed partially cold eggs onto plates. "No ETA for Aunt Tessa?" he asked. He set the food on the table and then went to the counter to boot up his laptop. As soon as he'd eaten, he'd pipe some cash into his sister's depleted bank account.

"She loves you." Sophie's eyes danced with anticipation. "She said she's got some stuff to do before she comes to Arizona, but she'll definitely be here before Christmas."

Tanner sat down and ate, but his brain was so busy, he barely tasted the eggs and toast. Which was probably good, since he wasn't the best cook in this or any other solar system. Then again, he wasn't the worst, either.

"You know what I want for Christmas?" Sophie asked, half an hour later as she washed dishes at the old-fashioned sink and Tanner sat at the table, tapping at the keyboard on his laptop. "And don't say, 'Your two front teeth,' either, because that would be a *really* lame joke."

Tanner grinned. "Okay, I won't," he said with mock resignation. "What do you want for Christmas?"

"I want you and me and Aunt Tessa to live here forever," she said. "Like a family. An aunt isn't the same as a mom, but we're all blood, the three of us. It could work."

Tanner's fingers froze in midtap. "Honey," he said quietly, "Aunt Tessa's young. She'll get married again eventually, and have a family of her own, just like you will when you grow up."

"I want to have a family *now*," Sophie said stubbornly. "I've been waiting long enough." With that, she turned back to the sink, rattling the dishes around, and her spine was rigid.

Tanner closed his eyes for a long moment, then forced himself to concentrate on the task at hand—transferring a chunk of money to Tessa's bank account.

He'd think about the mess he was in later.

OLIVIA MIGHT HAVE DRIVEN right past Starcross Ranch on her way to town if Ginger hadn't insisted that they stop and look in on Butterpie. In the cold light of a new day, Olivia wasn't eager to face Tanner Quinn.

Last night's wanton hussy had given way to *today's* embarrassed Goody Two-shoes.

And there were other things on her mind, too, most notably Ashley's statement on the phone the night before, that she thought she'd found their mother. No matter how Olivia had prodded, her sister had refused to give up any more information.

Olivia had already called the clinic, and she had a light caseload for the day, since another vet was on call. Normally that would have been a relief—she could buy groceries, get her hair trimmed, do some laundry. But she needed to check on Rodney, and Butterpie wasn't out of the woods yet, either. Yes, Sophie was home, so the pony would be ecstatic.

For as long as Tanner allowed his daughter to stay, that is.

For all Olivia knew, he was already making plans to shuttle the poor kid back to boarding school in a black helicopter.

And that thought led full circle back to her mother.

Had Ashley actually found Delia O'Ballivan—the *real* Delia O'Ballivan, not some ringer hoping to cash in on Brad's fame and fortune?

Olivia's feelings on that score were decidedly mixed.

She'd dreamed of a reunion with her lost mother, just as Ashley and Melissa had, and Brad, too, at least when he was younger. They'd all been bereft when Delia left, especially since their father had died so soon afterward.

If she hadn't been driving, Olivia would have closed her eyes against that memory. She'd been there, the tomboy child, always on horseback, riding with her dad after some stray cattle, when the lightning struck, killing both him and his horse instantly.

She'd jumped off her own panicked mount and run to her dad, kneeling beside him in the dirt while a warm rain pelted down on all of them. She'd screamed—and screamed—and screamed.

Screamed until her throat was raw, until Big John came racing out into the field in his old truck.

For a long time she'd thought he'd heard her cries all the way from the house, the better part of a mile away. Later, weeks after the funeral, when the numbness was just beginning to subside, she'd realized he'd been passing on the road, and had seen that bolt of lightning jag down out of the sky. Seen his own son killed, come running and stumbling to kneel in the pounding rain, just as Olivia had, gathering his grown boy into his strong rancher's arms, and rocking him.

*No,* Big John had wailed, over and over again, his craggy face awash with tears and rain. *No!*

All these years later Olivia could still hear those cries, and they still tore holes in her heart.

Tears washed her own cheeks.

Ginger, seated on the passenger side of the Suburban as usual, leaned over to nudge Olivia's shoulder.

Olivia sniffled, straightened her shoulders and dashed her face dry with the back of one hand. Her father's death had made the local and regional news, and for a while Olivia had hoped her mother would see the reports, on television or in a newspaper, realize how badly her family needed her and come home.

But Delia *hadn't* come home. Either she'd never learned that her ex-husband, the man to whom she'd borne four children, was dead, or she simply hadn't cared enough to spring for a bus ticket.

Fantasizing about her return had been one thing, though, and knowing it might *actually happen* was another.

She sucked in a deep breath and blew it out hard, making her bangs dance against her forehead.

Maybe Delia, if she *was* Delia, still wouldn't want to come home. That would be a blow to Ashley, starry-eyed optimist that she was. Ashley lived in a Thomas Kinkade sort of world, full of lighted stone cottages and bridges over untroubled waters.

The snow was melting, but the ground was frozen hard, and the Suburban bumped and jostled as Olivia drove up Tanner's driveway. She stopped the rig, intending to stay only a few minutes, and got out. Ginger jumped after her without waiting to use the ramp.

The barn, alas, was empty. Shiloh's and Butterpie's stall doors stood open. Tanner and Sophie must have gone out riding, which should have been a relief—now she would have a little more time before she had to face him—but wasn't. For some reason she didn't want to examine too closely, nervous as she was, she'd been looking forward to seeing Tanner.

She came out of the barn, scanned the fields, saw them far off in the distance, two small figures on horseback. She hesitated only a few moments, then summoned Ginger and headed for the Suburban. She was about to climb behind the wheel when she noticed that the dog had stayed behind.

"You coming?" she called, her voice a little shaky.

*"I'll stay here for a while,"* Ginger answered without turning around. She was gazing off toward Sophie and Tanner.

Olivia swallowed an achy, inexplicable lump. "Don't go chasing after them, okay? Wait on the porch or something."

Ginger didn't offer a reply, or turn around. But she didn't streak off across the field as she had the morning before, either. Short of forcing the animal into the truck, Olivia didn't know what else to do besides leave.

Her first stop was Stone Creek Ranch. As she had at Starcross, she avoided the house and made for the barn. With luck, she wouldn't run into Brad, and have to go into all her concerns about Ashley's mother search.

Luck wasn't with her. Brad O'Ballivan, the world-famous, multi-Grammy-winning singer, was mucking out stalls, the reindeer tagging at his heels like a faithful hound as he worked.

He stopped, leaned on his pitchfork and offered a lopsided grin as Olivia approached, though his eyes were troubled.

"I see Rodney's getting along all right," Olivia said, her voice swelling, strangely thick, in her throat, and nearly cutting off her breath.

Brad gave a solemn nod. Tried for another grin and missed. "I'll have a blue Christmas if Santa comes to reclaim this little guy," he said. "I've gotten attached."

Olivia managed a smile, tried to catch it when it

slipped off her mouth by biting her lower lip, and failed. "Why the sad face, cowboy?"

"I was about to ask you the same question—sans the cowboy part."

"Ashley thinks she found Mom," Olivia said.

Brad nodded glumly, set the pitchfork aside, leaning it against the stable wall. Crouched to pet Rodney for a while before steering him back into his stall and shutting the door.

"I guess the time has come to talk about this," Brad said. "Pull up a bale of hay and sit down."

Olivia sat, but it felt more like sinking. Bits of hay poked her through the thighs of her jeans. All the starch, as Big John used to say, had gone out of her knees.

Brad sat across from her, studied her face and said— nothing.

"Where are Meg and Mac?" Olivia asked.

"Mac's with his grandma McKettrick," Brad answered. "Meg's shopping with Sierra and some of the others."

Olivia nodded. Knotted her hands together in her lap. "Brad, talk to me. Tell me what you know about Mom—because you know *something*. I can tell."

"She's alive," Brad said.

Olivia stared at him, astonished, and angry, too. "And you didn't think the rest of us might be interested in that little tidbit of information?"

"She's a drunk, Livie," Brad told her, holding her gaze steadily. He looked as miserable as Olivia felt. "I tried to help her—she wouldn't be helped. When she calls, I still cut her a check—against my better judgment."

Olivia actually felt the barn sway around her. She

had to lean forward and put her head between her knees and tell herself to breathe slowly.

Brad's hand came to rest on her shoulder.

She shook it off. *"Don't!"*

"Liv, our mother is not a person you'd want to know," Brad said quietly. "This isn't going to turn out like one of those TV movies, where everybody talks things through and figures out that it's all been one big, tragic misunderstanding. Mom left because she didn't want to be married, and she sure as hell didn't want to raise four kids. And there's no evidence that she's changed, except for the worse."

Olivia lifted her head. The barn stopped spinning like the globe Big John used to keep in his study. What had happened to that globe?

"What's she like?"

"I told you, Liv—she's a drunk."

"She's got to be more than that. The worst drunk in the world is more than just a drunk…."

Brad sighed, intertwined his fingers, let his hands fall between his knees. The look in his eyes made Olivia ache. "She's pretty, in a faded-rose sort of way. Too thin, because she doesn't eat. Her hair's blond, but not shiny and thick like it was when we knew her before. She's—hard, Olivia."

"How long have you been in touch with her?"

"I'm not 'in touch' with her," Brad answered gently, though his tone was gruff. "She called my manager a few years ago, told him she was my mother, and when Phil passed the word on to me, I went to see her. She didn't ask about Dad, or Big John, or any of you. She wanted to—" He stopped, looked away, his head slightly bowed under whatever he was remembering about that pilgrimage.

"Cash in on being Brad O'Ballivan's mother?" Olivia supplied.

"Something like that," Brad replied, meeting Olivia's eyes again, though it obviously wasn't easy. "She's bad news, Liv. But she won't come back to Stone Creek—not even if it means having a ticket to ride the gravy train. She flat out doesn't want anything to do with this place, or with us."

"Why?"

"Damn, Liv. Do you think I know the answer to that any better than you do? This has been harder on you and the twins—I realize that. Girls need a mother. But there were plenty of times when I could have used one, too."

Olivia reached out, touched her brother's arm. He'd had a hard time, especially after their dad was killed. He and Big John had butted heads constantly, mostly because they were so much alike—strong, stubborn, proud to a fault. And they'd been estranged after Brad ran off to Nashville and stayed there.

Oh, Brad had visited a few times over the years. But he'd always left again, over Big John's protests, and then the heart attack came, and it was too late.

"Are you thinking about Big John?" he asked.

It was uncanny, the way he could see into her head sometimes. "Yeah," she said. "His opinion of Delia was even lower than yours. He'd probably have stood at the door with a shotgun if she'd showed her face in Stone Creek."

"The door? He'd have been up at the gate, standing on the cattle guard," Brad answered with a slight shake of his head. "Liv, what are we going to do about Ashley? I think Melissa's levelheaded enough to deal with this. But Ash is in for a shock here. A pretty bad one."

"Is there something else you aren't telling me?"

Brad held up his right hand, as if to give an oath. "I've told you the whole ugly truth, insofar as I know it."

"I'll talk to Ashley," she said.

"Good luck," Brad said.

Olivia started to stand, planning to leave, but Brad stopped her by laying a hand on her shoulder.

"Hold on a second," he told her. "There *is* one more thing I need to say."

Olivia waited, wide-eyed and a little alarmed.

He drew a deep breath, let it out as a reluctant sigh. "About Tanner Quinn," he began.

Olivia stiffened. Brad could not possibly know what had happened between her and Tanner—could he? He wasn't *that* perceptive.

"What about him?"

"He's a decent guy, Liv," Brad told her. "But—"

"But?"

"Did he tell you about his wife? How she died?"

Olivia shook her head, wondering if Brad was about to say the circumstances had been suspicious, like in one of those reality crime shows on cable TV.

"Her name was Katherine," Brad said. "He called her Kat. He won the bid on a construction job in a place where, let's just say, Americans aren't exactly welcome. It was a dangerous project, but there were millions at stake, so he agreed. One day the two of them went to one of those open-air markets—a souk I think they call it. Tanner stopped to look at something, and Kat either didn't notice or didn't wait for him. When she reached the street…" Brad paused, his eyes as haunted as if he'd been there himself. "Somebody strafed the market with some kind of automatic weapon. Kat was hit I don't know how many times, and she died in Tanner's arms, on the sidewalk."

Olivia put a hand over her mouth. Squeezed her eyes shut.

"I know," Brad muttered. "It's awful even to imagine it. I met him a couple of years after it happened." He stopped. Sighed again. "The only reason I told you was, well, I've seen Tanner go through a lot of women, Liv. He can't—or won't—commit. Not to a woman, not to his daughter. He never stays in one place any longer than absolutely necessary. It's as if he thinks he's a target."

Olivia knew Brad was right. She had only to look at Sophie, forced to take drastic measures just to visit her father over the holidays, to see the truth.

"Why the warning?" she asked.

Brad leaned forward, clunked his forehead briefly against hers. "I know the signs, little sister," he answered. "I know the signs."

## CHAPTER SEVEN

AFTER LEAVING Stone Creek Ranch, the conversation with Brad draping her mind and heart like a lead net, Olivia stopped off at the clinic in town, just in case she might be needed.

She wasn't, actually, and that was kind of deflating. As the on-call vet for the current twenty-four-hour time slot, she could be sent anywhere in the county, at any moment. But today all was quiet on the Western front, so to speak.

She headed for Ashley's, fully intending to bite the mother bullet, but her sister's silly yellow car, usually parked in the driveway at that time of morning after a routine run to the post office, was gone. Crews of local college kids, home on vacation, swarmed the snowy front yard, though, bedecking every shrub and window and eave with holiday lights.

Olivia was momentarily reminded of Snoopy and his decorated doghouse in the cartoon Christmas special she'd watched faithfully since she was three years old. The image cheered her a little.

"Commercial dog," she muttered, though Ashley didn't qualify for the term species-wise, waving to the light crew before pulling away from the curb again.

She ought to see if she could swing a haircut, she thought, cruising the slush-crusty main street of Stone

Creek. Every street lamp and every store window was decorated, colored bulbs blinking the requisite bright red and green.

The Christmas-tree man had set up for business down by the supermarket—a new guy this year, she'd heard—and a plump Santa was already holding court in a spiffy-looking black sleigh with holly leaves and berries decorating its graceful lines. Its brass runners gleamed authentically, and eight life-size plastic reindeer had been hitched to the thing with a jingle-bell harness.

Olivia pulled into the lot—before she saw Tanner's red truck parked among other vehicles. She should have noticed it, she thought—it was the only clean one. She shifted into reverse, but it was too late.

Tanner, delectable in jeans and a black leather jacket, caught sight of her and waved. His young daughter, she of the dramatic helicopter arrival, stood beside him, clapping mittened hands together to keep warm as she inspected a tall, lush tree.

Annoyed by her own reticence, Olivia sighed, pulled into one of the few remaining parking spots and shut off the Suburban.

"Hey," Tanner said as she approached, working hard to smile.

Sophie was a very beautiful child—a Christmas angel in ordinary clothes. She probably looked just like her mother, the woman who had died so tragically, in Tanner's arms, no less. The one he'd loved too much to ever forget, according to Brad.

While they were making love the day before, had Tanner been pretending Olivia was Katherine?

Olivia blushed. Amped up her smile.

"Olivia O'Ballivan," Tanner said quietly, his eyes watchful, even a little pensive as he studied her face, "meet my daughter, Sophie."

Sophie turned, smiled and put out a hand. "Hello," she said. "Dad says you're a veterinarian, and you took care of Butterpie. Thank you."

Something melted, in a far and usually inaccessible corner of Olivia's heart. "You're welcome," she answered brightly. "And so is Butterpie."

"What do you think of this tree?" Sophie asked next, turning to the massive, fragrant blue spruce she'd been examining when Olivia drove in.

Olivia's gaze slid to Tanner's face, sprang away again. "It's—it's lovely," she said.

"Ho! Ho! Ho!" bellowed the hired Santa Claus. Apparently the guy hadn't heard that the line was now considered offensive to women.

"Would you believe this place is run by a man named Kris Kringle?" Sophie said to Olivia, drawing her in somehow, making her feel included, as though they couldn't buy the tree unless she approved of it.

Tanner nudged Sophie's shoulder with a light motion of one elbow. "It's an alias, kid," he said out of the side of his mouth in a pretty respectable imitation of an old-time gangster.

"Duh," Sophie said, but she beamed up at her father, her face aglow with adoration. "And I thought he was *really* Santa Claus."

"Go get Mr. Kringle, so we can wrap this deal up," Tanner told her.

Did he see, Olivia wondered, how much the child loved him? How much she needed him?

Sophie hurried off to find the proprietor.

"I take it Sophie will be around for Christmas," Olivia ventured.

"Until New Year's," Tanner said with a nod. "Then she goes straight back to Connecticut. Butterpie's going along—he'll board in a stable near the school until Briarwood's is built—so you won't have to worry about a depressed horse."

Olivia's throat thickened. All her emotions were close to the surface, she supposed because of the holidays and the situation with her mother, which might well morph into a Situation, and the knowledge that all good things seemed to be temporary.

"I'll miss Butterpie," she managed, shoving her cold hands into the pockets of her old down vest. It was silly to draw comparisons between her own issues and Sophie's, but she couldn't seem to help it. She was entangled.

"I'll miss Sophie," Tanner said.

Olivia wanted to beat at his chest with her fists, which just went to prove she needed therapy. *She needs you!* she wanted to scream. *Don't you see that you're all she has?*

Patently none of her business. She pretended an interest in a small potted tree nearby, a Charlie Brownish one that suited her mood. Right then and there she decided to buy it, take it home and toss some lights onto it.

It was an act of mercy.

"Olivia—" Tanner began, and his tone boded something serious, but before he could get the rest of the sentence out of his mouth, Sophie was back with Kris Kringle.

Olivia very nearly didn't believe what she was seeing.

The man wore ordinary clothes—quilted snow pants, a heavy plaid flannel shirt, a blue down vest and a Fargo hat with earflaps. But he had a full white beard and kind—okay, *twinkly*—blue eyes. Round red cheeks, and a bow of a mouth.

"A fine choice indeed," he told Olivia, noting her proximity to the pathetic little tree no one else was likely to buy. Only the thought of it, sitting forgotten on the lot when Christmas arrived, amid a carpet of dried-out pine needles, kept her from changing her mind. "I could tie on some branches for you with twine. Thicken it up a little."

Olivia shook her head, rummaged in her pocket for money, being very careful not to look at Tanner and wondering why she felt the need to do that. "It's fine the way it is. How much?"

Kringle named a figure, and Olivia forked over the funds. She felt stupid, being so protective of a tree, and she didn't even own any decorations, but Charlie Brown was going home with her anyway. They'd just have to make the best of things.

"Dad told me you found a real reindeer," Sophie said to Olivia when she would have grabbed her tree, said goodbye and made a hasty retreat.

This drew Kris Kringle's attention, Olivia noted out of the corner of her eye. He perked right up, listening intently. Zeroing in. If he thought he was going to use that poor little reindeer to attract customers, he had another think coming.

Sure enough, he said, "I just happen to be missing a reindeer."

Olivia didn't believe him, and even though she knew that was because she didn't *want* to believe him, her radar was up and her antennae were beeping. "Is that so?" she asked somewhat stiffly, while Tanner and Sophie looked on with heightened interest. "How did you happen to misplace this reindeer, Mr.—?"

"Kringle," the old man insisted with a smile in his eyes. "We did a personal appearance at a birthday party, and he just wandered off."

"I see," Olivia said. "Didn't you look for him?"

"Oh, yes," Kringle replied, looking like a right jolly old elf and all that. "No tracks to be found. We hunted and hunted. Is Rodney all right?"

Olivia's mouth fell open. Kringle *must* be the reindeer's rightful owner if he knew his name. It would be too much of a coincidence otherwise. "He's—he's fine," she said.

Kringle smiled warmly. "The other seven have been *very* worried, and so have I, although I've had an idea all along that Rodney was on a mission of some kind."

Olivia swallowed. She'd wanted to find Rodney's rightful owner so he could go home. So why did she feel so dejected?

"The other seven what?" Tanner asked with a dry note in his voice.

"Why, the other seven reindeer, of course," Kringle answered merrily after tossing a conspiratorial glance Sophie's way. "If Rodney is safe and well taken care of, though, we won't fret about him. Not until Christmas Eve, anyway. We'll need him back by then for sure."

If Olivia had had a trowel handy, she would have handed it to the guy, so he could lay it on thicker. He really knew how to tap into Christmas, that was for sure.

"I thought Santa's reindeer had names like Prancer and Dancer," Sophie said, sounding serious.

Tanner, meanwhile, got out his wallet to pay for the big spruce.

"Well, they do," Kringle said, still in Santa mode. "But they're getting older, and Donner's developed a touch of arthritis. So I brought Rodney up out of the ranks, since he showed so much promise, especially at flying. He's only been on trial runs so far, but this Christmas Eve he's on the flight manifest for the whole western region."

Tanner and Olivia exchanged looks.

"You don't need Rodney back until Christmas Eve?" Olivia asked. An owner was an owner, crazy or not. She took one of her dog-eared business cards out of her vest pocket, wrote Brad's private number on the back with a pen Tanner provided and handed it to Kringle. "He's at Stone Creek Ranch."

"I'll pick him up after I close the lot on the twenty-fourth," Kringle said, still twinkling, and even going so far as to tap a finger to the side of his nose. If there had been a chimney handy, he probably would have rocketed right up it. He examined the card, nodded to himself and tucked it away. "Around six o'clock," he added. "Even the last-minute Louies will have cleared out by then."

"Right," Olivia murmured, wondering if she'd made a mistake telling him where to find Rodney.

"Let me load up that tree for you," Tanner said, hoisting Charlie Brown by his skinny, crooked trunk before Olivia could get a hold on it. Brown needles rained to the pavement.

Sophie tagged along with Tanner and Olivia while Kringle carried the big spruce to Tanner's pickup truck.

Branches of the lush tree rustled, and the evergreen scent intensified.

A few fat flakes of snow wafted down.

Olivia felt like a figure in a festive snow globe. Man, woman and child, with Christmas tree. Which was silly.

"My tree weighs all of three pounds," she pointed out to Tanner under her breath. "Aren't you supposed to be working on the new shelter?"

"More like thirty, with this pot." Tanner grinned and held the little tree out of her reach. "Nothing much gets done on a holiday weekend," he added, as if it was some big news flash or something. "Shouldn't you be helping a cow give birth?"

"Cows don't commonly give birth at this time of year," Olivia pointed out. "It's a springtime sort of thing."

"Yeah, Dad," Sophie interjected, rolling her eyes. "Yeesh."

Olivia had to laugh. "Yeah," she said, opening the rear doors of the Suburban to receive Charlie Brown. *"Yeesh."*

"How about joining Sophie and me for supper tonight?" Tanner asked, blocking the way when she would have closed the doors again.

"We live in a dump," Sophie said philosophically. "But it's home."

Olivia felt another pang at the word *home.* The rental she lived in definitely didn't qualify, and though she had a history at Stone Creek Ranch, it belonged to Brad and Meg and Mac now, which was as it should be. "Well…"

"Please?" Sophie asked, suddenly earnest.

Tanner grinned, waited. The kid was virtually irresistible, and nobody knew that better than he did.

"Okay," Olivia said. For Sophie's sake and not—not *at all*—because she wanted to get in any deeper with Tanner Quinn than she already was.

"Six o'clock?" Tanner asked.

"Six o'clock," Olivia confirmed, casting another glance at Kris Kringle, now busy instructing the hired Santa Claus on how to hold the sleigh reins. She'd call Wyatt Terp, the marshal over in Indian Rock, the county seat, she decided, and get him to run a background check on this dude, just in case he had a rap sheet or the men in white coats were looking for him.

Tanner and Sophie said their goodbyes and left, and Olivia sat in the driver's seat of her Suburban for a few moments, working up the courage to call Wyatt. The only name she could give him was Kris Kringle, and *that* was bound to liven up an otherwise dull day in the cop shop.

"You mean there really *is* a Kris Kringle?" she asked ten minutes later, her cell phone pressed to one ear as she pulled into the lot at the hardware store to buy lights and tinsel for Charlie Brown.

"You'd be surprised how many there are," Wyatt said drolly.

"So you have something on him, then? You're sure it's the same guy?"

"Kristopher Kringle, it says here. Christmas-tree farmer with a place up near Flagstaff. Only one traffic violation—he was caught driving a horse-drawn sleigh on the freeway two winters ago."

Olivia shut off the Suburban, eyes popping. The painted sign on the weathered brick side of the hardware store read, in time-faded letters, "Smoke Caliber Cigarettes. They're Good for You!"

"Nothing like, say, animal cruelty?"

"Nope," Wyatt said. Olivia could hear some yukking going on in the background. Either the cops were celebrating early or the marshal had the phone on "speaker." "Santa's clean, Doc."

Olivia sighed. She was relieved, of course, to learn that Kringle was neither an escaped maniac nor a criminal, but on some level, she realized, she'd been hoping *not* to find Rodney's owner.

How crazy was that?

She got out of the car, after promising Charlie Brown she'd be back soon, and went inside to shop for a tree wardrobe. She bought two strands of old-fashioned bubbling lights, a box of shiny glass balls in a mixture of red, gold and silver, and some tinsel.

*Ho, ho, ho,* she thought, stashing her purchases in the back of the rig, next to Charlie. *Deck the halls.*

EVEN THOUGH THEY HAD a million things to do, Sophie insisted on stopping at Stone Creek Middle School when they drove past it. It was a small brick building, and the reader board in front read "Closed for Thanksgiving Vacation! See You Monday!"

The whole town, Tanner thought, feeling grumbly, was relentlessly cheerful. And what was up with that Kris Kringle yahoo, back at the tree lot, claiming he had seven reindeer at home, waiting to lift off on Christmas Eve?

Sophie cupped her hands and peered through the plate-glass door at the front of the school, her breath fogging it up. "Wow," she said. "The computer room at Briarwood is bigger than this whole place."

"Can we go now, Soph? We still need to pick up

lights and ornaments and some things for you to wear, not to mention groceries."

Sophie turned and made a face at him. "Bah humbug," she said. "Why are you so crabby all of a sudden?" She paused to waggle her eyebrows. "You looked real happy when Olivia was around."

"That guy at the tree lot…"

"What?" Sophie said, skipping back down the snowy steps to the walk. "You think he's a serial killer or something, just because he claims to be Santa?"

"Where do you get these things?" Tanner asked.

"He's delusional, that's all," said the doctor's daughter. "And probably harmless."

"Probably," Tanner agreed. He knew then what was troubling him—Olivia clearly didn't want to surrender custody of the reindeer until she knew "Kris Kringle" was all right. And he cared, more than he liked, what Olivia wanted and didn't want.

"Danger lurks everywhere!" Sophie teased, making mitten claws with her hands in an attempt to look scary. "You just can't be *too careful!*"

"Cut it out, goofball," Tanner said, chuckling in spite of himself as they both got back in the truck. "You don't know anything about the world. If you did, you wouldn't have run away from the field trip and tried to board an iron horse headed west."

"Are we going to talk about *that* again?" Sophie fastened her seat belt with exaggerated care. "I'm a proactive person, Dad. Don't you want me to be *proactive?*"

Tanner didn't answer. Whatever he said would be wrong.

"That Santa shouldn't be saying 'ho, ho, ho,'" Sophie informed him as they pulled away from the curb.

Next stop, the ranch, to drop off the tree, then on to a mall he'd checked on MapQuest, outside Flagstaff. "It isn't politically correct."

"Ask me what I think of political correctness," Tanner retorted.

"Why would I do that when I already know?" Sophie responded cheerfully. "At Briarwood we call Valentine's Day 'Special Relationship Day' now."

"What's next? 'Significant Parental Figure Day' for Father's and Mother's Day?"

Sophie laughed, her cheeks bright with cold and excitement. "It does sound kind of silly, doesn't it?"

"Big-time," Tanner said. He couldn't even tell a woman on his executive staff that her hair looked nice without risking a sexual-harassment suit. Where would it all end?

At home, Tanner unloaded the tree and set it on the front porch so the branches could settle, while Sophie went out to the barn to eyeball the horses. In looks she resembled Kat, but she sure took after Tessa when it came to hay-burners.

"That dog is still here," she reported when she came back. "The one that was waiting on the porch when we got back from riding this morning. Shouldn't we take her home or something?"

"Ginger lives next door, with Olivia," Tanner reminded Sophie. "If she wants to go home, she can get there on her own."

"I hope she isn't depressed, like Butterpie was," Sophie fretted.

Tanner grinned, gave her ponytail a light tug. "She and Butterpie are buddies," he said, recalling finding the dog in the pony's stall. "Olivia will take her home after supper tonight, most likely."

"You like Olivia, don't you?" Sophie asked, with a touch of slyness, as she climbed back into the truck.

Tanner got behind the wheel, started the engine. Olivia was right. The rig was too clean—it had stood out like the proverbial sore thumb back in town, at the tree lot. Maybe he could find a creek to run it through or something. With the ground frozen hard, it wouldn't be easy to come up with mud.

So where were the other guys getting all that macho dirt streaking their rigs and clogging their grilles?

"Of course I like her," he said. "She's a friend."

"She's pretty."

"I'll grant you that one, shorty. She's very pretty."

"You could marry her."

Tanner, in the process of turning the truck around, stopped it instead. "Don't go there, Soph. Olivia's a hometown girl, with a family and a veterinary practice. I'll be moving on to a new place after Stone Creek. And neither one of us is looking for a serious relationship."

Sophie sighed, and her shoulders sloped as though the weight of the world had just been laid on them. "I almost wish that Kris Kringle guy really was Santa Claus," she said. "Then I could tell him I want a mom for Christmas."

Tanner knew he was being played, but his eyes burned and his throat tightened just the same. No accounting for visceral reactions. "That was pretty underhanded, Soph," he said. "It was blatant manipulation. And guilt isn't going to work with me. You should know that by now."

Sophie folded her arms and sulked. Only twelve and

already she'd mastered the you're-too-stupid-to-live look teenage girls were so good at. Tessa had been world champ, but clearly the torch had been passed. "What-*ever*."

"I know you'd like to have a mother, Sophie."

"You know, but you don't care."

"I *do* care."

A tear slid down Sophie's left cheek, and Tanner knew it wasn't orchestrated to win his sympathy, because she turned her head quickly, so he wouldn't see.

"I do care, Sophie," he repeated.

She merely nodded. Gave a sniffle that tore at his insides.

Maybe someday she'd understand that he was only trying to protect her. Maybe she wouldn't.

He wondered if he could deal with the latter possibility. Suppose, even as a grown woman, Sophie still resented him?

Well, he thought grimly, this wasn't *about* him. It was about keeping Sophie safe, whether she liked it or not.

He took the turnoff for Flagstaff, bypassing Stone Creek completely. Sophie was female. Shopping would make her feel better, and if that didn't work, there was still the Christmas tree to set up, and Olivia coming over for supper.

They'd get through this, he and Sophie.

"The time's going to go by really fast," Sophie lamented, breaking the difficult silence and still not looking at him. "Before I know it, I'll be right back at Briarwood. Square one."

Tanner waited a beat to answer, so he wouldn't snap at the kid. God knew, being twelve years old in this day and age couldn't be easy, what with all the drugs and the underground websites and the movement to rename *Valentine's Day,* for God's sake. No, it would be difficult with two ordinary parents and a mortgaged house, and Sophie didn't have two parents.

She didn't even have *one,* really.

"Everything's going to be all right, Soph," he said. Was he trying to convince her, or himself? Both, probably.

"I could live with Aunt Tessa on Starcross—couldn't I? And go to Stone Creek Middle School, like a regular kid?"

Tanner nearly had to pull over to the side of the road. Instead, he clamped his jaw down tight and concentrated harder on navigating the slick high-country road curving ever upward into the timbered area around Flagstaff.

He should have seen this coming, after the way Sophie had made him stop at the school in town so she could look in the windows, but the kid had a gift for blindsiding him.

"Aunt Tessa," he said evenly, "is only visiting for the holidays."

"She's bringing her horses."

"Okay, a few months at most. Can we not talk about this for a little while, Soph? Because it's a fast track to nowhere."

That was when she brought out the big guns. "They have drugs at Briarwood, you know," she said with a combination of defiance and bravado. "It's not an ivory tower, no matter *how* good the security is."

That time he *did* pull over, with a screech of tires and a lot of flying slush. *"What?"* he rasped.

"Meth," Sophie said. "Ice. That's—"

"I *know* what ice is," Tanner snapped. "So help me God, Sophie, if you're messing with me—"

"It's true, Dad."

He believed her. That was the worst thing of all. His stomach rolled, and for a moment he thought he might have to shove open the door and get sick, right then and there.

"It's a pervasive problem," Sophie said, sounding like a venerable news commentator instead of a pre-adolescent girl.

"Has anyone offered you drugs? Have you taken any?" He kept his hand on the door handle, just in case.

"I'm not stupid, Dad," she answered. "Drugs are for losers, people who can't cope unless their brains have been chemically altered."

"Would you talk like a twelve-year-old for a few minutes? Just to humor me?"

"I don't take drugs, Dad," Sophie reiterated quietly.

"How are they getting in? The drugs, I mean?"

"Kids bring them from home. I think they mostly steal them from their parents."

Tanner laid his forehead on the steering wheel and drew slow, deep breaths. *From their parents.* In his mind, he started drawing up blueprints for an ivory tower. Not that he'd use ivory, even if he could get it from a legitimate supplier.

Sophie touched his arm. "Dad, I'm trying to make a point here. Are you okay? Because you look kind of... gray. You're not having a heart attack or anything, are you?"

"Not the kind you're thinking of," Tanner said,

straightening. Pulling himself together. He was a father. He needed to act like one.

When he was sure he wasn't a menace to Sophie, himself and the general driving public, he pulled back out onto the highway. Sophie fiddled with the radio until she found a station she liked, and a rap beat filled the truck cab.

Tanner adjusted the dial. Brad O'Ballivan's voice poured out of the speakers. "Have Yourself a Merry Little Christmas."

It figured. Tessa was practically being stalked by the song, according to her, and now he probably would be, too.

"Is that the guy who hired you to build the animal shelter?" Sophie asked.

Beyond relieved at the change of subject, Tanner said, "Yes."

"He has a nice voice."

"That's the word on the street."

"Even if the song *is* kind of hokey."

Tanner laughed. "I'll tell him you said so."

After that they talked about ordinary things—not drugs at Briarwood, not Sophie's longing for a mother, destined to be unrequited, not weird Kris Kringle, the reindeer man. No, they discussed a new saddle for Butterpie, and what to get Tessa for Christmas, and the pros and cons of nuking a package of frozen lasagna for supper.

Reaching the mall, Tanner parked the truck and the two of them waded in. They bought ornaments and lights and tinsel. They cleaned out the "young juniors" department in an upscale store, and chose a yellow cashmere sweater for Tessa's gift. They had a late lunch in the food court, watching as the early shoppers rushed by with their treasures.

On the way out of town they stopped at a Western supply store for the new saddle, and after that, a supermarket, where they filled two carts. When they left the store, Tanner almost tripped over a kid in ragged jeans, a T-shirt and a thin jacket, trying to give away squirmy puppies from a big box. The words "Good Xmas Presents" had been scrawled on the side in black marker.

Tanner lengthened his stride, making the shopping cart wheels rattle.

Sophie stopped her cart.

"Oh, they're so cute," she said.

"Only two left," the kid pointed out unnecessarily. There were holes in the toes of his sneakers. Had he dressed for the part?

"Sophie," Tanner said in warning.

But she'd picked up one of the puppies—a little golden-brown one of indeterminate breed, with floppy ears and big, hopeful eyes. Then the other, a black-and-white version of the dog Tanner remembered from his first-grade reader.

"Dad," she whispered, drawing up close to his side, the full cart she'd been pushing left behind by the boy and the box, to show him the puppies. "Look at that kid. He probably needs the money, and who knows what might happen to these poor little things if they don't get sold?"

Tanner couldn't bring himself to say the obvious— that Sophie would be leaving for a new school in a few weeks, since Briarwood was definitely out of the question now that he knew about the drugs. He'd just have to buy the dogs and hope that Olivia would be able to find them good homes when the time came.

At the moment, turning Sophie down wasn't an option, even if it was the right thing to do. He'd had to say no to one too many things already.

So Tanner gave the boy a ridiculous amount of money for the puppies, and Sophie scared them half to death with a squeal of delight, and they loaded up the grub and the dogs and headed back to Starcross Ranch.

## CHAPTER EIGHT

OLIVIA HADN'T BEEN ABLE to track Ashley down, even after hunting all over town, and no emergency veterinary calls came in, either. She had her hair cut at the Curly-Q, bought some groceries and cleaning supplies at the supermarket, then she and Charlie Brown went home.

Ginger was waiting on the back porch when she arrived, balls of snow clinging to her legs and haunches from the walk across the very white field between Olivia's place and Tanner's.

*"It's about time you got here,"* the dog said, rising off her nest of blankets next to the drier.

Freezing, Olivia hustled through the kitchen door and set Charlie Brown on the table, root-bound in his bulky plastic pot. "You're the one who insisted on staying at Starcross," she said before going back out for the bags from the hardware store and supermarket.

A pool of melted snow surrounded Ginger when Olivia finished carrying everything inside. After setting the last of the bags on the counter, she threw an old towel into the drier to warm it up and adjusted the thermostat for the temperamental old furnace. She started a pot of coffee—darn, she should have picked up a new brewing apparatus at the hardware store—and filled Ginger's kibble bowl.

While the dog ate and the coffee brewed, Olivia fished the towel out of the drier and knelt on the scuffed and peeling linoleum floor to give Ginger a rubdown.

*"Were they out of good Christmas trees?"* Ginger asked, eyeing Charlie Brown, whose sparse branches seemed to droop a little at the insult.

"Be nice," Olivia whispered. "You'll hurt his feelings."

*"I suppose I should be happy that you're decorating this year,"* Ginger answered, giving Olivia's face an affectionate lick as thanks for the warm towel. *"Since you're so Christmas-challenged and all."*

Olivia stood, chuckling. "I saw these stick-on reindeer antlers for dogs at the hardware store," she said. "They have jingle bells and they light up. Treat me right or I'll buy you a pair, take your picture and post it on the internet."

Ginger sighed. She hated costumes.

A glance at the clock told Olivia she had an hour before she was due at Starcross for supper. After her shower, she decided, she'd dig through her closet and bureau drawers again, and find something presentable to wear, so Sophie wouldn't think she was a rube.

Ginger padded after her, jumped up onto her unmade bed and curled up in the middle. Olivia laid out clean underwear, her second-best pair of jeans and a red sweatshirt from two years ago, when Ashley had been on a fabric-painting kick. It had a cutesy snowman on the front, with light-up eyes, though the battery was long dead.

Toweling off after her shower and pulling on her clothes quickly, since even with the thermostat up, the house was drafty, Olivia told Ginger about the invitation to Starcross.

*"I'll stay here,"* Ginger said. *"Reinforcements have arrived."*

"What kind of reinforcements?" Olivia asked, peering at Ginger through the neck hole as she tugged the sweatshirt on over her head.

*"You'll see,"* Ginger answered, her eyes already at half-mast as she drifted toward sleep. *"Take your kit with you."*

"Is Butterpie sick?" Olivia asked, alarmed.

*"No,"* came the canine reply. *"I would have told you right away if she was. But you'll need the kit."*

"Okay," Olivia said.

Ginger's snore covered an octave, somewhere in the alto range.

Olivia wasn't musical.

AT SIX O'CLOCK, straight up, she drove up in front of the ranch house at Starcross. Colored lights glowed through the big picture window, a cheering sight in the snow-flecked twilight.

Bringing her medical kit as far as the porch, Olivia set it down and knocked.

Sophie opened the door, her small face as bright as the tree lights. The scents of piney sap and something savory cooking or cooling added to the ambience.

"Wait till you *see* what we got at the supermarket!" Sophie whooped, half dragging Olivia over the threshold.

Tanner stood framed in the entrance to the living room, one shoulder braced against the woodwork. He wore a blue Henley shirt, with a band around the neck instead of a collar, open at the throat, and jeans that looked as though they'd seen some decent wear. "Yeah," he drawled with an almost imperceptible roll of his eyes, "wait till you see."

A puppy bark sounded from behind him.

"You didn't," Olivia said, secretly thrilled.

"There are *two* of them!" Sophie exulted as the pair gamboled around Tanner to squirm and yip at Olivia's feet.

She crouched immediately, laughing and ruffling small, warm ears. So *this* was the reason Ginger had wanted her to bring the kit. These were mongrels, not purebreds, up to date on their vaccinations before they left the kennel, and they'd need their shots.

"I named them Snidely and Whiplash," Sophie said. "After the villain in *The Dudley Do-Right Show*."

"I suggested Going and Gone," Tanner interjected humorously, "but the kid wouldn't go for it."

"Which is which?" Olivia asked Sophie, ignoring Tanner's remark. Her heart was beating fast—did this mean he was thinking of staying on at Starcross after the shelter was finished?

"That's Snidely," Sophie said, pointing to the puppy with gold fur. They looked like some kind of collie-shepherd-retriever mix. "The spotted one is Whiplash."

"Let's just have a quick look at them," Olivia suggested. "My kit is on the porch. Would you get it for me, please?"

Sophie rushed to comply.

"Going and Gone?" Olivia asked very softly, watching Tanner. Now that she'd shifted, she could see the blue spruce behind him, in front of the snow-laced picture window.

But Sophie was back before he could answer.

"Later," he mouthed, and his eyes looked so serious that some of the spontaneous Christmas magic drifted to the floor like tired fairy dust.

Olivia examined the puppies, pronounced them healthy and gave them each their first round of shots. They were "box" puppies, giveaways, and that invariably meant they'd had no veterinary care at all.

"Does that hurt them?" Sophie asked, her blue eyes wide as she watched Olivia inject serum into the bunched-up scruffs of their necks with a very small needle. They'd all gathered in the living room, near the fragrant tree and the fire dancing on the hearth, Olivia employing the couch as an examining table.

"No," she said gently, putting away her doctor gear. "The injections will prevent distemper and parvo, among other things. The diseases *would* hurt, and these girls will need to be spayed as soon as they're a little older."

Sophie nodded solemnly. "They wet on the floor," she said, "but I promised Dad I'd clean up after them myself."

"Good girl," Olivia said. "If you take them outside every couple of hours, they'll get the idea." Her gaze was drawn to Tanner, but she resisted. *Going and Gone?* The names didn't bode well. Had he actually brought these puppies home intending to get rid of them as soon as Sophie went back to school?

*No,* she thought. *He couldn't have. He couldn't be that cold.*

There was lasagna for supper, and salad. Sophie talked the whole time they were eating, fairly bouncing in her chair while the puppies tumbled and played under the table, convinced they had a home.

Even though she was hungry, Olivia couldn't eat much.

When the meal was over, Sophie and Olivia put on coats and went out to the barn to see Butterpie and Shiloh while Tanner, strangely quiet, stayed behind to clean up the kitchen.

"We bought a new saddle for Butterpie," Sophie said excitedly as they entered the hay-scented warmth of the barn. "And Dad's having all the stalls fixed up so Aunt Tessa's horses will be comfortable here."

"Aunt Tessa?" Olivia asked, admiring the saddle. She'd had one much like it as a young girl; Big John had bought it for her thirteenth birthday, probably secondhand and at considerable sacrifice to the budget.

Now, she thought sadly, she didn't even own a horse.

"Tessa's my dad's sister. She has a whole bunch of horses, and she's getting a divorce, so Dad sent her money to come out here to Arizona." Sophie drew a breath and rushed on. "Maybe you saw her on TV. She starred in *California Women* for years—and a whole bunch of shows before that."

Olivia remembered the series, though she didn't watch much television. Curiously, her viewing was mostly limited to the holidays—she always tried to catch *It's a Wonderful Life, The Bishop's Wife* and, of course, *A Charlie Brown Christmas.*

"I think I've seen it once or twice," she said, but she couldn't place Tessa's character.

Sophie sagged a little as she opened Butterpie's stall. "I think Dad's going to ask Aunt Tessa to stay here and look after Starcross Ranch and Shiloh and the puppies after he leaves," she said.

"Oh," Olivia said, deflated but keeping up a game face for Sophie's sake.

Butterpie looked fit, and she was eating again.

"I'm still hoping he'll change his mind and let me stay here," Sophie confided quietly. "My education shouldn't be interrupted—at least we agree on that much—so I get to go to Stone Creek Middle School, starting Monday, until they let out for Christmas vacation."

Olivia didn't know what to say. She had opinions about boarding schools and adopting puppies he didn't intend to raise, that was for sure, but sharing them with Sophie would be over the line. Satisfied that Butterpie was doing well, she let herself into Shiloh's stall to stroke his long side.

He nuzzled her affectionately.

And her cell phone rang.

Here it was. The sick-cow call Olivia had been expecting all day.

But the number on the caller ID panel was Melissa's private line at the law office. What was she doing working this late, and on a holiday weekend, too?

"Mel? What's up?"

"It's Ashley," Melissa said quietly. "She just called me from some Podunk town in Tennessee. She caught the shuttle to the airport early this morning, evidently, and flew out of Phoenix without telling any of us."

"Tennessee?" Olivia echoed, momentarily confused. Or was she simply trying to deny what she already knew, deep down?

"I guess Mom's living there now," Melissa said.

Sophie stepped out of Butterpie's stall just as Olivia stepped out of Shiloh's, her face full of concern. They turned their backs on each other to work the latches, securing both horses for the night.

"Oh, my God," Olivia said.

"She's a wreck," Melissa went on, sounding as numb as Olivia felt. "Ashley, I mean. Things turned out badly—so badly that Brad's chartering a jet to go back there and pick up the pieces."

Sophie caught hold of Olivia's arm, steered her to a bale of hay and urged her to sit down.

She sat, gratefully. Standing up any longer would have been impossible, with her knees shaking the way they were.

"Should I go get my dad?" Sophie asked.

Olivia shook her head, then closed her eyes. "What happened, Mel? What did Ashley say on the phone?"

"She just said she should have listened to you and Brad. She was crying so hard, I could hardly understand her. She told me where she was staying and I called Brad as soon as we hung up."

Ashley. The innocent one, the one who believed in happy endings. She'd just run up against an ugly reality, and Olivia was miles away, unable to help her. "I'm going to call Brad and tell him I want to go, too," she said, about to hang up.

"I tried that," Melissa answered immediately. "He said he wanted to handle this alone. My guess is he's already on his way to Flagstaff to board the jet."

Olivia fought back tears of frustration, fury and resignation. "When did Ashley call?" she asked, fighting for composure. Sophie was already plenty worried—

the look on her face proved that—and it wouldn't do
to fall apart in front of a child.

"About half an hour ago. I called Brad right away,
and we were on the phone for a long time. As soon as
we hung up, I called you."

"Thanks," Olivia said woodenly.

"Are you all right?" Melissa asked.

"No," Olivia replied. "Are you?"

"No," Melissa admitted. "And I won't be until the
twin-unit is back home in Stone Creek, where she belongs. I know you want to call Brad and beat your head
against a brick wall trying to get him to let you go to
Tennessee with him, so I'll let you go."

"Go home," Olivia told her kid sister. "It's a holiday
weekend and you shouldn't be working."

Melissa's chuckle sounded more like a sob. Olivia
was terrified, so Melissa, what with the twin bond and
all, had to be ready to dissolve. "Like *you* have any
room to talk," she said. "Can I come out to your place,
Liv, and spend the night with you and Ginger?"

"Meet you there," Olivia said, following up with a
goodbye. She speed-dialed Brad in the next moment.

"No," he said instead of the customary hello.

"Where are you?"

"Almost to Flagstaff. The jet's waiting. When I know
anything, I'll call you."

Clearly, asking him to come back for her, or wait till
she could get to the airport, would, as her sister had pre-
dicted, be a waste of breath. Besides, Melissa needed
her, or she wouldn't have asked to spend the night.

"Okay," Olivia said. A few moments later she shut
her cell phone.

Sophie stood watching her. "Did something bad happen?"

Olivia stood. Her knees were back in working order, then. That was something. "It's a family thing," she said. "Nothing you need to worry about. I have to go home right away, though."

Sophie nodded sagely. "Shall I go get your doctor bag?" she asked. "I'll explain to Dad and everything."

"Thanks," Olivia said, heading for the Suburban.

Sophie raced for the house, but it was Tanner who brought the medical kit out to her.

"Anything I can do?" he asked, handing it through the open window of the Suburban.

Olivia shook her head, not trusting herself to speak.

To her utter surprise, Tanner leaned in, cupped his hand at the back of her head and planted a gentle but electrifying kiss on her mouth. Then he stepped away, and she put the Suburban into gear and drove out.

TANNER STOOD IN THE COLD, watching Olivia's taillights disappear in the thickening snowfall.

The shimmering colors on the Christmas tree in the front room seemed to mock him through the steam-fogged glass. Whatever Olivia's problem was, he probably couldn't make it right. It was a "family thing," according to Sophie's breathless report, and he wasn't family.

He shoved his hands into his hip pockets—he hadn't bothered with a coat—and thought about, of all things, the puppies. There was no way he could ask Olivia to find them homes after he moved on. Tessa might or might not be willing to stay on at Stone Creek and look after Snidely and Whiplash.

He'd dug himself a big hole, with Sophie *and* with Olivia, and getting out was going to take some doing. Fast-talking wouldn't pack it.

Inside the house, Sophie was making a bed for the puppies in a cardboard box fluffed up with an old blanket.

"Did somebody die?" she asked when Tanner entered the living room.

The question poleaxed him. Sophie had lost her mother when she was seven years old. Did every crisis prompt her to expect a funeral?

"I don't think so, honey," he said gruffly. He should have hugged her, but he couldn't move. He just stood there, like a fool, in the middle of the living room.

Sophie looked at the Christmas tree. "Maybe we could finish decorating tomorrow," she said. "I don't feel much like it now."

"Me, either," Tanner admitted. "Let's take the puppies outside before you bed them down."

Sophie nodded, and they put on their coats and each took a puppy.

The dogs squatted obediently in the thickening snow.

"I like Olivia," Sophie said.

"I do, too," Tanner replied. *Maybe a little too much.*

"It was fun having her here to eat supper with us."

Tanner nodded, draped an arm around Sophie's small shoulders. She felt so little, so insubstantial, inside her bulky nylon jacket.

"I showed her my new saddle."

"It's a nice piece of gear."

The puppies were finished. Tanner scooped one up, and Sophie collected the other. They plodded toward the house, with its half-decorated Christmas tree, peeling wallpaper and outdated plumbing fixtures.

Flipping *this* house, Tanner thought ruefully, was going to be a job.

Once Sophie and the dogs were settled upstairs, in the room she'd declared to be hers, Tanner unplugged the tree lights and wandered into the kitchen to log on at his laptop. He had some supply invoices to look over, fortunately, and that would keep his mind occupied. Keep him from worrying about what had happened in Olivia's family to knock her off balance like that.

He could call Brad and ask, of course, but he wasn't going to do that. It would be an intrusion.

So he poured himself a cup of lukewarm coffee, drew up a chair at the table and opened his laptop.

The invoices were there, all right. But they might as well have been written in Sanskrit, for all the sense he could make of them.

After half an hour he gave up.

It was too early to go to sleep, so he snapped on the one TV set in the house, a little portable in the living room, and flipped through channels until he found a weather report.

Snow, snow and more snow.

He sighed and changed channels again, settled on a holiday rerun of *Everybody Loves Raymond*. Here, at least, was a family even more dysfunctional than his own.

In a perverse sort of way, it cheered him up.

MELISSA ARRIVED WITH AN overnight case only twenty minutes after Olivia got home. Her blue eyes were red rimmed from crying.

Of all the O'Ballivan siblings, Melissa was the least emotional. But she stood in Olivia's kitchen, her shoulders stooped and dusted with snowflakes, and choked up when she tried to speak.

Olivia immediately took her younger sister into her arms. "It's okay," she said. "Everything will work out, you'll see."

Melissa nodded, sniffled and pulled away. "God," she said, trying to make a joke, "this place is *such* a dive."

"It'll do until I can move in above the new shelter," Olivia said, pointing toward the nearby hall. "The guest room is ready. Put your stuff away and we'll talk."

Melissa had spotted Charlie Brown, still standing in his nondescript pot in the center of the kitchen table. "You bought a Christmas tree?" she marveled.

Olivia set her hands on her hips. "Why is that such a surprise to everybody?" she asked, realizing only when the words were out of her mouth that *Ginger* had offered the only other comment on the purchase.

Melissa sighed and shook her head. Ginger escorted her to the spare room, and back. Melissa had shed her coat, and she was pushing up the sleeves of her white sweater as she reentered the kitchen.

"Let's get the poor thing decorated," she said.

"Good idea," Olivia agreed.

The tree was fairly heavy, between the root system and the pot, and Melissa helped her lug it into the living room.

Olivia pushed an end table in front of the window, after moving a lamp, and Charlie was hoisted to eye level.

"This is sort of—cheerful," Melissa said, probably

being kind, though whether she felt sorry for Olivia or the tree was anybody's guess.

Olivia pulled the bubble lights and ornaments from the hardware-store bags. "Maybe I should make popcorn or something."

"That," Melissa teased after another sniffle, "would constitute *cooking.* And you promised you wouldn't try that at home."

Olivia laughed. "I'm glad you're here, Mel."

"Me, too," Melissa said. "We should get together more often. We're always working."

"You work more than I do," Olivia told her good-naturedly. "You need to get a life, Melissa O'Ballivan."

"I *have* a life, thank you very much," Melissa retorted, heading for Olivia's CD player and putting on some Christmas music. "Anyway, if anybody's going to preach to me about overdoing it at work and getting a life, it isn't going to be you, Big Sister."

"Are you dating anybody?" Olivia asked, opening one of the cartons of bubble lights. When they were younger, Big John had hung lights exactly like them on the family tree every year. Then they'd become a fire hazard, and he'd thrown them out.

"The last one ended badly," Melissa confessed, busy opening the ornament boxes and putting hangers through the little loops. So busy that she wouldn't meet Olivia's gaze.

"How so?"

"He was married," Melissa said. "Had me fooled, until the wife sent me a photo Christmas card showing them on a trip to the Grand Canyon last summer. Four kids and a dog."

"Yikes," Olivia said, wanting to hug Melissa, or at

least lay a hand on her shoulder, but holding back. Her sister seemed uncharacteristically brittle, as though she might fall apart if anyone touched her just then. "You really cared about him, huh?"

"I cared," Melissa said. "What else is new? If there's a jerk within a hundred miles, I'll find him, rope him in and hand him my heart."

"Aren't you being a little hard on yourself?"

Melissa shrugged offhandedly. "The one before that wanted to meet Brad and present him with a demo so he could make it big in showbiz." She paused. "But at least *he* didn't have children."

"Mel, it happens. Cut yourself a little slack."

"You didn't see those kids. Freckles. Braces. They all looked so happy. And why not? How could they know their dad is a class-A, card-carrying schmuck?"

Once again Olivia found herself at a loss for words. She concentrated on clipping the lights to Charlie Brown's branches.

"Par-ump-pah-pum…" Bing Crosby sang from the CD player.

"I might as well tell you it's the talk of the family," Melissa said, picking up the conversational ball with cheerful determination, "that you skipped out of Thanksgiving to sneak off with Tanner Quinn."

Olivia stiffened. "I didn't 'sneak off' with him," she said.

*Not much,* said her conscience.

"Don't be so defensive," Melissa replied, widening her eyes. "He's a hunk. I'd have left with him, too."

"It wasn't—"

"It wasn't what I think?" Melissa challenged, smiling now. "Of course it was. Are you in love with him?"

Olivia opened her mouth, closed it again.

Bing Crosby sang wistfully of orange groves and sunshine. He was dreaming of a white Christmas.

He could have hers.

"Are you?" Melissa pressed.

"No," Olivia said.

"Too bad," Melissa answered.

Olivia looked at her watch, pretending she hadn't heard that last remark. By now Brad was probably in the air, jetting toward Tennessee.

*Hold on, Ashley,* she thought. *Hold on.*

The call didn't come until almost midnight, and when it did, both Melissa and Olivia, snacking on leathery egg rolls snatched from the freezer and thawed in the oven, dived for the kitchen phone.

Olivia got there first. Home-court advantage.

"She's okay," Brad said. "We'll be back sometime tomorrow."

"Put her on," Olivia replied anxiously.

"I don't think she's up to that right now," Brad answered.

"Tell her Melissa's here with me, and we'll be waiting when she gets home."

Brad agreed, and the call ended.

"She's all right, then?" Melissa asked carefully.

Olivia nodded, but she wasn't entirely convinced it was the truth. The only thing to do now was get some sleep—Melissa needed a night's rest, and so did she.

In her room, with Ginger sharing the bed, Olivia stared up at the ceiling and worried. Across the hall, in the tiny spare room, Melissa was probably doing the same thing.

TANNER, WATCHING FROM HIS bedroom window, saw the lights go out across the field, in Olivia's house. He went to look in on Sophie and the puppies one more time, then showered, brushed his teeth, pulled on sweats and stretched out for the night.

Sleep proved elusive, and when it came, it was shallow, a partial unconsciousness ripe for lucid dreams. And not necessarily good ones.

He found himself in what looked like a hospital corridor, near the nurses' desk, and when a tall, dark-haired woman came out of a room, wearing scrubs and carrying a chart, he thought it was Kat.

She was back, then. The last dream hadn't been a goodbye after all.

He tried to speak to her, but it was no use. He was no more articulate than the droopy Christmas garlands and greeting cards taped haphazardly to the walls and trimming the desk.

The general effect was forlorn, rather than festive.

The woman in scrubs slapped the chart down on the counter and sighed.

There were shadows under her eyes, and she was too thin. No wedding ring on her left hand, either.

"Nurse?" she called.

A heavy woman appeared from a back room. "Do you need something, Dr. Quinn?"

Dr. Quinn, medicine woman. It was a joke he and Sophie shared when they talked about her career plans.

Sophie. This was *Sophie*—some kind of ghost of Christmas future.

Tanner tried hard to wake up, but it didn't happen for him. During the effort, he missed whatever Sophie said in reply to the nurse's question.

"I thought you'd go home for Christmas this year," the nurse said chattily. "I'd swear I saw your name on the vacation list."

Sophie studied the chart, a little frown forming between her eyebrows. "I swapped with Dr. Severn," she answered distractedly. "He has a family."

Tanner felt his heart break. *You* have a family, Sophie, he cried silently.

"Anyway, my dad's overseas, building something," Sophie went on. "We don't make a big deal about Christmas."

*Sophie,* Tanner pleaded.

But she didn't hear him. She snapped the chart shut and marched off down the hospital corridor again, disappearing into a mist.

*My dad's overseas, building something. We don't make a big deal about Christmas.*

Sophie's words lingered in Tanner's head when he opened his eyes. He ran the back of his arm across his wet face, alone in the darkness.

So much for sleep.

## CHAPTER NINE

OVER WHAT WAS LEFT of the weekend, the snow melted and the roads were lined with muddy slush. It made the decorations on Main Street look as though they were trying just a shade too hard, by Olivia's calculations.

Brad and Ashley didn't get back to Stone Creek until Monday afternoon. Melissa and Olivia were waiting at Ashley's, along with Ginger, when Brad's truck pulled up outside. They'd considered turning on the outside lights to welcome Ashley home, but in the end it hadn't seemed like a good idea.

Olivia had brewed fresh coffee, though.

Melissa had brought a box of Ashley's favorite doughnuts from the bakery.

As they peered out the front window, watching as Brad helped Ashley out of the truck and held on to her arm as they approached the gate, both Olivia and Melissa knew coffee and doughnuts weren't going to be enough.

Ashley looked thinner—was that possible after only a couple of days?—and even from a distance, Olivia could see that there were deep shadows under her eyes.

Melissa rushed for the door and opened it as Brad brought Ashley up the steps. He shot a look of bruised warning at Melissa, then Olivia.

"I don't want to talk about it," Ashley said.

"You don't have to," Olivia told her softly, reaching for Ashley and drawing back when her sister flinched, huddled closer to Brad, as though she felt threatened. She wouldn't look at either Olivia or Melissa, but she did stoop to pat Ginger's head. "I just want to sleep."

Once Ashley was inside the house, Melissa urged her toward the stairs. The railing was buried under an evergreen garland.

"That must have been a very bad scene," Olivia said to Brad when the twins were on their way upstairs, followed by Ginger.

He nodded, his expression glum. Now that Olivia looked at him, she realized that he looked almost as bad as Ashley did.

"What happened?" Olivia prompted when her brother didn't say anything.

"She wouldn't tell me any more than she just told you." There was more, though. Olivia knew that, by Brad's face, even before he went on. "A desk clerk at Ashley's hotel told me she checked in, all excited, and a woman came to see her—the two of them met in the hotel restaurant for lunch. The woman was Mom, of course. She swilled a lot of wine, and things went sour, fast. According to this clerk, Mom started screaming that if she'd wanted 'a bunch of snot-nosed brats hanging off her,' she'd have stayed in Stone Creek and rotted."

The words, and the image, which she could picture only too well, struck Olivia like blows. It didn't help that she would have expected something similar out of any meeting with her mother.

"My God," she whispered. "Poor Ashley."

"It gets worse," Brad said. "Mom raised such hell

in the restaurant that the police were called. Turns out she'd violated probation by getting drunk, and now she's in jail. Ashley's furious with me because I wouldn't bail her out."

A sudden headache slammed at Olivia's temples with such ferocity that she wondered if she was blowing a blood vessel in her brain. She nodded to let Brad know she'd heard, but her eyes were squeezed shut.

"I tried to get Ashley to stop at the doctor's office on the way into town a little while ago—maybe get some tranquilizers or something—but she said she just wanted to go home." He paused. "Liv, are you okay?"

"I've been better," she answered, opening her eyes. "Right now I'm not worried about myself. I should have known Ashley would have done something like this—tried to stop her—"

"It isn't your fault," Brad said.

Olivia nodded, but she probably wasn't very convincing, to Brad or herself.

"I've got to get home to Meg and the baby," Brad told her. "Can you and Melissa take it from here?"

Again Olivia nodded.

"You'll call if she seems to be losing ground?"

Olivia stood on tiptoe and kissed her brother's unshaven, wind-chilled cheek. "I'll call," she promised.

After casting a rueful glance toward the stairs, Brad turned and left.

Olivia was halfway up those same stairs when Melissa appeared at the top, a finger to her lips.

"She's resting," she whispered. Apparently Ginger had elected to stay in Ashley's room.

Together, Olivia and Melissa retreated to the kitchen.

"Did she say anything?" Olivia prodded.

"Just that it was terrible," Melissa replied, "and that she still doesn't want to talk about it."

Olivia's cell phone chirped. Great. After the slowest weekend on record, professionally speaking anyway, she was suddenly in demand.

"Dr. O'Ballivan," she answered, having seen the clinic's number on the ID panel.

"There's a horse colicking at the Wildes' farm," the receptionist, Becky, told her. "It's bad and Dr. Elliott is on call, but he's busy...."

Colic. The ailment could be deadly for a horse. "I'm on my way," Olivia said.

"Go," Melissa said when she'd hung up. "I'll look after Ashley. Ginger, too."

Having no real choice, Olivia hurried out to the Suburban and headed for the Wildes'.

The next few hours were harrowing, with teenaged Sherry Wilde, the owner of the sick horse, on the verge of hysteria the whole time. Olivia managed to save the bay mare, but it was a fight.

She was so drained afterward that she pulled over and sat in the Suburban with her head resting on the steering wheel, once she'd driven out of sight of the house and barn, and cried.

Presently she heard another rig pull up behind her and, since she was about halfway between Stone Creek and Indian Rock, she figured it was Wyatt Terp or one of his deputies, out on patrol, stopping to make sure she was okay. Olivia sniffled inelegantly and lifted her head.

But the face on the other side of the window was Tanner's, not Wyatt's.

She hadn't seen him since supper at his place a few nights before.

He gestured for her to roll down the window.

She did.

"Engine trouble?" he asked.

Olivia shook her head. She must look a sight, she thought, with her eyes all puffy and her nose red enough to fly lead for Kris Kringle. She was a professional, good under pressure, and it was completely unlike her to sit sniveling beside the road.

"Move over," he said after locking his own vehicle by pressing a button on the key fob. "I'm driving."

"I'm all right—really…"

He already had the door open, and he was standing on the running board.

Olivia scrambled over the console to the passenger side once she realized he wasn't going to give in.

"Where to?" he asked.

"Home, I guess," Olivia said. She'd called the bed-and-breakfast before leaving the Wildes' farm, and Melissa had told her Ashley still wanted to be left alone. The family doctor had dropped by, at Brad's request, and given Ash a mild sedative.

Melissa planned to stay overnight.

"When you're ready to talk," Tanner said, checking the rearview mirror before pulling onto the road, "I'll be ready to listen."

"It might be a while," Olivia said, after a few moments spent struggling to get a grip. "Where's Sophie?"

Tanner grinned. "She stayed after school to watch the drama department rehearse for the winter play," he said. "We'll pick her up on our way if you don't mind."

It went without saying that Olivia didn't mind, but she said it anyway.

Sophie was waiting with friends when they pulled up in front of the middle school. She looked puzzled for a moment, then rushed, smiling, toward the Suburban.

"We really should go back and get your truck," Olivia fretted, glancing at Tanner as Sophie climbed into the rear seat.

"Maybe it will get dirty," Tanner said cheerfully. Then, when Olivia didn't smile, he added, "I'll send somebody from the construction crew to pick it up."

"Can we get pizza?" Sophie wanted to know.

"We have horses to feed," Tanner told her. "Not to mention Snidely and Whiplash. We'll order pizza after the chores are done."

"Our tree is all decorated," Sophie told Olivia. "You should come and see it."

"I will," Olivia said.

"Are you coming down with a cold?" Sophie wanted to know. "You sound funny."

"I'm all right," Olivia answered, touched.

They were about a mile out of town, on the far side of Stone Creek, when they spotted Ginger trudging alongside the road. Olivia's mouth fell open—she'd thought the dog was still at Ashley's.

"What's Ginger doing out here all alone?" Sophie demanded.

"I don't know," Olivia said, struggling in vain to open the passenger-side door even as Tanner stopped the Suburban, got out and lifted the weary dog off the ground. Carried her in his arms to the back of the rig and settled her on the blankets.

"I don't think she's hurt," Tanner said once he was behind the wheel again. "Just tired and pretty footsore."

A tear slipped down Olivia's cheek, and she wiped it away, but not quickly enough.

"Hey," he said, his voice husky. "It can't be that bad."

Olivia didn't answer.

Ashley would be all right.

Ginger would be, too.

But she wasn't so sure about herself.

At some point, without even realizing it, she'd fallen in love with Tanner Quinn. Talk about a dismal revelation.

Reaching her place, Tanner let Sophie stay behind with Olivia and Ginger while he went on to Starcross to feed Butterpie and Shiloh and see to the puppies, as well.

Holding off tears with everything she had, Olivia peeled off her vest, turned up the heat and gave Ginger a quick but thorough exam. Tanner's diagnosis had been correct—she was worn out, and she'd need some salve on the pads of her feet, but otherwise she was fine. "Why didn't you stay at Ashley's?" she asked. "I would have come back for you."

Ginger just looked up at her, eyes full of exhaustion and devoted trust.

"Can I order pizza?" Sophie asked, hovering by the phone.

Olivia smiled a fragile smile, nodded. *Keep busy,* she thought. *Keep busy.* She filled Ginger's water and kibble bowls and dragged her fluffy Ashley-made bed into the kitchen. Ginger turned a few circles and collapsed, obviously spent and blissfully happy to be home.

Sophie placed the pizza order and sat down cross-legged on the floor to pet Ginger, who slumbered on.

"Did Ginger run away?" she asked.

Olivia was making coffee. Maybe Santa would bring her a new percolator. Was it too late to write to him? Did he have an email address?

Was she losing her ever-loving *mind?*

Yes, if she'd fallen for Tanner. He was as unavailable as Melissa's last guy.

"She and I were visiting my sister in town earlier," Olivia explained, amazed at how normal she sounded. "Ginger must have decided to come home on her own."

"I ran away once," Sophie confessed.

"So I heard," Olivia answered, listening more intently now. Watching the girl out of the corner of her eye.

"It was a stupid thing to do," Sophie elaborated.

"And dangerous," Olivia agreed.

"I just wanted to come home," Sophie said. "Like Ginger."

Olivia's throat thickened again. "How do you like Stone Creek Middle School?" she asked, forging bravely on. *Oh, and by the way, I'm hopelessly in love with your father.*

"They're doing *Our Town,* the week between Christmas and New Year's," Sophie said. "I would have tried out for the part of Emily if I lived here."

"They do *Our Town* every year," Olivia answered. "It's a tradition."

"Were you in it when you were in middle school?"

"No. I had stage fright. So I worked sets and costumes. But my older brother, Brad, had a leading role one year, and both my sisters, Ashley and Melissa, had parts when their turn came."

"You have stage fright?"

"I didn't get the show-business gene. That went to Brad."

"Dad has some of his CDs. I kind of like the way he sings."

"Me, too," Olivia said.

"Did you always want to be a veterinarian?"

Olivia left the coffeepot and sat down at the table, near Sophie and the sweetly slumbering Ginger. "For as long as I can remember," she said.

"I want to be a people doctor," Sophie said. "Like my mom was."

"I'm sure you'll be a good one."

Sophie looked very solemn, and she might have been about to say something more about her mother, but the Suburban rolled noisily up alongside the house just then. A door slammed.

Tanner was back from feeding horses and puppies, and the pizza would be arriving soon, no doubt.

*Maybe I'm over him,* Olivia thought. *Maybe fighting for a horse's life made me overemotional.*

He knocked and came inside, shivering. Flecks of hay decorated his clothes. "It's cold out there," he said.

Nope, she wasn't over him.

Olivia's hand shook a little as she gestured toward the coffeepot. "Help yourself," she told him. She was ridiculously glad he was there, he and Sophie both.

Sophie got up from the floor while Tanner poured coffee, and wandered into the living room.

"Hey," she called right away. "Your little tree looks pretty good."

"Thanks," Olivia called back as she and Tanner exchanged low-wattage smiles.

*I love you,* Olivia said silently. *How's that for foolish?*

"How come there aren't any presents under it?"

"Soph," Tanner objected.

Sophie appeared in the doorway between the kitchen and living room.

"There are a lot of guys at our house, fixing up the barn," she told Olivia. "It's a good thing, too, because Aunt Tessa's horses will be tired when they get here."

"Are they on their way?" Olivia asked Tanner.

He nodded. "Tessa's bringing them herself," he said. "I wanted her to fly and let a transport company bring them, but she has a head as hard as Arizona bedrock."

"I think I'm going to like her," Olivia said.

Sophie beamed, nodding in agreement. "Once she's out here with us, she'll get over her break-up in no time!"

Olivia looked at Tanner. "Break-up?"

"Divorce," he said. "None of them are easy, but this one's a meat grinder."

"I'm sorry," Olivia told him, and she meant it. She remembered how broken up her dad had been after Delia skipped out. Knew only too well how *she* would feel when Tanner left Stone Creek for good.

"Can I plug in your Christmas tree?" Sophie asked.

"Sure," Olivia said.

Sophie disappeared again.

Tanner and Olivia looked at each other in silence.

Mercifully, the pizza delivery guy broke the spell by honking his car horn from the driveway.

Tanner grinned and started for the door.

"My turn to provide supper," Olivia said, easing past him.

When she came back with the goods, snow-speckled and wishing she'd taken the time to put on her coat, Tanner was setting the table.

Ginger roused herself long enough to sniff the air. Pizza was one of her favorites, although Olivia never gave her more than a few bites.

Supper was almost magical—they might have been a family, Tanner and Olivia and Sophie, talking around the table as they ate in the warm, cozy kitchen.

Sophie snuck a few morsels to Ginger, and Olivia pretended not to see.

Because Tanner's truck had been picked up and driven to Starcross, Olivia gave her neighbors a ride home when the time came. She waited until they'd both gone inside, after waving from the porch, and watched as the tree lights sprang to life in the front window.

Sophie's doing, she supposed.

On the way back to her place, because she still wanted to cry, Olivia called Ashley's house again.

"She's fine, mother hen," Melissa told her. "I talked her into having some soup a little while ago, and a cup of tea, too. She says she'll be her old self again after a bubble bath."

Olivia's relief was so great that she didn't ask if anybody had noticed Ginger's escape. Nor, of course, did she announce that she was in love.

"I can't seem to find the dog, though," Melissa said. "It's a big house. She must be here somewhere."

"She's home," Olivia said.

"You picked her up?"

"She walked."

"Oh, God, Livie, I'm sorry—she must have slipped out through Ashley's pet door in the laundry room—"

"Ginger's fine," Olivia assured her worried sister.

"Thank God," Melissa replied. "Why do you suppose she put in a pet door—Ashley, I mean—when she doesn't have a *pet?*"

"Maybe she wants one."

"I could stop by the shelter and adopt a kitten for her or something."

"Don't you dare," Olivia said. "Adopting an animal is a commitment, and Ashley has to make that decision on her own."

"Okay, Dr. Dolittle," Melissa teased. "*Okay.* Spare me the responsible pet owner lecture, all right? I was just thinking out loud."

"Why don't *you* adopt a dog or a cat?"

"I'm allergic, remember?" Melissa answered, giving a sneeze right on cue. It was the first sign of Melissa's hypochondria that Olivia had seen in recent days.

"Right," Olivia replied.

By then the snow was coming down so thick and fast, she could barely see her driveway. *Please God,* she prayed silently, *no emergencies tonight.*

She and Melissa swapped goodbyes, and she ended the call.

A nice hot bubble bath didn't sound half-bad, she thought when the cold air hit her as she got out of the Suburban. Maybe she'd light a few candles, put on her snuggly robe after the bath, make cocoa and watch something Christmasy and sentimental on TV.

Talk herself out of loving a no-strings-attached kind of man.

Ginger got up when she came in, ate a few kibbles and immediately headed for the back door.

So much for getting warm.

Olivia went outside with the dog.

*"It's not as if I plan to run away, you know,"* Ginger remarked.

Through the storm, Olivia could just make out the lights over at Starcross. The sight comforted her and, at the same time, made her feel oddly isolated.

"I wouldn't have thought you'd try to walk all the way home from Stone Creek," Olivia scolded. "Ginger, it's at least five miles."

*"I made it, didn't I?"* Having completed her outside enterprise, Ginger headed for the back porch, stopping to shake off the snow before going on into the kitchen.

Olivia tromped in after her, hugging herself. Shut the door and locked it.

"I'm taking a bubble bath," she said. "Don't bother me unless you're bleeding or the place catches fire."

Ginger took hold of her dog bed with her teeth and hauled it into the living room, in front of the tree. In the softer light, Charlie Brown looked almost—well—*bushy.* Downright festive, even.

She'd unplugged the bubble lights before leaving to take Tanner and Sophie home. Now she bent to plug them in again, waited until the colorful liquid in the little glass vials began to bubble cheerfully.

She immediately thought of Big John, but tonight the memory of her grandfather didn't hurt. She smiled, remembering what a big deal he'd always made over Christmas, spending money he probably didn't have, taking them all up into the timber country to look for just the right tree, sitting proud and straight-backed in the audience at each new production of *Our Town*. In retrospect, she knew he'd been trying to make up for the losses in their lives—hers, Brad's, Ashley's and Melissa's.

The year Brad was in the play, Ashley had cried all the way home to the ranch. Big John had carried her into the house and demanded to know what the "waterworks" were all about.

"All those dead people sitting in folding chairs!" Ashley had wailed. "Is Daddy someplace like that, all in shadow, sitting in a folding chair?"

Big John's face had been a study in manfully controlled emotion. "No, honey," he'd said gruffly, there in the kitchen at Stone Creek Ranch, while Brad and Olivia and Melissa peeled out of their coats. "*Our Town* is just a story. Your daddy isn't sitting around in a folding chair, and you can take that to the bank. He's too busy riding horses, I figure. The way I figure it, they've got some mighty good trails up there in heaven, and there aren't any shadows to speak of, either."

Ashley's eyes had widened almost to saucer size, but she'd stopped crying. "How do you know, Big John?" she'd asked, gazing up at him. "Is it in the Bible?"

Brad, a pretty typical teenager, had given a snort at that.

Big John had quelled him with a look. "No," he told Ashley, resting a hand on her shoulder. "It probably isn't in the Bible. But there are some things that just make sense. How many cowboys would want to go to heaven if there weren't any horses to ride?"

Ashley had brightened at the question. In her child's mind, the argument made sense.

Blinking, Olivia returned to the present moment.

"Time for that hot bath I promised myself," she told Ginger.

*"I wouldn't mind one either,"* Ginger said.

And so it was that Olivia bathed the dog first, toweled her off and then scrubbed out the tub for her own turn.

When she finished, she put on flannel pajamas and her favorite bathrobe and padded out to the living room.

Ginger had the TV on, watching *Animal Planet.*

"How did you do that?" Olivia asked. There were some things that strained even an animal communicator's credulity.

*"If you step on the remote just right, it happens,"* Ginger replied.

"Oh, good grief," Olivia said, glancing in Charlie Brown's direction.

*"I wouldn't have thought he could look that good,"* Ginger observed, following Olivia's gaze.

She reclaimed the remote. Checked the channel guide.

"We're watching *The Bishop's Wife,*" she told Ginger.

Ginger didn't protest. She liked Cary Grant, too.

*"After it's over,"* the dog said, *"we can talk about how you're in love with Tanner."*

"I DON'T WANT TO TALK about it," Ashley said, for the fourth or fifth time, the next morning when Olivia stopped by her house on the way to the clinic, Ginger in tow. Melissa had already gone to work.

Olivia was still in love, but she was adjusting.

"Fair enough," she replied. Ashley looked almost like her old self, and she was expecting paying guests later in the day. Rolling out piecrusts in preparation for some serious baking.

Some people drank when they were upset. Others chain-smoked.

Ashley baked.

"Tell me about the guests," Olivia said, trying to snitch a piece of pie dough and getting her hand slapped for her trouble.

"They're long-term," Ashley answered, rolling harder, so the flour flew. Some of it was in her hair, and a lot more decorated her holly-sprigged chef's apron. "Tanner Quinn called and booked the rooms. He said he needed space for four people, and he'd vouch for their character because they all work for him."

Olivia raised an eyebrow. "I see," she said, considering another attempt at the pie dough and doing a pretty good job of hiding the fact that Tanner's name made the floor tremble under her feet.

"Don't even think about it," Ashley said, sounding like her old self. *Almost* her old self, anyway. She was still pretty ragged around the edges, but if she didn't want to talk about their mother just yet, Olivia would respect that.

Even if it killed her.

"Nice of him," she said. "Tanner, I mean. He could have put the crew up at the Sundowner Motel, or over in Indian Rock."

Ashley pounded at the pie dough and rolled vigorously again. It looked like a good upper-arm workout. "All I know is they're paying top dollar, and they'll be here until next spring. Merry Christmas to me. For a few months, anyway, I won't need any more 'loans' from Brad to keep the business going."

Olivia didn't miss the slight edge in her sister's voice. "Ash," she said. "This will get easier. I promise it will."

"I should have listened to you."

"But you didn't, and that's okay. You're a grown woman, with a perfect right to make your own decisions."

"She's *horrible*, Liv."

"Let it go, Ash."

"Do you know why she was on probation? For shoplifting, and writing bad checks, and—and God knows what else."

"Brad said you were miffed because he wouldn't bail her out."

Ashley set down the rolling pin, backed away from the counter. Flour drifted down onto Ginger's head like finely sifted snow. "He was right," Ashley said. "He was right not to bail that—that *woman* out!"

"I can stay if you want me to," Olivia said.

Ashley shook her head, hard. "No," she insisted. "But I wouldn't mind if Ginger were here to keep me company."

Olivia looked at Ginger. Knew instantly that she wanted to stay.

"Don't you dare try to walk home again," she told the dog. "I'll pick you up after I finish my last call."

"Oh, for Pete's sake," Ashley said. Like Brad and Melissa, she had always taken the Dr. Dolittle thing with a grain of salt. Make that a barrel. Only Big John had really understood—he'd said his grandmother could talk to animals, too.

"Later," Olivia said, and dashed out through the back, though she did stop briefly to secure the latch on the pet door, in case Ginger got another case of wanderlust.

NOW THAT HE HAD CREWS working, the shelter project took off. The barn at Starcross was coming along nicely, too. Tanner was pleased.

Or he *should* have been.

Sophie loved school—specifically Stone Creek Middle School. She'd already found some friends, and she was making good progress at house-training the puppies, too. She did her chores without being asked, exercising Butterpie every day.

That morning, when he came back inside from feeding the horses, she was already making breakfast.

"I used your laptop," she'd confessed immediately.

"Is that why you're trying to make points?"

Sophie had laughed. "Nope. I had to check my email. All hell's breaking loose at Briarwood."

He hadn't been surprised to hear that, since he'd called both Jack McCall and Ms. Wiggins soon after the drug conversation with Sophie that day in the truck, and read them every line of the riot act, twice over.

Ms. Wiggins had promised a thorough and immediate investigation.

Jack had asked if he was sure Sophie wasn't playing him, so she could stay with him in Stone Creek.

"I *really* can't go back there now, Dad," Sophie had told him, turning serious again. "Everybody knows I'm the one who blew the whistle, and that won't win me the Miss Popularity pin."

He'd ruffled her hair. "Don't worry about it. You'll be going to a new school, anyway." He'd found a good one in Phoenix, just over two hours away by car, but he was saving the details for a surprise. He wanted Tessa to be there when he broke the good news, and Olivia, too, if possible.

Olivia.

Now, there was a gift he'd like to unwrap again.

As soon as Tessa got there and he had somebody to hold down the fort with Sophie, he was going to ask Olivia O'Ballivan, DVM, out on a real date. Take her to dinner somewhere fancy, up in Flagstaff, or in nearby Sedona.

In the meantime, he'd have to tough it out. Work hard. Take a lot of cold showers.

A worker went by, whistling "Have Yourself a Merry Little Christmas."

Tanner almost told him to shut the hell up.

# CHAPTER TEN

THERE WAS NO SLOWING down Christmas. It was bearing down on Stone Creek at full throttle, hell-bent-for-election, as Big John used to say. Watering Charlie Brown in her living room before braving snowy roads to get to the clinic for a full day of appointments, Olivia hummed a carol under her breath.

The week since Ashley had come home from Tennessee had been a busy one, rushing by. Olivia had had supper with Sophie and Tanner twice, once at her place, once at theirs.

And she hadn't been able to shake off loving him.

It was for real.

The big tree in the center of town would be lighted as soon as the sun went down that night, to the noisy delight of the whole community, and after that, over at the high school gymnasium, the chamber of commerce was throwing their annual Christmas carnival, with a dance to follow.

In the kitchen Ginger began to bark.

Olivia frowned and went to investigate. They'd already been outside, and she hadn't heard anybody drive in.

Passing the kitchen window, she saw a late-model truck pulling in at Starcross, pulling a long, mud-splashed horse trailer behind it.

Sophie's much-anticipated aunt Tessa, Tanner's sister, had finally arrived. That would be a relief to Tanner—more than once over the past week he'd admitted he was on the verge of heading out to look for Tessa. Even though Tessa called every night, according to Sophie, to report her progress, Tanner had been jumpy.

"He worries a lot about what *could happen*," Sophie had told Olivia, on the q.t., while the two of them were frying chicken in the kitchen at Starcross. Then, as if concerned that Olivia might be turned off by the admission, she'd added, "But he's *really* brave. He saved Uncle Jack's life *twice* in the Gulf War."

"And modest, too," Olivia had teased.

But Sophie's expression was serious. "Uncle Jack told me about it," she'd said. "Not Dad."

Now, with Ginger barking fit to deafen her, Olivia made an executive decision. She'd stop by Starcross on the way to town and offer a brief welcome to Tessa. It was the neighborly thing to do, after all.

And if she was more than a little curious about the soon-to-be-divorced former TV star, well, nothing wrong with that. Brad would have to share his local-celebrity status, at least temporarily.

Showing up would be an intrusion of sorts, though, Olivia reasoned as she and Ginger slipped and slid down the icy driveway to the main road. Who knew what kind of shape Tessa Quinn Whoever might be in after driving practically across country with a load of horses and a broken heart?

All the more reason to offer a friendly greeting, Olivia decided.

Tanner had probably already left for the construction site in town, and Sophie was surely in school, secretly lusting after the role of Emily in next year's production of *Our Town*. Stone Creek never got tired of that play—perhaps because it reminded them to be grateful for ordinary blessings.

It bothered Olivia to think Tessa might have no one to welcome her, help her unload her prized horses and settle them into stalls. Since all her morning appointments were things a veterinary assistant could handle, Olivia decided she'd offer whatever assistance she could.

Only, Tanner was there when Olivia arrived, and so was Sophie.

She and Tessa—a tall, dark-haired woman who resembled Tanner—were just breaking up a hug. Tanner was pulling out the ramp on the horse trailer, but he stopped and smiled as Olivia drove up.

Her heart beat double time.

Sophie was obviously filling Tessa in on the new arrival as Olivia got out of the Suburban, leaving Ginger behind in the passenger seat. Tessa's wide-set gray eyes, friendly but reserved, too, took Olivia's measure as she approached, hands in the pockets of her down vest.

What, if anything, Olivia wondered, had Tanner told his sister about the veterinarian-next-door?

Nothing, Olivia hoped. And everything.

Except for a few stolen kisses when Sophie happened to be out of range, nothing had happened between Olivia and Tanner since Thanksgiving.

For all that she was playing with fire and she knew it, Olivia was past ready for another round of hot sex with the first man she'd ever loved—and probably the last.

Tanner made introductions; Tessa wiped her palms

down the slim thighs of her gray corduroy pants before offering Olivia a handshake. The caution lingered in her eyes, though, and she slipped an arm around Sophie's shoulders after the hellos had been said, and pulled her against her side.

"I'm trying to talk Tessa into going to the tree-lighting and the Christmas carnival and dance tonight," Tanner said, watching his sister with an expression of fond, worried relief. "So far, it's no-go."

"It's been a long drive," Tessa said, smiling somewhat feebly. "I'd rather stay here. Maybe I'll stop feeling as if the road is still rolling under me."

"I'll stay with you," Sophie told her aunt, clinging with both arms and looking up with a delight that made Olivia feel an unbecoming rush of envy. "We can order pizza."

"You don't want to miss the tree-lighting," Tessa said to Sophie, squeezing her once and kissing the top of her head. "Or the carnival. *That* sounds like a lot of fun." The woman looked almost shell-shocked, the way Ashley had when Brad brought her home from Tennessee, and it wasn't because of the endless highways and roadside hotels.

*Will I look like that when Tanner's gone?* Olivia asked herself, even though she already knew the answer.

"Dad could bring me back after," Sophie insisted. "Couldn't you, Dad?"

Tanner looked at Olivia.

Tessa's glance bounced between the two of them.

"Are you up for a Christmas dance, Doc?" Tanner asked. It was a simple question, but it sounded grave under the watchful eyes of Tessa and Sophie.

"I guess so," Olivia said, because jumping up and down and shouting "Yes, yes, yes!" would have given her away.

"Note the wild enthusiasm," Tanner said, grinning.

"I *think* she said yes," Tessa remarked, her smile warming noticeably.

"Do you have a dress?" Sophie inquired, her brow furrowed. Clearly she was worried that Olivia would skip off to the Christmas festivities in her customary cow-doctor getup.

"Maybe I'll buy one," Olivia said, after chuckling. She still felt as if she'd swallowed a handful of jumping beans, though.

Buying a dress she'd probably never wear again?

*What I did for love.*

When she was a creaky old spinster veterinarian, she'd show the dress to her brother's and sisters' kids and tell them the story. The G-rated part, anyway.

She checked her watch, which was a perfectly normal thing to do. She even smiled. "I guess I'd better get to the clinic," she said. Then, achingly aware of Tanner standing at the edge of her vision, she added, "Unless you need some help unloading those horses?"

"I think I can handle it, Doc," he said good-naturedly. "But if you're in a favor-doing mood, you can drop Sophie off at school."

"Sure," Olivia said, pleased.

"I thought I'd take today off," Sophie piped up.

"You're in or you're out, kiddo," Tanner told her. "You were dead set on continuing your education, remember?"

"Go," Tessa told her niece. "I'll probably be asleep all day anyway."

Sophie nodded, very reluctantly, but in that quick-silver way of children, she had a warm smile going by the time she climbed into the front seat of the Suburban. Ginger, always accommodating, when it came to Sophie, anyway, had already moved to the back, her big furry head blocking the rearview mirror.

"Where are you going to plant Charlie Brown when Christmas is over?" Sophie asked, snapping her seat belt into place and settling in.

"I hadn't thought about it," Olivia admitted. "Maybe in town, on the grounds of the new shelter. I'll be living upstairs when it's finished."

"I wish all Christmas trees came in pots, so they could be planted afterward," Sophie said. "That way, they wouldn't die."

"Me, too," Olivia said.

"Do you think trees have feelings?"

Ginger had shifted just enough to allow Olivia a glance in the rearview. Olivia caught a glimpse of Tanner, leading the first horse down the ramp and toward the newly refurbished barn.

"I don't know," Olivia answered belatedly, "but they're living things, and they deserve good treatment."

Mercifully, the conversation took a different track after that, though the subject of trees lingered in Olivia's mind, leading to Kris Kringle at the lot in town, and finally to Rodney, who was living the high life in Brad's barn at Stone Creek Ranch. For that little stretch of time, she didn't think about Tanner.

Much.

"Aunt Tessa is pretty, don't you think?" Sophie asked as ramshackle country fences whizzed by on both sides of the Suburban.

"She certainly is," Olivia agreed, feeling unusually self-conscious about her clothes and her bobbed hair. Tessa's locks flowed, wavy and almost as dark as Tanner's, past her shoulders. "I don't recall seeing her on TV, though."

"We got you the season one DVD of *California Women* for Christmas," Sophie said with a spark of mischief in her eyes. "It was supposed to be a surprise, though."

Sophie and Tanner had bought her a Christmas present?

Lord, what was she going to give them in return? She hadn't even shopped for Mac yet, let alone Brad and Meg, Ashley and Melissa, and the office staff and the other vets she worked with at the clinic.

"It's no big deal," Sophie assured her, evidently reading her expression.

Fruitcake? Olivia wondered, distracted. One of those things that came in a colorful tin and had a postapocalyptic sell-by date? If they didn't eat it, it could double as a doorstop.

"How come you're frowning like that?" Sophie pressed.

"I'm just thinking," Olivia said as they reached the outskirts of town. The hardware store had fruitcake; she'd seen a display when she bought the lights and ornaments for Charlie Brown.

And what kind of loser bought bakery goods in a hardware store?

This was a job for super-Ashley, she of the wildly wielded rolling pin and the flour-specked hair. Olivia would drop in on her on her lunch break, she decided, to (a) borrow a dress for the dance, thereby saving posterity from the tale, and (b) persuade her sister to whip up something impressive for the Quinns' Christmas present.

"This is cool," Sophie said a few minutes later when Olivia pulled up to the curb in front of Stone Creek Middle School. "Almost like having a mom." Having dropped that one, she turned to say a quick goodbye to Ginger, and then she disappeared into the gaggle of kids milling on the lawn.

Olivia's hands trembled on the steering wheel as she eased out of a tangle of leaving and arriving traffic.

*"We still have half an hour before you're due at the clinic,"* Ginger said, brushing Olivia's face with her plumy tail as she returned to the front seat. *"Let's go by the tree lot and have a word with Kris Kringle. For Rodney's sake, we need to know he's on the level."*

"Not going to happen," Olivia said firmly. "I've got some paperwork to catch up on before I start seeing patients and, besides, Kringle checked out with Indian Rock PD. Plus, Rodney's doing okay at the homeplace. I get daily reports from either Meg or Brad, and we've been to visit our reindeer buddy twice in the last three days."

Ginger was determined to be helpful, apparently. Or just to butt in. *"How's your mother?"*

"I do not want to talk about my mother."

*"Denial,"* Ginger accused. *"Sooner or later, you're going to have to see her, just to get closure."*

"You need to stop watching talk-TV while I'm at work," Olivia said. "Besides, Mommy dearest is in the clink right now."

*"No, she isn't. Brad got her a lawyer and had her moved to a swanky 'recovery center' in Flagstaff."*

Olivia almost ran the one red light in Stone Creek. "How do you know these things?"

*"Rodney told me the last time we visited. He heard Brad and Meg talking about it in the barn."*

"And you're just getting around to mentioning this now?"

*"I knew you wouldn't take it well. And there's the being in love with Tanner thing."*

Olivia grabbed her cell phone and speed-dialed her sneaky brother. Mr. Tough, refusing to bail their mom out of the hoosegow back in Tennessee. He hadn't said a single word to her about bringing Delia to Arizona, or to the twins, either. They'd have told her if he had.

"Is Mom in a treatment center in Flagstaff?" she demanded the moment Brad said hello.

"How did you know that?" Brad asked, sounding both baffled and guilty.

"Never mind how I know. I just do."

Brad heaved a major sigh. "Okay. Yes. Mom's in Flagstaff. I was going to tell you and the twins after Christmas."

"Why the change of heart, Brad?" Olivia snapped, annoyed for the obvious reason and, also, because Ginger was right. If she wanted any closure, she'd have to visit her mother, and after what had happened to Ashley, the prospect had all the appeal of locking herself in a cage with a crazed grizzly bear.

"She's our mother," Brad said after a long silence. "I wanted to turn my back on her, the way she turned hers on us, but in the end I couldn't do it."

Olivia's eyes stung. Good thing she was pulling into the clinic lot, because she couldn't see well enough to drive at the moment. "I know you did the right thing," she said as Ginger nudged her shoulder sympathetically. "But I'll be a while getting used to the idea of Mom living right up the road, after all these years."

"Tell me about it," Brad said. "It's a long-term thing, Liv. Basically, the prognosis for her recovery isn't good."

Olivia sat very still in the Suburban, nosed up to the wall of the clinic, clutching the phone so tightly in her right hand that her knuckles ached. "Are you telling me she's dying?"

"We're all dying," Brad answered. "I'm telling you that, in this case, 'treatment center' is a euphemism for one of the best mental hospitals in the world. She could live to be a hundred, but she'll probably never leave Palm Haven."

"She's crazy?"

"She's fried her brain, between the booze and snorting a line of coke whenever she could scrape the money together. So, yeah. *She's crazy.*"

"Oh, God."

"They're adjusting her medication, and she'll eat regularly, anyway. I'm not planning to pay her a visit until sometime after the first, and I'd suggest you wait, too. This is Mac's first Christmas, and I plan to enjoy it."

Becky, the receptionist, beckoned from the side door of the clinic.

"I've got to go," Olivia said, nodding to Becky that she'd be right in. "Will you and Meg be at the tree-lighting and all that?"

"Definitely the tree-lighting. Probably the carnival, too. But maybe not the dance. Mac's getting a tooth, so he's not his usual sunny self."

Olivia laughed, blinked away tears.

This was life, she supposed. Their mother's tragedy on the one hand, a baby having his first Christmas and sprouting teeth on the other.

Falling in love with the wrong man at the wrong time.

What could you do but tough it out?

THE SOPHIE-OF-CHRISTMAS-FUTURE haunted Tanner—she still came to him almost every night in his dreams, and of course he mulled them over during the days. In one memorable visit he'd found her living alone in an expensive but sparsely furnished apartment, with only a little ceramic tree to mark the presence of a holiday. He'd counted two Christmas cards tacked to her wall. In another, she tried to get through to him by phone, wanting to wish him a Merry Christmas. He'd been unreachable. And in a third installment he'd seen her standing wistfully at the edge of a city playground, watching a flock of young mothers and their children skating on a frozen pond.

Was this really a glimpse of the future, Ebenezer Scrooge–style, or was he just torturing himself with parental guilt?

Either way, he'd come to dread closing his eyes at night.

"Sophie looks happy," Tessa remarked from her seat at the kitchen table. Now that she'd finally arrived safely at Starcross at least, Tanner had one fewer thing to worry about. "And I like Olivia. Something special going on between the two of you?"

"What makes you think that?" he asked, hedging.

Tessa smiled at him over the rim of her coffee cup.

"Oh, maybe the way you sort of held your breath when you asked her to the dance, until she said yes, and the way she blushed—"

"If I remember correctly," Tanner broke in, "she said 'I guess so.'"

"Could it be you're finally thinking of settling down, Big Brother?"

Tanner dragged back a chair and sat. "A week ago, even a *day* ago, I probably would have said no. Emphatically. But I'm getting pretty worried about Sophie."

Tessa arched an eyebrow, waited in silence.

"I've been having these crazy dreams," he confessed, after a few moments spent trying to convince himself that Tessa would think he was nuts if he told her about them.

"What kind of crazy dreams?" Tessa asked gently, pushing her coffee cup aside, folding her arms and resting them on the table's edge.

Tanner shoved a hand through his hair. "It's as if I travel through time," he admitted, every word torn out of him like a strip of hide. "Sophie's in her thirties, and she's a doctor, but she's alone in the world."

"Hmmm," Tessa said. "The doctor is in. Advice, five cents."

Tanner gave a raw chuckle. "Put it on my bill," he said.

"How do you fit into these dreams?"

"I'm off building something, in some other part of the world. At the same time, I'm there somehow, watching Sophie. And who knows where you are. I don't want to scare you or anything, but you haven't been a guest star."

"Go on," Tessa said.

"I love my daughter, Tessa," Tanner said. "I don't want her to end up—well, alone like that."

Tessa's gray eyes widened, and a smile flicked at the corner of her mouth. She was still beautiful, and she still got acting offers, but she always turned them down because it would mean leaving her horses. "Sophie's been miserable at boarding school," she said. "Last fall, when it was time for her to go back, she begged me to let her stay on with me at the farm. I wanted so much to say yes, and damn *your* opinion in the matter, but things were going downhill fast between Paul and me even then. She'd heard us fighting all summer, and I knew it wasn't good for her."

"I thought she was *safe* at school."

"'Thought'? Past tense? What's happened, Tanner?"

Briefly Tanner explained what Sophie had told him about the easy availability of meth and ice at Briarwood. "It's not like Stone Creek is Brigadoon or anything." He sighed. "A kid can probably score any kind of drug right here in rural America. But I really thought I had all the bases covered."

"Give Sophie a little credit," Tessa said, and though her tone was firm, she reached across the table to touch Tanner's hand. "She's way too smart to do drugs."

"I know," Tanner answered. "But I've always thought she'd be happy when she grew up—that she'd come to understand that I had her best interests at heart, sending her away to school…."

"And the dreams made you question that?"

Tanner nodded. "They're so—so *real,* Tess. I can't shake the feeling that Sophie's going to have no life outside her work—all because she doesn't know how to be part of a family."

"Heavy stuff," Tessa said. "Are you in love with Olivia?"

"I don't know what I feel," Tanner answered, after a long silence. "And I don't necessarily have to get married to give Sophie a home, do I? I could sell off the overseas part of the business, or just close it down. I'd still have to do some traveling, but if you were here—"

"Hold it," Tessa broke in. "I can't promise I'm going to stay, Tanner. And one way or the other, I don't intend to live off your generosity like some poor relation."

"You won't have to," Tanner said. "There's money, Tess. Kat and I set it aside for you a long time ago."

Tessa's cheeks colored up. Her pride was kicking in, just as Tanner had known it would. *"What?"*

"You put me through college on what you earned when you were acting, Tessa," he reminded her. "You took care of Gram while I was in the service and then getting the business started. You're *entitled* to all the help I can give you."

Tessa went from pink to pale. Her eyes narrowed. "I can provide for myself," she said.

"Can you?" Tanner countered. "Good for you. Because that's more than I could do when I was in college and for a long time after that, and it's more than Gram could have managed, too, with just her Social Security and the take from that roadside vegetable stand of hers."

"How *much* money, Tanner?"

"Enough," Tanner said. He got up, walked to the small desk in the corner of the kitchen and jerked a bound folder out of the drawer. Returning to the table, he tossed it down in front of her.

Tessa opened the portfolio and stared at the figures, her eyes rounding at all those zeroes.

"The magic of compound interest," Tanner said.

"This money should be Sophie's," Tessa whispered, her voice thin and very soft. "My God, Tanner, this is a *fortune.*"

"Sophie has a trust fund. I started it with Kat's life insurance check, and the last time I looked, it was around twice that much."

Tessa swallowed, looked up at him in shock, momentarily speechless.

"You can draw on it, or let it grow. My accountant has the tax angle all figured out, and it's in my name until the divorce is final, so Paul can't touch it." Still standing, Tanner folded his arms. "It's up to you, Tess. You're real good at giving. How are you at *receiving?*"

Tessa huffed out a stunned breath. "I could buy out Paul's half of the horse farm—"

"*Or* you could start over, right here, with a place of your own. No bad memories attached. Times are hard, and there are a lot of good people looking to sell all or part of their land."

"I can't think. Tanner, this is—this is unbelievable! I knew you were doing well, but I had no idea…"

"I'm late," he said.

On his way out, he checked on the puppies, found them sleeping in their box by the stove, curled up together as if they were still in the womb. They were so small, so helpless, so wholly trusting.

His throat tightened as he took his coat off the peg on the wall by the back door. He couldn't help drawing a parallel between the pups and Sophie.

"I'll be at the job site in town," he said. "You have my cell number if you need anything."

Tessa was still hunched over the portfolio. Her shoulders were shaking a little, so Tanner figured she was crying, though he couldn't be sure, with her back to him and all.

"Will you be okay here alone?" he asked gruffly.

She nodded vigorously, but didn't turn around to meet his gaze.

That damnable pride again.

Grabbing up his truck keys from the counter, he left the house. It was snowing so hard by then, he figured he'd probably let the construction crew off an hour or two early.

And Olivia had agreed to go to the dance with him that night.

It wasn't quite the date he'd had in mind, but she was planning to wear a dress, and Tessa would be on hand to keep an eye on Sophie after the tree-lighting and the carnival.

This was shaping up to be a half-decent Christmas.

Climbing behind the wheel of the truck, Tanner started the engine, whistling "Jingle Bells" under his breath, and headed for town.

ASHLEY, WITH THE HELP of a few very tall elves in college sweatshirts, was on a high ladder decorating her annual mongo Christmas tree when Olivia and Ginger showed up at noon.

"I need to borrow a dress for the dance," Olivia said.

"Hello to you, too," Ashley replied. She still looked a little feeble, but she was obviously into the holiday spirit, or she wouldn't have been decking the halls. And if she had a clue that Delia was in Flagstaff, luxuriously hospitalized, it didn't show. "I'm taller than you are. Anything I loaned you would have to be hemmed. I don't have time for that, and you can't sew."

"I sew all the time. It's called surgery. Ashley, this is an emergency. Can I raid your closet? Please? The hardware store doesn't sell dresses, and I don't have time to drive up to Flagstaff and shop."

Ashley waved her toward the stairs. "Anything but the blue velvet number with the little beads. I'm wearing that myself."

Olivia wiggled her eyebrows. Ginger snugged herself up on the hooked rug in front of the crackling blaze in the fireplace and relaxed into a power nap. That dog was at home anywhere. And everywhere.

"You have a date?" Olivia asked.

"As a matter of fact, I do," Ashley replied, carefully draping a single strand of tinsel over a branch. She'd do that two jillion times, to make the tree look perfect. "It's a blind date, if you must know. A friend of Tanner Quinn's—he's going to be staying here. The friend, not Tanner."

Olivia paused at the base of the stairway. "I hope it goes well," she said. "It could be awkward living under the same roof with a bad date until next spring."

"Thanks a heap, Liv. Now I'm *twice* as nervous."

Olivia hurried up the stairs. She still had to broach the subject of Ashley whipping up something spectacular for her to give Tanner, Sophie and Tessa for Christmas. An ice castle, made of sugar, she thought. Failing that, fancy cookies would work—the kind with colored frosting and sugar sparkles.

But the outfit had to come first.

Ashley's room was almost painfully tidy—the bed made, all the furniture matching, the prints tastefully arranged on the pale pink walls. Everywhere she looked, there was lace, or ruffles, or both.

It was almost impossible to imagine a man in that room.

Olivia sighed, thinking of her own jumbled bed, liberally sprinkled with dog hair. Her clothes were all over the floor, and she hadn't seen the surface of the dresser in weeks.

Yikes. If the date with Tanner went the way she hoped it would, she'd wish she'd spruced the place up a little—but at least he wouldn't have to contend with lace and ruffles.

She would cut out of the clinic an hour early that afternoon, assuming there were no disasters in the interim. Run the vacuum cleaner, dust a little, change the sheets.

She turned her mind back to the task at hand. Ashley's closet was jammed, but organized. Even color coded, for heaven's sake. Olivia swiped a pair of black velvet palazzo pants—probably gaucho pants on Ashley—and tried them on. If she rolled them up at the waist and wore her high-heeled boots, she probably wouldn't catch a toe in a hem and fall on her face.

A red silk tank top and a glittering silver shawl completed the ensemble.

Piece of cake, Olivia thought smugly, heading out of the room and back down the stairs with the garments draped over one arm.

At the bottom of the steps, just opening her mouth to pitch the sugar-ice-castle idea to Ashley, she stopped in her tracks.

A guy stood just inside the front door, and what a guy he was. Military haircut, hard body, straight back and shoulders. Wearing black from head to foot. Only the twinkle in his hazel eyes as he looked up at Ashley saved him from looking like a CIA agent trying to infiltrate a terrorist cell.

Ashley, staring back at him, seemed in imminent danger of toppling right off the ladder.

The air sizzled.

"Jack McCall," Ashley marveled. "You son of a bitch!"

## CHAPTER ELEVEN

JACK MCCALL GRINNED and saluted. "Good to see you again, Ash," he said, admiring her with a sweep of his eyes. "Are we still going to the dance together tonight?"

Ashley shinnied down the ladder, which was no mean trick in a floor-length Laura Ashley jumper. "I wouldn't go *anywhere* with you, you jerk," she cried. "Get out of my house!"

Olivia's mouth fell open. Ashley was the consummate bed-and-breakfast owner. She *never* screamed at guests—and Mr. McCall was clearly a guest, since he had a suitcase—much less called them sons of bitches.

"Sorry," McCall said, crossing his eyes a little at the finger Ashley was about to shake under his nose. "The deal's made, the lease is signed and I'm here until spring. On and off."

The college-student elves had long since fled, but Olivia and Ginger remained, both of them fascinated.

*"She's crazy about him,"* Ginger said.

"Look, Ash," McCall went on smoothly, "I know we had that little misunderstanding over the cocktail waitress, but don't you think we ought to let bygones be bygones?"

This man worked for Tanner? Olivia thought, trying to catch up with the conversation. He didn't look like the type to work for anyone but himself—or maybe the president.

Where had Ashley met him?

And what was the story with the cocktail waitress?

"I was young and stupid," Ashley spouted, putting her hands on her hips.

"But very beautiful." Jack McCall sighed. "And you still are, Ash. It's good to see you again."

"I bet you said the same thing to the cocktail waitress!" Ashley cried.

Jack looked, Olivia thought, like a young, modern version of Cary Grant. Impishly chagrined and way too handsome. And where had she heard his name before?

"She meant nothing to me," Jack said.

Olivia rolled her eyes. What a charmer he was. But he and Ashley looked perfect together, even if Ashley *was* trembling with fury.

It was time to step in, before things escalated.

Olivia hurried over and took her sister by the arm, tugging her toward the kitchen and, at the same time, chiming rapid-fire at McCall, over one shoulder, "Hi. I'm Olivia O'Ballivan, Ashley's sister. Glad to meet you. Make yourself at home while I talk her into building an ice castle out of sugar, will you? Thanks."

"An *ice castle?*" Ashley demanded once they were in the kitchen.

"With turrets, and lights inside. I'll pay you big bucks. Who *is* that guy, Ash?"

Ashley's shoulders sagged. She blew out a breath, and her bangs fluttered in midair. "He's nobody," she said.

"Get real. I know passion when I see it."

"I knew him in college," Ashley admitted.

"You never mentioned dating the reincarnation of Cary Grant."

"He dropped me for a cocktail waitress. Why would I want to mention that? I felt like an idiot."

"That was a while ago, Ash."

"Don't you have to get back to work or something?"

Ginger meandered in. *"There'll be a hot time in the old town tonight,"* she said.

"Hush," Olivia said.

"I will *not* hush," Ashley said. "And what's this about a sugar ice castle with lights inside?"

"I need something special to give the Quinns for Christmas, and you're the only one I know with that kind of—"

"Time on her hands?" Ashley finished ominously.

"Talent," Olivia said sweetly. "The only one with that kind of *talent.*"

"You are *so* full of it."

Olivia batted her eyelashes. "But I'm your big sister, and you love me. I'm always there for you, and if you ever had a pet, I'd give it free veterinary care. For life."

"No sugar castle," Ashley said. "I have a million things to do, with all these guests checking in." She paused. "If I murdered Jack McCall, would you testify that I was with you and give me an alibi?"

"Only if you made me a few batches of your stupendous Christmas cookies so I could give them to Sophie and Tanner."

Ashley smiled in spite of her earlier ire, but pain lingered in her eyes, old and deep. Jack McCall *had* hurt her, and suddenly he seemed a whole lot less charming than before. "I'll bake the cookies," she said. "God knows where I'll find the time, but I'll do it."

Olivia kissed her sister's cheek. "I'm beyond grateful. Are you really going to refuse to rent McCall a room?"

"It's Christmas," Ashley said musingly. "And anyway, if he's here, under my roof, I can find lots of ways to get back at him. By New Year's, he'll be *begging* to break the lease."

Olivia laughed, held up the armload of clothes. "Thanks, Ash," she said. "In this getup, I'll be a regular Cinderella."

*"Shall I stay here and spy, or go back to the clinic with you?"* Ginger inquired, looking from Ashley to Olivia.

"You're going with me," Olivia said on the way back to the living room. She'd have gone out the back way, as the fleeing elves probably had, but she wanted one more look at Jack McCall.

"I'm not going anywhere," Ashley argued, following. "I've still got to tie at least a hundred bows on the branches of the Christmas tree."

"I was talking to Ginger," Olivia explained breezily.

"And I suppose she talked back?" Ashley asked.

"Skeptic," Olivia said.

Jack McCall had taken off his coat, and his bag sat at the base of the stairs. Evidently he was planning to stay on. The poor guy probably had no idea how many passive-aggressive ways there were for a crafty bed-and-breakfast owner to make an unwanted guest hit the road.

Too much starch in the sheets.

Too much salt in the stew.

The possibilities were endless.

Olivia was smiling broadly as she and Ginger descended Ashley's front steps, headed for the Suburban.

FAT FLAKES OF SNOW drifted down from a heavy sky as the entire population of Stone Creek and half of Indian Rock gathered in the town's tiny park for the annual tree-lighting ceremony.

Sophie stood at Olivia's left side, Tanner at her right.

Brad had been roped into being the MC, but it was an informal gig, and he didn't have to sing. He announced that the high school gym was all decked out for the carnival and the dance afterward, and reminded the crowd that all the proceeds would go to worthy causes.

An enormous live spruce awaited splendor, its branches dark and fragrant, strings of extension cord running from beneath it. Roots enclosed in burlap, it would be planted when the ground thawed, like all the other Stone Creek Christmas trees before it.

"Are we ready?" Brad asked, holding the switch.

"YES!" roared the townspeople in one happy voice.

Brad flipped the plastic lever, and what seemed like millions of tiny colored lights shimmered in the cold winter night, like stars trapped in the branches.

The applause sounded like a herd of cattle stampeding.

The din had barely subsided when sleigh bells jingled, right on cue.

Tanner grinned down at Olivia and took her hand. She felt a little trill, though she was a bit nervous because she'd already had to surreptitiously roll up her borrowed palazzo pants a couple of times.

"Could it be?" Brad said into the mic. "Could *Santa Claus* be right here in Stone Creek?"

The smaller children in the crowd waited in breathless silence, their eyes huge with wonder and anticipation.

It happened every year. Santa arrived on a tractor from the heavy-equipment rental place, bells jingling an accompaniment through a scratchy PA system, the man in the red suit waving and tossing candy and shouting, "Ho! Ho! *Ho!*"

This year was a little different, it turned out.

Kris Kringle himself drove the fancy tree-lot sleigh, the one with the brass runners, into the center of the park—pulled by seven real live reindeer and a donkey. He wore hands-down the best Santa suit Olivia had ever seen, and instead of candy, he had a huge, bulky green velvet bag in the back of the sleigh.

"Very authentic," Tanner told Olivia, his eyes sparkling.

There were actual wrapped presents in the bag, they soon saw, and Kris Kringle distributed them, making sure every child received one.

Even Sophie, too old at twelve to believe in Santa, got a small red-and-white striped package.

Brad must have been behind the gifts, Olivia thought. Times were hard, and a lot of Stone Creek families had been out of work since late summer. It would be just like her brother to see that they got something for Christmas in a pride-sparing way like this.

"Wow," Sophie said, staring at the package, then casting a sidelong glance at Tanner. "Can I open it?"

"Why not?" Tanner asked, looking mystified. Olivia knew he was throwing a turkey-and-trimmings feast for the whole community on Christmas Day, down at the senior citizens' center—Sophie had spilled the beans about that—but he didn't seem to be in on the presents-for-every-kid-in-town thing.

Sophie ripped into the package, drew in a breath when

she saw what it was—an exquisite miniature snow globe with horses inside, one like Shiloh, the other the spitting image of Butterpie.

"Is this from you, Dad?" she asked after swallowing hard.

Tanner was staring curiously at Kris Kringle, who glanced his way and smiled before turning his attention back to the children clamoring to pet the lone donkey and the seven reindeer.

"Gently, now," Kringle called, a right jolly old elf. "They have a long trip to make on Christmas Eve and they're not used to crowds."

"Can they fly?" one child asked. Olivia spotted the questioner, a little boy in outgrown clothes, clutching an unopened package in both hands. She'd gone to high school with his parents, both of whom had been drawing unemployment since the sawmill closed down for the winter. It was rumored that the husband had just been hired as a laborer at Tanner's construction site, but of course that didn't mean their Christmas would be plush. The family would have bills to catch up on.

"Why, of course they can fly, Billy Johnson," Kringle replied jovially.

"Oh, brother," Tanner sighed.

Mr. Kringle had gotten to know everybody in town, Olivia thought, just since the day after Thanksgiving. Otherwise he wouldn't have known Billy's name.

"What about the donkey?" a little girl inquired. Like Billy's, her clothes showed some wear, and she had a package, too, also unopened. Olivia didn't recognize her, figuring she and her family must be new in town. "There wasn't any *donkey* in the St. Nicholas story."

"I've had to improvise, Sandra," Kringle explained

kindly. "One of my reindeer—" here he paused, sought and unerringly found Olivia's face in the gathering, and winked "—has been on vacation."

"Oh," said the little girl.

Brad, having left the stage after lighting up the tree, had made his way through the crowd, carrying a snow-suited, gurgling Mac on one hip. Like every other kid, Mac had a present, and he was bonking Brad on the head with it as they approached.

"The packages were a nice touch," Olivia said, drawing her brother aside.

"I was expecting Fred Stevens, stuffed into the chamber of commerce's ratty old corduroy suit and driving a tractor," Brad said, looking puzzled. Even when *they* were kids, Mr. Stevens, a retired high school principal and the grand poo-bah at the lodge, had done the honors. "And I don't know anything about the presents."

No one else in Stone Creek, besides Tanner, had the financial resources to buy and wrap so many gifts. Olivia narrowed her eyes. "You can level with me," she whispered. "I know you and Meg arranged for this, just like when you made a lot of toys and food baskets magically appear on certain people's porches last Christmas Eve. You put one over on poor Fred somehow and paid Kringle to fill in."

Brad frowned. Took the present from Mac's hand, putting an end to the conking. "No, I didn't," he said. "Fred loves this job. I wouldn't have talked him out of it."

"Okay, but you must have bought the presents. I *know* the town council, the chamber of commerce, both churches *and* the lodge couldn't have pulled this off."

"I haven't got a clue where these packages came

from," Brad insisted, and his gaze strayed to Kris Kringle, who was preparing to drive away in his sleigh. "Unless…"

"Don't be silly," Olivia said. "The man runs a Christmas-tree lot and makes personal appearances at birthday parties. Wyatt ran a background check on him, and there's no way he could afford a giveaway on this scale. Nor, my dear brother, is he Santa Claus."

Brad shoved a hand through his hair, scanning the crowd, probably looking for his wife. "Look, I admit Meg and I are planning to scatter a few presents around town this year," he told her earnestly. "But if I was in on this one, believe me, I'd tell you."

Sophie stood nearby, shaking her snow globe for Mac's benefit. The baby strained over Brad's shoulder, trying to grab it.

Olivia turned to Tanner. "Then you must have done it."

"I wish I had," Tanner said thoughtfully. "The turkey dinner on Christmas Day seemed more practical to me." He grinned, putting one arm around Sophie and one around Olivia. "Let's go check out that carnival."

A look passed between Brad and Tanner.

"Have fun," Brad said, with a note of irony and perhaps warning in his voice.

"We will," Tanner replied lightly, slugging Brad in the Mac-free arm.

Brad gave him an answering slug.

*Men,* Olivia thought.

THE CARNIVAL, LIKE THE tree-lighting ceremony, was crowded. The gym had been decorated with red and green streamers and giant gold Christmas balls, and there were booths set up on all four walls—fudge for sale in this one, baked goods in that one. Adults settled in for a rousing evening of bingo, the prizes all donated by local merchants, and there were games for the children—the "fishing hole" being the most popular.

For a modest fee, a child could dangle a long wooden stick with a string on the end of it over a shaky blue crepe-paper wall. After a tug, they'd pull in their line and find an inexpensive toy attached.

Sophie was soon bored, though good-naturedly so. She kept taking the snow globe out of her purse and shaking it to watch the snow swirl around Shiloh and Butterpie.

Tanner bought her a chili dog and a Coke and asked if she was ready to go home. She said she was.

"Ride along?" Tanner asked Olivia.

"I think I'll sit in on a round of bingo," she answered. The ladies from her church were running the game, and they'd been beckoning her to join in from the beginning.

Tanner nodded. "Save the first dance for me," he whispered into her ear. "And the last. And all the ones in between."

Feeling like a teenager at her first prom, Olivia nodded.

"It's weird that that guy knows about Butterpie and Shiloh," Sophie commented, munching on the chili dog as she and Tanner headed for Starcross in the truck. The snow was coming down so thick and fast that Tanner had the windshield wipers on. "A *nice* kind of weird, though."

"It must have been a coincidence, Soph."

"Heaven forbid," Sophie said loftily, "that I might want to believe in one teeny, tiny Christmas *miracle*."

He thought of the dreams. Sophie as a lonely adult, working too hard, with no life outside her medical practice. A chill rippled down his spine, even though the truck's heater was going full blast. "Believe, Sophie," he said quietly. "Go ahead and believe."

He felt her glance, quick and curious. "What?"

"Maybe I *have* been too serious about things."

"Ya think?" Sophie quipped, but there was a taut thread of hope strung through her words, and it sliced deep into Tanner's heart.

"Look, I've been thinking—how would you like to go to school in Phoenix? There's a good one there, with an equestrian program and excellent security. I was going to wait until Christmas to bring it up, but—"

"I'd rather go to Stone Creek Middle School."

What had he expected her to say? The place was still a boarding school, even if it did have horse facilities. "I know that, Sophie. But I travel a lot and—"

"And Aunt Tessa will be here, so I'd be fine if you were away." Sophie was watching him closely. "What are you so afraid of, Dad?"

He thrust out a sigh. "That you'll be hurt. Your mom—"

"Dad, this is Stone Creek. There aren't any terrorists here. There's nobody to be mad and want to shoot at us because you built some bridge for the U.S. government where the local bomb-brewers didn't *want* a bridge."

Tanner's hands tightened on the steering wheel. He'd had no idea Sophie knew that much. Did she know about the periodic death threats, too? The ones that had prompted him to hire Jack McCall's men-in-black to guard Briarwood? Hell, he'd even had a detail looking out for Sophie when she was on the horse farm every summer, with Tessa.

"I feel safe here, Dad," Sophie went on gently. "I want you to feel safe, too. But you don't, because Uncle Jack wouldn't be in town if you did."

"How did you know Jack was here? He didn't get in until today."

"I saw him at the carnival with a pretty blond lady who didn't seem to like him," Sophie answered matter-of-factly. "Some kids play 'Where's Waldo?' Thanks to you, *I* play 'Where's Jack?' And I'm *real* good at spotting him."

"He's here on personal business," Tanner said. "Not to trail you."

"What kind of personal business?"

"How would I know? Jack doesn't tell me everything—he's got a private side." A "private side"? The man rappelled down walls of compounds behind enemy lines. He rescued kidnap victims and God knew what else. Tanner didn't have a lot of information about Jack's operation, beyond services rendered on Sophie's behalf at very high fees, and he didn't want to.

He slept better that way, and Jack, the secretive bastard, wouldn't have told him anyhow.

Oh, yeah. He was *way* happier. Except when he dreamed about Dr. Sophie Quinn, ghost of Christmas future, or thought about leaving Stone Creek and probably never seeing Olivia again.

"Soph," he said, skidding a little on the turnoff to Starcross, "when you grow up, are you going to hate me for making you go to boarding school?"

"I could never hate you, Dad." She said the words

with such gentle equanimity that Tanner's throat constricted. "I know you're doing the best you can."

Sigh.

"I thought you'd be happy about Phoenix," he said after a pause. "It's only two hours from here, you know."

"What will that matter, if you're in some country where they want to put your head on a pike because you build things?"

It was a good thing they'd reached the driveway at Starcross; if they'd still been on the highway, Tanner might have run the truck into the ditch. "Is that what you think is going to happen?"

"I worry about it all the time. I'm human, you know."

"You're way too smart to be human. You're an alien from the Planet Practical."

She laughed, but there wasn't much humor in the sound. "I watch CNN all the time when you're out of the country," she confessed. "Sometimes really bad things happen to contractors working overseas."

Tanner pulled the truck up close to the house. He was anxious to get back to Olivia, but not so anxious that he'd leave Sophie in the middle of a conversation like this one. "What if I promised not to work outside the U.S.A., Soph? Ever again?"

The look of reluctant hope on the face Sophie turned to Tanner nearly broke him down. "You'd do that?"

"I'd do that, shorty."

She flung herself across the console, after springing the seat belt, and threw both arms around his neck, hugging him hard. He felt her tears against his cheek, where their faces touched. "Can I tell Aunt Tessa?" she sniffled.

"Yes," he said gruffly, holding on to her. Wishing she'd always be twelve, safe with him and Tessa at Starcross Ranch, and never become a relationship-challenged adult working eighteen-hour days out of loneliness as much as ambition.

It would be his fault if Sophie's life turned out that way. He'd been the one to set the bad example.

"I love you, Soph," he said.

She gave him a smacking kiss on the cheek and pulled away. "Love you, too, Dad," she replied, turning to get out of the truck.

He walked her inside the house, torn between wanting to stay home and wanting to be with Olivia.

Tessa had the tree lights on, and she and the puppies were cozied up together on the couch, watching a Christmas movie on TV.

"Dad is never going to work outside the country again!" Sophie shouted gleefully, bounding into the room like a storm trooper.

"Is that so?" Tessa asked, smiling, her gaze pensive as she studied Tanner. Was that skepticism he saw in her eyes?

"Dad's going back to dance the night away with Olivia," Sophie announced happily. "How about some hot chocolate, Aunt Tessa? I know how to make it."

"Good idea," Tessa said.

Sophie said a quick goodbye to Tanner as she passed him on her way to the kitchen.

"I hope you're going to keep your word," Tessa told him when Sophie was safely out of earshot.

"Why wouldn't I?"

"It's tempting, all that money. All those adrenaline rushes."

"I can resist temptation."

Tessa grinned. "Except where Olivia O'Ballivan is concerned, I suspect. Go ahead and 'dance the night away.' I'll take good care of Sophie, and if the place is overrun by revenge-seeking foreign extremists, I'll be sure and give you a call."

Tanner chuckled. Something inside him let go suddenly, something that had held on for dear life ever since that awful day on a street thousands of miles away, when Kat had died in his arms. "I *have* been a little paranoid, haven't I?" he asked.

"A little?" Tessa teased.

"There's a lady waiting at the bingo table," he told his sister. "Gotta go."

"See you tomorrow," Tessa said knowingly.

He let that one pass, waggling his fingers in farewell. "Later, Soph!" he called.

And then he left the house, sprinting for his truck.

"I NEED TO GET OUT of these pants before I kill myself," Olivia confided several hours later, when they'd both worn out the soles of their shoes dancing to the lodge orchestra's Christmas retrospective.

Tanner laughed. "Far be it from me to interfere," he said. Then he tilted his head back and looked up. "Is that mistletoe?"

"No," Olivia said. "It's three plastic Christmas balls hanging from a ribbon."

"Have you no imagination? No vision?"

"I can imagine myself in something a lot more comfortable than my sister's clothes," she told him. "I really hate to face it, but I'm going to have to *shop*."

"A woman who hates shopping," Tanner commented. "Will you marry me, Olivia O'Ballivan?"

It was a joke, and Olivia knew that as well as he did, but an odd, shivery little silence fell between them just the same. She seemed to draw away from him a little, even though he was holding her close as they swayed to the music.

"Let's get out of here," he said. Not exactly a mood enhancer, he reflected ruefully, but it was an honest sentiment.

She nodded. The pulse was beating at the base of her throat again.

The snow hadn't let up—it was worse, if anything— and Tanner drove slowly back over the same course he'd followed with Sophie earlier that evening.

"Seriously," he began, picking up the conversation they'd had on the dance floor as though there had been no interval between then and now, "do you plan on getting married? Someday, I mean? Having kids and everything?"

Olivia gnawed on her lower lip for a long moment. "Someday, maybe," she said at last.

"What kind of guy would you be looking for?"

She smiled, until she saw that he was serious. The realization, like the pulse, was visible. "Well, he'd have to love animals, and be okay with my getting called out on veterinary emergencies at all hours of the day and night. It would be nice if he could cook, since I'm in the remedial culinary group." She paused, watching him. "And the sex would have to be very, very good."

He laughed again. "Is there an audition?"

"As a matter of fact, there is," she said. "Tonight."

Heat rushed through Tanner. If she kept talking like that, the windshield would fog up, making visibility even worse.

When they arrived at Olivia's place Ginger greeted them at the door, wanting to go outside.

*He'd have to love animals...*

Tanner took Ginger out and waited in the freezing cold until she'd done what she had to do.

Olivia was waiting when he got back inside. "Hungry?" she asked.

*It would be nice if he could cook....*

Was she testing him?

"I could whip up an omelet," he offered.

She crossed to him, put her arms around his neck. "Later," she said.

*And the sex would have to be very, very good.*

Five minutes later, after some heavy kissing, he was helping her out of the palazzo pants. And everything *else* she was wearing.

## CHAPTER TWELVE

HE'D GONE AND FALLEN in love, Tanner realized, staring up at the ceiling as the first light of dawn crept across it. Olivia, sleeping in the curve of his arm, naked and soft, snuggled closer.

*He loved her.*

When had it happened? The first time they met, in his barn? Thanksgiving afternoon, before, during or after the kind of sex he'd never expected to have again? Or last night, at the dance?

Did it matter?

It was irrevocable. A no-going-back kind of thing.

He stirred to look at the clock on the bedside stand. Almost eight—Sophie would be up and on her way to school on the bus, well aware that dear old Dad hadn't come home last night.

What had Tessa told her?

He spoke Olivia's name.

She sighed and cuddled up closer.

"Doc," he said, more forcefully. "It's morning."

She bolted upright, looked at the clock. Shot out of bed. Realizing she was naked, she pulled on a pink robe. Her cheeks were the same color. "What are you doing here?" she demanded.

"You *know* what I'm doing here," he pointed out, in no hurry to get out of the warm bed.

"That was last night," she said, shoving a hand through her hair.

"Was I supposed to sneak out before sunrise? If I was, you didn't mention it."

Her color heightened. "What will Sophie think?"

"She's probably praying we'll get married, so she'll have a mom. She wants to grow up in Stone Creek."

To his surprise, Olivia's eyes filled with tears.

"Hey," he said, flinging back the covers and going to her, and the cold be damned. "What's the matter, Doc?" he asked, taking her into his arms.

"I love you," she sobbed into his bare shoulder. "That's what's wrong!"

He held her away, just far enough to look into her up-turned face. "No, Doc," he murmured. "That's what's *right*."

"What?"

"I love you, too," he said. "And it's cold out here. Can I share that bathrobe?"

She laughed and tried to stretch the sides of it around him. Her face felt wet against his chest. "This all happened so fast," she said. Then she tilted her head back and looked up at him again. "Are you sure? It wasn't just—just the sex?"

"The sex was world-class," he replied, kissing the top of her head. "But it's a lot more than that. The way you tried to cheer Butterpie up. That goofy reindeer you rescued, and the fact that you ran a background check on his owner. The old Suburban, and your grandfather's jacket, and that pitiful-looking little Christmas tree."

"What happens now?"

"We have sex again?"

She punched him, but she was grinning, all wet faced

and happy. And his butt was freezing, since the robe didn't cover it. "Not that. Tomorrow. Next week. Next month…"

"We date. We sleep together, whenever we get the chance." He caught his hand under her chin and gently lifted. "We rename the ranch and renovate the house."

"Rename the ranch?"

"You said it once. 'Starcross' isn't a happy name. What do you want to call it, Doc?"

She wriggled against him. "How about 'Star*fire* Ranch'?" she asked.

"Works for me," he said, about to kiss her. Steer her back to bed. Hell, they were both late—might as well make it count.

"Wait," she said, pulling back. Her eyes were huge and blue and if he fell into them, he'd drown. And count himself lucky for it. "What about Sophie? Does she get to stay in Stone Creek?"

"She stays," Tanner said, after heaving a sigh.

"We'll keep her safe, Tanner," Olivia said. "To-gether."

He nodded.

And they went back to bed, though the lovemaking came a long time later.

Tanner told Olivia all about Kat, and how she'd died, and how he'd blamed himself and feared for Sophie.

And Olivia told him about her mother, and how she'd left the family. How her father had died, and her grand-father had carried on after that as best he could. How it was when animals talked to her.

When the deepest, most private things had been said, and only then, they made love.

ON THE MORNING OF Christmas Eve, Olivia stood in a hospital corridor, peering through a little window at the main reason she'd been afraid to get married, long before she met Tanner Quinn.

He waited downstairs, in the lobby. She had to do this alone, but it was better than nice to know he was there.

Olivia closed her eyes for a moment, rested her forehead against the glass.

Restless, unhappy, Delia had left a husband and four children behind one blue-skyed summer day. Just gotten on a bus and boogied.

Olivia's worst fear, one she'd successfully sublimated for as long as she could remember, was that the same heartless streak might be buried somewhere in *her,* as well. That it might surface suddenly, causing her to abandon people and animals who loved and trusted her.

It was a crazy idea—she knew that. She was the steady type, brave, thrifty, loyal and true.

But then, Delia had seemed that way, too. She'd read Ashley and Melissa bedtime stories and listened to their prayers, played hide-and-seek with them while she was hanging freshly laundered sheets in the backyard, let Olivia wear clear nail polish even over her dad's protests. She'd taken all four of them to afternoon movies, sometimes even on school days, where they shared a big bucket of popcorn. She'd helped Brad with his homework practically every night.

And then she'd left.

Without a word of warning she'd simply vanished.

Why?

Olivia opened her eyes.

The woman visible through that window didn't look

as though she could answer that question or any other. She'd retreated inside herself, according to her doctors, and she might not come out again.

It happened with people who had abused alcohol and drugs over a long period of time, the doctors had said.

Olivia drew a deep breath, pushed open the door and went in.

Everyone had a dragon to fight. This was hers.

Delia looked too small to have caused so much trouble and heartache, and too broken. Huddled in a chair next to a tabletop Christmas tree decorated with paper chains and nothing else, she looked at Olivia with mild interest, then looked away again.

Olivia crossed to her, touched her thin shoulder.

She flinched away. Though she didn't speak, the look in her eyes said, *Leave me alone.*

"It's me, Mom," she said. "Olivia."

Delia simply stared, giving no sign of recognition.

Olivia dropped to a crouch beside her mother's chair. "I guess I'll never know why you left us," she said moderately, "and maybe it doesn't matter now. We turned out well, all of us."

Delia's vacant eyes were a soft, faded blue, like worn denim, or a fragile spring sky. Slowly, almost imperceptibly, she nodded.

Tears burned Olivia's eyes. "I'm in love, Mom," she said. "His name is Tanner. Tanner Quinn, and he has a twelve-year-old daughter, Sophie. I—I want to be a good stepmother to Sophie, and I guess, in some strange way, I needed to see you to know I could do this. That I could really be a wife and a mother—"

Delia didn't speak. She didn't cry or embrace her

daughter or ask for a second chance. In short, there was no miracle.

And yet Olivia felt strangely light inside, as though there had been.

"Anyway, I'm planning to come back and see you as often as I can." She stood up straight again, opened her purse. Took out a small wrapped package. It was a bulb in a prepared planter, guaranteed to bloom even in the dead of winter. She'd wanted to bring perfume—one of her memories of Delia was that she'd loved smelling good—but that was on the hospital's forbidden gift list, because of the alcohol content. "Merry Christmas, Mom."

*I'm not you.*

She laid the parcel in Delia's lap, bent to kiss the top of her head and left.

Downstairs, Tanner drew her into a hug. Kissed her temple. "You gonna be okay, Doc?" he asked.

"Better than okay," she answered, smiling up at him. "Oh, much, much better than okay."

AT SIX O'CLOCK STRAIGHT UP, Kris Kringle officially closed the tree lot. He'd sold every one—nothing left now but needles and twine. The plastic reindeer and the hired Santa were gone, but the sleigh was still there.

He looked up and down the street.

Folks were inside their warm lighted houses and their churches now, as they should be on Christmas Eve. When he was sure nobody was looking, he gave a soft whistle.

The reindeer came—all except Rodney, that is. Took their usual places in front of the sleigh, waiting to be hitched up.

He frowned. Where was that deer?

The clippity-clop of small hooves sounded behind him on the pavement. He turned, and there was Rodney, coming toward him out of that snowy darkness, ready to take his first flight. The donkey had filled in willingly at the tree-lighting, but this was the real deal—and everybody knew donkeys couldn't fly.

"Ready?" he asked, bending over Rodney and stroking his silvery back.

He fitted the harnesses gently, having had years of practice. Climbed into the sleigh and took up the reins. They'd have to stop off at home, so he could change into his traveling clothes and, of course, fetch the first bag of gifts.

First stop, he decided: Olivia O'Ballivan's house. She'd been so kind to that little tree—next year at this time, he knew, it would be growing tall and strong on the grounds of the new shelter, glowing with colored lights.

Yes, sir. He'd deliver her present first.

That woman needed a new coffeepot.

CHRISTMAS EVE, THE WEATHER was crisp and clear with the promise of snow, and Olivia felt renewed as she watched Tanner's respectably muddy extended-cab truck coming up the driveway. They were all invited to Stone Creek Ranch for the evening—she and Tanner, Tessa and Sophie—and she knew it would be like old times, when Big John was alive. He'd always roped in half the countryside to share in the celebration.

Her heart soared a little when she heard Tanner's footsteps on the back porch, followed by his knock.

She opened the door, looked up at him with shining eyes.

He took in her red velvet skirt and matching crepe sweater with an appreciative grin, looking pretty darn handsome himself in jeans, a white shirt and his black leather jacket.

"Olivia O'Ballivan," he said with a twinkling grin. "You *shopped*."

"I sure did," she replied happily. "That big box of presents you passed on the porch is further proof. How about loading it up for me, cowboy?"

Tanner bent to greet Ginger, who could barely contain her glee at his arrival. "Anything for you, ma'am," Tanner drawled, still admiring Olivia's Christmas getup. "Tessa and Sophie went on ahead in Tessa's rig," he added, to explain their absence. "I told them we'd be right behind them."

He straightened, and Ginger went back to her bed.

"She's not going with us?" Tanner asked, referring, of course, to the dog.

"She claims she's expecting a visitor," Olivia said.

Tanner's grin quirked one corner of his kissable mouth. "Well, then," he said, making no move to leave the kitchen *or* load up the box of presents.

"What?" Olivia asked, shrugging into her good coat.

"I have something for you," Tanner said, and for all his worldliness, he looked and sounded shy. "But I'm wondering if it's too soon."

Olivia's heartbeat quickened. She waited, watching him, hardly daring to breathe.

It couldn't be. They'd only just agreed that they loved each other….

Finally Tanner gave a decisive, almost rueful sigh, crossed to her, laid his hands on her shoulders and gently pressed her into one of the chairs at the kitchen table.

Then, just like in an old movie, or a romantic story, he dropped to one knee.

"Will you marry me, Olivia O'Ballivan?" he asked. "When you're darn good and ready and the time is right?"

*"Say yes,"* Ginger said from the dog bed.

As if Olivia needed any canine input. "Yes," she said with soft certainty. "When we're *both* darn good and ready, and we *agree* that the time is right."

Eyes shining with love, and what looked like relief—had he really thought she might refuse?—Tanner reached into his jacket pocket and brought out a small white velvet box. An engagement ring glittered inside, as dazzling as a captured star.

"I love you," Tanner said. "But if you don't want to wear this right away, I'll understand."

Because she couldn't speak, Olivia simply extended her left hand. Tears of joy blurred her vision, making the diamond in her engagement ring seem even bigger and brighter than it was.

Tanner slid it gently onto her finger, and it fit perfectly, gleaming there.

Olivia laughed, sniffled. "To think I got you a bathrobe!" she blubbered.

Tanner laughed, too, and stood, pulling Olivia to her feet, drawing her into his arms and sealing the bargain with a long, slow kiss.

"We'd better get going," he said with throaty reluctance when it was over.

Olivia nodded.

Tanner went to lug the box of gifts to the truck, while Olivia lingered to unplug Charlie Brown's bubbling lights.

"You're sure you won't come along?" she asked Ginger, pausing in the kitchen.

*"I'll just settle my brains for a long winter's nap,"* Ginger said, muzzle on forepaws, gazing up at Olivia with luminous brown eyes. *"Don't be surprised if Rodney's gone when you get to the ranch. It's Christmas Eve, and he has work to do."*

"I'll miss him," Olivia said, reaching for her purse.

But Ginger was already asleep, perhaps with visions of rawhide sugarplums dancing in her head.

Stone Creek Ranch was lit up when Olivia and Tanner arrived, and the yard was crowded with cars and trucks.

"There's something I need to do in the barn," Olivia told Tanner as he wedged the rig into one of the few available parking spaces. "Meet you inside?"

He smiled, leaned across the console and kissed her lightly. "Meet you inside," he said.

Rodney's stall was empty, and Olivia felt a pang at that.

She stood there for a while, marveling at the mysteries of life in general and Christmas in particular, and was not surprised when Brad joined her.

"When I came out to feed the horses," he told Olivia, "there was no sign of Rodney the reindeer. I figured he got out somehow and wandered off, but there were no tracks in the snow. It's as if he vanished."

Olivia dried her eyes. "It's Christmas Eve," she said, repeating Ginger's words. "He has work to do." She turned, looked up at her brother. "He's all right, Brad. Trust me on that."

Brad chuckled and wrapped an arm around her

shoulders. "If you say so, Doc, I believe you, but I'm going to miss the little guy, just the same."

"Me, too," Olivia said.

Brad took her hand, examined the ring. "That's quite the sparkler," he said gravely. "Are you sure about this, Liv?"

"Very sure," she said.

He kissed her forehead. "That's good enough for me," he told her.

Together they went into the house, where there was music and laughter and a tall tree, all alight. Olivia spotted Ashley and Melissa right away, and some of Meg's family, the McKettricks, were there, too.

Sophie rushed to greet Olivia. "I get to stay in Stone Creek!" she confided, her face aglow with happiness. "Dad said so!"

Olivia laughed and hugged the child. "That's wonderful news, Sophie," she said.

"I've been thinking I might want to be a veterinarian when I grow up, like you," Sophie said seriously.

"Plenty of time to decide," Olivia replied gently. Just as she'd fallen in love with Tanner, hard, fast and forever, she'd fallen in love with Sophie, too. She'd never try to replace Kat, of course, but she'd be the best possible stepmother.

"Dad told me he was going to ask you to marry him," Sophie added, her voice soft now as she took Olivia's hand and smiled to see her father's engagement ring shining on the appropriate finger. "He wanted to know if it was okay with me, and I said yes." A mischievous smile curved the girl's lips. "I see you did, too."

"I've never been a stepmother before, Sophie," Olivia said, her eyes burning again. "Will you be patient with me until I get the hang of it?"

"I'm almost a teenager," Sophie reminded her sagely. "I suppose you'll have to be patient with me, too."

"I can manage," Olivia assured her.

Sophie's gaze strayed, came to rest on Tessa, who was off by herself, sipping punch and watching the hectic proceedings with some trepidation, like a swimmer working up the courage to jump into the water. "I'm a little worried about Aunt Tessa, though," the child admitted. "She's been hurt a lot worse than she's letting on."

"This crowd can be a little overwhelming," Olivia replied. "Let's help her get to know some of her new neighbors."

Sophie nodded, relieved and happy.

Arm in arm, she and Olivia went to join Tessa.

"You're coming to my open house tomorrow, right?" Ashley asked hopefully, sometime later, when they'd all had supper and opened piles of gifts, and the two sisters had managed a private moment over near the fireplace.

"Of course," Olivia said, pleased that Ashley looked and sounded like her old self. "Did you manage to get rid of Jack McCall yet?"

Ashley's blue eyes shone like sapphires. "The man is impossible to get rid of," she said, nodding toward the Christmas tree, where Jack stood talking quietly with Keegan McKettrick. As if sensing Ashley's gaze, he lifted his punch cup to her in a saucy toast and nodded. "But I'm having fun trying."

Olivia laughed. "Maybe you shouldn't try *too* hard," she said.

Soon after that, with little Mac nodding off, exhausted by all the excitement, people started leaving for their own homes.

Merry Christmases were exchanged all around.

Olivia left with Tanner, delighted to see a soft snow falling as they drove toward home.

"I meant to congratulate you on how dirty this truck is," Olivia teased.

"I finally found a mud puddle," Tanner admitted with a grin.

It felt good to laugh with him.

They parted reluctantly, on Olivia's back porch. She'd be going to Ashley's tomorrow, while Tanner spent Christmas Day with Tessa and Sophie, at *Starfire* Ranch.

He kissed her thoroughly and murmured a Merry Christmas, and finally took his leave.

Olivia went inside, found Ginger waiting just on the other side of the kitchen door.

"Did your visitor show up?" Olivia asked as Ginger went past her for a necessary pit stop in the back yard.

*"See for yourself,"* Ginger said as she climbed the porch steps again, to go inside with Olivia.

Puzzled, Olivia looked around. Nothing seemed different—and yet something was. But what?

Ginger waited patiently, until Olivia finally noticed. A brand-new coffeemaker gleamed on the countertop, topped with a fluffy red bow.

Tanner couldn't have brought it, she thought, mystified. Perhaps Tessa and Sophie had dropped it off? But that wasn't possible, either—they'd already been at Stone Creek Ranch when Tanner and Olivia arrived.

"Ginger, who—?"

Ginger didn't say anything at all. She just turned and padded into the living room.

Olivia followed, musing. Brad? Ashley or Melissa?

No. Brad and Meg had given her a dainty gold bracelet for Christmas, and the twins had gone together on a spa day at a fancy resort up in Flagstaff.

The living room was dark, and Christmas Eve was almost over, so Olivia decided to light the tree and sit quietly for a while with Ginger, reliving all the wonderful moments of the day, tucking them away, one by one, within the soft folds of her heart.

Tanner, proposing marriage on one knee, in her plain kitchen.

Sophie, thrilled that she'd be a permanent resident of Stone Creek from now on. She could ride Butterpie every day, and she was already boning up on Emily's lines in *Our Town,* determined to be ready for the auditions next fall.

Ashley, so recently broken, now happily bedeviling a certain handsome boarder.

Olivia cherished these moments, and many others besides.

She leaned over to plug in Charlie Brown's lights, and that was when she saw the card tucked in among the branches.

Her fingers trembled a little as she opened the envelope.

The card showed Santa and his reindeer flying high over snowy rooftops, and the handwriting inside was exquisitely old-fashioned and completely unfamiliar.

Happy Christmas, Olivia. Think of us on cold winter mornings, when you're enjoying your coffee. With appreciation for your kindness, Kris Kringle and Rodney.

"No way," Olivia marveled, turning to Ginger.

*"Way,"* Ginger said. *"I told you I was expecting company."*

And just then, high overhead, sleigh bells jingled.

"YOU LOOK MIGHTY HANDSOME in that apron, cowboy," Olivia said, joining Tanner, Tessa and Sophie behind the cafeteria counter at Stone Creek High School on Christmas Day. It was almost two o'clock—time for the community Christmas dinner—and there was a crowd waiting outside. "You're understaffed, though."

Tanner's blue-denim eyes lit at the sight of Olivia taking her place beside him and tying on an apron she'd brought from home. Tessa and Sophie exchanged pleased looks, but neither spoke.

A fancy catering outfit out of Flagstaff had decorated the tables and prepared the food—turkey and prime rib and ham, and every imaginable kind of trimming and salad and holiday dessert—and they'd be clearing tables and cleaning up afterward. But Olivia knew, via Sophie, that Tanner had insisted on doing more than paying the bill.

A side door opened, and Brad and Meg came in, followed by Ashley and Melissa, fresh from Ashley's open house at the bed-and-breakfast. They were all pushing up their sleeves as they approached, ready to lend a hand. Meg was especially cheerful, since Carly had shared in the festivities, via speaker-phone. She'd be back in Stone Creek soon after New Year's, eager to take Sophie under her wing and 'show her the ropes.'

Of course, having spent the morning at Ashley's herself, Olivia had been expecting them.

Tanner swallowed, visibly moved. "I never thought—I mean, it's Christmas, and…"

Olivia gave him a light nudge with her elbow. "It's what country people do, Tanner," she told him. "They help. Especially if they're family."

"Shall I let them in before they break down the doors?" Brad called, grinning. He didn't seem to mind that he looked a little silly in the bright red sweater Ashley had knitted for his Christmas gift. On the front, she'd stitched in a cowboy Santa Claus, strumming a guitar.

Tanner nodded, after swallowing again. "Let them in," he said. Then he turned to Olivia, Tessa and Sophie. "Ready, troops?"

They had serving spoons in hand. Sophie even sported a chef's hat, strung with battery-operated lights.

"Ready!" chorused the three women who loved Tanner Quinn.

Brad opened the cafeteria doors and in they came, the ones who were down on their luck, or elderly, or simply lonely. The children were spruced up in their Sunday best, wide-eyed and shy. Some carried toys they'd received from Brad and Meg in last night's secret-Santa front-porch blitz, others wore new clothes and a few of the older ones were rocking to MP3 players.

Ashley, Melissa and Meg ushered the elderly ladies and gentlemen to tables, took their orders and brought them plates.

Everyone else went through the line—proud, hardworking men who might have been ashamed to partake of free food, even on a holiday, if the whole town hadn't been invited to join in, tired-looking women who'd had one too many disappointments but were daring to hope things could be better, teenagers doing their best to be cool.

As she filled plate after plate, Olivia felt her throat constrict with love for these townspeople—*her* people, the home folks—and for Tanner Quinn. After all, this dinner had been his idea, and he'd spent a fortune to make it happen.

She was most touched, though, when the mayor showed up, and a dozen of the town's more prosperous families. They had fine dinners waiting at home, and Christmas trees surrounded by gifts—but they'd come to show that this was no charity event.

It was for everybody, and their presence made that plain.

When the last straggler had been served, when plates had been wrapped in foil for delivery to shut-ins, and the caterers had loaded the copious leftovers in their van for delivery to the nursing home, the people of Stone Creek lingered, swapping stories and jokes and greetings.

*This,* Olivia thought, watching them, seeing the new hope in their eyes, *is Christmas.*

Inevitably, Brad's guitar appeared.

He sat on the edge of one of the tables, tuned it carefully and cleared his throat.

A silence fell, fairly buzzing with anticipation.

"I'm not doing this alone," Brad said, grinning as he addressed the gathering. All these people were his friends and, by extension, his family. To Olivia, it was a measure of his manhood that he could wear that sweater in public. He knew how hard Ashley had worked to prepare her gift, and because he loved his kid sister, he didn't mind the amused whispers.

A few chuckles rose from the tables. It was partly because of his words, Olivia supposed, and partly because of the sweater.

He strummed a few notes, and then he began to sing.

"Silent night, holy night…"

And voice by voice, cautious and confident, old and young, warbling alto and clear tenor, the carol grew, until all of Stone Creek was singing.

Olivia looked up into Tanner's eyes, and something passed between them, something silent and fundamental and infinitely precious.

"Do I qualify?" he asked her when the song faded away.

"As what?"

"A real cowboy," Tanner said with a grin teetering at the corners of his mouth.

Olivia stood on tiptoe and kissed him lightly. "Yes," she told him happily. "You're the real deal, Tanner Quinn."

"Was it the muddy truck?" he teased.

She laughed. "No," she answered, laying a hand to his chest and spreading her fingers wide. "It's that big, wide-open-spaces heart of yours."

He looked up, frowned ruefully. "No mistletoe," he said.

Olivia slipped her arms around his neck, right there in the cafeteria at Stone Creek High School, with half the town looking on. "Who needs mistletoe?"

\* \* \* \* \*

# AT HOME IN STONE CREEK

**For Karen Beaty, with love.**

## CHAPTER ONE

ASHLEY O'BALLIVAN dropped the last string of Christmas lights into a plastic storage container, resisting an uncharacteristic urge to kick the thing into the corner of the attic instead of stacking it with the others. For her, the holidays had been anything *but* merry and bright; in fact, the whole year had basically sucked. But for her brother, Brad, and sister Olivia, it qualified as a personal best—both of them were happily married. Even her workaholic twin, Melissa, had had a date for New Year's Eve.

Ashley, on the other hand, had spent the night alone, sipping nonalcoholic wine in front of the portable TV set in her study, waiting for the ball to drop in Times Square.

How lame was that?

It was worse than lame—it was *pathetic*.

She wasn't even thirty yet, and she was well on her way to old age.

With a sigh, Ashley turned from the dusty hodgepodge surrounding her—she went all out, at the Mountain View Bed and Breakfast, for every red-letter day on the calendar—and headed for the attic stairs. As she reached the bottom, stepping into the corridor just off the kitchen, a familiar car horn sounded from the driveway in front of the detached garage. It could only be Olivia's ancient Suburban.

Ashley had mixed feelings as she hoisted the ladder-steep steps back up into the ceiling. She loved her older sister dearly and was delighted that Olivia had found true love with Tanner Quinn, but since their mother's funeral a few months before, there had been a strain between them.

Neither Brad nor Olivia nor Melissa had shed a single tear for Delia O'Ballivan—not during the church service or the graveside ceremony or the wake. Okay, so there wasn't a greeting card category for the kind of mother Delia had been—she'd deserted the family long ago, and gradually destroyed herself through a long series of tragically bad choices. For all that, she'd still been the woman who had given birth to them all.

Didn't that count for something?

A rap sounded at the back door, as distinctive as the car horn, and Olivia's glowing, pregnancy-rounded face filled one of the frost-trimmed panes in the window.

Oddly self-conscious in her jeans and T-shirt and an ancient flannel shirt from the back of her closet, Ashley mouthed, "It's not locked."

Beaming, Olivia opened the door and waddled across the threshold. She was due to deliver her and Tanner's first child in a matter of days, if not hours, and from the looks of her, Ashley surmised she was carrying either quadruplets or a Sumo wrestler.

"You know you don't have to knock," Ashley said, keeping her distance.

Olivia smiled, a bit wistfully it seemed to Ashley, and opened their grandfather Big John's old barn coat to reveal a small white cat with one blue eye and one green one.

"Oh, no you don't," Ashley bristled.

Olivia, a veterinarian as well as Stone Creek, Arizona's one and only real-deal animal communicator, bent awkwardly to set the kitten on Ashley's immaculate kitchen floor, where it meowed pitifully and turned in a little circle, pursuing its fluffy tail. Every stray dog, cat or bird in the county seemed to find its way to Olivia eventually, like immigrants gravitating toward the Statue of Liberty.

Two years ago, at Christmas, she'd even been approached by a reindeer named Rodney.

"Meet Mrs. Wiggins," Olivia chimed, undaunted. Her china-blue eyes danced beneath the dark, sleek fringe of her bangs, but there was a wary look in them that bothered Ashley…even shamed her a little. The two of them had always been close. Did Olivia think Ashley was jealous of her new life with Tanner and his precocious fourteen-year-old daughter, Sophie?

"I suppose she's already told you her life story," Ashley said, nodding toward the cat, scrubbing her hands down the thighs of her jeans once and then heading for the sink to wash up before filling the electric kettle. At least *that* hadn't changed—they always had tea together, whenever Olivia dropped by—which was less and less often these days.

After all, unlike Ashley, Olivia had a life.

Olivia crooked up a corner of her mouth and began struggling out of the old plaid woolen coat, flecked, as always, with bits of straw. Some things never changed— even with Tanner's money, Olivia still dressed like what she was, a country veterinarian.

"Not much to tell," Livie answered with a slight lift of one shoulder, as nonchalantly as if telepathic exchanges with all manner of finned, feathered and furred creatures were commonplace. "She's only four-teen weeks old, so she hasn't had time to build up much of an autobiography."

"I do not want a cat," Ashley informed her sister.

Olivia hauled back a chair at the table and collapsed into it. She was wearing gum boots, as usual, and they looked none too clean. "You only *think* you don't want Mrs. Wiggins," she said. "She needs you and, whether you know it or not, you need her."

Ashley turned back to the kettle, trying to ignore the ball of cuteness chasing its tail in the middle of the kitchen floor. She was irritated, but worried, too. She looked back at Olivia over one stiff shoulder. "Should you be out and about, as pregnant as you are?"

Olivia smiled, serene as a Botticelli Madonna. "Preg-nancy isn't a matter of degrees, Ash," she said. "One either is or isn't."

"You're pale," Ashley fretted. She'd lost so many loved ones—both parents, her beloved granddad, Big John. If anything happened to any of her siblings, what-ever their differences, she wouldn't be able to bear it.

"Just brew the tea," Olivia said quietly. "I'm perfectly all right."

While Ashley didn't have her sister's gift for talk-ing to animals, she *was* intuitive, and her nerves felt all twitchy, a clear sign that something unexpected was about to happen. She plugged in the kettle and joined Olivia at the table. "Is anything wrong?"

"Funny you should ask," Olivia answered, and though the soft smile still rested on her lips, her eyes were solemn. "I came here to ask *you* the same question. Even though I already know the answer."

As much as she hated the uneasiness that had sprung up between herself and her sisters and brother, Ashley tended to bounce away from any mention of the subject like a pinball in a lively game. She sprang right up out of her chair and crossed to the antique breakfront to fetch two delicate china cups from behind the glass doors, full of strange urgency.

"Ash," Olivia said patiently.

Ashley kept her back to her sister and lowered her head. "I've just been a little blue lately, Liv," she admitted softly. "That's all."

She would never get to know her mother.

The holidays had been a downer.

Not a single guest had checked into her Victorian bed-and-breakfast since before Thanksgiving, which meant she was two payments behind on the private mortgage Brad had given her to buy the place several years before. It wasn't that her brother had been pressing her for the money—he'd offered her the deed, free and clear, the day the deal was closed, but she'd insisted on repaying him every cent.

On top of all that, she hadn't heard a word from Jack McCall since his last visit, six months ago. He'd suddenly packed his bags and left one sultry summer night, while she was sleeping off their most recent bout of lovemaking, without so much as a good-bye.

Would it have killed him to wake her up and explain? Or just leave a damn note? Maybe pick up a phone?

"It's because of Mom," Olivia said. "You're grieving for the woman she never was, and that's okay, Ashley.

But it might help if you talked to one of us about how you feel."

Weary rage surged through Ashley. She spun around to face Olivia, causing her sneakers to make a squeaking sound against the freshly waxed floor, remembered that her sister was about to have a baby, and sucked all her frustration and fury back in on one ragged breath.

"Let's not go there, Livie," she said.

The kitten scrabbled at one leg of Ashley's jeans and, without thinking, she bent to scoop the tiny creature up into her arms. Minute, silky ears twitched under her chin, and Mrs. Wiggins purred as though powered by batteries, snuggling against her neck.

Olivia smiled again, still wistful. "You're pretty angry with us, aren't you?" she asked gently. "Brad and Melissa and me, I mean."

"No," Ashley lied, wanting to put the kitten down but unable to do so. Somehow, nearly weightless as that cat was, it made her feel anchored instead of set adrift.

"Come on," Olivia challenged quietly. "If I weren't nine and a half months along, you'd be in my face right now."

Ashley bit down hard on her lower lip and said nothing.

"Things can't change if we don't talk," Olivia persisted.

Ashley swallowed painfully. Anything she said would probably come out sounding like self-pity, and Ashley was too proud to feel sorry for herself, but she also knew her sister. Olivia wasn't about to let her off the hook, squirm though she might. "It's just that nothing seems to be working," she confessed, blinking back tears. "The business. Jack. That damn computer you insisted I needed."

The kettle boiled, emitting a shrill whistle and clouds of steam.

Still cradling the kitten under her chin, Ashley unplugged the cord with a wrenching motion of her free hand.

"Sit down," Olivia said, rising laboriously from her chair. "I'll make the tea."

"No, you won't!"

"I'm pregnant, Ashley," Olivia replied, "not incapacitated."

Ashley skulked back to the table, sat down, the tea forgotten. The kitten inched down her flannel work shirt to her lap and made a graceful leap to the floor.

"Talk to me," Olivia prodded, trundling toward the counter.

Ashley's vision seemed to narrow to a pinpoint, and when it widened again, she swayed in her chair, suddenly dizzy. If her blond hair hadn't been pulled back into its customary French braid, she'd have shoved her hands through it. "It must be an awful thing," she murmured, "to die the way Mom did."

Cups rattled against saucers at the periphery of Ashley's awareness. Olivia returned to the table but stood beside Ashley instead of sitting down again. Rested a hand on her shoulder. "Delia wasn't in her right mind, Ashley. She didn't suffer."

"No one cared," Ashley reflected, in a miserable whisper. "She died and no one even *cared*."

Olivia didn't sigh, but she might as well have. "You were little when Delia left," she said, after a long time. "You don't remember how it was."

"I remember praying every night that she'd come home," Ashley said.

Olivia bent—not easy to do with her huge belly—and rested her forehead on Ashley's crown, tightened her grip on her shoulder. "We all wanted her to come home, at least at first," she recalled softly. "But the reality is, she didn't—not even when Dad got killed in that lightning storm. After a while, we stopped needing her."

"Maybe *you* did," Ashley sniffled. "Now she's gone forever. I'm never going to know what she was really like."

Olivia straightened, very slowly. "She was—"

"Don't say it," Ashley warned.

"She drank," Olivia insisted, stepping back. The invisible barrier dropped between them again, a nearly audible shift in the atmosphere. "She took drugs. Her brain was pickled. If you want to remember her differently, that's your prerogative. But don't expect me to rewrite history."

Ashley's cheeks were wet, and she swiped at them with the back of one hand, probably leaving streaks in the coating of attic dust prickling on her skin. "Fair enough," she said stiffly.

Olivia crossed the room again, jangled things around at the counter for a few moments, and returned with a pot of steeping tea and two cups and saucers.

"This is getting to me," she told Ashley. "It's as if the earth has cracked open and we're standing on opposite sides of a deep chasm. It's bothering Brad and Melissa, too. We're *family,* Ashley. Can't we just agree to disagree as far as Mom is concerned and go on from there?"

"I'll try," Ashley said, though she had to win an inner skirmish first. A long one.

Olivia reached across the table, closed her hand around Ashley's. "Why didn't you tell me you were having trouble getting the computer up and running?" she asked. Ashley was profoundly grateful for the change of subject, even if it did nettle her a little at the same time. She hated the stupid contraption, hated anything electronic. She'd followed the instructions to the letter, and the thing *still* wouldn't work.

When she didn't say anything, Olivia went on. "Sophie and Carly are cyberwhizzes—they'd be glad to build you a website for the B&B and show you how to zip around the internet like a pro."

Brad and his wife, the former Meg McKettrick, had adopted Carly, Meg's half sister, soon after their marriage. The teenager doted on their son, three-year-old Mac, and had befriended Sophie from the beginning.

"That would be…nice," Ashley said doubtfully. The truth was, she was an old-fashioned type, as Victorian, in some ways, as her house. She didn't carry a cell phone, and her landline had a rotary dial. "But you know me and technology."

"I also know you're not stupid," Olivia responded, pouring tea for Ashley, then for herself. Their spoons made a cheerful tinkling sound, like fairy bells, as they stirred in organic sugar from the chunky ceramic bowl in the center of the table.

The kitten jumped back into Ashley's lap then, startling her, making her laugh. How long had it been since she'd laughed?

Too long, judging by the expression on Olivia's face.

"You're really all right?" Ashley asked, watching her sister closely.

"I'm better than 'all right,'" Olivia assured her. "I'm married to the man of my dreams. I have Sophie, a barn full of horses out at Starcross Ranch, and a thriving veterinary practice." A slight frown creased her forehead. "Speaking of men…?"

"Let's not," Ashley said.

"You still haven't heard from Jack?"

"No. And that's fine with me."

"I don't think it *is* fine with you, Ashley. He's Tanner's friend. I could ask him to call Jack and—"

"No!"

Olivia sighed. "Yeah," she said. "You're right. That would be interfering, and Tanner probably wouldn't go along with it anyhow."

Ashley stroked the kitten even as she tried not to bond with it. She was zero-for-zero on that score. "Jack and I had a fling," she said. "It's obviously over. End of story."

Olivia arched one perfect eyebrow. "Maybe you need a vacation," she mused aloud. "A new man in your life. You could go on one of those singles' cruises—"

Ashley gave a scoffing chuckle—it felt good to engage in girl talk with her sister again. "Sure," she retorted. "I'd meet guys twice my age, with gold chains around their necks and bad toupees. Or worse."

"What could be worse?" Olivia joked, grinning over the gold rim of her teacup.

"Spray-on hair," Ashley said decisively.

Olivia laughed.

"Besides," Ashley went on, "I don't want to be out of town when you have the baby."

Olivia nodded, turned thoughtful again. "You should get out more, though."

"And do what?" Ashley challenged. "Play bingo in the church basement on Mondays, Wednesdays and Fridays? Join the Powder Puff bowling league? In case it's escaped your notice, O pregnant one, Stone Creek isn't exactly a social whirlwind."

Olivia sighed again, in temporary defeat, and glanced at her watch. "I'm supposed to meet Tanner at the clinic in twenty minutes—just a routine checkup, so don't panic. Meet us for lunch afterward?"

The kitten climbed Ashley's shirt, its claws catching in the fabric, nestled under her neck again. "I have some errands to run," she said, with a shake of her head. "You're going to stick me with this cat, aren't you, Olivia?"

Olivia smiled, stood, and carried her cup and saucer to the sink. "Give Mrs. Wiggins a chance," she said. "If she doesn't win your heart by this time next week, I'll try to find her another home." She took Big John's ratty coat from the row of pegs next to the back door and shoved her arms into the sleeves, reclaimed her purse from the end of the counter, where she'd set it on the way in. "Shall I ask Sophie and Carly to come by after school and have a look at your computer?"

Ashley enjoyed the girls, and it would be nice to bake a batch of cookies for someone. Besides, she was tired of being confronted by the dark monitor, tower and printer every time she went into the study. "I guess," she answered.

"Done deal," Olivia confirmed brightly, and then she was out the door, gone.

Ashley held the kitten in front of her face. "You're not staying," she said.

"Meow," Mrs. Wiggins replied.

"Oh, all right," Ashley relented. "But I'd better not find any snags in my new chintz slipcovers!"

THE HELICOPTER SWUNG abruptly sideways in a dizzying arch, setting Jack McCall's fever-ravaged brain spinning. He hoped the pilot hadn't seen him grip the edges of his seat, bracing for a crash.

His friend's voice sounded tinny, coming through the earphones. "You belong in a hospital," he said. "Not some backwater bed-and-breakfast."

All Jack really knew about the toxin raging through his system was that it wasn't contagious—the CDC had ordered him into quarantine until that much had been determined—but there was still no diagnosis and no remedy except a lot of rest and quiet. "I don't like hospitals," he responded, hoping he sounded like his normal self. "They're full of sick people."

Vince Griffin chuckled at that, but it was a dry sound, rough at the edges. "What's in Stone Creek, Arizona?" he asked. "Besides a whole lot of nothin'?"

*Ashley O'Ballivan* was in Stone Creek, and she was a whole lot of somethin', but Jack had neither the strength nor the inclination to explain. Given the way he'd ducked out on her six months before, after taking an emergency call on his cell phone, he didn't expect a welcome, knew he didn't deserve one. But Ashley, being Ashley, would take him in, whatever her misgivings, same as she would a wounded dog or a bird with a broken wing.

He had to get to Ashley—he'd be all right then.

He closed his eyes, letting the fever swallow him.

There was no telling how much time had passed when he surfaced again, became aware of the chopper blades slowing overhead. The magic flying machine bobbed on its own updraft, sending the broth he'd sipped from a thermos scalding its way up into the back of his throat.

Dimly, he saw the ancient ambulance waiting on the airfield outside Stone Creek; it seemed that twilight had descended, but he couldn't be sure. Since the toxin had taken him down, he hadn't been able to trust his perceptions.

Day turned into night.

Up turned into down.

The doctors had ruled out a brain tumor, but he still felt as though something was eating his brain.

"Here we are," Vince said.

"Is it dark or am I going blind?"

Vince tossed him a worried look. "It's dark," he said.

Jack sighed with relief. His clothes—the usual black jeans and black turtleneck sweater—felt clammy against his flesh. His teeth began to chatter as two figures unloaded a gurney from the back of the ambulance and waited for the blades to stop so they could approach.

"Great," Vince remarked, unsnapping his seat belt. "Those two look like volunteers, not real EMTs. The CDC parked you at Walter Reed, and that wasn't good enough for you because—?"

Jack didn't answer. He had nothing against the famous military hospital, but he wasn't associated with the U.S. government, not officially at least. He couldn't see taking up a bed some wounded soldier might need, and, anyhow, he'd be a sitting duck in a regular facility.

The chopper bounced sickeningly on its runners, and Vince, with a shake of his head, pushed open his door and jumped to the ground, head down.

Jack waited, wondering if he'd be able to stand on his own. After fumbling unsuccessfully with the buckle on his seat belt, he decided not.

When it was safe, the EMTs came forward, following Vince, who opened Jack's door.

Jack hauled off his headphones and tossed them aside.

His old friend Tanner Quinn stepped around Vince, his trademark grin not quite reaching his eyes.

"You look like hell warmed over," he told Jack cheerfully.

"Since when are you an EMT?" Jack retorted.

Tanner reached in, wedged a shoulder under Jack's right arm, and hauled him out of the chopper. His knees immediately buckled, and Vince stepped up, supporting him on the other side.

"In a place like Stone Creek," Tanner replied, "everybody helps out."

"Right," Jack said, stumbling between the two men keeping him on his feet. They reached the wheeled gurney—Jack had thought they never would, since it seemed to recede into the void with every awkward step—and he found himself on his back.

Tanner and the second man strapped him down, a process that brought back a few bad memories.

"Is there even a hospital in this hellhole of a place?" Vince asked irritably, from somewhere in the cold night.

"There's a pretty good clinic over in Indian Rock," Tanner answered easily, "and it isn't far to Flagstaff." He paused to help his buddy hoist Jack and the gurney into the back of the ambulance. "You're in good hands, Jack. My wife is the best veterinarian in the state."

Jack laughed raggedly at that.

Vince muttered a curse.

Tanner climbed into the back beside Jack, perched on some kind of fold-down seat. The other man shut the doors.

"I'm not contagious," Jack said to Tanner.

"So I hear," Tanner said, as his partner climbed into the driver's seat and started the engine. "You in any pain?"

"No," Jack struggled to quip, "but I might puke on those Roy Rogers boots of yours."

"You don't miss much, even strapped to a gurney." Tanner chuckled, hoisted one foot high enough for Jack to squint at it and hauled up the leg of his jeans to show off the fancy stitching on the boot shaft. "My brother-in-law gave them to me," he said. "Brad used to wear them onstage, back when he was breaking hearts out there on the concert circuit. Swigged iced tea out of a whiskey bottle all through every performance, so everybody would think he was a badass."

Jack looked up at his closest and most trusted friend and wished he'd listened to Vince. Ever since he'd come down with the illness, a week after snatching a five-year-old girl back from her noncustodial parent—a small-time drug runner with dangerous aspirations and a lousy attitude—he hadn't been able to think about anyone or anything but Ashley. When he *could* think.

Now, in one of the first clearheaded moments he'd experienced since checking himself out of the hospital the day before, he realized he might be making a major mistake—not by facing Ashley; he owed her that much and a lot more. No, he could be putting her in danger, and putting Tanner and his daughter and his pregnant veterinarian wife in danger, as well.

"I shouldn't have come here," he said, keeping his voice low.

Tanner shook his head, his jaw clamped down hard, as though irritated by Jack's statement. Since he'd gotten married, settled down and sold off his multinational construction company to play at being an Arizona rancher, Tanner had softened around the edges a little, but Jack knew his friend was still one tough SOB.

"This is where you belong," Tanner insisted. Another grin quirked one corner of his mouth. "If you'd had sense enough to know that six months ago, old buddy, when you bailed on Ashley without so much as a fare-thee-well, you wouldn't be in this mess."

*Ashley.* The name had run through his mind a million times in those six months, but hearing somebody say it out loud was like having a fist close around his insides and squeeze hard.

Jack couldn't speak.

Tanner didn't press for further conversation.

The ambulance bumped over country roads, finally hit smooth blacktop.

"Here we are," Tanner said. "Ashley's place."

"I KNEW SOMETHING WAS going to happen," Ashley told Mrs. Wiggins, peeling the kitten off the living room curtains as she peered out at the ambulance stopped in the street. "I *knew* it."

Not bothering to find her coat, Ashley opened the door and stepped out onto the porch. Tanner got out on the passenger side and gave her a casual wave as he went around back.

Ashley's heart pounded. She stood frozen for a long moment, not by the cold, but by a strange, eager sense of dread. Then she bolted down the steps, careful not to slip, and hurried along the walk, through the gate.

"What…?" she began, but the rest of the question died in her throat.

Tanner had opened the back of the ambulance, but then he just stood there, looking at her with an odd expression on his face.

"Brace yourself," he said.

Jeff Baxter, part of a rotating group of volunteers, like Tanner, left the driver's seat and came to stand a short but eloquent distance away. He looked like a man trying to brace himself for an imminent explosion.

Impatient, Ashley wedged herself between the two men, peered inside.

Jack McCall sat upright on the gurney, grinning stupidly. His black hair, military-short the last time she'd seen him, was longer now, and sleekly shaggy. His eyes blazed with fever.

"Whose shirt is that?" he asked, frowning.

Still taken aback, Ashley didn't register the question right away. Several awkward moments had passed by the time she glanced down to see what she was wearing.

"Yours," she answered, finally.

Jack looked relieved. "Good," he said.

Ashley, beside herself with surprise until that very instant, landed back in her own skin with a jolt. "What are you doing here?" she demanded.

Jack scooted toward her, almost pitched out of the

ambulance onto his face before Tanner and Jeff moved in to grab him by the arms.

"Checking in," he said, once he'd tried—and failed—to shrug them off. "You're still in the bed-and-breakfast business, aren't you?"

*You're still in the bed-and-breakfast business, aren't you?*

Damn, the man had nerve.

"You belong in a hospital," she said evenly. "Not a bed-and-breakfast."

"I'm willing to pay double," Jack offered. His face, always strong, took on a vulnerable expression. "I need a place to lay low for a while, Ash. Are you game?"

She thought quickly. The last thing in the world she wanted was Jack McCall under her roof again, but she couldn't afford to turn down a paying guest. She'd have to dip into her savings soon if she did, and not just to pay Brad.

The bills were piling up.

"Triple the usual rate," she said.

Jack squinted, probably not understanding at first, then gave a raspy chuckle. "Okay," he agreed. "Triple it is. Even though it *is* the off-season."

Jeff and Tanner half dragged, half carried him toward the house.

Ashley hesitated on the snowy sidewalk.

First the cat.

Now Jack.

Evidently, it was her day to be dumped on.

## CHAPTER TWO

"WHAT *HAPPENED* TO HIM?" Ashley whispered to Tanner, in the hallway outside the second-best room in the house, a small suite at the opposite end of the corridor from her own quarters. Jeff and Tanner had already put the patient to bed, fully dressed except for his boots, and Jeff had gone downstairs to make a call on his cell phone.

Jack, meanwhile, had sunk into an instant and all-consuming sleep—or into a coma. It was a crapshoot, guessing which.

Tanner looked grim; didn't seem to notice that Mrs. Wiggins was busily climbing his right pant leg, her infinitesimal claws snagging the denim as she scaled his knee and started up his thigh with a deliberation that would have been funny under any other circumstances.

"All I know is," Tanner replied, "I got a call from Jack this afternoon, just as Livie and I were leaving the clinic after her checkup. He said he was a little under the weather and wanted to know if I'd meet him at the airstrip and bring him here." He paused, cupped the kitten in one hand, raised the little creature to nose level, and peered quizzically into its mismatched eyes before lowering it gently to the floor. Straightening from a crouch, he added, "I offered to put him up at our place, but he insisted on coming to yours."

"You might have called me," Ashley fretted, still keeping her voice down. "Given me some warning, at least."

"Check your voice mail," Tanner countered, sounding mildly exasperated. "I left at least four messages."

"I was out," Ashley said, defensive, "buying kitty litter and kibble. Because *your wife* decided I needed a cat."

Tanner grinned at the mention of Olivia, and something eased in him, gentling the expression in his eyes. "If you'd carry a cell phone, like any normal human being, you'd have been up to speed, situationwise." He paused, with a mischievous twinkle. "You might even have had time to bake a welcome-back-Jack cake."

*"As if,"* Ashley breathed, but as rattled as she was over having Jack McCall land in the middle of her life like the flaming chunks of a latter-day Hindenburg, there was something else she needed to know. "What did the doctor say? About Olivia, I mean?"

Tanner sighed. "She's a couple of weeks overdue— Dr. Pentland wants to induce labor tomorrow morning."

Worry made Ashley peevish. "And you're just telling me this now?"

"As I said," Tanner replied, "get a cell phone."

Before Ashley could come up with a reply, the front door banged open downstairs, and a youthful female voice called her name, sounding alarmed.

Ashley went to the upstairs railing, leaned a little, and saw Tanner's daughter, Sophie, standing in the living room, her face upturned and so pale that her freckles stood out, even from that distance. Sixteen-year-old Carly, blond and blue-eyed like her sister, Meg, appeared beside her.

"There's an ambulance outside," Sophie said. "What's happening?"

Tanner started down the stairs. "Everything's all right," he told the frightened girl.

Carly glanced from Tanner to Ashley, descending behind him. "We meant to get here sooner, to set up your computer," Carly said, "but Mr. Gilvine kept the whole Drama Club after school to rehearse the second act of the new play."

"How come there's an ambulance outside," Sophie persisted, gazing up at her father's face, "if nobody's sick?"

"I didn't say nobody was sick," Tanner told her quietly, setting his hands on her shoulders. "Jack's upstairs, resting."

Sophie's panic rose a notch. "Uncle Jack is sick? What's wrong with him?"

*That's what* I'd *like to know,* Ashley thought.

"From the symptoms, I'd guess it's some kind of toxin."

Sophie tried to go around Tanner, clearly intending to race up the stairs. "I want to see him!"

Tanner stopped her. "Not now, sweetie," he said, his tone at once gruff and gentle. "He's asleep."

"Do you still want us to set up your computer?" Carly asked Ashley.

Ashley summoned up a smile and shook her head. "Another time," she said. "You must be tired, after a whole day of school and then play practice on top of that. How about some supper?"

"Mr. Gilvine ordered pizza for the whole cast," Carly answered, touching her flat stomach and puffing out her cheeks to indicate that she was stuffed. "I already called home, and Brad said he'd come in from the ranch and get us as soon as we had your system up and running."

"It can wait," Ashley reiterated, glancing at Tanner.

"I'll drop you off on the way home," he told Carly, one hand still resting on Sophie's shoulder. "My truck's parked at the fire station. Jeff can give us a lift over there."

Having lost her mother when she was very young, Sophie had insecurities Ashley could well identify with. The girl adored Olivia, and looked forward to the birth of a brother or sister. Tanner probably wanted to break the news about Livie's induction later, with just the three of them present.

"Call me," Ashley ordered, her throat thick with concern for her sister and the child, as Tanner steered the girls toward the front door.

Tanner merely arched an eyebrow at that.

Jeff stepped out of the study, just tucking away his cell phone. "I'm in big trouble with Lucy," he said. "Forgot to let her know I'd be late. She made a soufflé and it fell."

"Uh-oh," Tanner commiserated.

"We get to ride in an ambulance?" Sophie asked, cheered.

"Awesome," Carly said.

And then they were gone.

Ashley raised her eyes to the ceiling. Recalled that Jack McCall was up there, sprawled on one of her guest beds, buried under half a dozen quilts. Just how sick was he? Would he want to eat, and if so, what?

After some internal debate, she decided on homemade chicken soup.

That was the cure for everything, wasn't it?

Everything, that is, except a broken heart.

JACK MCCALL AWAKENED to find something furry standing on his face.

Fortunately, he was too weak to flail, or he'd have sent what his brain finally registered as a kitten flying before he realized he wasn't back in a South American jail, fighting off rats willing to settle for part of his hide when the rations ran low.

The animal stared directly into his face with one blue eye and one green one, purring as though it had a motor inside its hairy little chest.

He blinked, decided the thing was probably some kind of mutant.

"Another victim of renegade genetics," he said.

"Meooooow," the cat replied, perhaps indignant.

The door across the room opened, and Ashley elbowed her way in, carrying a loaded tray. Whatever was on it smelled like heaven distilled to its essence, or was that the scent of her skin and that amazing hair of hers?

"Mrs. Wiggins," she said, "get down."

"Mrs.?" Jack replied, trying to raise himself on his pillows and failing. This was a fortunate thing for the cat, who was trying to nest in his hair by then. "Isn't she a little young to be married?"

"Yuk-yuk," Ashley said, with an edge.

Jack sighed inwardly. All was not forgiven, then, he concluded.

Mrs. Wiggins climbed down over his right cheek and curled up on his chest. He could have sworn he felt some kind of warm energy flowing through the kitten, as though it were a conduit between the world around him and another, better one.

Crap. He was really losing it.

"Are you hungry?" Ashley asked, as though he were any ordinary guest.

A gnawing in the pit of Jack's stomach told him he was—for the first time since he'd come down with the mysterious plague. "Yeah," he ground out, further weakened by the sight of Ashley. Even in jeans and the flannel shirt he'd left behind, with her light hair springing from its normally tidy braid, she looked like a goddess. "I think I am."

She approached the bed—cautiously, it seemed to Jack, and little wonder, after some of the acrobatics they'd managed in the one down the hall before he left—and set the tray down on the nightstand.

"Can you feed yourself?" she asked, keeping her distance. Her tone was formal, almost prim.

Jack gave an inelegant snort at that, then realized, to his mortification, that he probably couldn't. Earlier, he'd made it to the adjoining bathroom and back, but the effort had exhausted him. "Yes," he fibbed.

She tilted her head to one side, skeptical. A smile flittered around her mouth, but didn't come in for a landing. "Your eyes widen a little when you lie," she commented.

He sure hoped certain members of various drug and gunrunning cartels didn't know that. "Oh," he said.

Ashley dragged a fussy-looking chair over and sat down. With a little sigh, she took a spoon off the tray and plunged it into a bright-blue crockery bowl. "Open up," she told him.

Jack resisted briefly, pressing his lips together— he still had *some* pride, after all—but his stomach betrayed him with a long and perfectly audible rumble. He opened his mouth.

The fragrant substance turned out to be chicken soup, with wild rice and chopped celery and a few other things he couldn't identify. It was so good that, if he'd been able to, he'd have grabbed the bowl with both hands and downed the stuff in a few gulps.

"Slow down," Ashley said. Her eyes had softened a little, but her body remained rigid. "There's plenty more soup simmering on the stove."

Like the kitten, the soup seemed to possess some sort of quantum-level healing power. Jack felt faint tendrils of strength stirring inside him, like the tender roots of a plant splitting through a seed husk, groping tentatively toward the sun.

Once he'd finished the soup, sleep began to pull him downward again, toward oblivion. There was something different about the feeling this time; rather than an urge to struggle against it, as before, it was more an impulse to give himself up to the darkness, settle into it like a waiting embrace.

Something soft brushed his cheek. Ashley's fingertips? Or the mutant kitten?

"Jack," Ashley said.

With an effort, he opened his eyes.

Tears glimmered along Ashley's lashes. "Are you going to die?" she asked.

Jack considered his answer for a few moments; not easy, with his brain short-circuiting. According to the doctors at Walter Reed, his prognosis wasn't the best. They'd admitted that they'd never seen the toxin before, and their plan was to ship him off to some secret government research facility for further study.

Which was one of the reasons he'd bolted, conned a

series of friends into springing him and then relaying him cross-country in various planes and helicopters.

He found Ashley's hand, squeezed it with his own. "Not if I can help it," he murmured, just before sleep sucked him under again.

THEIR BRIEF CONVERSATION echoed in Ashley's head, over and over, as she sat there watching Jack sleep until the room was so dark she couldn't see anything but the faintest outline of him, etched against the sheets.

*Are you going to die?*

*Not if I can help it.*

Ashley overcame the need to switch on the bedside lamp, send golden light spilling over the features she knew so well—the hazel eyes, the well-defined cheekbones, the strong, obstinate jaw—but just barely. Leaving the tray behind, she rose out of the chair and made her way slowly toward the door, afraid of stepping on Mrs. Wiggins, frolicking at her feet like a little ghost.

Reaching the hallway, Ashley closed the door softly behind her, bent to scoop the kitten up in one hand, and let the tears come. Silent sobs rocked her, making her shoulders shake, and Mrs. Wiggins snuggled in close under her chin, as if to offer comfort.

*Was* Jack truly in danger of dying?

She sniffled, straightened her spine. Surely Tanner wouldn't have agreed to bring him to the bed-and-breakfast—to her—if he was at death's door.

On the other hand, she reasoned, dashing at her cheek with the back of one hand, trying to rally her scattered emotions, Jack was bone-stubborn. He always got his way.

So maybe Tanner was simply honoring Jack's last wish.

Holding tightly to the banister, Ashley started down the stairs.

Jack hadn't wanted to *live* in Stone Creek. Why would he choose to *die* there?

The phone began to ring, a persistent trilling, and Ashley, thinking of Olivia, dashed to the small desk where guests registered—not that *that* had been an issue lately—and snatched up the receiver.

"Hello?" When had she gotten out of the habit of answering with a businesslike, "Mountain View Bed and Breakfast"?

"I hear you've got an unexpected boarder," Brad said, his tone measured.

Ashley was unaccountably glad to hear her big brother's voice, considering that they hadn't had much to say to each other since their mother's funeral. "Yes," she assented.

"According to Carly, he was sick enough to arrive in an ambulance."

Ashley nodded, remembered that Brad couldn't see her, and repeated, "Yes. I'm not sure he should be here—Brad, he's in a really bad way. I'm not a nurse and I'm—" She paused, swallowed. "I'm scared."

"I can be there in fifteen minutes, Ash."

Fresh tears scalded Ashley's eyes, made them feel raw. "That would be good," she said.

"Put on a pot of coffee, little sister," Brad told her. "I'm on my way."

True to his word, Brad was standing in her kitchen before the coffee finished perking. He looked more like a rancher than a famous country singer and sometime movie star, in his faded jeans, battered boots, chambray shirt and denim jacket.

Ashley couldn't remember the last time she'd hugged her brother, but now she went to him, and he wrapped her in his arms, kissed the top of her head.

"Olivia…" she began, but her voice fell away.

"I know," Brad said hoarsely. "They're inducing labor in the morning. Livie will be fine, honey, and so will the baby."

Ashley tilted her head back, looked up into Brad's face. His dark-blond hair was rumpled, and his beard was growing in, bristly. "How's the family?"

He rested his hands on her shoulders, held her at a little distance. "You wouldn't have to ask if you ever stopped by Stone Creek Ranch," he answered. "Mac misses you, and Meg and I do, too."

The minute Brad had known she needed him, he'd been in his truck, headed for town. And now that he was there, her anger over their mother's funeral didn't seem so important.

She tried to speak, but her throat had tightened again, and she couldn't get a single word past it.

One corner of Brad's famous mouth crooked up. "Where's Lover Boy?" he asked. "Lucky thing for him that he's laid up—otherwise I'd punch his lights out for what he did to you."

The phrase *Lover Boy* made Ashley flinch. "That's over," she said.

Brad let his hands fall to his sides, his eyes serious now. "Right," he replied. "Which room?"

Ashley told him, and he left the kitchen, the inside door swinging behind him long after he'd passed through it.

She kept herself busy by taking mugs down from the cupboard, filling Mrs. Wiggins's dish with kibble the size of barley grains, switching on the radio and then switching it off again.

The kitten crunched away at the kibble, then climbed onto its newly purchased bed in the corner near the fireplace, turned in circles for a few moments, kneaded the fabric, and dropped like the proverbial rock.

After several minutes had passed, Ashley heard Brad's boot heels on the staircase, and poured coffee for her brother; she was drinking herbal tea.

As if there were a hope in hell she'd sleep a wink that night by avoiding caffeine.

Brad reached for his mug, took a thoughtful sip.

"Well?" Ashley prompted.

"I'm not a doctor, Ash," he said. "All I can tell you for sure is, he's breathing."

"*That's* helpful," Ashley said.

He chuckled, and the sound, though rueful, consoled her a little. He turned one of the chairs around backward, and straddled it, setting his mug on the table.

"Why do men like to sit like that?" Ashley wondered aloud.

He grinned. "You've been alone too long," he answered.

Ashley blushed, brought her tea to the table and sat down. "What am I going to do?" she asked.

Brad inclined his head toward the ceiling. "About McCall? That's up to you, sis. If you want him out of here, I can have him airlifted to Flagstaff within a couple hours."

This was no idle boast. Even though he'd retired from the country-music scene several years before, at least as far as concert tours went, Brad still wrote and recorded songs, and he could have stacked his royalty checks like so much cordwood. On top of that, Meg was a McKettrick, a multimillionaire in her own right. One phone call from either one of them, and a sleek jet would be landing outside of town in no time at all, fully equipped and staffed with doctors and nurses.

Ashley bit her lower lip. God knew why, but Jack wanted to stay at her place, and he'd gone through a lot to get there. As impractical as it was, given his condition, she didn't think she could turn him out.

Brad must have read her face. He reached out, took her hand. "You still love the bastard," he said. "Don't you?"

"I don't know," she answered miserably. She'd definitely loved the man she'd known before, but this was a new Jack, a different Jack. The *real* one, she supposed. It shook her to realize she'd given her heart to an illusion.

"It's okay, Ashley."

She shook her head, started to cry again. "Nothing is okay," she argued.

"We can make it that way," Brad offered quietly. "All we have to do is talk."

She dried her eyes on the sleeve of Jack's old shirt. It seemed ironic, given all the things hanging in her closet, that she'd chosen to wear that particular garment when she'd gotten dressed that morning. Had some part of her known, somehow, that Jack was coming home?

Brad was waiting for an answer, and he wouldn't break eye contact until he got one.

Ashley swallowed hard. "Our mother died," she said, cornered. "Our *mother.* And you and Olivia and Melissa all seemed—relieved."

A muscle in Brad's jaw tightened, relaxed again. He

sighed and shoved a hand through his hair. "I guess I *was* relieved," he admitted. "They said she didn't suffer, but I always wondered—" He paused, cleared his throat. "I wondered if she was in there somewhere, hurting, with no way to ask for help."

Ashley's heart gave one hard beat, then settled into its normal pace again. "You didn't hate her?" she asked, stunned.

"She was my mother," Brad said. "Of course I didn't hate her."

"Things might have been so different—"

"Ashley," Brad broke in, "things *weren't* different. That's the point. Delia's gone, for good this time. You've got to let go."

"What if I can't?" Ashley whispered.

"You don't have a choice, Button."

*Button.* Their grandfather had called both her and Melissa by that nickname; like most twins, they were used to sharing things. "Do you miss Big John as much as I do?" she asked.

"Yes," Brad answered, without hesitation, his voice still gruff. He looked down at his coffee mug for a second or so, then raised his gaze to meet Ashley's again. "Same thing," he said. "He's gone. And letting go is something I have to do about three times a day."

Ashley got up, suddenly unable to sit still. She brought the coffee carafe to the table and refilled Brad's cup. She spoke very quietly. "But it was a one-time thing, letting go of Mom?"

"Yeah," Brad said. "And it happened a long, long time ago. I remember it distinctly—it was the night my high school basketball team took the state championship. I was sure she'd be in the bleachers, clapping and cheering like everybody else. She wasn't, of course, and that was when I got it through my head that she wasn't coming back—ever."

Ashley's heart ached. Brad was her big brother; he'd always been strong. Why hadn't she realized that he'd been hurt, too?

"Big John *stayed,* Ashley," he went on, while she sat there gulping. "He stuck around, through good times and bad. Even after he'd buried his only son, he kept on keeping on. Mom caught the afternoon bus out of town and couldn't be bothered to call or even send a postcard. I did my mourning long before she died."

Ashley could only nod.

Brad was quiet for a while, pondering, taking the occasional sip from his coffee mug. Then he spoke again. "Here's the thing," he said. "When the chips were down, I basically did the same thing as Mom—got on a bus and left Big John to take care of the ranch and raise the three of you all by himself—so I'm in no position to judge anybody else. Bottom line, Ash? People are what they are, and they do what they do, and you have to decide either to accept that or walk away without looking back."

Ashley managed a wobbly smile. Sniffled once. "I'm sorry I'm late on the mortgage payments," she said.

Brad rolled his eyes. "Like I'm worried," he replied, his body making the subtle shifts that meant he'd be leaving soon. With one arm, he gestured to indicate the B&B. "Why won't you just let me sign the place over to you?"

"Would you do that," Ashley challenged reasonably, "if our situations were reversed?"

He flushed slightly, got to his feet. "No," he admitted, "but—"

"But what?"

Brad grinned sheepishly, and his powerful shoulders shifted slightly under his shirt.

"But you're a man?" Ashley finished for him, when he didn't speak. "Is that what you were going to say?"

"Well, yeah," Brad said.

"You'll have the mortgage payments as soon as I get a chance to run Jack's credit card," she told her brother, rising to walk him to the back door. Color suffused her cheeks. "Thanks for coming into town," she added. "I feel like a fool for panicking."

In the midst of pulling on his jacket, Brad paused. "I'm a big brother," he said, somewhat gruffly. "It's what we do."

"Are you and Meg going to the hospital tomorrow, when Livie…?"

Brad tugged lightly at her braid, the way he'd always done. "We'll be hanging out by the telephone," he said. "Livie swears it's a normal procedure, and she doesn't want everyone fussing 'as if it were a heart transplant,' as she put it."

Ashley bit down on her lower lip and nodded. She already had a nephew—Mac—and two nieces, Carly and Sophie, although technically Carly, Meg's half sister, whom her dying father had asked her to raise, wasn't really a niece. Tomorrow, another little one would join the family. Instead of being a nervous wreck, she ought to be celebrating.

She wasn't, she decided, so different from Sophie. Having effectively lost Delia when she was so young, she'd turned to Olivia as a substitute mother, as had Melissa. Had their devotion been a burden to their sister, only a few years older than they were, and grappling with her own sense of loss?

She stood on tiptoe and kissed Brad's cheek. "Thanks," she said again. "Call if you hear anything."

Brad gave her braid another tug, turned and left the house.

Ashley felt profoundly alone.

JACK HAD NEARLY flung himself at the singing cowboy standing at the foot of his bed, before recognizing him as Ashley's famous brother, Brad. Even though the room had been dark, the other man must have seen him tense.

"I know you're awake, McCall," he'd said.

Jack had yawned. "O'Ballivan?"

"Live and in person," came the not-so-friendly reply.

"And you're sneaking around my room because…?"

O'Ballivan had chuckled at that. Hooked his thumbs through his belt loops. "Because Ashley's worried about you. And what worries my baby sister worries *me*, James Bond."

Ashley was worried about him? Something like elation flooded Jack. "Not for the same reasons, I suspect," he said.

Mr. Country Music had gripped the high, spooled rail at the foot of the bed and leaned forward a little to make his point. "Damned if I can figure out why you'd come back here, especially in the shape you're in, after what happened last summer, except to take up where you left off." He paused, gripped the rail hard enough that his knuckles showed white even in the gloom. "You hurt her again, McCall, and you have my solemn word—I'm gonna turn right around and hurt *you*. Are we clear on that?"

Jack had smiled, not because he was amused, but because he liked knowing Ashley had folks to look after her when he wasn't around—and when he was. "Oh, yeah," Jack had replied. "We're clear."

Obviously a man of few words, O'Ballivan had simply nodded, turned and walked out of the room.

Remembering, Jack raised himself as high on the pillows as he could, strained to reach the lamp switch. The efforts, simple as they were, made him break out in a cold sweat, but at the same time, he felt his strength returning.

He looked around the room, noting the flowered wallpaper, the pale rose carpeting, the intricate woodwork on the mantelpiece. Two girly chairs flanked the cold fireplace, and fat flakes of January snow drifted past the two sets of bay windows, both sporting seats beneath, covered by cheery cushions.

It was a far cry from Walter Reed, he thought.

An even further cry from the jungle hut where he'd hidden out for nearly three months, awaiting his chance to grab little Rachel Stockard, hustle her out of the country by boat and then a seaplane, and return her to her frantic mother.

He'd been well paid for the job, but it was the memory of the mother-daughter reunion, after he'd surrendered the child to a pair of FBI agents and a Customs official in Atlanta, that made his throat catch more than two weeks after the fact.

Through an observation window, he'd watched as Rachel scrambled out of the man's arms and raced toward her waiting mother. Tears pouring down her face,

Ardith Stockard had dropped to her knees, arms out-spread, and gathered the little girl close. The two of them had clung to each other, both trembling.

And then Ardith had raised her eyes, seen Jack through the glass, and mouthed the words, "Thank you."

He'd nodded, exhausted and already sick.

Closing his eyes, Jack went back over the journey to South America, the long game of waiting and watching, finally finding the small, isolated country estate where Rachel had been taken after she was kidnapped from her maternal grandparents' home in Phoenix, almost a year before.

Even after locating the child, he hadn't been able to make a move for more than a week—not until her father and his retinue of thugs had loaded a convoy of jeeps with drugs and firepower one day, and roared off down the jungle road, probably headed for a rendezvous with a boat moored off some hidden beach.

Jack had soon ascertained that only the middle-aged cook—and he had reason not to expect opposition from her—and one guard stood between him and Rachel. He'd waited until dark, risking the return of the jeep convoy, then climbed to the terrace outside the child's room.

"Did you come to take me home to my mommy?" Rachel had shrilled, her eyes wide with hope, when he stepped in off the terrace, a finger to his lips.

Her voice carried, and the guard burst in from the hallway, shouting in Spanish.

There had been a brief struggle—Jack had felt something prick him in the side as the goon went down—but, hearing the sound of approaching vehicles in the distance, he hadn't taken the time to wonder.

He'd grabbed Rachel up under one arm and climbed over the terrace and back down the crumbling rock wall of the house, with its many foot- and handholds, to the ground, running for the trees.

It was only after the reunion in Atlanta that Jack had suddenly collapsed, dizzy with fever.

The next thing he remembered was waking up in a hospital room, hooked up to half a dozen machines and surrounded by grim-faced Feds waiting to ask questions.

# CHAPTER THREE

ASHLEY DID NOT EXPECT to sleep at all that night; she had too many things on her mind, between the imminent birth of Olivia's baby, lingering issues with her mother and siblings, and Jack McCall landing in the middle of her formerly well-ordered days like the meteor that allegedly finished off the dinosaurs.

Therefore, sunlight glowing pink-orange through her eyelids and the loud jangle of her bedside telephone came as a surprise.

She groped for the receiver, nearly throwing a disgruntled Mrs. Wiggins to the floor, and rasped out a hoarse, "Hullo?"

Olivia's distinctive laugh sounded weary, but it bubbled into Ashley's ear and then settled, warm as summer honey, into every tuck and fold of her heart. "Did I wake you up?"

"Yes," Ashley admitted, her heart beating faster as she raised herself onto one elbow and pushed her bangs back out of her face. "Livie? Did you—is everything all right—what—?"

"You're an aunt again," Olivia said, choking up again. "Twice over."

Ashley blinked. Swallowed hard. "Twice over? Livie, you had *twins?*"

"Both boys," Olivia answered, in a proud whisper.

"And before you ask, they're fine, Ash. So am I." There was a pause, then a giggle. "I'm not too sure about Tanner, though. He's only been through this once before, and Sophie didn't bring along a sidekick when she came into the world."

Ashley's eyes burned, and her throat went thick with joy. "Oh, Livie," she murmured. "This is wonderful! Have you told Melissa and Brad?"

"I was hoping you'd do that for me," Olivia answered. "I've been working hard since five this morning, and I could use a nap before visiting hours roll around."

First instinct: Throw on whatever clothes came to hand, jump in the car and head straight for the hospital, visiting hours be damned. Ashley wanted a look at her twin nephews, wanted to see for herself that Olivia really was okay.

In the next instant, she remembered Jack.

She couldn't leave a sick guest alone, which meant she'd have to rustle up someone to keep an eye on him before she could visit Olivia and the babies.

"You're in Flagstaff, right?" she asked, sitting up now.

"Good heavens, no," Olivia replied, with another laugh. "We didn't make it that far—I went into labor at three-thirty this morning. I'm at the clinic over in Indian Rock—thanks to the McKettricks, they're equipped with incubators and just about everything else a new baby could possibly need."

"Indian Rock?" Ashley echoed, still a little groggy. Forty miles from Stone Creek, Meg's hometown was barely closer than Flagstaff, and lay in the opposite direction.

"I'll explain later, Ash," Olivia said. "Right now, I'm beat. You'll call Brad and Melissa?"

"Right away," Ashley promised. Happiness for her sister and brother-in-law welled up into her throat, a peculiar combination of pain and pleasure. "Just one more thing—have you named the babies?"

"Not yet. We'll probably call one John Mitchell, for Big John and Dad, and the other Sam. Even though Tanner and I knew we were having two babies—our secret—we need to give it some thought."

Practically every generation of the O'Ballivan family boasted at least one Sam, all the way back to the founder of Stone Creek Ranch. For all her delight over the twins' birth, Ashley felt a little pang. She'd always planned to name her own son Sam.

Not that she was in any danger of having children.

"C-Congratulations, Livie. Hug Tanner for me, too."

"Consider it done," Olivia said.

Good-byes were said, and Ashley had to try three times before she managed to hang up the receiver.

After drawing a few deep breaths and wiping away *mostly* happy tears, Ashley regained her composure, remembered that she'd promised to pass the news along to the rest of her family.

Brad answered the telephone out at the ranch, sounding wide-awake. The sun couldn't have been up for long, but by then, he'd probably fed all the dogs, horses and cattle on the place and started breakfast for Meg, Carly, Mac and himself. "That's great," he said, once Ashley had assured him that both Olivia and the babies were doing well. "But what are they doing in Indian Rock?"

"Olivia said she'd explain later," Ashley answered.

The next call she placed was to her own twin, Melissa, who lived on the other side of town. A lawyer and an absolute genius with money, Melissa owned the spacious two-family home, renting out one side and thereby making the mortgage payment without touching her salary.

A man answered, and the voice wasn't familiar.

A little alarmed—reruns of *City Confidential* and *Forensic Files* were Ashley's secret addiction—she sat up a little straighter and asked, "Is this 555-2293?"

"I think so," he said. "Melissa?"

Melissa came on the line, sounding breathless. "Olivia?"

"Your *other* sister," Ashley said. "Livie asked me to call you. The babies were born this morning—"

*"Babies?"* Melissa interrupted. "Plural?"

"Twins," Ashley answered.

"Nobody said anything about twins!" Being something of a control freak, Melissa didn't like surprises—even good ones.

Ashley smiled. "They do run in the family, you know," she reminded her sister. "And apparently Tanner and Olivia wanted to surprise us. She says all is well, and she's going to catch some sleep before visiting hours."

"Boys? Girls? One of each?" Melissa asked, rapid-fire.

"Both boys," Ashley said. "No for-sure names yet. And who is that man who just answered your phone?"

"Later," Melissa said, lowering her voice.

Ashley's imagination spiked again. "Just tell me you're all right," she said. "That some stranger isn't forcing you to pretend—"

"Oh, for Pete's sake," Melissa broke in, sounding almost snappish. She'd been worried about Olivia, too, Ashley reasoned, calming down a little, but still unsettled. "I'm not bound with duct tape and being held captive in a closet. You're watching too much crime-TV again."

"Say the code word," Ashley said, just to be absolutely sure Melissa was safe.

"You are so paranoid," Melissa griped. Ashley could just see her, pushing back her hair, which fell to her shoulders in dark, gleaming spirals, picture her eyes flashing with irritation.

"Say it, and I'll leave you alone."

Melissa sighed. "Buttercup," she said.

Ashley smiled. After a rash of child abductions when they were small, Big John had helped them choose the secret word and instructed them never to reveal it to anyone outside the family. Ashley never had, and she was sure Melissa hadn't, either.

They'd liked the idea of speaking in code—their version of the twin-language phenomenon, Ashley supposed. Between the ages of three and seven, they'd driven everyone crazy, chattering away in a dialect made up of otherwise ordinary words and phrases.

If Melissa had said, "I plan to spend the afternoon sewing," for instance, Ashley would have called out the National Guard. Ashley's signal, considerably less autobiographical, was, "I saw three crows sitting on the mailbox this morning."

"Are you satisfied?" Melissa asked.

"Are you PMS-ing?" Ashley countered.

"I wish," Melissa said.

Before Ashley could ask what she'd meant by that, Melissa hung up.

"She's PMS-ing," Ashley told Mrs. Wiggins, who

was curling around her ankles and mewing, probably ready for her kitty kibble.

Hastily, Ashley took a shower, donned trim black woolen slacks and an ice-blue silk blouse, brushed and braided her hair, and went out into the hallway.

Jack's door was closed—she was sure she'd left it open a crack the night before, in case he called out— so she rapped lightly with her knuckles.

"In," he responded.

Ashley rolled her eyes and opened the door to peek inside the room. Jack was sitting on the edge of the bed, his back very straight. He needed a shave, and his eyes were clear when he turned his head to look at her.

"You're better," she said, surprised.

He gave a slanted grin. "Sorry to disappoint you."

Ashley felt her temper surge, but she wasn't about to give Jack McCall the satisfaction of getting under her skin. Not today, when she'd just learned that she had twin nephews. "Are you hungry?"

"Yeah," he said. "Bacon and eggs would be good."

Ashley raised one eyebrow. He'd barely managed chicken soup the night before, and now he wanted a trucker's breakfast? "You'll make yourself sick," she told him, hiking her chin up a notch.

"I'm already sick," he pointed out. "And I still want bacon and eggs."

"Well," Ashley said, "there aren't any. I usually have grapefruit or granola."

"You serve paying guests *health food?*"

Ashley sucked in a breath, let it out slowly. She wasn't about to admit, not to Jack McCall, at least, that she hadn't had a guest, paying or otherwise, in way too long. "Some people," she told him carefully, "care about good nutrition."

"And some people want bacon and eggs."

She sighed. "Oh, for heaven's sake."

"It's the least you can do," Jack wheedled, "since I'm paying triple for this room and the breakfast that's supposed to come with the bed."

"All right," she said. "But I'll have to go to the store, and that means *you'll* have to wait."

"Fine by me," Jack replied lightly, extending his feet and wriggling his toes, his expression curious, as though he wasn't sure they still worked. "I'll be right here." The wicked grin flashed again. "Get a move on, will you? I need to get my strength back."

Ashley shut the door hard, drew another deep breath in the hallway, and started downstairs, careful not to trip over the gamboling Mrs. Wiggins.

Reaching the kitchen, she poured kibble for the kitten, cleaned and refilled the tiny water bowl, and gathered her coat, purse and car keys.

"I'll be back in a few minutes," she told the cat.

The temperature had dropped below freezing during the night, and the roads were sheeted in ice. Ashley's trip to the supermarket took nearly forty-five minutes, the store was jammed, and by the time she got home, she was in a skillet-banging mood. She was an innkeeper, not a nurse. Why hadn't she insisted that Tanner and Jeff take Jack to one of the hospitals in Flagstaff?

She built a fire on the kitchen hearth, hoping to cheer herself up a little—and take the chill out of her bones—then started a pot of coffee brewing. Next, she laid four strips of bacon in the seasoned cast-iron frying pan that had been Big John's, tossed a couple of slices of bread into the toaster slots, and took a carton of eggs out of her canvas grocery bag.

She knew how Jack liked his eggs—over easy—just as she knew he took his coffee black and strong. It galled her plenty that she remembered those details—and a lot more.

Cooking angrily—so much for her motto that every recipe ought to be laced with love—Ashley nearly jumped out of her skin when she heard his voice behind her.

"Nice fire," he said. "Very cozy."

She whirled, openmouthed, and there he was, standing in the kitchen doorway, but leaning heavily on the jamb.

"What are you doing out of bed?" she asked, once the adrenaline rush had subsided.

Slowly, he made his way to the table, dragged back a chair and dropped into the seat. "I couldn't take that wallpaper for another second," he teased. "Too damn many roses and ribbons."

Knowing that wallpaper was a stupid thing to be sensitive about, and sensitive just the same, Ashley opened a cupboard, took down a mug and filled it, even though the coffeemaker was still chortling through the brewing process. Set the mug down in front of him with a thump.

"Surely you're not *that* touchy about your décor," Jack said.

"Shut up," Ashley told him.

His eyes twinkled. "Do you talk to all your guests that way?"

As so often happened around Jack, Ashley spoke without thinking first. "Only the ones who sneaked out of my bed in the middle of the night and disappeared for six months without a word."

Jack frowned. "Have there been a lot of those?"

Jack McCall was the first—and only—man Ashley had ever slept with, but she'd be damned if she'd tell him so. After all, she realized, he hadn't just broken her heart once—he'd done it *twice.* She'd been shy in high school, but the day she and Jack met, in her freshman year of college at the University of Arizona, her world had undergone a seismic shift.

They talked about getting married after Ashley finished school, had even looked at engagement rings. Jack had been a senior, and after graduation, he'd enlisted in the Navy. After a few letters and phone calls, he'd simply dropped out of her life.

She'd gotten her BA in liberal arts.

Melissa had gone on to law school, Ashley had returned to Stone Creek, bought the B&B with Brad's help and tried to convince herself that she was happy.

Then, just before Christmas, two years earlier, Jack had returned. She'd been a first-class fool to get involved with him a second time, to believe it would last. He came and went, called often when he was away, showed up again and made soul-wrenching love to her just when she'd made up her mind to end the affair.

"I haven't been hibernating, you know," she said stiffly, turning the bacon, pushing down the lever on the toaster and sliding his perfectly cooked eggs off the burner. "I date."

Right. Melissa had fixed her up twice, with guys she knew from law school, and she'd gone out to dinner once, with Melvin Royce, whose father owned the Stone Creek Funeral Home. Melvin had spent the whole evening telling her that death was a beautiful thing—not to mention lucrative—cremation was the way to go, and corpses weren't at all scary, once you got used to them.

She hadn't gone out with anyone since.

Oh, yes, she was a regular party girl. If she didn't watch out, she'd end up as tabloid fodder.

Not. The tabloids were Brad's territory, and he was welcome to them, as far as she was concerned.

"I'm sorry, Ashley," Jack said quietly, when they'd both been silent for a long time. She couldn't help noticing that his hand shook slightly as he took a sip of his coffee and set the mug down again.

"For what?"

"For everything." He thrust splayed fingers through his hair, and his jaw tightened briefly, under the blue-black stubble of his beard.

"Everything? That covers a lot of ground," Ashley said, sliding his breakfast onto a plate and setting it down in front of him with an annoyed flourish.

Jack sighed. "Leaving you. It was a dumb thing to do. But maybe coming back is even dumber."

The remark stung Ashley, made her cheeks burn, and she turned away quickly, hoping Jack hadn't noticed. "You arrived in an ambulance," she said. "Feel free to leave in one."

"Will you sit down and talk to me? Please?"

Ashley faced him, lest she be thought a coward.

Mrs. Wiggins, the little traitor, started up Jack's right pant leg and settled in his lap for a snooze. He picked up his fork, broke the yolk on one of his eggs, but his eyes were fastened on Ashley.

"What happened to you?" Ashley asked, without

planning to speak at all. There it was again, the Jack Phenomenon. She wasn't normally an impulsive person.

Jack didn't look away, but several long moments passed before he answered. "The theory is," he said, "that a guy I tangled with on a job injected me with something."

Ashley's heart stopped, started again. She joined Jack at the table, but only because she was afraid her knees wouldn't support her if she remained standing. "A job? What kind of job?"

"You know I'm in security," Jack hedged, avoiding her eyes now, concentrating on his breakfast. He ate slowly, deliberately.

"Security," Ashley repeated. All she really knew about Jack was that he traveled, made a lot of money and was often in danger. These were not things he'd actually told her—she'd gleaned them from telephone conversations she'd overheard, stories Sophie and Olivia had told her, comments Tanner had made.

"I've got to leave again, Ashley," Jack said. "But this time, I want you to know why."

She *wanted* Jack to leave. So why did she feel as though a trapdoor had just opened under her chair, and she was about to fall down the rabbit hole? "Okay— why?" she asked, in somebody else's voice.

"Because I've got enemies. Most of them are in prison—or dead—but one has a red-hot grudge against me, a score to settle, and I don't want you or anybody else in Stone Creek to get hurt. I should have thought things through before I came here, but the truth is, all I could focus on was being where you are."

The words made her ache. Ashley longed to take

Jack's hand, but she wouldn't let herself do it. "What kind of grudge?"

"I stole his daughter."

Ashley's mouth dropped open. She closed it again.

Jack gave a mirthless little smile. "Her name is Rachel. She's seven years old. Her mother went through a rebellious period that just happened to coincide with a semester in a university in Venezuela. She fell in with a bad crowd, got involved with a fellow exchange student—an American named Chad Lombard, who was running drugs between classes. Her parents ran a background check on Lombard, didn't like the results and flew down from Phoenix to take their daughter home. Ardith was pregnant—the folks wanted her to give the baby up and she refused. She was nineteen, sure she was in love with Lombard, waited for him to come and get her, put a wedding band on her finger. He didn't. Eventually, she finished school, married well, had two more kids. The new husband wanted to adopt Rachel, and that meant Lombard had to sign off, so the family lawyers tracked him down and presented him with the papers and the offer of a hefty check. He went ballistic, said he wanted to raise Rachel himself, and generously offered to take Ardith back, too, if she'd leave the other two kids behind and divorce the man she'd married. Naturally, she didn't want to go that route. Things were quiet for a while, and then one day Rachel disappeared from her backyard. Lombard called that night to say Phoenix P.D. was wasting its time looking for Rachel, since he had the child and they were already out of the country."

Although Ashley had never been a mother herself, it

was all too easy to understand how frantic Ardith and the family must have been.

"And they hired you to find Rachel and bring her home?"

"Yes," Jack answered, after another long delay. The long speech had clearly taken a lot out of him, but the amazed admiration she felt must have been visible in her eyes, because he added, "But don't get the idea that I'm some kind of hero. I was paid a quarter of a million dollars for bringing Rachel back home safely, and I didn't hesitate to accept the money."

"I didn't see any of this in the newspapers," Ashley mused.

"You wouldn't have," Jack replied. He'd finished half of his breakfast, and although he had a little more color than before, he was still too pale. "It was vital to keep the story out of the press. Rachel's life might have depended on it, and mine definitely did."

"Weren't you scared?"

"Hell," Jack answered, "I was terrified."

"You should lie down," she said softly.

"I don't think I can make it back up those stairs," Jack said, and Ashley could see that it pained him to admit this.

"You're just trying to avoid the wallpaper," she joked, though she was dangerously close to tears. Carefully, she helped him to his feet. "There's a bed in my sewing room. You can rest there until you feel stronger."

His face contorted, but he still managed a grin. "You're strong for a woman," he said.

"I was raised on a ranch," Ashley reminded him, ducking under his right shoulder and supporting him as she steered him across the kitchen to her sewing room.

"I used to help load hay bales in our field during harvest, among other things."

Jack glanced down at her face, and she thought she saw a glimmer of respect in his eyes. "*You* bucked bales?"

"Sure did." They'd reached the sewing-room door, and Ashley reached out to push it open. "Did you?"

"Are you kidding?" Jack's chuckle was ragged. "My dad is a dentist. I was raised in the suburbs—not a hay bale for miles."

Like the account of little Rachel's rescue, this was news to Ashley. She knew nothing about Jack's background, wondered how she could have fallen so hard for a man who'd never mentioned his family, let alone introduced her to them. In fact, she'd assumed he didn't *have* a family.

"Exactly what *is* your job title, anyway?"

He looked at her long and hard, wavering just a few feet from the narrow bed. "Mercenary," he said.

Ashley took that in, but it didn't really register, even after the Rachel story. "Is that what it says on your tax return, under *Occupation?*"

"No," he answered.

They reached the bed, and she helped him get settled. Since he was on top of the blankets, she covered him with a faded quilt that had been passed down through the O'Ballivan clan since the days when Maddie and Sam ran the ranch.

"You do file taxes, don't you?" Ashley was a very careful and practical person.

Jack smiled without opening his eyes. "Yeah," he said. "What I do is unconventional, but it isn't illegal."

Ashley stepped back, torn between bolting from the

room and lying down beside Jack, enfolding him in her arms. "Is there anything I can get you?"

"My gear," he said, his eyes still closed. "Tanner brought it in. Leather satchel, under the bed upstairs."

Ashley gave a little nod, even though he wouldn't see it. What kind of *gear* did a mercenary carry? Guns? Knives?

She gave a little shudder and left the door slightly ajar.

Upstairs, she found the leather bag under Jack's bed. The temptation to open it was nearly overwhelming, but she resisted. Yes, she was curious—*beyond* curious—but she wasn't a snoop. She didn't go through guests' luggage any more than she read the postcards they gave her to send for them.

When she got back to the sewing room, Jack was sleeping. Mrs. Wiggins curled up protectively on his chest.

Ashley set the bag down quietly and slipped out. Busied herself with routine housekeeping chores, too soon finished.

She was relieved when Tanner showed up at the kitchen door, looking worn out but blissfully happy.

"I came to babysit Jack while you go and see Olivia and the boys," he said, stepping past her and helping himself to a cup of lukewarm coffee. "How's he doing?"

Ashley watched as her brother-in-law stuck the mug into the microwave and pushed the appropriate buttons. "Not bad—for a mercenary."

Tanner paused, and his gaze swung in Ashley's direction. "He told you?"

"Yes. I need some answers, Tanner, and Jack is too sick to give them."

The new father turned away from the counter, the microwave whirring behind him, leaned back and folded his arms, watching Ashley, probably weighing the pros and cons of spilling what he knew—which was plenty, unless she missed her guess.

"He's talking about leaving," Ashley prodded, when Tanner didn't say anything right away. "I'm used to that, but I think I deserve to know what's going on."

Tanner gave a long sigh. "I'd trust Jack with my life—I trusted him with *Sophie's,* when she ran away from boarding school right after we moved here, but the truth is, I don't know a hell of a lot more about him than you do."

"He's your best friend."

"And he plays his cards close to the vest. When it comes to security, he's the best there is." Tanner paused, thrust a hand through his already mussed hair. "I can tell you this much, Ashley—if he said he loved you, he meant it, whatever happened afterward. He's never been married, doesn't have kids, his dad is a dentist, his mother is a librarian, and he has three younger brothers, all of whom are much more conventional than Jack. He likes beer, but I've never seen him drunk. That's the whole shebang, I'm afraid."

"Someone injected him with something," Ashley said in a low voice. "That's why he's sick."

"Good God," Tanner said.

A silence fell.

"And he's leaving as soon as he's strong enough," Ashley said. "Because some drug dealer named Chad Lombard has a grudge against him, and he's afraid of putting all of us in danger."

Tanner thought long and hard. "Maybe that's for the

best," he finally replied. Ashley knew Tanner wasn't afraid for himself, but he had to think about Olivia and Sophie and his infant sons. "I hate it, though. Turning my back on a friend who needs my help."

Ashley felt the same way, though Jack wasn't exactly a friend. In fact, she wasn't sure how to describe their relationship—if they had one at all. "This is Stone Creek," she heard herself say. "We have a long tradition of standing shoulder to shoulder and taking trouble as it comes."

Tanner's smile was tired, but warm. "Go," he said. "Tuckered out as she is, Olivia is dying to show off those babies. I'll look after Jack until you get home."

Ashley hesitated, then got her coat and purse and car keys again, and left for the clinic in Indian Rock.

# CHAPTER FOUR

OLIVIA WAS SITTING UP in bed, beaming, a baby tucked in the crook of each arm, when Ashley hurried into her room. There were flowers everywhere—Brad and Meg had already been there and gone, having brought Carly and Sophie to see the boys before school.

"Come and say hello to John and Sam," Olivia said gently.

Ashley, clutching a bouquet of pink and yellow carnations, hastily purchased at a convenience store, moved closer. She felt stricken with wonder and an immediate and all-encompassing love for the tiny red-faced infants snoozing in their swaddling blankets.

"Oh, Livie," she whispered, "they're beautiful."

"I agree," Olivia said proudly. "Do you want to hold them?"

Ashley swallowed, then reached out for the bundle on the right. She sat down slowly in the chair closest to Olivia's bed.

"That's John," Olivia explained, her voice soft with adoring exhaustion.

"How can you tell?" Ashley asked, without lifting her eyes from the baby's face. He seemed to glow with some internal light, as though he were trailing traces of heaven, the place he'd so recently left.

Livie chuckled. "The twins aren't identical, Ashley,"

she said. "John is a little smaller than Sam, and he has my mouth. Sam looks like Tanner."

Ashley didn't respond; she was too smitten with young John Mitchell Quinn. By the time she swapped one baby for the other, she could tell the difference between them.

A nurse came and collected the babies, put them back in their incubators. Although they were healthy, like most twins they were underweight. They'd be staying at the clinic for a few days after Olivia went home.

Olivia napped, woke up, napped again.

"I'm so glad you're here," she said once.

Ashley, who had been rising from her chair to leave, sat down again. Remembered the carnations and got up to put them in a water-glass vase.

"How did you wind up in Indian Rock instead of Flagstaff?" Ashley asked, when Olivia didn't immediately drift off.

Olivia smiled. "I was on a call," she said. "Sick horse. Tanner wanted me to call in another vet, but this was a special case, and Sophie was spending the night at Brad and Meg's, so he came with me. We planned to go on to Flagstaff for the induction when I was finished, but the babies had other ideas. I went into labor in the barn, and Tanner brought me here."

Ashley shook her head, unable to hold back a grin. Her sister, nine and a half months pregnant by her own admission, had gone out on a call in the middle of the night. It was just like her. "How's the horse?"

"Fine, of course," Olivia said, still smiling. "I'm the best vet in the county, you know."

Ashley found a place for the carnations—they looked pitiful among all the dozens and dozens of roses, yellow from Brad and Meg, white from Tanner, and more arriving at regular intervals from friends and coworkers. "I know," she agreed.

Olivia reached for her hand, squeezed. "Friends again?"

"We were never *not* friends, Livie."

Olivia shook her head. Like all O'Ballivans, she was stubborn. "We were always *sisters,*" she said. "But sisters aren't necessarily friends. Let's not let the mom-thing come between us again, okay?"

Ashley blinked away tears. "Okay," she said.

Just then, Melissa streaked into the room, half-hidden behind a giant potted plant with two blue plastic storks sticking out of it. She was dressed for work, in a tailored brown leather jacket, beige turtleneck and tweed trousers.

Setting the plant down on the floor, when she couldn't find any other surface, Melissa hurried over to Olivia and kissed her noisily on the forehead.

"Hi, Twin-Unit," she said to Ashley.

"Hi." Ashley smiled, glanced toward the doorway in case the mystery man had come along for the ride. Alas, there was no sign of him.

Melissa looked around for the babies. Frowned. She did everything fast, with an economy of motion; she'd come to see her nephews and was impatient at the delay. "Where are they?"

"In the nursery," Olivia answered, smiling. "How many cups of coffee have you had this morning?"

Melissa made a comical face. "Not nearly enough," she said. "I'm due in court in an hour, and where's the nursery?"

"Down the hall, to the right," Olivia told her. A worried crease appeared in her otherwise smooth forehead. "The roads are icy. Promise me you won't speed all the way back to Stone Creek after you leave here."

"Scout's honor," Melissa said, raising one hand. But she couldn't help glancing at her watch. "Yikes. Down the hall, to the right. Gotta go."

With that, she dashed out.

Ashley followed, double-stepping to catch up.

"Who was the man who answered your phone this morning?" she asked.

Melissa didn't look at her. "Nobody important," she said.

"You spent the night with him, and he's 'nobody important'?"

They'd reached the nursery window, and since Sam and John were the only babies there, spotting them was no problem.

"Could we not discuss this now?" Melissa asked, pressing both palms to the glass separating them from their nephews. "Why are they in incubators? Is something wrong?"

"It's just a precaution," Ashley answered gently. "They're a little small."

"Aren't babies *supposed* to be small?" Melissa's eyes were tender as she studied the new additions to the family. When she turned to face Ashley, though, her expression turned bleak.

"He's my boss," she said.

Ashley took a breath before responding. "The one who divorced his latest trophy wife about fifteen minutes ago?"

Melissa stiffened. "I knew you'd react that way. Honestly, Ash, sometimes you are such a prig. The marriage was over years ago—they were just going through the motions. And if you think I had anything to do with the breakup—well, you ought to know better."

Ashley closed her eyes briefly. She *did* know better. Her twin was an honorable person; nobody knew that better than she did. "I wasn't implying that you're a home-wrecker, Melissa. It's just that you're not over Daniel yet. You need time."

Daniel Guthrie, the last man in Melissa's life, owned and operated a fashionably rustic dude ranch between Stone Creek and Flagstaff. An attractive widower with two young sons, Dan was looking for a wife, someone to settle down with, and he'd never made a secret of it. Melissa, who freely admitted that she *could* love Dan and his children if she half tried, wanted a career—after all, she'd worked hard to earn her law degree.

It was a classic lose-lose situation.

"I didn't have sex with Alex," Melissa whispered, though Ashley hadn't asked. "We were just *talking.*"

"I believe you," Ashley said, putting up both hands in a gesture of peace. "But Stone Creek is a small town. If some bozo's car was parked in your driveway all night, word is bound to get back to Dan."

"Dan has no claim on me," Melissa snapped. "*He's* the one who said we needed a time-out." She sucked in a furious breath. "And Alex Ewing is *not* a bozo. He's up for the prosecutor's job in Phoenix, and he wants me to go with him if he gets it."

Ashley blinked. "You would move to—to Phoenix?"

Melissa widened her eyes. "Phoenix isn't Mars, Ashley," she pointed out. "It's less than two hours from here. And just because you're content to quietly fade away in

Stone Creek, quilting and baking cookies for visiting strangers, that doesn't mean *I* am."

"But—this is home."

Melissa looked at her watch again, shook her head. "Yeah," she said. "That's the problem."

With that, she walked off, leaving Ashley staring after her.

*I am* not *"content to quietly fade away in Stone Creek,"* she thought.

But wasn't that exactly what she was doing?

Making beds, cooking for guests, putting up decorations for various holidays only to take them down again? And, yes, quilting. That was her passion, her artistic outlet. Nothing wrong with that.

But Melissa's remarks *had* brought up the question Ashley usually avoided.

When was her *life* supposed to start?

JACK WOKE WITH A violent start, expecting darkness and nibbling rats.

Instead, he found himself in a small, pretty room with pale green walls. An old-fashioned sewing machine, the treadle kind usually seen only in antiques malls and elderly ladies' houses stood near the door. The quilt covering him smelled faintly of some herb—probably lavender—and memories.

Ashley.

He was at her place.

Relief flooded him—and then he heard the sound. Distant—a heavy step—definitely *not* Ashley's.

Leaning over the side of the bed, which must have been built for a child, it was so short and so narrow, Jack found his gear, fumbled to open the bag, extracted his trusty Glock, that marvel of German engineering. Checked to make sure the clip was in—and full.

The mattress squeaked a little as he got to his feet, listening not just with his ears, but with every cell, with all the dormant senses he'd learned to tap into, if not to name.

There it was again—that thump. Closer now. Definitely masculine.

Jack glanced back over one shoulder, saw that the kitten was still on the bed, watching him with curious, mismatched eyes.

"Shhh," he told the animal.

"Meooow," it responded.

The sound came a third time, nearer now. Just on the other side of the kitchen doorway, by Jack's calculations.

*Think,* he told himself. He knew he was reacting out of all proportion to the situation, but he couldn't help it. He'd had a lot of practice at staying alive, and his survival instincts were in overdrive.

Chad Lombard couldn't have tracked him to Stone Creek; there hadn't been time. But Jack was living and breathing because he lived by his gut as well as his mind. The small hairs on his nape stood up like wire.

Using one foot, the Glock clasped in both hands, he eased the sewing room door open by a few more inches.

Waited.

And damn near shot the best friend he'd ever had when Tanner Quinn strolled into the kitchen.

"Christ," Jack said, lowering the gun. With his long outgoing breath, every muscle in his body seemed to go slack.

Tanner's face was hard. "That was my line," he said.

Jack sagged against the doorframe, his eyes tightly shut. He forced himself to open them again. "What the hell are you doing here?"

"Playing nursemaid to you," Tanner answered, crossing the room in a few strides and expertly removing the Glock dangling from Jack's right hand. "Guess I should have stuck with my day job."

Jack opened his eyes, sick with relief, sick with whatever that goon in South America had shot into his veins. "Which is what?" he asked, in an attempt to lighten the mood.

Tanner set the gun on top of the refrigerator and pulled Jack by the arm. Squired him to a chair at the kitchen table.

"Raising three kids and being a husband to the best woman in the world," he answered. "And if it's all the same to you, I'd like to stick around long enough to see my grandchildren."

Jack braced an elbow on the tabletop, covered his face with one hand. "I'm sorry," he said.

Tanner hauled back a chair of his own, making plenty of noise in the process, and sat down across from Jack, ignoring the apology. "What's going on, McCall?" he demanded. "And don't give me any of your bull crap cloak-and-dagger answers, either."

"I need to get out of here," Jack said, meeting his friend's gaze. "Now. Today. Before somebody gets hurt."

Tanner flung a scathing glance toward the Glock, gleaming on top of the brushed-steel refrigerator. "Seems to me, *you're* the main threat to public safety around here. Dammit, you could have shot Ashley—or Sophie or Carly—"

"I said I was sorry."

"Oh, well, that changes everything."

Jack sighed. And then he told Tanner the same story he'd told Ashley earlier. Most of it was even true.

"You call this living, Jack?" Tanner asked, when he was finished. "When are you going to stop playing Indiana Jones and settle down?"

"Spoken like a man in love with a pregnant veterinarian," Jack said.

At last, Tanner broke down and grinned. "She's not pregnant anymore. Olivia and I are now the proud parents of twin boys."

"As of when?" Jack asked, delighted and just a shade envious. He'd never thought much about kids until he'd gotten to know Sophie, after Tanner's first wife, Katherine, was killed, and then Rachel, the bravest seven-year-old in Creation.

"As of this morning," Tanner answered.

"Wow," Jack said, with a shake of his head. "It would *really* have sucked if I'd shot you."

"Yeah," Tanner agreed, going grim again.

"All the more reason for me to hit the road."

"And go where?"

"Dammit, I don't know. Just away. I shouldn't have come here in the first place—I was out of my mind with fever—"

"You were out of your mind, all right," Tanner argued. "But I think it has more to do with Ashley than the toxin. There's a pattern here, old buddy. You always leave—and you always come back. That ought to tell you something."

"It tells me that I'm a jerk."

"You won't get any argument there," Tanner said, without hesitation.

"I can't keep doing this. Every time I've left that woman, I've meant to stay gone. But Ashley haunts me, Tanner. She's in the air I breathe and the water I drink—"

"It's called *love,* you idiot," Tanner informed him.

"Love," Jack scoffed. "This isn't the Lifetime channel, old buddy. And it's not as if I'm doing Ashley some big, fat favor by loving her. My kind of romance could get her *killed.*"

Tanner's mouth crooked up at one corner. "You watch the *Lifetime channel?*"

"Shut up," Jack bit out.

Tanner laughed. "You are so screwed," he said.

"Maybe," Jack snapped. "But you're not being much help here, in case you haven't noticed."

"It's time to stop running," Tanner said decisively. "Take a stand."

"Suppose Lombard shows up? He'd like nothing better than to take out everybody I care about."

Tanner's expression turned serious again, and both his eyebrows went up. "What about your dad, the dentist, and your mom, the librarian, and your three brothers, who probably have the misfortune to look just like you?"

Something tightened inside Jack, a wrenching grab, cold as steel. "Why do you think I haven't seen them since I got out of high school?" he shot back. "Nobody knows I *have* a family, and I want it to stay that way."

Tanner leaned forward a little. "Which means your name isn't Jack McCall," he said. "Who the hell are you, anyway?"

"Dammit, you *know* who I am. We've been through a lot together."

"Do I? Jack is probably your real first name, but I'll bet it doesn't say *McCall* on your birth certificate."

"My birth certificate conveniently disappeared into cyberspace a long time ago," Jack said. "And if you think I'm going to tell you my last name, so you can tap into a search engine and get the goods on me, you're a bigger sucker than I ever guessed."

Tanner frowned. He loved puzzles, and he was exceptionally good at figuring them out. "Wait a second. You and Ashley dated in college, and she knew you as Jack McCall. Did you change your name in high school?"

"Let this go, Tanner," Jack answered tightly. He had to give his friend something, or he'd never get off his back—that much was clear. And while they were sitting there planning his segment on *Biography,* Chad Lombard was looking for him. By that scumbag's watch, it was payback time. "I was one of those difficult types in high school—my folks, with some help from a judge, sent me to one of those military schools where they try to scare kids into behaving like human beings. One of the teachers was a former SEAL. Long story short, the Navy tapped me for their version of Special Forces and put me through college. I never went home after that, and the name change was their idea, not mine."

Tanner let out a long, low whistle. "Hot damn," he muttered. "Your folks must be frantic, wondering what happened to you."

"They think I'm dead," Jack said, stunned at how much he was giving up. That toxin must be digesting his brain. "There's a grave and a headstone; they put flowers on it once in a while. As far as they're concerned, I was blown to unidentifiable smithereens in Iraq."

Tanner glared at him. "How could you put them through that?"

"Ask the Navy," Jack said.

Outside, snow crunched under tires as Ashley pulled into the driveway.

"End of conversation," Jack told Tanner.

"That's what *you* think," Tanner replied, pushing back his chair to stand.

"I'll be out of here as soon as I can arrange it," Jack warned quietly.

Tanner skewered him with a look that might have meant "Good riddance,' though Jack couldn't be sure.

The back door opened, and Ashley blew in on a freezing wind. Hurrying to Tanner, she threw her arms around his waist and beamed up at him.

"The babies are *beautiful!*" she cried, her eyes glistening with happy tears. "Congratulations, Tanner."

Tanner hugged her, kissed the top of her head. "Thanks," he said gruffly. Then, with one more scathing glance at Jack, he put on his coat and left, though not before his gaze strayed to the Glock on top of the refrigerator.

Fortunately, Ashley was too busy taking off her own coat to notice.

Jack made a mental note to retrieve the weapon before she saw it.

"You're up," she told him cheerfully. "Feeling better?"

He'd never left her willingly, but this time, the prospect nearly doubled him over. He sat up a little straighter. "I love you, Ashley," he said.

She'd been in the process of brewing coffee; at his words, she stopped, stiffened, stared at him. "What did you say?"

"I love you. Always have, always will."

She sagged against the counter, all the joy gone from her eyes. "You have a strange way of showing it, Jack McCall," she said, after a very long time.

"I can't stay, Ash," he said hoarsely, wishing he could take her into his arms, make love to her just once more. But he'd done enough damage as it was. "And this time, I won't be back. I promise."

"Is that supposed to make me feel better?"

"It would if you knew what it might mean if I stayed."

"What would it mean, Jack? If you stayed, that is."

"I told you about Lombard. He's the vindictive type, and if he ever finds out about you—"

"Suppose he does," Ashley reasoned calmly, "and you're not here to protect me. What then?"

Jack closed his eyes. "Don't say that."

"Stone Creek isn't a bad place to raise a family," she forged on, with a dignity that broke Jack's heart into two bleeding chunks. "We could be happy here, Jack. Together."

He got to his feet. "Are you saying you love me?"

"Always have," she answered, "always will."

"It wouldn't work," Jack said, wishing he hadn't been such a hooligan back in his teens. None of this would be happening if he hadn't ended up in military school and shown a distinct talent for covert action. He'd probably be a dentist in the Midwest, with a wife and kids and a dog, and his parents and his brothers would be dropping by for Sunday afternoon barbecues instead of visiting an empty grave.

"Wouldn't it?" Ashley challenged. "Make love to me, Jack. And then tell me it wouldn't work."

The temptation burned in his veins and hardened his groin until it hurt. "Ashley, don't."

She began to unbutton her blue silk blouse.

"Ashley."

"What's the matter, Jack? Are you chicken?"

"Ashley, *stop* it." It wasn't a command, it was a plea. "I'm not who you think I am. My name isn't Jack Mc-Call, and I—"

Her blouse was open. Her lush breasts pushed against the lacy pink fabric of her bra. He could see the dark outline of her nipples.

"I don't care what your name is," she said. "I love you. You love me. Whoever you are, take me to bed, unless you want to have me on the kitchen floor."

He couldn't resist her any more than he'd been able to resist coming back every time he left. She was an addiction.

He held out his hand, and she came to him.

Somehow, they managed to get up the stairs, along the hallway, into her bedroom.

He didn't remember undressing her, or undressing himself.

It was as though their clothes had burned away in the heat.

Even a few minutes before, Jack wouldn't have believed he had the strength for sex, but the drive was deep, elemental, as much a part of him as Ashley herself.

There was no foreplay—their need for each other was too great.

The two of them fell sideways onto her bed, kissing as frantically as half-drowned swimmers trying to breathe, their arms and legs entwined.

He took her in one hard stroke, and found her ready for him.

She came instantly, shouting his name, clawing at his back with her fingernails. He drove in deep again, and she began the climb toward another pinnacle, writhing beneath him, flinging her hips up to meet his.

"Jack," she sobbed, *"Jack!"*

He fought to keep control, wondered feverishly if he'd die from the exertion. Oh, but what a way to go.

"Jack—"

"For God's sake, Ashley, lie still—"

Of course she didn't. She went wild beneath him.

Jack gave a ragged shout and spilled himself into her. He felt her clenching around him as she erupted in an orgasm of her own, with a long, continuous cry of exultant surrender.

Afterward, they lay still for a long time, spent, gasping for breath.

Jack felt himself hardening within her, thickening.

"Say it, Jack," she said, burying her in his hands. "Say you're going to leave me. I dare you."

He couldn't; he searched for the words, but they were nowhere to be found.

So he kissed her instead.

ASHLEY AWAKENED ALONE, at dusk, naked and soft-boned in her bed.

The aftershocks of Jack's lovemaking still thrummed in her depths, even as panic surged within her. Damn, he'd done it again—he'd driven her out of her mind with pleasure and then left her.

She scrambled out of bed, pulled on her ratty chenille robe, and hurried downstairs.

"Jack?" She felt like a fool, calling his name when she knew he was already gone, but the cry was out of her mouth before she could stop it.

"In here," he called back.

Ashley's heart fluttered, and so did the pit of her stomach.

She followed the echo of his voice as far as the study doorway, found him sitting at her computer. The monitor threw blue shadows over the planes of his face.

"Hope you don't mind," he said. "My laptop came down with a case of jungle rot, so I trashed it somewhere in the mountains of Venezuela, and I haven't had a chance to get another one."

Ashley groped her way into the room, like someone who'd forgotten how to walk, and landed in the first available chair, a wingback she'd reupholstered herself, in pink, green and white chintz. "Make yourself at home," she said, and then blushed because the words could be taken so many ways.

His fingers flew over the keyboard, with no pause when he looked her way. "Thanks," he said.

"You've made a remarkable recovery, it seems to me," Ashley observed.

"The restorative powers of good sex," Jack said, "are legendary."

*He* was legendary. It had been hours since they'd made love, but Ashley still felt a deliciously orgasmic twinge every few moments.

"Answering email?" she asked, to keep the conversation going.

Jack shook his head. "I don't get email," he said.

"After I booted this thing up and ran all the setups, I did a search. Noticed you didn't have a website. You can't run a business without some kind of presence on the internet these days, Ashley—not unless you want to go broke."

"You're building a *website?*"

"I'm setting up a few prototypes. You can have a look later, see if you like any of them."

"You're a man of many talents, Jack McCall."

He grinned. He'd showered and shaved since leaving her bed, she noticed. And he was wearing fresh clothes—blue jeans and a white T-shirt. "I began to suspect you thought that while you were digging your heels into the small of my back and howling like a she-wolf calling down the moon."

Ashley laughed, but her cheeks burned. She *had* acted like a hussy, abandoning herself to Jack, body and soul, and she didn't regret a moment of it. "Pretty cocky, aren't you?" she said.

Jack swiveled the chair around. "Come here," he said gruffly.

Her heart did a little jig, and her breath caught. "Why?"

"Because I want you," he replied simply.

She stood up, crossed to him, allowed him to set her astraddle on his lap. Moaned as he opened her bathrobe, baring her breasts.

Jack nibbled at one of her nipples, then the other. "Ummm," he murmured, shifting in the chair. He continued to arouse delicious feelings in her breasts with his lips and tongue.

Her eyes widened when she realized he'd opened his jeans. He drew his knees a little farther apart, and she gave a crooning gasp when she felt him between her legs, hot and hard, prodding.

Just as he entered her, he leaned forward again, took her right nipple into his mouth, tongued it and then began to suckle.

Ashley choked out an ecstatic sob and threw back her head, her hair falling loose down her back. "Oh, God," she whimpered. "Oh, God, not yet—"

But her body seized, caught in a maelstrom of pleasure, spasmed wildly, and seized again. Taken over, possessed, she rode him relentlessly, recklessly, her very soul ablaze with a light that blinded her from the inside.

Jack waited until she'd gone still, the effort at restraint visible in his features, and when he let himself go, the motions of his body were slow and graceful. Ashley watched his face, spellbound, until he'd stopped moving.

He sighed, his eyes closed.

And then they flew open.

"You *are* on the pill, aren't you?" he asked.

She had been, before he left. After he was gone, there had been no reason to practice birth control.

Ashley shook her head.

*"What?"* Jack choked out.

Ashley closed her robe, moved to rise off his lap.

But he grasped her hips and held her firmly in place. "Ashley?" he rasped.

"No, Jack," she said evenly. "I'm not on the pill."

He swore under his breath.

"Don't worry," she told him, hiding her hurt. "I'm not going to trap you."

He was going hard inside her again—angry hard. His eyes smoldering, his hands still holding her by the hips, he began to raise and lower her, raise and lower her, along the growing length of his shaft.

She buckled with the first orgasm, bit back a cry of response.

Jack settled back in the chair, watching her face, already driving her toward another, stronger climax.

And then another, and still another.

When his own release came, much later, he didn't utter a sound.

# CHAPTER FIVE

IN SOME WAYS, that last bout of lovemaking had been the most satisfying, but it left Ashley feeling peevish, just the same. When it was over, and she'd solidified her sex-weakened knees by an act of sheer will, she tugged her bathrobe closed and cinched the belt with a decisive motion.

"Good night," she told Jack, her chin high, her face hot.

"'Night," he replied. Having already refastened his jeans, he turned casually back to the computer monitor. To look at him, nobody would have guessed they'd been having soul-bending sex only a few minutes before.

"I'll need a credit card," Ashley said.

Jack slanted a look at her. "I beg your pardon?" he drawled.

Ashley's blush deepened to crimson. "Not for the sex," she said primly. "For the room."

Jack's attention was fixed on the monitor again. "My wallet's in the bag with my other gear. Help yourself."

As she stormed out, she thought she heard him chuckle.

Fury zinged through her, like a charge.

Since she was no snoop, she snatched up the leather bag, resting on the sewing room floor, and marched right back to the study. Set it down on the desk with a hard thump, two inches from Jack's elbow.

He sighed, flipped the brass catch on the bag, and rummaged inside until he found his wallet. Extracted a credit card.

"Here you go, Madam," he said, holding it between two fingers.

Ashley snatched the card, unwilling to pursue the word *Madam.* "How long will you be staying?"

The question hung between them for several moments.

"Better put me down for two weeks," Jack finally said. "The food's good here, and the sex is even better."

Ashley glanced at the card. It was platinum, so it probably had a high limit, and the expiration date was three years in the future. The name, however, was wrong.

"'Mark Ramsey'?" she read aloud.

"Oops. Sorry." Jack took the card back.

"Is that your real name?"

"Of course not." Frowning with concentration, Jack thumbed through a stack of cards, more than most people carried, certainly.

"What *is* your name, then?" *Since I just had about fourteen orgasms straddling your lap, I think I have a right to know.*

"Jack McCall," he said sweetly, handing her a gold card. "Try this one."

"What name did you use when you rescued Rachel?"

"Not this one, believe me. But if a man calls here or, worse yet, comes to the door, asking for Neal Mercer, you've never heard of me."

Ashley's palms were sweaty. She sank disconsolately

into the same chair she'd occupied earlier, before the lap dance. "Just how many aliases do you have, anyway?"

Jack was focused on the keyboard again. "Maybe a dozen. Are you going to run that card or not?"

Ashley leaned a little, peered at the screen. A picture of her house, in full summer regalia, filled it. Trees leafed out. Flowers blooming. Lawn greener than green and neatly mowed. She could almost smell sprinkler-dampened grass.

"Where did you get that?" she asked.

"The picture?" Jack didn't look at her. "Downloaded it from the Chamber of Commerce website. I'm setting you up to take credit cards next—the usual?"

She sighed. "Yes."

"Why the sigh?" He was watching her now.

"I have so much to learn about computers," Ashley said, after biting her lip. That was only part of what was bothering her, of course. She loved this man, and he claimed to love her in return, and she didn't even know who he was.

How crazy was that?

"It's not so hard," he told her, switching to another page on the screen, one filled with credit card logos. "I'll show you how."

"What's your name?"

He chuckled. "Rumpelstiltskin?"

"Hilarious. Do you even *remember* who you really are?"

He turned in the swivel chair, gazing directly into her eyes. "Jack McKenzie," he said solemnly. "As if it mattered."

"Why wouldn't it matter?" Ashley asked in a whisper.

"Because Jacob 'Jack' McKenzie is dead. Buried at Arlington, with full military honors."

She stared at him, confounded.

"Get some sleep, Ashley," Jack said, and now he sounded weary.

She was too proud to ask if he planned on sharing her bed—wasn't even sure she wanted him there. Yes, she loved him, with her whole being, there was no escaping that. But they might as well have lived in separate universes; she wasn't an international spy. She was a small-town girl, the operator of a modest B&B. Intrigue wasn't in her repertoire.

Slowly, she rose from the chair. She walked into the darkened living room, flipped on a lamp and proceeded to the check-in desk. There, she ran Jack's credit card.

It went through just fine.

She returned the card to him. "There'll be a slip to sign," she said flatly, "but that can wait until morning."

Jack merely nodded.

Ashley left the study again, scooped up a mewing Mrs. Wiggins as she passed and climbed the stairs.

JACK WAITED UNTIL he'd heard Ashley's bedroom door close in the distance, then set up yet another hotmail account, and brought up the message page. Typed in his mother's email address at the library.

*Hi, Mom,* he typed. *Just a note to say I'm not really dead...*

Delete.

He clicked to the search engine, entered the URL of the website for his dad's dental office.

There was Dr. McKenzie, in a white coat, looking like a man you'd trust your teeth to without hesitation. The old man was broad in the shoulders, with a full head of silver hair and a confident smile—Jack supposed he'd look a lot like his dad someday, if he managed to live long enough.

The average web surfer probably wouldn't have noticed the pain in Doc's eyes, but Jack did. He looked deep.

"I'm sorry, Dad," he murmured.

His cell phone, buried in the depths of his gear bag, played the opening notes of "Folsom Prison Blues."

Startled, Jack scrabbled through T-shirts and underwear until he found the cell. He didn't answer it, but squinted at the caller ID panel instead. It read, "Blocked."

A chill trickled down Jack's spine as he waited to see if the caller would leave a voice mail. This particular phone, a throwaway, was registered to Neal Mercer, and only a few people had the number.

Ardith.

Rachel.

An FBI agent or two.

Chad Lombard? There was no way he could have it, unless Rachel or Ardith had told him. Under duress.

A cold sweat broke out between Jack's aching shoulder blades.

A little envelope flashed on the phone screen.

After sucking in a breath, Jack accessed his voice mail.

"Jack? It's Ardith." She sounded scared. She'd changed her name, changed Rachel's, bought a condo on a shady street in a city far from Phoenix and started a new life, hoping to stay under Lombard's radar.

Jack waited for her to go on.

"I think he knows where we are," she said, at long last. "Rachel—I mean, Charlotte—is sure she saw him drive by the playground this afternoon—oh, God, I hope you get this—" Another pause, then Ardith recited a number. "Call me."

Jack shuddered as he hit the call-back button. Cell calls were notoriously easy to listen in on, if you had the right equipment and the skill, and given the clandestine nature of his life's work, Lombard surely did. If Rachel *had* seen her father drive past the playground, and not just someone who resembled him, the bastard was already closing in for the kill.

"H-hello?" Ardith answered.

"It's Jack. This has to be quick, Ardith. You need to get *Charlotte* and leave. Right now."

"And go where?" Ardith asked, her voice shaking. "For all I know, he's waiting right outside my door!"

"I'll send an escort. Just be ready, okay?"

"But where—?"

"You'll know when you get here. My people will use the password we agreed on. Don't go with them unless they do."

"Okay," Ardith said, near tears now.

They hung up without good-byes.

Jack immediately contacted Vince Griffin, using Ashley's landline, and gave the order, along with the password.

"Call me after you pick them up," he finished.

"Will do," Vince responded. "I take it she and the kid are right where we left them?"

"Yes," Jack said. It was beyond unlikely that Ashley's phone was bugged, but Vince's could be. He had to take the chance, hope to God nobody was listening in, that his longtime friend and employee wouldn't be followed. "Be careful."

"Always," Vince said cheerfully, and hung up.

Jack heard a sound behind him, regretted that the Glock was hidden behind a pile of quilts in the sewing room.

Ashley stood, pale-faced, in the study doorway.

"They're coming here? Rachel and her mother?"

"Yes," Jack said, letting out his breath. *You could have shot Ashley,* he heard Tanner say. A chill burned through him. "They won't be here long—just until I can find them a safe place to start over."

"They can stay as long as they need to," Ashley said, but she looked terrified. "There's no safer place than Stone Creek."

It wouldn't be a safe place for long if Lombard tracked his ex-girlfriend and his daughter to the small Arizona town, but Jack didn't point that out. There was no need to say it aloud.

JACK SHUT DOWN the computer and retired to the sewing room.

Knowing she wouldn't sleep, Ashley showered, put on blue jeans and an old T-shirt, and returned to the kitchen, where she methodically assembled the ingredients for the most complicated recipe in her collection—her great-grandmother's rum-pecan cake.

The fourth batch was cooling when dawn broke, and Ashley was sitting at the table, a cup of coffee untouched in front of her.

Jack stepped out of the sewing room, a shaving kit under one arm. His smile was wan, and a little guilty.

"Smells like Christmas in here," he said, very quietly. "Did you sleep?"

Ashley shook her head, vaguely aware that she was covered in cake flour, the fallout of frenzied baking. "Did you?"

"No," Jack said, and she knew by the hollow look in his eyes that he was telling the truth. "Ashley, I'm sorry—"

"Please," Ashley interrupted, "stop saying that."

She couldn't help comparing that morning to the one before, when she'd virtually seduced Jack right there in the kitchen. Was it only yesterday that she'd visited Olivia and the babies at the clinic in Indian Rock, had that disturbing conversation with Melissa outside the nursery? Dear God, it seemed as though a hundred years had passed since then.

The wall phone rang.

Jack tensed.

Ashley got up to answer. "It's only Melissa," she said.

She always knew when Melissa was calling.

"I'm picking up twin-vibes," her sister announced. "What's going on?"

"Nothing," Ashley said, glancing at the clock on the fireplace mantel. "It's only six in the morning, Melissa. What are you doing up so early?"

"I told you, I've got vibes," Melissa answered, sounding impatient.

Jack left the kitchen.

"Nothing's wrong," Ashley said, winding the telephone cord around her finger.

"You're lying," Melissa insisted flatly. "Do I have to come over there?"

Ashley smiled at the prospect. "Only if you want a home-cooked breakfast. Blueberry pancakes? Cherry crepes?"

"You," Melissa accused, "are deliberately torturing me. Your own sister. You *know* I'm on a diet."

"You're five foot three and you weigh 110 pounds. If you're on a diet, I'm having you committed." Remembering that their mother had died in the psychiatric ward of a Flagstaff hospital, Ashley instantly regretted her choice of words. This was a subject she wanted to avoid, at least until she regained her emotional equilibrium. Melissa, like Brad and Olivia, had had a no-love-lost relationship with Delia.

"Cherry crepes," Melissa mused. "Ashley O'Ballivan, you are an evil woman." A pause. "Furthermore, you have some nerve, grilling me about Alex Ewing, when Jack McCall is back."

Ashley frowned. "How did you know that?"

"Your neighbor, Mrs. Pollack, works part-time in my office, remember? She told me he arrived in an ambulance, day before yesterday. Is there a reason you didn't mention this?"

"Yes, Counselor," Ashley answered, "there is. Because I didn't want you to know."

"Why not?" Melissa sounded almost hurt.

"Because I knew I'd look like an idiot when he left again."

"Not to be too lawyerly, or anything, but why invite me to breakfast if you were trying to hide a man over there?"

Ashley laughed, but it was forced, and Melissa probably picked up on that, though mercifully, she didn't comment. "Because I'm overstocked on cherry crepes and I need the freezer space?" she offered.

"You were supposed to say something like, 'Because you're my twin sister and I love you.'"

"That, too," Ashley responded.

"I'll be over before work," Melissa said. "You're really okay?"

*No,* Ashley thought. *I'm in love with a stranger, someone wants to kill him, and my bed-and-breakfast is about to become a stop on a modern underground railroad.*

"I will be," she said aloud.

"Damn right you will," Melissa replied, and hung up without a goodbye. Of course, there hadn't been a "hello," either.

Classic Melissa.

The upstairs shower had been running through most of her conversation with Melissa—Ashley had heard the water rushing through the old house's many pipes. Now all was silent.

Thinking Jack would probably be downstairs soon, wanting breakfast, Ashley fed Mrs. Wiggins and then took a plastic container filled with the results of her *last* cooking binge from the freezer.

A month ago she'd made five dozen crepes, complete with cherry sauce from scratch, when one of her college friends had called to say she'd just found out her husband was having an affair.

Before that, it had been a double-fudge brownie marathon—beginning the night of her mother's funeral. She'd donated the brownies to the residents of the nursing home three blocks over, since, in her own way, she was just as calorie-conscious as Melissa.

Baking therapy was one thing. Scarfing down the results was quite another.

Half an hour passed, and Jack didn't reappear.

Ashley waited.

A full hour had passed, and still no sign of him.

Resigned, she went upstairs. Knocked softly at his bedroom door.

No answer.

Her imagination kicked in. The man had *aliases,* for heaven's sake. He'd abducted a drug dealer's seven-year-old daughter from a stronghold in some Latin American jungle.

Maybe he'd sneaked out the front door.

Maybe he was lying in there, dead.

"Jack?"

Nothing.

She opened the door, her heart in her throat, and stuck her head inside the room.

He wasn't in the bed.

She raised her voice a little. "Jack?"

She heard the buzzing sound then, identified it as an electric shaver, and was just about to back out of the room and close the door behind her, as quietly as possible, when his bathroom door opened.

His hair was damp from the shower, and he was wearing a towel, loincloth style, and nothing else. He grinned as he shut off the shaver.

"I'm not here for sex," Ashley said, and then could have kicked herself.

Jack laughed. "Too bad," he said. "Nothing like a quickie to get the day off to a good start. So to speak."

*A quickie indeed.* Ashley gave him a look, meant to hide the fact that she found the idea more than appealing. "Breakfast will be ready soon," she said coolly. "And Melissa is joining us, so try to behave yourself."

He stepped out of the bathroom.

Her gaze immediately dropped to the towel. Shot back to his face.

He was grinning. "But we're alone *now,* aren't we?"

"I'm still not on birth control, remember?" Ashley's voice shook.

"*That* horse is pretty much out of the barn," Jack drawled. He was walking toward her.

She didn't move.

He took her hand, pulled her to him, pushed the door shut.

Kissed her breathless.

Unsnapped her jeans, slid a hand inside her panties.

All without breaking the kiss.

Ashley moaned into his mouth, wet where he caressed her.

He maneuvered her to the bed, laid her down.

Ashley was already trying to squirm out of her jeans. When it came to Jack McCall—McKenzie—*whoever*— she was downright easy.

Jack finally ended the kiss, proceeded to rid her of her shoes, of the binding denim, and then her practical cotton underpants.

She whimpered in anticipation when he knelt between her legs, parted her thighs, kissed her—*there.*

A shudder of violent need moved through her.

"Slow and easy," he murmured, between nibbles and flicks of his tongue.

*Slow and easy?* She was on fire.

She shook her head from side to side. "Hard," she pleaded. "Hard and fast, Jack. *Please...*"

He went down on her in earnest then, and after a few glorious minutes, she shattered completely, peaking and then peaking again.

Jack soothed her as she descended, stroking her thighs and murmuring to her until she sank into satisfaction.

She'd expected him to mount her, but he didn't.

Instead, he dressed her again, nipping her once through the moist crotch of her panties before tucking her legs into her jeans, sliding them up her legs, tugging them past her bottom. He even slipped her feet into her shoes and tied the laces.

"What about—the quickie?" she asked, burning again because he'd teased her with that little scrape of his teeth. Because as spectacular as her orgasm had been, it had left her wanting—*needing*—more.

"I guess that will have to wait," Jack said, sitting down beside her on the bed and easing her upright next to him. "Didn't you say your sister would be here for breakfast at any moment?"

She looked down at the towel—either it had miraculously stayed in place or he'd wrapped it around his waist again when she wasn't looking—and saw the sizable bulge of his erection. "You've got a hard-on," she said matter-of-factly.

Jack chuckled. "Ya think?"

Melissa's voice sounded from downstairs. "Ash? I'm here!"

Ashley bolted to her feet, blushing. "Coming!" she called back.

"You can say that again," Jack teased.

Smoothing her hair with both hands, tugging at her T-shirt, Ashley hurried out of the room.

"I'll be right down!" she shouted, from the top of the stairs.

Melissa's reply was inaudible.

Ashley dashed into her bathroom and splashed her face with cold water, then checked herself out in the full-length mirror on the back of the door.

She looked, she decided ruefully, like a woman who'd just had a screaming climax—and needed more.

Quickly, she applied powder to her face, but the tell-tale glow was still there.

Damn.

There was nothing to do but go downstairs, where her all-too-perceptive twin was waiting for cherry crepes. If she didn't appear soon, Melissa would come looking for her.

"You were having sex," Melissa said two minutes later, when Ashley forced herself to step into the kitchen.

"No, I wasn't," Ashley replied, with an indignant little sniff.

"Liar."

Ashley crossed the room, turned the oven on to pre-heat, and got very busy taking the frozen crepes out of their plastic container, transferring them to a baking dish. All the while, she was careful not to let Melissa catch her eye.

"Olivia and the twins are coming home today," Melissa said lightly, but something in her voice warned that she wasn't going to let the sex issue drop.

"I thought the babies had to stay until they were bigger," Ashley replied, still avoiding Melissa's gaze.

"Tanner hired special nurses and had two state-of-the-art incubators brought from Flagstaff," Melissa explained.

Once the crepes were in the oven, Ashley had no choice but to turn around and look at Melissa.

"You *were* having sex," Melissa repeated.

Ashley flung her hands out from her sides. "*Okay. Yes,* I was having sex!" She sighed. "Sort of."

"What do you mean, *sort of*? How do you 'sort of' have sex?"

"Never mind," Ashley snapped. "Isn't it enough that I admitted it? Do you want details?"

"Yes, actually," Melissa answered mischievously, "but I'm obviously not going to get them."

Jack pushed open the inside door and stepped into the kitchen.

*"Yet,"* Melissa added, in a whisper.

Ashley rolled her eyes.

"Hello, Jack," Melissa said.

"Melissa," Jack replied.

Like Brad and Olivia, Melissa wasn't in the Jack McCall fan club. They'd all turned in their membership cards the last time he ditched Ashley.

"Just passing through?" Melissa asked sweetly.

"Like the wind," Jack answered. "Your brother already threatened me, so maybe we can skip that part."

Ashley raised her eyebrows. Brad had *threatened* Jack?

"As long as somebody got the point across," Melissa chimed.

"Oh, believe me, I get it."

"Will you both stop bickering, please?" Ashley asked.

Melissa sneezed. Looked around. "Is there a *cat* in this house?"

Jack grinned. "I could find the little mutant, if you'd like to pet it."

Melissa sneezed again. "I'm—*allergic!* Ashley, you *know* I'm all—all—*atchoo!*"

Ashley had completely forgotten about Mrs. Wiggins, and about her sister's famous allergies. Olivia insisted it was all in Melissa's head, since she'd been tested and the results had been negative.

"I'm sorry, I—"

Another sneeze.

"Bless you," Jack said generously.

Melissa grabbed up her coat and purse and ran for the back door. Slammed it behind her.

"Well," Jack commented, "that went well."

"Shut up," Ashley said.

Jack let out a magnanimous sigh and spread his hands.

Ashley went to the cupboard, got out two plates, set them on the table with rather more force than necessary. "You," she said, "are complicating my life."

"Are you talking to me or the cat?" Jack asked, all innocence.

"You," Ashley replied tersely. "I'm not getting rid of the cat."

"But you *are* getting rid of me? After that orgasm?"

*"Shut up."*

Jack chuckled, pressed his lips together, and pretended to zip them closed.

Ashley served the crepes. They both ate.

All without a single word passing between them.

After breakfast, Jack retreated to the study, and Ashley cleaned up the kitchen. Melissa called just as she was closing the dishwasher door.

"It wasn't the cat," Melissa said, first thing.

"Duh," Ashley responded.

"I mean, I thought it was, but I'm probably catching cold or something—"

"Either that, or you're allergic to Jack."

"He's bad news, Ash," Melissa said.

"I guess I could take up with Dan," Ashley said mildly. "I hear he's looking for a domestic type."

"Don't you dare!"

Ashley smiled, even though tears suddenly scalded her eyes. She was destined to love one man—Jack Mc-Call—for the rest of her life, maybe for the rest of eternity.

And Melissa was right.

He was the worst possible news.

# CHAPTER SIX

"I'M GOING OUT TO Tanner and Olivia's after work today," Melissa said. "Gotta see my nephews in their natural habitat. Want to ride along?"

By the time Melissa left her office, even if she knocked off at five o'clock—a rare thing for her—it would be dark out. Ardith and Rachel would surely arrive that night, and Ashley wanted to be on hand to welcome the pair and help them settle in.

She'd already decided to put the secret guests in the room directly across from Jack's; it had twin beds and a private bathroom. Jack would surely want to be in close proximity to them in case of trouble, and the feeling was undoubtedly mutual.

"I didn't sleep very well last night," she confessed. "By the time you leave work, I'll probably be snoring."

"Whatever you say," Melissa said gently. "Be careful, Ash. When the sex is good, it's easy to get carried away."

"Sounds like you're speaking from experience," Ashley replied. "Have you seen Dan lately?"

Melissa sighed. "We're not speaking," she said, with a sadness she usually kept hidden. "The last time we did, he told me we should both start seeing other people." A sniffle. "I heard he's going out with some waitress from the Roadhouse, over in Indian Rock."

"Is that why you're considering leaving Stone Creek? Because Dan is dating someone else?"

Melissa began to cry. There was no sob, no sniffle, no sound at all, but Ashley knew her sister was in tears. That was the twin bond, at least as they experienced it.

"Why do I have to choose?" Melissa asked plaintively. "Why can't I have Dan *and* my career? Ash, I worked so hard to get through law school—even with Brad footing the bills, it was *really* tough."

Ashley hadn't been over this ground with Melissa, not in any depth, anyway, because they'd been semi-estranged since the day of their mother's funeral. "Is that what Dan wants, Melissa? For you to give up your law practice?"

"He has two young sons, Ash. The ranch is *miles* from anywhere. In the winter, they get snowed in—Dan homeschools Michael and Ray from the first blizzard, sometimes until Easter, because the ranch road is usually impassible. Unless I wanted to travel by dogsled, I couldn't possibly commute. I'd go bonkers." Melissa pulled in a long, quivery breath. "I might even pull a 'Mom,' Ashley. If I got desperate enough. Get on a bus one fine afternoon and never come back."

"I can't see you doing that, Melissa."

"Well, *I* can. I love Dan. I love the boys—way too much to do to them what Delia did to us."

"Mel—"

"Here's how much I love them. I'd rather Dan married that waitress than someone who was always looking for an escape route—like me."

"Have you and Dan talked about this, Melissa? *Really* talked about it?"

"Sort of," Melissa admitted wearily. "His stock response was, 'Mel, we can work this out.' Which means I stay home and cook and clean and sew slipcovers, while he's out on the trail, squiring around a bunch of executive greenhorns trying to find their inner cowboys."

"How do you *know* that's what it means? Did Dan actually say so, Melissa, or is this just your take on the situation?"

"*'Just'* my 'take' on the situation?" Melissa countered, sounding offended. "I'm not some naive Martha Stewart clone like—like—"

"Like me?"

"I didn't say that!"

"You didn't have to, Counselor." *A Martha Stewart clone?* Was that how other people saw her? Because she enjoyed cooking, decorating, quilting? Because she'd never had the kind of world-conquering ambition Brad and Melissa shared?

"Ashley, I truly didn't mean—"

Ashley had always been the family peacemaker, and that hadn't changed. "I know you didn't mean to hurt my feelings, Melissa," she said gently. *Oh, but you did.* "And maybe it *is* time I had a little excitement in my life."

With Jack around, excitement was pretty much a sure thing.

Out-of-the-stratosphere sex and a drug dealer bent on revenge.

Who could ask for more?

There was a smile in Melissa's voice, along with a tremulous note of relief. "Kiss the babies for me, if you see them before I do," she said.

Ashley hadn't decided whether or not she'd make the drive out to Starcross Ranch that day. It wasn't so far, but the roads were probably slick. Although she had snow tires, her car was a subcompact, and it didn't have four-wheel drive.

"I'll do that," she answered, and the call was over.

Jack, she soon discovered, was in the study, working on potential websites for the bed-and-breakfast. He was remarkably cool, calm and collected, considering the circumstances, but Ashley couldn't help noticing that his nondescript cell phone was within easy reach.

She went upstairs, cast one yearning look toward her bed. Climbing into it wasn't an option—she might have another wakeful night if she went to sleep at that hour of the day.

Using her bedside phone, she placed a call to Olivia.

Her sister answered on the second ring. "Dr. O'Ballivan," she said, all business. Olivia had taken Tanner's name when they married, but she still used her own professionally.

Olivia was managing marriage, motherhood and a career, at least so far. Why couldn't Melissa do the same thing?

"You sound very businesslike, for someone who just went through childbirth twice in the space of ten minutes," Ashley said.

Olivia laughed. "That's modern medicine for you. Have twins one day, go home the next. Tanner hired nurses to look after the babies round the clock until I've rested up, so I'm a lady of leisure these days."

"How are they?"

"Growing like corn in August," Olivia replied.

"Good," Ashley said. "Are you up for a visitor? Please say so if you're not—I promise I'll understand."

"I'd *love* to have a visitor," Olivia said. "Tanner's

out feeding the range cattle, Sophie's at school, and of course the day nurse is busy doting on the two new men in the house. Ginger isn't in the mood for chitchat, so I'm at loose ends."

Ashley couldn't help smiling. Ginger, an aging golden retriever, was Olivia's constant companion, and the two of them usually had a lot to say to each other. "I'll be out as soon as I've showered and dressed," she said. "Do you need anything from town?"

"Nope. Loaded up on groceries over the weekend," Olivia answered. "The roads have been plowed and sanded, but be careful anyway. There's another snowstorm rolling in tonight."

Ashley promised to drive carefully and said goodbye.

She tried to be philosophical about the approaching storm, but for her, once Christmas had come and gone, snow lost its charm. Unlike her siblings, she didn't ski.

The shower perked her up a little—she used her special ginseng-and-rice soap, and the scent was heavenly. After drying off with the kind of soft, thick towel one would expect a "Martha Stewart clone" to have on hand, she dressed in a long black woolen skirt, a lavender sweater with raglan sleeves, and high black boots.

She brushed her hair out and skillfully redid her braid.

Frowned at her image in the steamy mirror.

Maybe she ought to change her hair. Get one of those saucy, layered cuts, with a few shimmery highlights thrown in for good measure. Drive to one of the malls in Flagstaff and have a makeover at a department-store cosmetics counter.

Jazz herself up a little.

The trouble was, she'd never aspired to jazziness.

Her natural color, a coppery-blond, suited her just fine, and so did the style. The braid was tidy, feminine, and practical, considering the life she led.

On the other hand, she'd been wearing that same French braid since college. Spiral curls, like Melissa's, might look sexy on her.

Did she *want* to be sexier?

Look how much trouble she'd gotten herself into with the same old hairdo and minimal makeup.

Quickly, she applied lip gloss and a light coat of mascara and headed downstairs. Pausing in the study doorway, she allowed herself the pleasure of watching Jack for a few moments before saying, "I'm going out to Olivia and Tanner's. Want to come along?"

Jack turned in the swivel chair. "Maybe some other time," he said. "I think I'd better stick around, in case Vince shows up with Ardith and Rachel sooner than expected."

Ashley didn't know who Vince was, though she had caught the name when she accidentally-on-purpose overheard Jack's phone conversation with Ardith the night before.

"Did he call?" She wanted to ask Jack if he was feeling ill again, but something stopped her. "Vince, I mean?"

Jack nodded. "They're on their way."

"No trouble?"

His gaze was direct. "Depends on how you define *trouble*," he replied. "Ardith has a husband and two other children besides Rachel. She's had to leave them behind—at least for the time being."

Ashley's heart pinched. She knew what it was to

await the return of a missing mother. "Aren't the police doing anything?"

"They were willing to send a patrol car by Ardith's place every once in a while. Under civil law, unless Lombard actually attacks or kills her or Rachel, there isn't much the police can do."

"That's insane!"

"It's the law."

"The husband and the other children—aren't they in danger, too?" Wouldn't the whole family be better off together, Ashley wondered, even if they had to establish new identifies? At least they'd have each other.

"The more people involved," Jack told her grimly, "the harder it is to hide. For now, they're safer apart."

"A man like Lombard—wouldn't he go after the rest of the family, if only to force Ardith out into the open?"

"He might do anything," Jack admitted. "From what I've seen, though, Lombard is fixated on getting Rachel back and not much else. Ardith is in his way, and he won't hesitate to take her out to get what he wants."

Ashley hugged herself. Even inside, wearing warm clothes, she felt chilled. "But *why* is he so obsessed? He wasn't around when Rachel was born—he couldn't have bonded with her the way a father normally would."

"Why does he run drugs?" Jack countered. "Why does he kill people? We're not dealing with a rational person here, Ashley. If I had to hazard a guess at his motive, I'd say it's pure ego. Lombard is a sociopath, if not worse. He sees Rachel as an object, something that *belongs* to him." He paused, and she saw pain in his eyes. "Do me a favor?" he asked hoarsely.

"What?"

"Don't come back here tonight. Stay with Tanner and Olivia. Or with Brad and his wife."

Ashley swallowed. "You think Lombard's coming—here?" She'd known Jack thought exactly that, on some level, but it seemed so incredible that she had to ask.

"Let's just say I'd rather not take a chance."

"But you *will* be taking a chance, with your own life."

"That's one hell of a lot better than taking a chance with yours. Once I figure out what to do with Ardith and Rachel, make sure they're someplace Lombard will never find them, I'm going to draw that crazy son-of-a-bitch as far from Stone Creek as I can."

"This isn't going to end, is it? Not unless—"

"Not unless," Jack said, rising from the chair, approaching her, "I kill him, or he kills me."

"My God," Ashley groaned, putting a hand to her mouth.

Jack gripped her shoulders firmly, but with a gentleness that reminded her of their lovemaking. "I'll never be able to forgive myself if you get caught in the cross fire, Ashley. If you meant it when you said you loved me, then do what I ask. Take the cat, leave this house, and don't come back until I give the all clear."

"I *did* mean it, but—"

He brushed her chin with the pad of his thumb. "I understand that you come from sturdy pioneer stock and all that, Ashley. I know the O'Ballivans have always held their own against all comers, faced down any trouble that came their way. But Chad Lombard is no ordinary bad guy. He's the devil's first cousin. You don't want to know the things he's done—you wouldn't be able to get them out of your head."

Ashley stared into Jack's eyes, so deathly afraid for

him that it didn't occur to her to be afraid for herself. "When you went looking for Rachel in South America," she said, her mouth so dry that she almost couldn't get the words out, "that wasn't your first run-in with Lombard, was it?"

"No," he said, after a long, long time.

"What hap—?"

"You don't want to know. I sure as hell wish *I* didn't." He slid his hands down her upper arms, squeezed her elbows. "Go, Ashley. Do this for me, and I'll never ask you for another thing."

"That's what I'm afraid of," she told him.

He leaned in, kissed her forehead. Took a deep breath, seeming to draw in the scent of her and hold it as long as possible. "Go," he repeated.

She agonized in silence for a long moment, then nodded in reluctant agreement. She'd wanted to meet Ardith and Rachel, but maybe it would be better—for them as well as for her—if that never happened.

"You'll call when you get to your sister's place?" Jack asked.

"Yes," Ashley said.

She turned away from Jack slowly, went back upstairs, packed a small suitcase.

She didn't say good-bye to Jack; there was something too final about that. Instead, she collected Mrs. Wiggins and set out for Starcross Ranch, though when she arrived at Tanner and Olivia's large, recently renovated house, she left her suitcase and the kitten in the car.

The last thing the Quinns needed, with new babies and incubators and three shifts of nurses already in residence, was a relative looking for a place to hide out.

After the visit, she would drive on to Meg and Brad's, ask to spend the night in their guesthouse.

Although she knew she'd be welcome, Brad would want to know what was going on. After all, she had a perfectly good place of her own.

Lying wouldn't do any good—her brother knew Jack was there, knew their history, at least as a couple.

She would have to tell Brad the truth—but how much of it?

Jack hadn't asked her to keep any secrets. Given the situation, though, he might have thought that went without saying.

Tanner stepped out onto the porch as she came up the walk. He smiled, but his eyes were filled with unasked questions.

Ashley dredged up a tattered smile from somewhere inside, pasted it to her mouth. "Hello, Tanner," she said.

"Jack called," he told her.

Ashley stopped in the middle of the walk. A special system of wires kept the concrete clear of ice and snow, and she could feel the heat of it, even through the soles of her boots.

"Oh," she said.

He passed her on the walk without another word. Went to her car, reached in for the suitcase and the kitten.

"I was going to spend the night over at Brad and Meg's," she said, pausing on the porch steps.

"You're staying here," Tanner said. "It's not as though we don't have room, and I promise, the dogs won't eat your cat."

"But—the babies—Olivia—the last thing you need is—"

Beside her now, Tanner tried for a smile of his own

and fell short. "Brad and Meg will be over later, with the kids. Melissa's stopping by when she's through at work. Time for a family meeting, kiddo, and you're the guest of honor."

Curiously, Ashley felt both deflated and uplifted by this news. "If it's about giving up Jack, you can all forget it," she said firmly.

Tanner didn't respond to that. Somehow, even with a protesting cat in one hand and a suitcase handle in the other, he managed to open the front door. "Olivia's in the kitchen," he told her. "I'll put your things in the guestroom. Cat included."

In that house, the "guestroom" was actually a suite, with a luxurious bath, a flat-screen TV above the working fireplace, and its own kitchenette.

Ginger rose from her cushy bed, tail wagging, when Ashley stepped into the main kitchen. Ashley bent to greet the sweet old dog.

Dressed in jeans and an old flannel shirt, Olivia sat in the antique rocking chair in front of the bay windows, a receiving blanket draped discreetly over her chest, nursing one of the babies. Seeing Ashley, she smiled, but her eyes were troubled.

Ashley went to her sister, bent to kiss the top of her head.

"Tell me what's going on, Ashley," Olivia said. "Tanner gave me a few details after he talked to Jack on the phone earlier, but he was pretty cryptic."

Ashley pulled one of the high-backed wooden chairs over from the table and sat down, facing Olivia. Their knees didn't quite touch.

Tanner came into the room, went to the coffeepot and filled a cup for Ashley. "You look like you could use a shot of whiskey," he commented. "But now that Sophie's a teenager, always having friends over, we decided to remove all temptation. This will have to do."

"Thanks," Ashley said, smiling a little and taking the cup.

Olivia was rocking the chair a little faster, her gaze fixed on Ashley. "Talk to us," she ordered.

Ashley sighed. When Brad and Meg and Melissa arrived, she'd have to repeat the whole incredible story—what little she knew of it, anyway—but it was clear that Olivia would brook no delay. So Ashley told her sister and brother-in-law what she knew about Rachel's rescue, and Chad Lombard's determination to, one, get his daughter back and, two, take revenge on Jack for stealing her away.

Tanner didn't look surprised; he probably knew more than she did, since he and Jack were close friends. Ashley didn't risk as much as a glance in Olivia's direction. She hated worrying her sister, especially now.

"Jack sent someone to bring Ardith and Rachel to Stone Creek," she finished. "And he wanted me out of the house in case Lombard managed to follow them somehow."

"It was certainly generous of Jack," Olivia said, with a bite in her tone, "to bring all this trouble straight to *your* door."

Tanner glanced at Olivia, grimaced slightly. "He was sick, Liv," he told her. "Out of his head with fever."

Olivia sighed.

"I'm in love with Jack," Ashley said bravely. "You might as well know."

Olivia and Tanner exchanged looks.

"What a surprise," Tanner said, one corner of his mouth tilting up briefly.

"You do realize," Olivia said seriously, her gaze boring into Ashley's face, "that this situation is hopeless? Even if Jack manages to get the woman and her little girl to safety, this Lombard character will always be a threat."

Tanner pulled up a chair beside Olivia and took her hand. "Liv," he said, "Jack is the best at what he does. He won't let anything happen to Ashley."

Tears filled Olivia's expressive eyes, then spilled down her cheeks. Ginger gave a little whimper and lumbered over to lay her muzzle on her mistress's knee. Rolled her brown eyes upward.

"I will *not* calm down," Olivia told the dog. "This is serious!"

This time, Tanner and Ashley looked at each other.

"I agree with Ginger," Tanner told his wife quietly. "You need to stay calm. We all do." By now, he was used to Olivia's telepathic conversations with animals. Ashley couldn't remember a time when her big sister didn't communicate with four-legged creatures of all species.

"How can I, when my sister is in mortal danger?" Olivia snapped, watching Ashley. "All because of *your* friend."

"Jack *is* my friend," Tanner responded, his voice still even. "And that's why I'm going to do whatever I can to help him."

Olivia turned her head quickly, stared at her husband. *"What?"*

"I can't just turn my back on him, Liv," Tanner said. "Not even for you."

"What about Sophie? What about John and Sam? They need their father, and *I* need my husband!"

Tanner started to speak, then stopped himself. Ashley saw a small muscle bunch in his jaw, go slack.

Ginger whimpered again, still gazing up at Olivia in adoring sorrow, her dog eyes liquid.

"That's easy for *you* to say," Olivia told the dog.

"This is why I didn't want to stay here," Ashley told Tanner sadly. "I've been in this house for five minutes, and I'm already causing trouble."

"You didn't do anything wrong," Olivia said, her voice and expression softening, her eyes still shining with tears. "Before Big John died, when Brad was away from home, busy with his career, I promised our grandfather I'd look after you and Melissa, and I intend to keep my word, Ashley."

"I'm not a little girl anymore," Ashley reminded her sister.

Olivia didn't answer. She was intent on tucking either John or Sam against her shoulder, patting his tiny back. The receiving blanket still covered her. When the burp came, Olivia smiled proudly.

Tanner stood up, gently took his son and carried him out of the kitchen.

Olivia straightened her clothing and laid the blanket aside. Gave Ginger a few reassuring strokes on the head before sending the animal back to her bed nearby.

"You are going to be the most amazing mother," Ashley said.

"Don't try to change the subject," Olivia warned. She was smiling, but her eyes remained moist and fierce with determination to protect her little sister. "So, you really are in love with Jack McCall?"

"Afraid so," Ashley replied. "And I think it's forever."

"Is he planning to stay this time?" Olivia's tone was kind, if wary.

Ashley raised her shoulders slightly, lowered them again. "He paid for two weeks at the B&B," she said.

Olivia's eyes narrowed, then widened. "Two weeks? That's all?"

"It's something," Ashley said, feeling like a candidate for some reality show about women trying to get over the wrong man. She made a lame attempt at a joke. "If we decide to make this permanent, I won't be charging him for bed and board."

Olivia didn't laugh, or even smile. "What if he leaves?"

"I think there's a good chance that he will," Ashley admitted. Then, without thinking, she rested one hand against her lower belly.

Olivia read the gesture with unerring accuracy. "Ashley—are you *pregnant?*"

"It's too early to know, doctor," Ashley said. "Unless there's a second-day test out there that I haven't heard about."

"*Unprotected sex?* Ashley, what are you *thinking?*"

"For once, I'm not. And it's kind of a relief."

"What if there's a baby? Jack might not be around to help you raise it."

"I'd manage, Olivia, as other women do, and *have* since cave days, if not longer."

"A child needs a father," Olivia said.

"Spoken like a very lucky woman with a husband who adores her," Ashley answered, without a shred of malice.

Tanner returned before Olivia could answer, took

her by both hands, and gently hoisted her to her feet. "Time for your nap, Mama Bear," he told her.

Olivia didn't resist, but she did pin Ashley with a big-sister look and say, "We're not finished with this conversation."

Ashley simply spread her hands.

SHADE BY SHADE, shadow by shadow, night finally came.

Ashley had called from Olivia's place, as promised. They hadn't exchanged more than a few words, and those had been stiff and stilted.

It was no great wonder to Jack that Ashley was projecting a chill: She'd been banished from her own house by a man who had no damn business being there at all.

He was getting antsy.

He'd heard nothing about Ardith and Rachel since his first terse conversation with Vince Griffin, right after the pickup. On the bright side, the toxin seemed to be in abeyance, though he still broke out in cold sweats at irregular intervals, and spates of weakness invariably followed in their wake.

To keep from going crazy, or maybe to make sure he did, Jack logged on to his father's website again. Clicked to the Associates page.

There were his brothers, Dean and Jim. The last time Jack had seen them, they'd been in junior high, wannabe Romeos with braces and acne. Now, they looked like infomercial hosts.

He smiled.

A blurb at the bottom of the page showed a snapshot of Bryce, the youngest. In a wild break with McKenzie tradition, he was studying to be an optometrist.

There was no mention of Jack himself, of course. But his mother wasn't on the site, either, and that bothered him.

His dad had always been a big believer in family values.

*What a disappointment I must have been,* Jack thought, frowning as he left the website and ran another search. There might be a recent picture of his mom on the library's site. After all, she'd been the director when he'd left for military school.

The director's face beamed from the main page, and it wasn't his mother's.

Frowning, Jack ran another search, using her name.

That was when he found the obituary, dated three years ago, a week after her fifty-third birthday.

The picture was old, a close-up taken on a long-ago family vacation.

The headshot showed her beaming smile, the bright eyes behind the lenses of her glasses. Jack's own eyes burned so badly that he had to blink a few times before he could read beyond her name, Marlene Estes McKenzie.

She'd died at home, according to the writer of the obit, surrounded by family and friends. In lieu of flowers, her husband and sons requested that donations be made to a well-known foundation dedicated to fighting breast cancer.

Breast cancer.

Jack breathed deeply until his emotions were at least somewhat under control, then, against his better judgment, he reached for Ashley's phone, dialed the familiar number.

"Dr. McKenzie's residence," a woman's voice chimed.

Jack couldn't speak for a moment.

"Hello?" the woman asked pleasantly. "Is anyone there? Hello?"

He finally found his voice. "My name is—Mark Ramsey. Is the doctor around?"

"I'm so sorry," came the answer. "My husband is out of town at a convention, but either of his sons would be happy to see you if this is an emergency."

"It isn't," Jack said. Then, with muttered thanks, he quietly hung up.

He got out of the chair, walked to the window, looked out at the street. A blue pickup truck drove past. The house opposite Ashley's blurred.

All this time, Jack had imagined his mother visiting his grave at Arlington. Squaring her shoulders, sniffling a little, mourning her firstborn's "heroic" death in Iraq. Instead, she'd been lying in a grave of her own.

He rubbed his eyes with a thumb and forefinger.

How long had his dad waited, after his first wife's death, to remarry?

What kind of person was the new Mrs. McKenzie? Did Dean and Jim and Bryce like her?

Jack ached to call Ashley, needed to hear her voice.

But what would he say? *Hi, I just found out my mother died three years ago?* He wasn't sure he'd be able to get through the sentence without breaking down.

He moved away from the window. No sense making a target of himself.

The night grew darker, colder and lonelier.

And still Jack didn't turn on a light. Nor did he head for the kitchen to raid Ashley's refrigerator, even though he hadn't eaten since breakfast.

He'd done a lot of waiting in his life. He'd waited for

precisely the right moment to rescue children and dip-lomats and wealthy businessmen held for ransom. He'd waited to be rescued himself once, with nearly every bone in his body broken.

Waiting was harder now.

In his mind, he heard the voice of a young soldier. "You'll be all right now, sir. We're United States Ma-rines."

Jack's throat tightened further.

And then the throwaway cell phone rang.

Sweat broke out on Jack's upper lip. He'd spoken to Vince over Ashley's phone. He'd warned Ardith not to use the cell number again, in case it was being moni-tored.

It was unlikely that the FBI would be calling him up to chat. They had their own ways of getting in touch.

Holding his breath, he pressed the Talk button, but didn't speak.

"I'll find you," Chad Lombard said.

"Why don't I make it easy for you?" Jack answered lightly.

"Like, how?" Lombard asked, a smirk in his voice.

"We agree on a time and place to meet. One way or another, this thing will be over."

Lombard laughed. "I must be crazy. I kind of like that idea. It has a high-noon sort of appeal. But how do I know you'll come alone, and not with a swarm of FBI and DEA agents?"

"How do I know *you'll* come alone?" Jack countered.

"I guess we'll just have to trust each other."

"Yeah, right. When and where, hotshot?"

"I'll be in touch about that," Lombard said lightly. "Oh, and by the way, I've already killed you, for all intents and purposes. The poison ought to be in your bone marrow by now, eating up your red blood cells. Still, I'd like to be around to see you shut down, Robocop."

Jack's stomach clenched, but his voice came out sounding even and in charge.

"I'll be waiting to hear from you," he said, and hung up.

## CHAPTER SEVEN

*OH, AND BY THE WAY, I've already killed you, for all intents and purposes. The poison ought to be in your bone marrow by now, eating up your red blood cells.*

Lombard's words pulsed somewhere in the back of Jack's mind, like a distant drumbeat. The man was a skilled liar—and that was one of his more admirable traits, but this time, instinct said he was telling the truth.

Jack had never been afraid of death, and he still wasn't. But he was *very* afraid of leaving Ashley exposed to dangers she couldn't possibly imagine, even after all he'd told her. Tanner and her brother would *try* to protect her, and they were both men to be reckoned with, but were they in the same league with Lombard and his henchmen?

One-on-one, Lombard was no match for either of them.

The trouble was, Lombard never *went* one-on-one; he was too big a coward for that.

Coupled with the news of his mother's passing, *three years ago,* the knowledge that some concoction of jungle-plant extracts and nasty chemicals was already devouring his bone marrow left Jack reeling a little.

*Suck it up, McCall,* he thought. *One crisis at a time.*

It was after midnight when a local cab pulled up in front of Ashley's house.

Jack watched nervously from the study window as Vince got out of the front passenger seat, tucking his wallet into the back pocket of his chinos as he did so, and then opened the rear door, curbside.

Rachel scrambled out to the sidewalk, standing with her small hands on her hips like some miniature queen surveying her kingdom. She was soon followed by a much less confident Ardith, hunched over in a black trench coat and hooded scarf.

The cab drove away, and Vince steered Ardith and Rachel up the front walk.

Jack was quick to open the door; Rachel flashed past him, clad in jeans and a blue coat that looked like it might have been rescued from a thrift store, with Ardith slinking along behind.

"A *cab?*" Jack bit out, the minute he and Vince came face-to-face on the unlighted porch.

"Hide in plain sight," Vince said casually.

Jack let it pass for the moment, mainly because Rachel was tugging at the back of his shirt in a rapidly escalating effort to get his attention.

"My name is Charlotte now," she announced, "but you can still call me Rachel if you want to."

Jack grinned. He wanted to hoist the child into his arms, but didn't. After the conversation with Lombard, he couldn't quite shake the vision of his bones going hollow, caving in on themselves at the slightest exertion. He would need all his strength to deal with the inevitable.

*Get over it,* he told himself. If he lived long enough, he would check into a hospital, find out whether or not he was a candidate for a marrow transplant. In the meantime, there were other priorities, like keeping Rachel and Ashley and Ardith alive from one moment to the next.

"Are you hungry?" Jack asked, thinking of Ashley's freezer full of cherry crepes and other delicacies. God, what would it be like to live like a normal man—marry Ashley, live in this house, this Norman Rockwell town, for good?

"Just tired," Ardith said. Even trembling inside the bulky raincoat, she looked stick-thin, at least fifteen pounds lighter than the last time he'd seen her. And Ardith hadn't had all that much weight to spare in the first place.

"Yes!" Rachel blurted, the word toppling over the top of her mother's answer. "I'm *starved.*"

"I wouldn't mind something to gnaw on myself," Vince said, his gaze slightly narrowed as he studied his boss, there in the dimness of Ashley's entryway.

"We rode in a helicopter!" Rachel sang out, on the way to the kitchen.

Jack stopped at the base of the stairs, conscious of Ardith's exhaustion. She seemed to exude it through every pore. The unseen energy of despair vibrated around her, pervaded Jack's personal space.

"You two go on to the kitchen," Jack told Vince and the little girl, indicating the direction with a motion of one hand. "Help yourselves to whatever you find." Although he kept his tone even, the glance he gave the pilot said, *We'll talk about the cab later.*

Jack did not regard himself as a hard man to work for—sure, his standards were high, but he paid top wages, provided health insurance and a generous retirement plan for his few but carefully chosen employees. On the other hand, he didn't tolerate carelessness of any kind, and Vince knew that.

Vince grimaced slightly, keenly aware of Jack's meaning, and shepherded Rachel toward the kitchen.

"Don't burn too many lights," Jack added, "and stay away from the windows."

Vince stiffened at the predictability of the order, but he didn't turn around to give Jack a ration of crap, the way he might have done in less dire circumstances.

Jack shifted his gaze to Ardith, but she'd turned her face away. He put a hand to the small of her back and ushered her up the stairs.

"Are you all right?" he asked quietly.

"I'm scared to death," Ardith replied, still without looking at him.

Even through the raincoat and whatever she was wearing underneath, Jack could feel the knobbiness of her spine against the palm of his hand.

"When is this going to be over, Jack?" she blurted, when they'd reached the top. She was staring at him now, her eyes huge and black with sorrow and fear. "When can I go back to my husband and my children?"

"When it's safe," Jack said, but he was thinking, *When Chad Lombard is on a slab.*

*"When it's safe!"* Ardith echoed. "You know as well as I do that 'when it's safe' might be *never!*"

She was right about that; unless he took Lombard out, once and for all, she and Rachel would probably have to keep running.

"You can't think that way," Jack pointed out. "You'll drive yourself crazy if you do." He guided her toward the room across from his, the one Ashley had set aside for Ardith and Rachel.

Although he'd been the one to send Ashley away, he wished for a brief and fervent moment that she had stayed. Being a woman, she'd know how to calm and comfort Ardith in ways that would probably never enter his testosterone-saturated brain.

And he needed to tell *somebody* that his mother had died. He couldn't confide in Vince—they didn't have that kind of relationship. Ardith had enough problems of her own, and Rachel was a little kid.

Jack opened the door of the small but still spacious suite, with its flowery bedspreads, lace curtains and bead-fringed lamps. He'd closed the shutters earlier, and laid the makings of a fire on the hearth.

Taking a match from the box on the mantel, he lit the wadded newspaper and dry kindling, watched with primitive satisfaction as the blaze caught.

Ardith looked around, finally shrugged out of the raincoat.

"I want to call Charles," she said, clearly expecting a refusal. "I haven't talked to my husband since—"

"If you want to put him and the other kids in Lombard's crosshairs, Ardith," Jack said evenly, giving her a sidelong glance as he straightened, then stood there, soaking in the warmth of the fire, "you go right ahead."

She was boney as hell, beneath a turquoise running suit that must have been two sizes too big for her, and her once-beautiful face looked gaunt, her cheekbones protruding, her skin gray and slack. She'd aged a decade since gathering her small daughter close in that airport.

Ardith glanced toward the open door of the suite, then turned her gaze back to Jack's face. "I have two other children besides Rachel," she said slowly.

Jack added wood to the fire, now that it was crackling, and replaced the screen. Turned to Ardith with his arms folded across his chest.

"Meaning what?" he asked, afraid he already knew what she was about to say.

She sagged, limp-kneed, onto the side of one of the twin beds, her head down. "Meaning," she replied, after biting down so hard on her lower lip that Jack half expected to see blood, "that Chad is wearing me down."

Jack went to the door, peered out into the hall, found it empty. In the distance, he could hear Vince and Rachel in the kitchen. Pans were clattering, and the small countertop TV was on.

He shut the door softly. "Don't even tell me you're thinking of turning Rachel over to Lombard," he said.

A tear slithered down one of Ardith's pale cheeks, and she didn't move to wipe it away. Maybe she wasn't even aware that she was crying. Her eyes blazed, searing into Jack. "Are you judging me, Mr. McCall? May I remind you that you work for me?"

"May I remind you," Jack retorted calmly, "that Lombard is an international drug runner? That he tortures and kills people on a regular basis—for fun?"

Ardith dragged in a breath so deep it made her entire body quiver. "I wish I'd never gotten involved with him."

"Get in line," Jack said. "I'm sure your parents would agree, along with your present husband. The fact is, you *did* 'get involved,' in a big way, and now you've got a seven-year-old daughter who deserves all the courage and strength you can muster up."

"I'm running on empty, Jack. I can't keep this up much longer."

"Where does that leave Rachel?"

Misery throbbed in her eyes. "With you?" she asked, in a small voice. "She'd be safe, I know she would, and—"

"And you could go back home and pretend none of this ever happened? That you never met Lombard and gave birth to his child—*your* child?"

"You make me sound horrible!"

Jack thrust out a sigh. "Look, I know this is hard. It's *worse* than hard. But you can't bail on that little girl, Ardith. Deep down, you don't even want to. You've got to tough this out, for Rachel's sake and your own."

"What if I can't?" Ardith whispered.

"You can, Ardith, because you don't have a choice."

"Couldn't the FBI or the DEA help? Find her another family—?"

*"Christ,"* Jack said. "You can't be serious."

Ardith fell onto her side on the bed, her knees drawn up to her chest in a fetal position, and sobbed, deeply and with a wretchedness that tore at the fabric of his soul. It was one of the worst sounds Jack had ever heard.

"You're exhausted," he said. "You'll feel different when you've had something to eat and a good night's sleep. We'll come up with some kind of solution, Ardith. I promise."

Footsteps sounded on the stairs, then in the hallway, and Rachel burst in. "Mommy, we found beef stew in the fridge and—" she stopped, registering the sight her mother made, lying there on the bed. Worry contorted the child's face, made her shoulders go rigid. "Why are you crying?"

Stepping behind Rachel so she couldn't see him, Jack glared a warning at Ardith.

Ardith stopped wailing, sat up, sniffled and dashed at her cheeks with the backs of both hands. "I was just missing your daddy and the other kids," she said. She straightened her spine, snatched tissues from a decorative box on the table between the beds, and blew her nose.

"I miss them, too," Rachel said. "And Grambie and Gramps, too."

Ardith nodded, set the tissue aside. "I know, sweetheart," she said. Somehow, she summoned up a smile, misty and faltering, but a smile nonetheless. "Did someone mention beef stew? I could use something like that."

Rachel's attention had shifted to the cheery fireplace. "We get our own *fireplace?*" she enthused.

Jack thought back to the five days he and Rachel had spent navigating that South American jungle after he'd nabbed her from Lombard's remote estate. They'd dealt with mosquitoes, snakes, chattering monkeys with a penchant for throwing things at them, and long, dark nights with little to cover them but the stars and the weighted, humid air.

Rachel hadn't complained once. When they were traveling, she got to ride on Jack's back or shoulders, and she enjoyed it wholeheartedly. She'd chattered incessantly, every waking moment, about all the things she'd have to tell her mommy, her stepfather, and her little brother and sister when they were together again.

"Your own fireplace," Jack confirmed, his voice husky.

He and Ardith exchanged glances, and then they all went downstairs, to the kitchen, for some of Ashley's beef stew.

ASHLEY WAITED UNTIL she was sure Olivia and Tanner were sound asleep, then crept out of the guest suite. The night nurse sat in front of the television set in the den, sound asleep.

Behind Ashley, Mrs. Wiggins mewed.

Ashley turned, a finger to her lips, hoisted the kitten up for a nuzzle, then carried the little creature back into the suite, set her down, and carefully closed the door.

Her eyes burned as the kitten meowed at being left behind.

Reaching the darkened and empty kitchen, Ashley let out her breath, going over the plan she'd spent several hours rehearsing in her head.

She would disable the alarm, then reset it before closing the door behind her. Drive slowly out to the main road, waiting until she reached the mailboxes before turning her headlights on.

Ginger, snoozing on her dog bed in the corner, lifted her golden head, gave Ashley a slow, curious once-over.

Ashley put a finger to her lips, just as she'd done earlier, with the kitten.

A voice bloomed in her mind.

*Don't go,* it said.

Ashley blinked. Stared at the dog. Shook her head.

No. She had *not* received a telepathic message from Olivia's dog. She was still keyed up from the family meeting, and worried about Jack, and her imagination was running away with her, that was all.

*I'll tell,* the silent, internal voice warned. *All I have to do is bark.*

"Hush," Ashley said, fumbling in her purse for her car keys. "I'm not hearing this. It's all in my head."

*"It's snowing."*

Unnerved, Ashley tried to ignore Ginger, who had now risen on all four paws, as though prepared to carry out a threat she couldn't possibly have made.

Ashley went to the nearest window, the one over the sink, and peered through it, squinting.

Snowflakes the size of golf balls swirled past the glass.

Ashley glanced back at Ginger in amazement. "Well, it *is* January," she rationalized.

*"You can't drive in this blizzard."*

"Stop it," Ashley said, though she couldn't have said whether she was talking to the golden retriever or to herself. Or both.

The dog simply stood there, ready to bark.

*Nonsense,* Ashley thought. *Olivia hears animals.* You don't.

Still, either her imagination or the dog had a point. Her small hybrid car wouldn't make it out of the driveway in weather like that. The yard was probably under a foot of snow, and visibility would be zero, if not worse.

She had to think.

As quietly as possible, she drew back a chair at the big kitchen table and sat down.

Ginger relaxed a little, but she was still watchful.

Just sitting at that table caused Ashley to flash back to the family meeting earlier that evening. Meg and Brad, Melissa, Olivia and Tanner—even Sophie and Carly and little Mac, had all been there.

As the eldest of the four O'Ballivan siblings, Brad had been the main spokesperson.

"Ashley," he'd said, "you're not going home until McCall is gone. And Tanner and I plan to make sure he is, first thing in the morning."

She'd gaped at her brother, understanding his reasoning but stung to fury just the same. Looking around, she'd seen the same grim determination in Tanner's face, Olivia's, even Melissa's.

Outraged, she'd reminded them all that she was an adult and would come and go as she pleased, thank you very much.

Only Sophie and Carly had seemed even remotely sympathetic, but neither of them had spoken up on her behalf.

"You can't hold me prisoner here," Ashley had protested, her heart thumping, adrenaline burning through her veins like acid.

"Oh, yeah," Brad had answered, his tone and expression utterly implacable. "We can."

She'd decided right then that she'd get out—yes, their intentions were good, but it was the principle of the thing—but she'd also kept her head. She'd pretended to agree.

She'd helped make supper.

She'd loaded the dishwasher afterward.

She'd even rocked one of the babies—John, she thought—to sleep after Olivia had nursed him.

The evening had seemed endless.

Finally, Meg and Brad had left, taking Mac and Carly with them. Sophie, having finished her homework, had given Ashley a hug before retiring to her room for the night.

Ashley had yawned a lot and vanished into her own lush quarters.

She'd taken a hot bath, put on her pajamas and one of Olivia's robes, watched a little television—some mindless reality show.

And she'd waited, listening to the old-new house settle around her, Mrs. Wiggins curled up on her lap, as though trying to hold her new mistress in her chair with that tiny, weightless body of hers.

Once she was sure the coast was clear, Ashley had quietly dressed, never thinking to check the weather. Such was her state of distraction.

Now, here she sat, alone in her sister's kitchen at one-thirty in the morning, engaged in a standoff with a talking dog.

"I can take the Suburban," she whispered to Ginger. "It will go anywhere."

*"What's so important?"* Ginger seemed to ask.

Ashley shook her head again, rubbed her temples with the fingertips of both hands. "Jack," she said, keeping her voice down because, one, she didn't want to be overheard and stopped from leaving and, two, she was talking to a *dog,* for pity's sake. "*Jack* is so important. He's sick. And something is wrong. I can feel it."

*"You could ask Tanner to go into town and help him out."*

Ashley blinked. Was this really happening? If the conversation *was* only in her mind, why did the other side of it just pop up without her framing the words first?

"I can't do that," she said. "Olivia and the babies might need him."

Resolved, she rose from her chair, crossed to the wooden rack where Olivia kept various keys, and helped herself to the set that would unlock and start the venerable old Suburban.

She jingled the key ring at Ginger.

"Go ahead," she said. "Bark."

Ginger gave a huge sigh. *"I'll give you a five-minute head start,"* came the reply, *"then I'm raising the roof."*

"Fair enough," Ashley agreed, scrambling into Big John's old woolen coat, the one Olivia wore when she was working, hoping it would give her courage. "Thanks."

*"I was in love once,"* Ginger said, sounding wistful.

Ashley moved to the alarm-control panel next to the back door. Racked her brain for the code, which Olivia had given to her in case of emergency, finally remembered it.

Grabbed her coat and dashed over the threshold.

The cold slammed into her like something solid and heavy, with sharp teeth.

Her car was under a mound of snow, the Suburban a larger mound beside it. Perhaps because of the emotions stirred by the family meeting, Tanner had forgotten to park the rigs in the spacious garage with his truck, the way he normally would have on a winter's night.

Hastily, she climbed onto the running board and wiped off the windshield with one arm, grateful for the heavy, straw-scented weight of her grandfather's old coat, even though it nearly swallowed her. Then she opened the door of the Suburban, got in and rammed the key into the ignition.

The engine sputtered once, then again, and finally roared to life.

Ashley threw it into Reverse, backed into the turn-around, spun her wheels for several minutes in the deep snow.

Swearing under her breath, she slammed the steering wheel with one fist, missed it, and hit the horn instead.

"Do. Not. Panic," she told herself out loud.

Just how many minutes had passed, she wondered frantically. Had Ginger already started barking? Had anyone heard the Suburban's horn when she hit it by accident?

She drew a deep breath, thrust it out in a whoosh.

No, she decided.

Lights would be coming on in the house if the dog were raising a ruckus. The howling wind had probably covered the bleat of the horn.

She shifted the Suburban into the lowest gear, tried again to get the old wreck moving. It finally tore free of the snowbank, the wheels grabbing.

As she turned the vehicle around and zoomed down the driveway, she heard the alarm system go off in the house, even over the wind and the noise of the engine.

Crap. She'd either forgotten to reset the system, or done it incorrectly.

Looking in the rearview mirror would have been useless, since the back window was coated with snow and frost, so Ashley sped up and raced toward the main road, praying she wouldn't hit a patch of ice and spin off into the ditch.

*I'm sorry,* she told Tanner and Olivia, the babies and Sophie and the night nurse, the alarm shrieking like a convention of angry banshees behind her. *I'm so sorry.*

HER KITCHEN WAS completely dark.

Shivering from the cold and from the harrowing ride into town, Ashley shut the door behind her, dropped her key into the pocket of Big John's coat and reached for the light switch.

"Don't move," a stranger's voice commanded. A *male* stranger's voice.

Flipping the switch was a reflex; light spilled from the fluorescent panels in the ceiling, revealing a man she'd never seen before—or had she?—seated at her table, holding a gun on her.

"Who are you?" she asked, amazed to discover that she could speak, she was so completely terrified.

The man stood, the gun still trained squarely on her central body mass. "The pertinent question here, lady, is who are *you?*"

A strange boldness surged through Ashley, fear borne high on a flood of pure, indignant rage. "I am Ashley O'Ballivan," she said evenly, "and this is my house."

"Oh," the man said.

Just then, the inside door swung open and Jack was there, brandishing a gun of his own.

What was this? Ashley wondered wildly. Tombstone?

"Lay it down, Vince," Jack said, his voice stone-cold.

Vince complied, though not with any particular grace. The gun made an ominous thump on the tabletop. "Chill, man," he said. "You told me to stand watch and that's all I was doing."

Ashley's gaze swung back to Jack. She was furious and relieved, and a host of other things, too, all at once.

"I do not allow firearms in my house," she said.

Vince chuckled.

Jack told him to get lost, shoving his own pistol into the front of his pants. The move was too expert, too deft, and the gun itself looked military.

Vince ambled out of the room, shaking his head once as he passed Jack.

"What are you doing here?" Jack asked, as though *she* were the intruder.

"Do I have to say it?" Ashley countered, flinging her purse aside, fighting her way out of Big John's coat, which suddenly felt like a straightjacket. *"I live here, Jack."*

"I thought we agreed that you wouldn't come back until I gave you a heads-up," Jack said, keeping his distance.

Considering Ashley's mood, that was a wise decision on his part, even if he *was* armed and almost certainly dangerous.

"I changed my mind," she replied, tight-lipped, her arms folded stubbornly across her chest. "And who is that—that *person,* anyway?"

"Vince works for me," Jack said.

Another car crunched into the driveway. A door slammed.

Jack swore, untucking his shirt so the fabric covered the gun in the waistband of his jeans.

Tanner slammed through the back door.

"Well," Jack observed mildly, "the gang's all here."

"Not yet," Tanner snapped. "Brad's on his way. What the *hell* is going on, Ashley? You set off the alarm, the dog is probably *still* barking her brains out, and the babies are permanently traumatized—not to mention Sophie and Olivia!"

"I'm sorry," Ashley said.

A cell phone rang, somewhere on Tanner's person.

He pulled the device from his coat pocket, after fumbling a lot, squinted at the caller ID panel and took the call. "She's at her place," he said, probably to Olivia. A crimson flush climbed his neck, pulsed in his jaw.

And his anger was nothing compared to what Brad's would be. "No, don't worry—I think things are under control…"

Ashley closed her eyes.

Brakes squealed outside.

Tanner's voice seemed to recede, and then the call ended.

Brad nearly tore down the door in his hurry to get inside.

Jack looked around, his expression drawn but pleasant.

"Cherry crepes, anyone?" he asked mildly.

## CHAPTER EIGHT

"I KNOW A PLACE the woman and the little girl will be safe," Brad said wearily, once the excitement had died down and Ashley, her brother, Jack and Tanner were calmly seated around her kitchen table, eating the middle-of-the-night breakfast she'd prepared to keep from going out of her mind with anxiety.

Vince, the man with the gun, was conspicuously absent, while Ardith and Rachel slept on upstairs. Remarkably, the uproar hadn't awakened them, probably because they were so worn-out.

Jack shifted in his chair, pushed back his plate. For a man who believed so strongly in bacon and eggs, he hadn't eaten much. "Where?" he asked.

"Nashville," Brad replied. Then he threw out the name of one of the biggest stars in country music. "She's a friend," he added, as casually as if just *anybody* could wake up a famous woman in the middle of the night and ask her to shelter a pair of strangers for an indefinite length of time. "And she's got more high-tech security than the president. Bodyguards, the whole works."

"She'd do that?" Jack asked, grimly impressed.

Brad raised one shoulder in a semblance of a shrug. "I'd do it for her, and she knows that," he said easily. "We go way back."

"Sounds good to me," Tanner put in, relaxing a little. Everyone, naturally, was showing the strain.

"Me, too," Jack admitted, and though he didn't sigh, Ashley sensed the depths of his relief. "How do we get them there?"

"Very carefully," Brad said. "I'll take care of it."

Jack seemed to weigh his response for a long time before giving it. "There's a woman's life at stake here," he said. "And a little girl's future."

"I get that," Brad answered. His gaze slid to Ashley, then moved back to Jack's face, hardening again. "Of course, I want something in return."

Ashley held her breath.

Jack maintained eye contact with Brad. "What?"

"You, gone," Brad said. "For good."

"Now, *wait just one minute*—" Ashley sputtered.

"He's right," Jack said. "Lombard wants me, Ashley, not you. And I intend to keep it that way."

"So when do we make the move?" Tanner asked.

"Now," Brad responded evenly, a muscle bunching in his jawline. He could surely feel Ashley's glare boring into him. "I can have a jet at the airstrip within an hour or two, and I think we need to get them out of here before sunrise."

"Can't you let Rachel and her mother rest, just for this one night?" Ashley demanded. "They must be absolutely exhausted by all this—"

"It has to be tonight," Brad insisted.

Jack nodded, sighed as he got to his feet. "Make the calls," he told Brad. "I'll get them out of bed."

Things were moving too fast. Ashley gripped the table edge, swaying with a sudden sensation of teetering on the brink of some bottomless abyss. "Wait," she said.

She might as well have been invisible, inaudible. A ghost haunting her own house, for all the attention anyone paid her.

Brad was already reaching for his cell phone. "When I get back from Nashville," he said, watching Jack, "I expect you to be history."

Jack nodded, avoiding Ashley's desperate gaze. "It's a deal," he said, and left the room.

Ashley immediately sprang out of her chair, without the faintest idea of what she would do next.

Tanner took a gentle hold on her wrist and eased her back down onto the cushioned seat.

Brad placed a call to his friend. Apologized for waking her up. Exchanged a few pleasantries—yes, Meg was fine and Mac was growing like a weed, and sure there would be other kids. Give him time.

Ashley listened in helpless sorrow as he went on to explain the Ardith-Rachel situation and ask for help.

The singer agreed immediately.

Brad called for a private jet. He might as well have been ordering a pizza, he was so casual about it. Only with a pizza, he would at least have had to give a credit card number.

When Brad said "jump," the response was invariably, "How high?"

Because she'd always known him as her big brother, the broad scope of his power always came as a surprise to her.

Things accelerated after the phone calls.

Resigned, Ashley got to work preparing food for the

trip, so Ardith and Rachel wouldn't starve, though the jet probably offered catered meals.

Her guests stumbled sleepily into the kitchen just as she was finishing, herded there by Jack, their clothes rumpled and hastily donned, their eyes glazed with confusion, weariness and fear.

The little girl favored Ashley with a wan, blinking smile. "Have you been taking care of Jack?" she asked.

Ashley's heart turned over. "I've been trying," she said truthfully, studiously ignoring Brad, Tanner and Jack himself.

Vince had wandered in behind them. "Want me to go along for the ride?" he asked, meeting no one's eyes.

"No," Jack said tersely. "You're done here."

"For good?" Vince asked.

"For now," Jack replied.

Vince turned to Brad. "Catch a ride to the airstrip with you?"

Jack gave the man a quick glance, his eyes ever so slightly narrowed. "I'll take you there myself," he said, adding a brisk, "Later."

"You stopped trusting me, boss?" Vince asked, with an odd grin.

"Maybe," Jack said.

Some of the color drained from Vince's face. "Am I fired?"

"Don't push it," Jack answered.

In the end, it was decided that Tanner would drive Vince back to his helicopter once Brad, Ardith and Rachel were aboard the jet, ready for takeoff. Later, Tanner would see that Jack boarded a commercial airliner in Flagstaff, bound for Somewhere Else.

Holding back tears, Ashley handed her brother the

food she'd packed, tucked into a basket with a cheery red-and-white-checkered napkin for a cover.

Something softened in Brad's eyes as he accepted the offering, but he didn't say anything.

And neither did Ashley.

A gulf had opened between Ashley and the big brother she had always loved and admired, far wider than the one created by their mother's death. Even knowing he was doing what he thought was right— what probably *was* right—Ashley felt steamrolled, and she resented it.

Soon, Brad was gone, along with Ardith and Rachel.

Approximately an hour later, Tanner and the chastened Vince left, too.

Jack and Ashley sat on opposite sides of the kitchen table, unable to look at each other.

After a long, long time, Jack said, "My mother died three years ago. And I didn't have a clue."

Startled, Ashley sat up straighter in her chair. "I'm sorry," she said.

"Breast cancer," Jack explained gruffly, his eyes moist.

"Oh, Jack. That's terrible."

He nodded. Sighed heavily.

"I guess this is our last night together," Ashley said, at some length.

"I guess so," Jack agreed miserably.

Purpose flowed through Ashley. "Then let's make it count," she said. She locked the back door. She flipped off the lights. And then she took Jack's hand, there in the darkness, and led him upstairs to her bed.

Every moment, every gesture, was precious, and very nearly sacred.

Jack undressed Ashley the way an archeologist might uncover a fragile treasure, with a cherishing tenderness that stirred not only her body, but her soul. Head back, she surrendered her naked breasts to him, reveled in the sensations wrought by his lips and tongue.

A low, crooning sound escaped her, and she found just enough control to open his shirt, her fingers fumbling with the buttons. She needed to feel his flesh, bare and hard, yet warm against her palms and splayed fingers.

They kissed, long and deep, with a sweet urgency all the better for the smallest delay.

In time, Jack eased her onto the bed, sideways, and spread her legs to nuzzle and then suckle her until she was gasping with need and exaltation.

She whispered his name, a ragged sound, and tears burned in her eyes. How would she live without him, without this? How colorless her days would be, when he was gone, and how empty her nights. He'd taught her body to crave these singular pleasures, to need them as much as she needed air and water and the light of the sun.

But, no, she thought sorrowfully. She mustn't spoil what was probably their last night together by leaving the moment, journeying into a lonely and uncertain future. It was *now* that mattered, and only now. Jack's hands on her inner thighs, Jack's mouth on the very center of her femininity.

Dear God, it felt so good, the way he was loving her, almost too good to be borne.

The first climax came softly, seizing her, making her buckle and moan in release.

"Don't stop," she pleaded, entangling her fingers in his hair.

She hoped he would *never* cut his hair short again.

He chuckled against her moist, straining flesh, nipped at her ever so lightly with his teeth and brought her to another orgasm, this one sharp and brief, a sudden and wild flexing deep within her. "Oh, I'm a long way from finished," he assured her gruffly, before falling to her again.

Ashley could never have said afterward how many times she rose and fell on the hot tide of primitive satisfaction, flailing and writhing and crying out with each new abandoning of her ordinary self.

When he finally took her, she gloried in the heat and length and hardness of him, in the pulsing and the renewed wanting. Her body became greedier than before, demanding, reaching, shuddering. And Jack drove deep, eventually losing control, but only after a long, delicious period of restraint.

They made love time and again that night, holding each other in silence while they recovered between bouts of fevered passion.

"I'll come back if I can," Jack told her, at one point, barely able to breathe, he was so spent. "Give me a year before you fall in love with somebody else, okay?"

A year. It seemed like an eternity to Ashley, she was so aware of every passing moment, every tick of the celestial clock. At the same time, though, she knew it was safe to promise. She'd wait a lifetime, a dozen lifetimes, because for her, there *was* no man but Jack.

She nodded, dampening his bare shoulder with her tears, and finally slept.

JACK EASED HIMSELF out of Ashley's arms, and her bed, around eight o'clock the next morning. It was one of those heartrendingly beautiful winter days, with sunlight glaring on pristine snow. Everything seemed to be draped in purity.

He dressed in his own room, gathered the few belongings he'd brought with him, and tucked them into his bag.

Given his druthers, he would have sat quietly in a chair, watching Ashley sleep, memorizing every line and curve of her, so he could hold her image in his mind and his heart until he died.

But Jack was the sort of man who rarely got his druthers.

He had things to do.

First, he'd meet with Chad Lombard.

If he survived that—and it was a crapshoot, whether he or Lombard or neither of them would walk away—he'd check himself into a hospital.

Feeling more alone than he ever had—and given some of the things he'd been through that was saying a lot—Jack gravitated to the computer in Ashley's study. He called up his dad's website, clicked to the Contact Us link, wrote an email he never intended to send.

*Hello, Dad. I'm alive, but not for long, probably...*

He went on to explain why he'd never come home from military school, why he'd let everyone in his family believe he was dead. He apologized for any pain they must have suffered because of his actions, and resisted the temptation to lay any of the blame on the Navy.

The mission had been a tough one, with a high price, but no one had held a gun to his head. He'd made the decision himself and, in most ways, he had never regretted it.

He went on to say that he hoped his mother hadn't had to endure too much pain, and asked for forgiveness. In sketchy terms, he described the toxin that was probably killing him.

In closing, he wrote, *You should know that I met a woman. If things were different, I'd love to settle down with her right here in this little Western town, raise a flock of kids with her. But some things aren't meant to be, and it's beginning to look as if this is one of them.*

*No matter how it may seem, I love you, Dad.*

*I'm sorry.*

*Jack.*

He was about to hit the Delete button—writing the piece had been a catharsis—when two things happened at once. His cell phone rang, and somebody knocked hard at the front door.

Simultaneously, Jack answered the call and admitted Tanner Quinn to the house he'd soon be leaving, probably forever.

No more cherry crepes.

No more mutant cat.

No more Ashley.

"Mercer?" Lombard asked affably, "is that you?"

Jack shifted to the Neal Mercer persona, because Lombard knew him by that name, gestured for Tanner to come inside, but be quiet about it.

Ashley was still sleeping, and Jack didn't want to wake her. Leaving was going to be hard enough, without a face-to-face good-bye.

On the other hand, didn't he owe her that much?

"What?" he asked Lombard.

"I've decided on a place for the showdown," Lombard said. "Tombstone, Arizona. Fitting, don't you think?"

"You're a regular John Wayne," Jack told him.

Tanner raised his eyebrows in silent question. Jack shook his head, pointed to his gear bag, waiting just inside the door.

Tanner picked up the bag, carried it out to his truck. The exhaust spewed white steam into the cold, bright air.

*Leavin' on a jet plane…* Jack thought.

"Tomorrow," Lombard went on. "High noon."

"High *drama,* you mean," Jack scoffed.

"Be there," Lombard ordered, dead serious now, and hung up.

Jack sighed and clicked the phone shut.

Glanced up at the ceiling.

Tanner returned from the luggage run, waiting with his big rancher's hands stuffed into the pockets of his sheepskin coat.

"Give me a minute," Jack said.

Tanner nodded, his eyes full of sympathy.

Jack turned from that. Sympathy wasn't going to help him now.

He had to be strong. Stronger than he'd ever been.

Upstairs, he entered Ashley's room, sat down on the edge of the bed, and watched her for a few luxurious moments, moments he knew he would cherish until he died, whether that was in a day, or several decades.

Ashley opened her eyes, blinked. Said his name.

For a lot of years, Jack had claimed he didn't have a heart. For all his money, love was something he simply couldn't afford.

Now he knew he'd lied—to himself and everyone else.

He had a heart, all right, and it was breaking.

"I love you," he said. "Always have, always will."

She sat up, threw her arms around his neck, clung to him for a few seconds. "I love you, too," she murmured, trembling against him. Then she drew back, looked deep into his eyes. "Thanks," she said.

"For—?" Jack ground out the word.

"The time we had. For not leaving without saying good-bye."

He nodded, not trusting himself to speak just then.

"If you can come back—"

Jack drew out of her embrace, stood. In the cold light of day, returning to Stone Creek, to Ashley, seemed unlikely, a golden dream he'd used to get through the night.

He nodded again. Swallowed hard.

And then he left.

HE WAS BOARDING a plane in Flagstaff, nearly two hours later, before he remembered that he hadn't closed the email he'd drafted on Ashley's computer, spilling his guts to his father.

Ashley wasn't exactly a techno-whiz, he thought, with a sad smile, but if she stumbled upon the message somehow, she'd know most of his secrets.

She might even send the thing, on some do-gooder impulse, though Jack doubted that. In any case, she'd know about the damage the toxin was doing to his bone marrow and be privy to his deepest regrets as far as his family was concerned.

She'd know he'd loved her, too. Wanted to spend his life with her.

That shining dream could still come true, he supposed, but a lot of chips would have to fall first, and land in just the right places. The odds, he knew, were against him.

Nothing new there.

He took his seat on the small commuter plane, fastened his seat belt, and shut off his cell phone.

Tanner had been right there when he'd bought his ticket—he'd chosen Phoenix, said he'd probably head for South America from there, and gone through all the proper steps, checking his gear bag and filling out a form declaring that there was a firearm inside, properly secured.

What he *didn't* tell his friend was that he planned to charter a flight to Tombstone as soon as he reached Phoenix and have it out with Chad Lombard, once and for all.

Takeoff was briefly delayed, due to some mechanical issue.

During the wait, Jack switched his phone on again, placed a short call that drew an alarmed stare from the woman sitting next to him and smiled as he put the cell away.

"Air marshal," he explained, in an affable undertone.

The woman didn't look reassured. In fact, she moved to an empty seat three rows forward. A word to the flight attendants about the man in 7-B and he'd be off the plane, tangled in a snarl with a pack of TSA agents until three weeks after forever.

For some reason, she didn't report him. Maybe she didn't watch the news a lot, or fly much.

Jack settled back, closed his eyes, and tried not to think about Ashley and the baby they might have conceived together, the future they might have shared.

That proved impossible, of course, like the old game of trying not to think about a pink elephant.

The plane lifted off, bucked through some turbulence and streaked toward his destiny—and Chad Lombard's.

CARLY MCKETTRICK O'BALLIVAN watched her aunt with concern, while Meg, who was both Carly's sister *and* her adoptive mother—how weird was that?—puttered around the big kitchen, trying to distract Ashley.

Meg was expecting a baby, and the news might have cheered Ashley up, but Carly and her mother-sister had agreed on the way into town to wait until Brad-dad was back from wherever he'd gone.

Unable to bear Ashley's pale face and sorrowful eyes any longer, Carly excused herself and wandered toward the study. She'd set up the computer, she decided. Use this strange morning constructively.

School was closed on account of megasnow, but nothing stopped members of the McKettrick clan when they wanted to get somewhere. Meg had told Carly they were going to town, fired up her new Land Rover right after breakfast, acting all mysterious and sad, buckled a squirmy Mac into his car seat, and off they'd gone.

Carly, a sucker for adventure, had enjoyed the ride into town, over roads buried under a foot of snow. Once, Meg had even taken an overland route, causing Mac to giggle and Carly to shout, "Yee-haw!"

Even the plows weren't out yet—that's how deep the stuff was.

To Carly's surprise, someone had beaten her to the computer gig. The monitor was dark, but the machine was on, whirring quietly away in the otherwise silent room.

She sat down in the swivel chair, touched the mouse.

An email message popped up on the monitor screen.

Since Brad and Meg were big on personal privacy, Carly didn't actually read the email, but she couldn't help noticing that it was signed, "Love, Jack."

She barely knew Jack McCall, but she'd liked him. Which was more than could be said for Brad and Meg.

They clearly thought the man was bad news.

Carly bit her lower lip. If Jack had gone to all the trouble of writing that long email, she reasoned, her heart thumping a little, surely he'd intended to send it.

With so much going on—Carly had no idea what any of it actually was, except that it had obviously done a real number on Ashley, so it must be pretty heavy stuff—he'd probably just forgotten.

Carly took a deep breath, moved the cursor, and hit Send.

"Carly!" Meg called, clearly approaching.

Carly closed the message panel. "What?"

Meg appeared in the doorway of the study. "School's open after all," she said. "I just heard it on the kitchen radio."

Carly sighed. "Awesome," she said, meaning exactly the opposite.

Meg chuckled. "Get a move on, kiddo," she ordered.

"Are there snowshoes around here someplace?" Carly countered. "Maybe a dogsled and a team, so I can *mush* to school?"

"Hugely funny," Meg said, grinning. Like all the other grown-ups, she looked tired. "I'd drive you to school in the Land Rover, but I don't think I should leave Ashley just yet."

Carly agreed, with the teenage reluctance that was

surely expected of her, and resigned herself to the loss of that greatest of all occasions, a snow day.

Trudging toward the high school minutes later, she wondered briefly if she should have left that email in the outbox, maybe told Meg or Ashley about it.

But her friends were converging up ahead, laughing and hurling snowballs at each other, and she hurried to join them.

ASHLEY BOTH HOPED FOR and dreaded a call from Jack, but none came.

Not while Meg and the baby were there, and not when they left.

A ranch hand from Starcross brought Mrs. Wiggins back home, and Ashley was glad and grateful, but still wrung out. She felt dazed, disjointed, as though she were truly beside herself.

She slept.

She cooked.

She slept some more, and then cooked some more.

At four o'clock that afternoon, Brad showed up.

"He's gone," she said, meaning Jack, meeting her taciturn-looking brother at the back door. "Are you happy now?"

"You know I'm not," Brad said, moving past her to enter the house when she would have blocked his way. He helped himself to coffee and, out of spite, Ashley didn't tell him it was decaf. If he expected a buzz from the stuff, something to jump-start the remainder of his day, he was in for a disappointment.

"Are Ardith and Rachel safe?" she asked.

"Yes," Brad answered, leaning back against the counter to sip his no-octane coffee and study her. "You all right?"

"Oh, I'm just fabulous, thank you."

"Ashley, give it up, will you? You know Jack couldn't stay."

"I also know the decision was mine to make, Brad— not yours."

Her brother gave a heavy sigh. She could see how drained he was, but she wouldn't allow herself to feel sorry for him. Much. "You'll get over this," he told her, after a long time.

"Gee, thanks," she said, wiping furiously at her already-clean counters, keeping as far from Brad as she could. "That makes it all better."

"Meg's going to have a baby," Brad said, out of the blue, a few uncomfortable moments later. "In the spring."

Ashley froze.

Olivia had twins.

Now Meg and Brad were adding to their family, something she should have been glad about, considering that Meg had suffered a devastating miscarriage a year after Mac was born and there had been some question as to whether or not she could have more children.

"Congratulations," Ashley said stiffly, unable to look at him.

"You'll get your chance, Ash. The right man will come along and—"

"The right man *came* along, Brad," Ashley snapped, "and now he's gone."

But at least, this time, Jack had said good-bye.

This time, he hadn't wanted to go.

Small consolations, but something.

Brad set his mug aside, crossed to Ashley, took her shoulders in his hands. "I'd have done anything," he said hoarsely, "to make this situation turn out differently."

Ashley believed him, but it didn't ease her pain.

She let herself cry, and Brad pulled her close and held her, big brother-style, his chin propped on top of her head.

"O'Ballivan tough," he reminded her. It was their version of something Meg's family, the McKettricks, said to each other when things got rocky.

"O'Ballivan tough," she agreed.

But her voice quavered when she said it.

She felt anything *but* tough.

She'd go on, just the same, because she had no other choice.

JACK ARRIVED IN Earp-country at eleven forty-five that morning and, after paying the pilot of the two-seat Cessna he'd chartered in Phoenix, climbed into a waiting taxi. Fortunately, Tombstone wasn't a big town, so he wouldn't be late for his meeting with Chad Lombard.

Anyway, he was used to cutting it close.

There were a lot of tourists around, as Jack had feared. He'd hoped the local police would be notified, find some low-key way to clear the streets before the shootout took place.

Some of them might be Lombard's men.

And some of them might be Feds.

Because of the innocent bystanders and because both the DEA and the FBI had valid business of their own with Lombard, Jack had taken a chance and tipped them off while waiting for the commuter jet to take off from Flagstaff.

He stashed his gear bag behind a toilet in a gas station restroom, tucked his Glock into his pants, covered it with his shirt and stepped out onto the windy street.

If he hadn't been in imminent danger of being picked off by Lombard or one of the creeps who worked for the bastard, he might have found the whole thing pretty funny.

He even amused himself by wishing he'd bought a round black hat and a gunslinger's coat, so he'd look the part.

Wyatt Earp, on the way to the OK Corral.

He was strolling down a wooden sidewalk, pretending to take in the famous sights, when the cell phone rang in the pocket of his jean jacket.

"Yo," he answered.

"You called in the Feds!" Lombard snarled.

"Yeah," Jack answered. "You're outnumbered, bucko."

"I'm going to take you out last," Lombard said. "Just so you can watch all these mommies and daddies and little kiddies in cowboy hats bite the freaking dust!"

Jack's blood ran cold. He'd known this was a very real possibility, of course—that was the main reason he'd called in reinforcements—but he'd hoped, against all reason, that even Lombard wouldn't sink that low.

After all, the man had a daughter of his own.

"Where are you?" Jack asked, with a calmness he sure as hell didn't feel. Worse yet, the weakness was rising inside him again, threatening to drop him to the ground.

Lombard laughed then, an eerie, brittle sound. "Look up," he said.

Jack lifted his eyes.

Lombard stood on a balcony overlooking the main street, opposite Jack. And he was wearing an Earp hat and a long coat, holding a rifle in one hand.

"Gun!" Jack yelled. "Everybody out of the street!"

The crowd panicked and scattered every which way, bumping into each other, screaming. Scrambling to shield children and old ladies and little dogs wearing neckerchiefs.

Lombard raised the rifle as Jack drew the Glock.

But neither of them got a chance to fire.

Another shot ripped through the shining January day, struck Lombard, and sent him toppling, in what seemed like slow motion, over the balcony railing, which gave way picturesquely behind him, like a bit from an old movie.

People shrieked in rising terror, as vulnerable to any gunmen Lombard might have brought along as backup as a bunch of ducks in a pond.

Feds rushed into the street, hustling the tourists into restaurants and hotel lobbies and souvenir shops, crowd control at its finest, if a little late.

Government firepower seemed to come out of the woodwork.

Somebody was taking pictures—Jack was aware of a series of flashes at the periphery of his vision.

He walked slowly toward the spot where Chad Lombard lay, either dead or dying, oblivious to the pandemonium he would have enjoyed so much.

Lombard stared blindly up at the blue, blue sky, a crimson patch spreading over the front of his collarless white shirt. Damned if he hadn't pinned a star-shaped badge to his coat, just to complete the outfit.

The Feds closed in, the sniper who had taken Lombard out surely among them. A hand came to rest on Jack's shoulder.

More pictures were snapped.

"Thanks, McCall," a voice said, through a buzzing haze.

He didn't look up at the agent, the longtime acquaintance he'd called from the plane in Flagstaff. Taking the cell phone out of his pocket, he turned it slowly in one hand, still studying Lombard.

Lombard didn't look like a killer, a drug runner. Jack could see traces of Rachel in the man's altar-boy features.

"We had trouble spotting him until he climbed out onto that balcony," Special Agent Fletcher said. "By our best guess, he stole the gunslinger getup from one of those old-time picture places—"

"Why didn't you clear the streets earlier?" Jack demanded.

"Because we got here about five seconds before you did," Fletcher answered. "Are you all right, McCall?"

Jack nodded, then shook his head.

Fletcher helped Jack to his feet. "Which is it?" he rasped. "Yes or no?"

Jack swayed.

His vision shrank to a pinpoint, then disappeared entirely.

"I guess it's no," he answered, just before he lost consciousness.

# *CHAPTER NINE*

THE FIRST SOUND Jack recognized was a steady *beep-beep-beep.* He was in a hospital bed, then, God knew where. Probably going about the business of dying.

"Jack?"

He struggled to open his eyes. Saw his father looming over him, a pretty woman standing wearily at the old man's side. If it hadn't been for her, Jack would have thought he was hallucinating.

Dr. William "Bill" McKenzie smiled, switched on the requisite lamp on the wall above Jack's head.

The spill of light made him wince.

"I see you've still got all your hair," Jack said, very slowly and in a dry-throated rasp. "Either that, or that's one fine rug perched on top of your head."

Bill laughed, though his eyes glistened with tears. Maybe they were good-bye tears. "You always were a smart-ass," he said. "This is my real hair. And speaking of hair, yours is too long. You look like a hippie."

People still used the word *hippie?*

Obviously, his dad's generation did. For all he knew, Bill McKenzie had been a hippie, once upon a time. There was so much they didn't know about each other.

"How did you find me?" Jack asked. The things he felt were too deep to leap right into—there had to be a transition here, a gradual shift.

"It wasn't too hard to track you down. You were all over the internet, the TV and the newspapers after that incident in Tombstone. You were treated in Phoenix, and then some congressman's aide got in touch with me—soon as you were strong enough, I had you brought home, where you belong."

*Home,* Jack thought. *To die?*

Jack's gaze slid to the woman, who looked uncomfortable. *My stepmother,* he thought, and felt a fresh pang of loss because his mom should have been standing there beside his dad, not this stranger.

"Abigail," Bill explained hoarsely. "My wife."

"If you'll excuse me," Abigail said, after a nod of greeting, and headed for the nearest exit.

Bill sighed, trailed her with his eyes.

Jack glimpsed tenderness in those eyes, and peace. "How long have I been here?" he asked, after a long time.

"Just a few days," Bill answered. He cleared his throat, looking for a moment as though he might make a run for the corridor, just as Abigail had done. "You're in serious condition, Jack. Not out of the woods by any means."

"Yeah," Jack said, trying to accept what was probably inevitable. "I know. And you're here to say goodbye?"

The old man's jaw clamped down hard, the way it used to when he was about to give one of his sons hell for some infraction and then ground him for a decade. "I'm *here,*" he said, almost in a growl, "because you're my son, and I thought you were dead."

"Like Mom."

Bill's eyes, hazel like Jack's own, flashed. "We'll

talk about your mother another time," he said. "Right now, boy, you're in one hell of a fix, and that's going to be enough to handle without going into all the *other* issues."

"It's a bone marrow thing," Jack recalled, but he was thinking about Ashley. She wasn't much for media, but even she had probably seen him on the news. "Something to do with a toxin manufactured especially for me."

"You need a marrow donor," Bill told him bluntly. "It's your only chance, and, frankly, it will be touch and go. I've already been tested, and so have your brothers. Bryce is the only match."

A chance, however small, was more than Jack had expected to get. He must have been mulling a lot of things over on an unconscious level while he was submerged in oblivion, though, because there was a sense of clarity behind the fog enveloping his brain.

"Bryce," he said. "The baby."

"He wouldn't appreciate being called that," Bill replied, with a moist smile. His big hand rested on Jack's, squeezed his fingers together. "Your brother will be ready when you are."

Jack imagined Ashley, the way she'd looked and smelled and felt, warm and naked beneath him. He saw her baking things, playing with the kitten, parking herself in front of the computer, her brow furrowed slightly with confusion and that singular determination of hers.

If he got through this thing, he could go back to her.

Swap his old life for a new one, straight across, and never look back.

But suppose some buddy of Lombard's decided to step up and take care of unfinished business?

No, he decided, discouraged to the core of his being.

There were too many unknown factors; he couldn't start things up with Ashley again, even if he got lucky and survived the ordeal he was facing, until he was sure she'd be in no danger.

"So when is this transplant supposed to go down?" he asked his dad.

"Yesterday wouldn't have been too soon," Bill replied. "They were only waiting for you to stabilize a little."

"I'd like to see my brothers," Jack said, but even as he spoke, the darkness was already sucking him back under, into the dreamless place churning like an ocean beneath the surface of his everyday mind. "If they're speaking to me, that is."

Bill dashed at his wet eyes with the back of one large hand. "They're speaking to you, all right," he replied. "But if you pull through, you can expect all three of them to read you the riot act for disappearing the way you did."

*If you pull through.*

Jack sighed. "Fair enough," he said.

REACHING DEEP INTO HER mind and heart in the days after Jack's leaving, Ashley had found a new strength. She'd absorbed the media blitz, with Jack and Chad Lombard playing their starring roles, with a stoicism that surprised even her. After the first wave, she'd stopped watching, stopped reading.

Enough was enough.

Every sound bite, every news clip, every article brought an overwhelming sense of sorrow and relief, in equal measures.

Two days after the Tombstone Showdown, as the reporters had dubbed it, a pair of FBI agents had turned up at Ashley's door.

They'd been long on questions and short on answers.

All they'd really been willing to divulge was that she was in no danger from Chad Lombard's organization; some of its members had been taken into federal custody in Arizona. The rest had scattered to the four winds.

And Jack was alive.

That gave her at least a measure of relief.

It was the questions that fed her sorrow, innocuous and routine though they were. Something about the tone of them, a certain sad resignation—there were no details forthcoming, either in the media or from the visiting agents, but she sensed that Jack was still in trouble.

*Had Jack McCall told her anything about his association with any particular government agencies and if so, what?* the agents wanted to know.

*Had he left anything behind when he went away?*

*If Mr. McCall agreed, would she wish to visit him in a location that would be disclosed at a later time?*

No, Jack hadn't told her anything, beyond the things the FBI already knew, and no, he hadn't left anything behind. Yes, she wanted to see him and she'd appreciate it if they'd disclose the mysterious location.

They refused, though politely, and left, promising to contact her later.

After that, she'd heard nothing more.

Since then, Ashley had been seized by a strange and fierce desperation, a need to do *something,* but she had no idea where Jack was, or what kind of condition he was in. She only knew that he'd collapsed in Tombstone—there had been pictures in the newspapers and on the web.

Both Brad and Tanner had "their people" beating the bushes for any scrap of information, but either they'd really come up with nothing, as they claimed, or they simply didn't want Jack McCall found. Ever.

Melissa was searching, too; even though she wasn't any fonder of Jack than Brad and Olivia were, she and Ashley had the twin link. Melissa knew, better than any of the others, exactly what her sister was going through.

The results of that investigation? So far, zip.

After a week, Jack disappeared from the news, displaced by accounts of piracy at sea, the president's latest budget proposal, and the like.

By the first of February, Ashley was very good at pretending she didn't care where Jack McCall was, what he was doing, whether or not he would—or could—come back.

She'd decided to Get on with Her Life.

Carly and Sophie had spent hours with her, after school, when they weren't rehearsing their parts in the drama club's upcoming play, fleshing out one of the websites Jack had created, showing her how to surf the Net, how to run searches, how to access and reply to email.

In fact, they'd both managed to earn special credit at school for undertaking the task.

Slowly, Ashley had begun to understand the mysteries of navigating cyberspace.

She quickly became proficient at web surfing, and especially at monitoring her modest but attractive website, already bringing in more business than she knew what to do with.

The B&B was booked solid for Valentine's Day weekend, and the profit margin on her "Hearts, Champagne and Roses" campaign looked healthy indeed.

With two weeks to go before the holiday arrived, she was already baking and freezing tarts, some for her guests to enjoy, and some for the annual dance at the Moose Lodge. This year, the herd was raising money to resurface the community swimming pool.

She'd agreed to serve punch and help provide refreshments, not out of magnanimity, but because she baked for the dance every year. And, okay, partly because she knew everybody in town was talking about her latest romantic disaster—this one had gone national, with CNN coverage and an article in *People,* not that she'd been specifically mentioned—and she wanted to show them all that she wasn't moping. No, sir, not her.

She was O'Ballivan tough.

If she still cried herself to sleep once in a while, well, nobody needed to know that. Nobody except Mrs. Wiggins, her small, furry companion, always ready to comfort her with a cuddle.

As outlined in the piece in *People,* Ardith and Rachel were back home, in a suburb of Phoenix, happily reunited with the rest of the family.

Yes, Ashley thought, sitting there at her computer long after she should have taken a bubble bath and gone to bed, day by day, moment by moment, she was getting over Jack.

Really and truly.

Or not.

Glancing out the window, she saw Melissa's car, a red glow under the streetlight, swinging into her driveway.

"Good," Ashley said to Mrs. Wiggins, who was

perched on her right shoulder like a parrot. "I could use a little distraction."

Melissa was just coming through the back door when Ashley reached the kitchen. Her hair was flecked with snow and her grin was wide. Looking askance at Mrs. Wiggins, now nestling into her basket in front of the fireplace, Ashley's twin gave a single nose twitch and carefully kept her distance.

"It happened!" she crowed, hauling off her red tailored coat. "Alex got the prosecutor's job, and I'm going to be one of his assistants! I start the first of March and I've already got a line on a condo in Scottsdale—"

"Wonderful," Ashley said.

Melissa narrowed her beautiful eyes in mock suspicion. "Well, *that* was an enthusiastic response," she replied, draping the coat over the back of one of the chairs at the table.

Ashley's smile felt wobbly on her mouth, and a touch too determined. "If this is what you want, then I'm happy for you. I'm going to miss you a lot, that's all. Except for when you were in law school, we've never really been apart."

Melissa approached, laid a winter-chilled hand on each of Ashley's shoulders. "I'll only be two hours away," she said. "You'll visit me a lot, and of course I'll come back to Stone Creek as often as I can."

"No, you won't," Ashley said, turning away to start some tea brewing, so she wouldn't have to struggle to keep that stupid, slippery smile in place any longer. "You'll be too busy with your caseload, and you know it."

"I need to get away," Melissa said, so sadly that Ashley immediately turned to face her again, no longer concerned about hiding her own misgivings.

"Because?" Ashley prompted.

Melissa rarely looked vulnerable—a good lawyer appeared confident at all times, she often said—but she did then. That sheen in her eyes—was she crying?

"Because," Melissa said, after pushing back her spirally mane of hair with one hand, "things are heating up between Dan and the waitress. Her name is Holly and according to one of the receptionists at the office, they've been in Kruller's Jewelry Store three times in the last week, looking at rings."

Ashley sighed, wiped her hands on her patchwork apron, her own creation, made up of quilt scraps. "Sit down, Melissa," she said.

To her amazement, Melissa sat.

Of the two of them, Melissa had always been the leader, the one who decided things and gave impromptu motivational speeches.

Forgetting the tea preparations, Ashley took the chair closest to her sister's. "That's why you're leaving Stone Creek?" she asked quietly. "Because Dan and this Holly person might get married?"

"'Might,' nothing," Melissa huffed, but her usually straight shoulders sagged a little beneath her very professional white blouse. "As hot and heavy as things were between Dan and me, he never said a *word* about looking at engagement rings. If he's shopping for diamonds, he's *serious* about this woman."

"And?"

Melissa flushed a vibrant pink, with touches of crimson. "And I *might* still be *just a little* in love with him," she admitted.

"You can't have it all, Melissa," Ashley reminded her sister gently. "No one does. You made a choice and now you either have to change it or accept things as they are and move on."

Melissa blinked. "That's easy for *you* to say!"

"Is it?" Ashley asked.

"What am I saying?" Melissa immediately blurted out. "Ash, I'm sorry—I know the whole Jack thing has been—"

"We're not talking about Jack," Ashley said, a mite stiffly. "We're talking about Dan—and you. He's probably marrying this woman on the rebound—if the rumors about the rings are even true in the first place—because he really cared about you. And he might be making the mistake of a lifetime."

"That's *his* problem," Melissa snapped.

"Don't be a bitch," Ashley replied. "You didn't want him, or the life he offered, remember? What did you expect, Melissa? That Dan would wait around until you retire from your seat on the Supreme Court someday, and write your memoirs?"

"Whose side are you on, anyway?" Melissa asked peevishly.

"Yours," Ashley said, and she meant it. "Just talk to Dan before you take the job in Phoenix, Melissa. Please?"

"*He's* the one who broke it off!"

"Don't you want to be sure things can't be patched up?"

"Have you been paying attention? It's *too late,* Ashley."

"Maybe it is, maybe it isn't," Ashley said, getting up

to resume the tea making. "You'll never know if you don't talk things over with Dan while there's still time."

"What am I supposed to do?" Melissa demanded, losing a little steam now. "Drive out there to the back of beyond, knock on his door, and ask him if he'd like to live in a city and be Mr. Melissa O'Ballivan? I can tell you right now what the answer would be—and besides, what if I interrupted—well—*something*—?"

"Like what? Chandelier-swinging sex? Dan has kids, Melissa—he and Holly Hot-Biscuits probably don't go at it in the living room on a regular basis."

Melissa sputtered out a laugh, wholly against her will. *"Holly Hot-Biscuits?"* she crowed. "Ashley O'Ballivan, could it be that you actually have a *racy* side?"

"You'd be surprised," Ashley said, recalling, with a well-hidden pang, some of the sex she and Jack had had. A chandelier would have been superfluous.

"Maybe I wouldn't," Melissa teased. At least she'd cheered up a little. Perhaps that could be counted as progress. "You miss Jack a lot, don't you?"

"When I let myself," Ashley admitted, though guardedly, concentrating on scooping tea leaves into a china pot. "The other night, I dreamed he was—he was standing at the foot of my bed. I could see through him, because he was—dead."

Melissa softened, in that quicksilver way she had. Tough one minute, tender the next—that was Melissa O'Ballivan. "Jack can't be dead," she reasoned, looking as though she wanted to get up from her chair, cross the room, and wrap Ashley in a sisterly embrace, but wisely refraining.

Ashley wasn't accepting hugs these days—from anybody.

She felt too bruised, inside and out.

"Why not?" she asked reasonably, over the sound of the water she ran to fill the kettle.

"Because someone would have told Tanner," Melissa said, very gently. "Come to Scottsdale with me, Ash. Right now, this weekend. Help me decide on the right condo. It would be good for you to get away, change your perspective, soak up some of that delicious sunshine—"

The idea had a certain appeal—she was sick of snow, for one thing—but there was the B&B to think about. She had guests coming for Valentine's Day, after all, and lots of preparations to make. She'd even rented out her private quarters, planning to sleep on the couch in her study.

"Maybe after the holiday," she said. Except that she'd have skiers then, with any luck at all—she'd been pitching that on her new blog, on the website. And after that, it would be time to think about Easter.

"Can you handle Valentine's Day, Ash?" Melissa asked, with genuine concern. "You're still pretty raw."

"And you're not?" Ashley challenged, but gently. "Yes, I can 'handle' it, because I have to." She brought two cups to the table, along with milk and sugar cubes. "What is it with us, Melissa? Brad got it right with Meg, and Olivia with Tanner. Why can't we?"

"I think we're romantically challenged," Melissa decided.

"Or stubborn and proud," Ashley pointed out archly. Her meaning was clear: *Melissa* was stubborn and proud. *She* would have crawled over broken glass for Jack McCall, if it meant they could be together.

Not that she particularly wanted anyone else to know that.

All of which probably made her a candidate for an episode of *Dr. Phil,* during Unhealthy Emotional Dependency week. She would serve as the bad example. *This could happen to you.*

"Don't knock pride," Melissa said cheerfully. "And some people call stubbornness 'persistence.'"

"*Some* people can put a spin on anything," Ashley countered. "Are you going to clear things up with Dan before you leave, or not?"

"Not," Melissa said brightly.

"Chicken."

"You got it. If that man looks me in the eye and says he's in love with Holly Hot-Biscuits, I'll die of mortification on the spot."

"No, you won't. You're too strong. And at least you'd know where you stand." *I'd give anything for another chance with Jack.*

"I *know* where I stand," Melissa answered, pouring tea for Ashley and then for herself, and then warming her hands around the cup instead of drinking the brew. "Up the creek without a paddle."

"That's a mixed metaphor," Ashley couldn't help pointing out.

"Whatever," Melissa said.

And that, for the time being, was the end of the discussion.

A WEEK AFTER THE transplant, the jury was still out on whether the procedure had been successful or not, but by pulling certain strings Jack had been reluctantly released from the hospital, partly on the strength of his well-respected father's promise to make sure he was looked after and did not overexert himself. He went home to Oak Park, Illinois, his old hometown, and let Abigail and the old man install him in his boyhood bedroom in the big brick Federal on Shady Lane.

Not that there were any leaves on the trees to provide shade.

Abigail, though shy around him, had taken pains to get his room ready for occupancy—she'd put fresh sheets on the bed, dusted, aired the place out.

The obnoxious rock-star posters, a reminder of his checkered youth, were still on the walls. The antiquated computer, one of the earliest models, which he'd built himself from scavenged components, remained on his desk, in front of the windows. Hockey sticks and baseball bats occupied every corner.

The sight of it all swamped Jack, made him miss his mother more acutely than ever.

And that was nothing compared to the way he missed Ashley.

Bryce, soon to be an optometrist, appeared in the doorway. He was in his mid-twenties, but he looked younger to Jack.

"You're going to make it, Jack," Bryce said, and he spoke in a man's voice, not a boy's.

So many things had changed.

So many hadn't.

"Thanks to you, maybe I will."

"No maybe about it," Bryce argued.

There was a brief, awkward pause. "What do you think of Abigail?" Jack asked, pulling back the chair at his desk and sitting down. He still tired too easily.

Bryce closed the door, took a seat on the edge of

Jack's bed. Loosely interlaced his fingers and let his hands dangle between his blue-jeaned knees. "She's been good for Dad. He was a real wreck after Mom died."

"I guess that must have been a hard time," Jack ventured, turning his head to look out over the street lined with skeleton trees, waiting for spring.

"It was pretty bad," Bryce admitted. "Did Dad tell you the government is having your headstone removed from the cemetery at Arlington, and the empty box dug up?"

"Guess they need the space," Jack said, as an infinite sadness washed over him. Once, he'd been a hotshot. Now he was sick of guns and violence and war.

"Yeah," Bryce agreed quietly. "Who's the woman?"

Jack tensed. "What woman?"

"The one you mentioned in the email you sent to Dad's office."

Jack closed his eyes briefly, longing for Ashley. Wondering if she'd finally mastered the fine art of computing well enough to check out the Sent Messages folder.

"I'm getting engaged on Valentine's Day," Bryce said, to fill the gap left by Jack's studied silence. "Her name is Kathy. We went to college together."

"Congratulations," Jack managed.

"I wanted to be like you, you know," Bryce went on. "Raise hell. Get sent away to military school. Maybe even bite the sand in Iraq."

Jack managed a tilt at one corner of his mouth, enough to pass for a grin—he hoped. "Thank God you changed your mind," he said. "Mom and Dad—after I disappeared—how were they?"

"Devastated," Bryce answered.

Jack shoved a hand through his hair. Sighed. What had he expected? That they'd go merrily on, as if nothing had happened? *Oh, well, Jack's gone, but we still have three sons left, don't we, and they're all going to graduate school.*

"I need to see Mom's grave," he said.

"I'll take you there," Bryce responded immediately. "After my last class, of course."

Jack smiled. "Of course."

Bryce rose, made that leaving sound by huffing out his breath. "Be nice to Abigail, okay?" he said. "Dad loves her a lot, and she's really trying to fit in without usurping Mom's place."

"I haven't been nice?"

"You've been…reserved."

"Staying alive has been taking up all my time," Jack answered. "Again, thanks to you, I've got a fighting chance. I'll never forget what you did, Bryce. No two ways about it, donating marrow hurts."

Bryce cleared his throat, reached for the doorknob, but didn't quite turn it. "It could take time," he said, letting Jack's comment pass. "All of us being a family again, I mean. But don't give up on us, okay? Don't just take off or something, because I can't even tell you how hard that would be for Dad. He's already lost so much."

"I'm not going anywhere," Jack promised. "I might need that grave at Arlington after all, you know. Maybe they shouldn't be too quick to lay the new resident to rest."

Bryce flushed. "Who's the woman?" he asked again.

Jack met his brother's gaze. "Her name is Ashley

O'Ballivan. She runs a bed-and-breakfast in Stone Creek, Arizona. Do me a favor, little brother. Don't get any ideas about calling her up and telling her where I am."

"Why don't *you* call her?"

"Because I still don't know if I'm going to live or die."

Bryce finally turned the knob, opened the door to go. "Maybe she'd like to hear from you, either way. Spend whatever time you have left—"

"And maybe she'd like to get on with her life," Jack broke in brusquely.

After Bryce was gone, Jack booted up the ancient computer—or tried to, anyhow. The cheapest pay-as-you-go cell phone on the market probably had more power.

Giving up on surfing the web, catching up on all he'd missed since Tombstone, he tried to interest himself in the pile of high-school yearbooks stacked on a shelf in his closet.

What a hotheaded little jerk he'd been, he thought. A throwback, especially in comparison to his brothers.

He revisited his junior year, flipping pages until he found Molly Henshaw, the love of his adolescent life. Although he hadn't been a praying man, Jack had begged God to let him marry Molly someday.

Looking at her class picture, he remembered that she'd had acne, which she tried to cover with stuff closer to orange than flesh tone. Big hair, too. And a come-hither look in her raccoonlike eyes. Even in the photograph, he could see the clumps of mascara coating her lashes.

Must have been the come hither, he decided.

And thank God for unanswered prayers.

Having come to that conclusion, Jack decided to go downstairs, where Abigail was undoubtedly flitting around the kitchen. Time to make a start at getting to know his father's new wife, though their acquaintance might be a short one if his body rejected Bryce's marrow.

For his dad's sake, because there were so many things he couldn't make up for, he had to give it a shot. Ironically, he knew it was what his mother would have wanted.

Later, he'd log on to his dad's computer, in the den.

See if Ashley's website was up and running.

With luck, there would be a picture of her, smiling like the welcoming hostess she was, dressed in something flowered, with her hair pulled back into that prim French braid he always wanted to undo.

For now, that would have to be enough.

Abigail was in the kitchen, the room where Jack had had so many conversations with his mother. Feminine and modestly pretty, Abigail wore a flowered apron, her hair was pinned up in a loose chignon at her nape, and her hands were white with flour.

She smiled shyly at Jack. "Your father likes peach pie above all things," she confided.

"I'm pretty fond of it myself," Jack answered, grinning. "You're a baker, Abigail?"

His stepmother shrugged. She couldn't have been more different, physically anyway, from his mom. She'd been tall and full-figured, always lamenting humorously that she should have lived in the 1890s, when women with bosoms and hips were appreciated. Abigail was petite and trim; she probably gardened, maybe knitted and crocheted.

His mother had loved to play golf and sail, and to Jack's recollection, she'd never baked a pie or worn an apron in her life.

"A baker and a few other things, too," Abigail said, with a quirky little smile playing briefly on her mouth. "I retired from real estate a year before Bill and I met. Sold my company for a chunk of cash and decided to spend the rest of my life doing what I love…baking, planting flowers, sewing. Oh, and fussing over my husband."

Jack swiped a slice of peach from the bowl waiting to be poured into the pie pan, and she didn't slap his hand. "Married before?" he asked casually. "Any kids?"

Abigail shook her head, and a few tendrils of her graying auburn hair escaped the chignon. "I was too busy with my career," she said, without a hint of regret. "Besides, I always promised myself I'd wait for the right man, no matter how long it took. Turned out to be Bill McKenzie."

He'd underestimated Abigail, that much was clear. She was an independent woman, living the life she chose to live, not someone looking for an easy life married to a prosperous dentist. In fact, Abigail probably had a lot more money than his dad did, and that was saying something.

"He's happy, Abigail. Thank you for that." Jack reached for a second slice, and this time she did swat his hand, smiling and shaking her head.

She took a cereal bowl from the cupboard, scooped in a generous portion of fruit with a soup spoon, and handed him the works.

Jack decided he knew all he needed to know about

Abigail—she loved his father, and that was as good as it got. Leaning in a little, he kissed her cheek.

"Welcome aboard, Abigail," he said hoarsely.

She smiled. "Thanks," she replied, and went back to building the pie.

# CHAPTER TEN

"Ms. O'Ballivan? My name is Bryce McKenzie and I—"

Ashley shifted the telephone receiver from her left ear to her right, hunching one shoulder to hold it in place, busy rolling out pie dough on the butcher's block next to the counter. "I'm sorry, Mr. McKenzie," she said, distracted, "but we're all booked up for Valentine's Day—"

The man replied with an oddly familiar chuckle. Something about the timbre of it struck a chord somewhere deep in Ashley's core. "Excuse me?" he said.

"The bed-and-breakfast—I guess I just assumed you were calling because of the publicity my website's been getting—"

Again, that sense of familiarity flittered, in the pit of Ashley's stomach now.

"I'm Jack McKenzie's brother," Bryce explained.

*McKenzie.* The name finally registered in Ashley's befuddled memory, the one Jack had admitted leaving behind so long ago. "Oh," she said, stretching the phone cord taut so she could collapse into a kitchen chair. *"Oh."*

"I probably shouldn't be calling you like this, but—well—"

"Is Jack all right?"

Bryce McKenzie sighed. "Yes and no," he said carefully.

Ashley put a floury hand to her heart, smearing her T-shirt with white finger marks. "Tell me about the 'no' part, Mr. McKenzie," she said.

"Bryce," he corrected. And then, after clearing his throat, he explained that Jack had needed a bone marrow transplant. The patient was up and around, and he was taking antirejection drugs, but he didn't seem to be recovering—or regressing—and his family was worried.

They'd had a family meeting, Bryce concluded, one Jack hadn't been privy to, and decided as a unit that seeing Ashley again might be the boost he needed to get better.

Ashley listened with her eyes closed and her heart hammering.

"Where is he now?" she asked, very quietly, when Bryce had finished.

"We live in Chicago, so he's here," he answered. "There's plenty of room at my dad's place, if you wanted to stay there. I mean, if you even want to come in the first place, that is."

Ashley's heart thrummed. Valentine's Day was a week away and she had to be there to greet her guests, make them comfortable—didn't she? This was her chance to take the business to a whole new level, make some progress, stay caught up on her payments to Brad and fortify her faltering savings.

And none of that was as important as seeing Jack again.

"I think," she said shakily, "that if Jack wanted to see me, he would have called himself."

"He wants to make sure he's going to live through this first," Bryce answered candidly. Then, after sucking in an audible breath, he added, "Will you come? It could make all the difference in his recovery—or, at least, that's what we're hoping."

Ashley looked around her kitchen, cluttered now with the accoutrements of serious cooking. The freezer was full, the house was ready for the onslaught of lovers planning a romantic getaway.

How could she leave now?

How could she *stay?*

"I'll be there as soon as I can book a flight," she heard herself say.

"One of us will pick you up at O'Hare," Bryce said, his voice light with relief. "Just call back with your flight number and arrival time."

Ashley wrote down the cell numbers he gave her and promised to get in touch with him as soon as she had the necessary information.

"This is crazy," she told Mrs. Wiggins, as soon as she'd hung up.

"Meooow," Mrs. Wiggins replied, curling against Ashley's ankle.

Having made the decision, Ashley was full of sudden energy. She made airline reservations for the next day, flying out of Flagstaff, connecting in Phoenix, and then going on to Chicago. When that was done, she called Bryce back.

"You're sure Jack wants to see me?" she asked, having second thoughts.

"I'm sure," Bryce said, with a smile in his voice.

The next call was to Melissa, at her office, and Ashley was almost panicking by then. The moment Melissa greeted her with a curious "Hello"—Ashley never called her at work—the whole thing spilled out.

Ashley held her breath, after the spate of words, awaiting Melissa's response.

"I see," Melissa said cautiously.

"I might be back before Valentine's Day," Ashley blurted, anxious to assuage her sister's misgivings about Jack, "but I can't be absolutely sure, and I need you to cover for me if necessary."

"I don't know beans about running a bed-and-break-fast," Melissa said gamely, "much less *cooking*. But I'll be there, Ash. Get your bags packed."

Tears burned Ashley's eyes. She could always count on Melissa, on any member of her family, to come through in a pinch. Why had she doubted that, even for a moment? "Thanks, Melissa."

"You'll have to send the cat to Olivia's place," Melissa warned, though her tone was good-natured. "You know how my allergies flare up when I'm around anything with fur."

"I know," Ashley said sweetly, "that you're a hypochondriac. But I love you anyway."

"Gee, thanks," Melissa replied. "No cat," she clarified firmly. "The deal's off if Olivia won't take him."

*"Her,"* Ashley said, smiling. "How many male cats do you know with the name 'Mrs. Wiggins'?"

"I don't know *any* cats, whatever the gender," Melissa answered, "and I don't want to, either."

Ashley grinned to herself. "I'm sure Olivia will cat-sit," she conceded. "One more thing. Could you serve punch at the Valentine's Day dance? I promised and I did all this baking and I'm not sure I'll be back in time—"

"Oh, for Pete's sake," Melissa said. "*Yes,* if it comes to that, but you'd better do your darnedest to be home before the first guests arrive. I mean well, but we're taking a risk here. I'm not the least bit domestic, remember, and I could put you out of business without half trying."

Ashley laughed, sniffled once. "I promise I'll do my O'Ballivan best," she said. "Have you seen Dan yet?"

"No," Melissa said, "and don't mention his name again, if you don't mind."

After the call ended, Ashley wrestled her one and only suitcase down from the attic—she rarely traveled—and set it on her bed, open.

Mrs. Wiggins immediately climbed into it, as though determined to make the journey with her mistress.

"Not this time," Ashley said, gently removing the furball.

The next dilemma was, what did a person pack for a trip to Chicago in the middle of winter?

She decided on her trademark broomstick skirts, lightweight tunic sweaters, and some jeans, for good measure.

When she called Starcross Ranch, hoping to speak to Olivia, Tanner answered instead. Ashley asked if Mrs. Wiggins could bunk in for a few days.

"Sure," Tanner said, as Ashley had known he would. But he also wanted an explanation. "Where are you off to, in such a hurry?"

Tanner was Jack's friend, and he'd surely been as worried about him as Ashley had. Although it was possible that the two men had been in touch, her instincts told her they hadn't.

Ashley drew a deep breath, let it out slowly, and

hoped she was doing the right thing by telling Tanner. And by jetting off to Chicago when Jack hadn't asked her to come.

"Jack's in Chicago," she said. "He's had a bone marrow transplant—something to do with the toxin—and his family is worried about him. He's not getting worse, but he's not getting better, either."

Tanner murmured an exclamation. "I see," he said. "Jack didn't call you himself?"

"No," Ashley admitted, her shoulders sagging a little.

Tanner considered that, must have decided against giving an opinion, one way or the other. "You'll keep me in the loop?" he asked presently.

"Yes," Ashley said.

"I'll be there to get the cat sometime this afternoon. Do you want a ride to the airport?"

"I've got that covered," Ashley replied. "Thanks, Tanner. I really appreciate this."

"We're family," Tanner pointed out. "Brad could probably charter a jet—"

"I don't need a jet," Ashley interrupted, though gently. "And I'm not really ready to discuss any of this with Brad. Not just yet, anyhow."

"Is there a plan?" Tanner asked. "And if so, what is it?"

Ashley smiled, even though her eyes were burning again. "No plan," she said. "I'm not even sure Jack wants me there. But I have to see him, Tanner."

"Of course you do," Tanner agreed, sounding both relieved and resigned. "Brad is going to wonder where you've gone, though. He keeps pretty close tabs on his three little sisters, you know. But don't worry about that—I'll handle him."

She heard Olivia's voice in the background, asking what was going on.

"Let me talk to her," Ashley said, and told the whole story all over again.

"I don't like it that you're going alone," Olivia told her, a minute or so later. "I've got the babies to look after, and I think Sophie is coming down with a cold, but maybe Melissa could go along—"

"Melissa is going to house-sit," Ashley said. "And she'll have her hands full holding down the fort, especially if I'm not back before Valentine's Day. I'll be *fine,* Livie."

"You're sure? What if Jack—?"

"What if he doesn't want to see me? I'll handle it, Liv. I'm a big girl now, remember?"

Olivia's laugh was warm, and a little teary. "Godspeed, little sister," she said. "And call us when you get there."

"I will," Ashley said, thinking how lucky she was.

The next few hours passed in a haze of activity— there were project lists to make for Melissa, and dozens of other details, too.

As promised, Tanner showed up late that afternoon to collect a mewing Mrs. Wiggins in the small pet carrier Olivia had sent along.

"Tell Jack I said hello," Tanner said, as he was leaving.

Ashley nodded, and her brother-in-law planted a light kiss on the top of her head.

"Take care," he told her. And then he was gone.

Melissa showed up when she got off work, and she

and Ashley went over the lists—which guests to put where, how to reheat the food she'd prepared ahead of time, frozen and carefully labeled, how to take reservations and run credit cards, and a myriad of other things.

Melissa looked overwhelmed, but in true O'Ballivan spirit, she vowed to do her best.

Knowing she wouldn't sleep if she stayed in Stone Creek that night, Ashley loaded her suitcase into the car and set out for Flagstaff, intending to check into a hotel near the airport and have a room-service supper.

Her flight was leaving at six-thirty the next morning.

Along the way, though, she pulled off onto the snowy road leading to the cemetery where her mother was buried, parked near Delia's grave, and waded toward the headstone.

There were no heartfelt words, no tears.

Ashley simply felt a need to be there, in that quiet place. Somehow, a sense of closure had stolen into her heart when she wasn't looking. She could let go now, move on.

The weather was bitterly cold, though, and she soon got back in her car and made her steady, careful way toward Flagstaff.

She would always love the mother she'd longed to have, she reflected, but it was time to go forward, appreciate the *living* people she loved, those who loved her in return: Brad and Meg, Olivia and Tanner, Melissa and little Mac and Carly and sweet Sophie and the babies.

And Jack.

She didn't obsess over what might happen when she

arrived in Chicago. For once in her life, she was taking a risk, going for what she wanted.

And she wanted Jack McCall—McKenzie—whoever he was.

Once she'd arrived in Flagstaff, she chose a hotel and checked in, ordered a bowl of cream of broccoli soup, ate it, and soaked in a warm bath until the chill seeped out of her bones. Most of it, anyway.

A part of her would remain frozen until she'd seen Jack for herself.

"YOU DID *WHAT?*" Jack demanded, after supper that night, when he and Bryce wound up the evening sitting in chairs in front of the fireplace. It had been a hectic thing, supper, with brothers and their wives, nieces and nephews, and even a few neighbors there to share in the meal celebrating Jack's return from the dead.

"I called Ashley O'Ballivan," Bryce repeated, with no more regret than he'd shown the first time. "She'll be here late tomorrow afternoon. I'm picking her up at O'Hare."

Jack sat back, absorbing the news. A part of him soared, anticipating Ashley's arrival. Another part wanted to find a place to hide out until she was gone again.

"You've got a lot of nerve, little brother," he finally said, with no inflection in his voice at all. "Especially considering that I told you I'm not ready to see her."

"Until you're sure you won't die," Bryce confirmed confidently. "Jack, *all* of us are terminal. Maybe you won't be around long. Maybe you'll live to be a hundred. But in the meantime, you need to see *this woman,* even if it's only to say good-bye."

Saying good-bye to Ashley the last time had been one of the hardest things Jack had ever had to do. Saying good-bye to her again, especially for eternity, might be more than he could bear.

His conscience niggled at him. What about what *Ashley* had to bear?

Jack closed his eyes. "I'll get you for this," he told his brother.

Bryce chuckled. "You'll have to get well first," he replied.

"You think you can take me?" Jack challenged, grinning now, both infuriated and relieved.

"I'm not a little kid anymore," Bryce pointed out. "I might be able to take you—even with all your paramilitary skills."

Jack opened his eyes, looked at his younger brother with new respect. "Maybe you could," he said.

Bryce stood, stretched and yawned mightily. "Better get back to my apartment," he said. "Busy day tomorrow."

*Ashley,* Jack thought, full of conflicting emotions he couldn't begin to identify. What was he so afraid of? Not commitment, certainly—at least as far as Ashley was concerned.

"After this," he told his departing brother, "mind your own business."

"Not a chance," Bryce said lightly.

And then he was gone.

THE FIRST SIGNS OF AN approaching blizzard hit Chicago five minutes after Ashley's plane landed at O'Hare, and the landing had been so bumpy that her knuckles were white from gripping the armrests—letting go of them was a slow and deliberate process.

She was such a homebody, completely unsuited to an adventurer like Jack. If she'd had a brain in her head, she decided, gnawing at her lower lip, she would have turned right around and flown back to Arizona where she belonged, blizzard or no blizzard.

She waited impatiently while all the passengers in the rows ahead of hers gathered their coats and carry-ons and meandered up the aisle at the pace of spilled peanut butter.

They had all the time in the world, probably.

Ashley knew she might not.

She hurried up the Jetway when her turn finally came, having returned the flight attendant's farewell smile with a fleeting one of her own.

Finding her way along a maze of moving walkways took more time, and she was almost breathless when she finally stepped out of the secure area, scanning the waiting sea of strange faces. Bryce had promised to hold up a sign with her name on it, so they could recognize each other, but even standing on tiptoe, she didn't see one.

"Ashley?"

She froze, turned to see Jack standing at her elbow. A strangled cry, part sob and part something else entirely, escaped her.

He looked so thin, so pale. His eyes were, as Big John used to say, like two burned holes in a blanket.

"Hey," he said huskily.

Ashley swallowed, still unable to move. "Hey," she responded.

He grinned, resembling his old self a little more, and crooked his arm, and she took it.

"You're glad to see me?" she asked, afraid of the answer. His grin, after all, could have been a reflex.

"If I'd been given a choice," he replied, "I would have asked you not to come. But, yeah, I'm glad to see you."

"Good," Ashley said uncertainly, aware of the strangeness between them. And the ever-present electrical charge.

"My interfering brother is waiting over in baggage claim," he said. "Let's go find him, before this storm gets any worse and we get stuck in rush-hour traffic. It's a long drive out to Oak Park."

Ashley nodded, overjoyed to be there and, at the same time, wishing she'd stayed home.

Once she'd met Bryce McKenzie—he was taller than his brother, though not so broad in the shoulders—and collected her solitary, out-of-style suitcase, the three of them headed for the parking garage, Bryce carrying the bag.

Fortunately, Bryce drove a big SUV with four-wheel drive, and he didn't seem a bit worried about the weather. Ashley sat in the front passenger seat, while Jack climbed painfully into the back.

The snow was coming down so hard and so fast by then, and the traffic was so intense, that Ashley wondered if they would reach Oak Park alive.

They did, eventually, and all the McKenzies were waiting in the entryway of the large brick house when they pulled into the circular driveway out front.

Introductions were made—Jack's father and stepmother, his brothers and their wives, Bryce's fiancée, Kathy—and most of their names went out of Ashley's head as soon as she'd heard them.

She could think of nothing—and no one—but Jack.

Jack, who'd sat silent in the backseat of his brother's SUV all the way from the airport. Bryce, bless his heart, had tried hard to keep the conversation going, asking Ashley if her flight had been okay, inquiring about Stone Creek and what it was like there.

Ashley, as uncomfortable in her own way as Jack was in his, had given sparse answers.

She shouldn't have come.

Just as she'd feared, Jack didn't want her there.

The McKenzies welcomed her heartily, though, and Mrs. McKenzie—Abigail—served a meat-loaf supper so delicious that Ashley made a mental note to ask for the recipe.

Jack, seated next to her, though probably not by his own choosing, ate sparingly, as she did, and said almost nothing.

"You must be tired," Jack's father said to her, when the meal was over and Ashley automatically got up to help clear the table. The older man's gaze shifted to his eldest son. "Jack, why don't you show Ashley to her room so she can rest?"

Jack nodded, gestured for Ashley to precede him, and followed her out of the dining room.

The base of the broad, curving staircase was just ahead.

Ashley couldn't help noticing how slowly Jack moved. He was probably exhausted. "You don't have to—"

"Ashley," he interrupted blandly, "I can still climb stairs."

She lowered her gaze, then forced herself to look at him again. "I'm sorry, Jack—I—I shouldn't have come, but—"

He drew the knuckles of his right hand lightly down the side of her cheek. "Don't be sorry," he said. "I guess—well—it's hard on my pride, your seeing me like this."

Ashley was honestly puzzled. Sure, he'd lost weight, and his color wasn't great, but he was still *Jack*. "Like what?"

Jack spread his arms, looked down at himself, met her eyes again. She saw misery and sorrow in his expression. "I might be dying, Ashley," he said. "I wanted you to remember me the way I was before."

Ashley stiffened. "You are *not* going to die, Jack McCall. I won't tolerate it."

He gave a slanted grin. "Is that so?" he replied. "What do you intend to do to prevent it, O'Ballivan?"

"Take a pregnancy test," Ashley said, without planning to at all.

Jack's eyes widened. "You think you're—?"

"Pregnant?" Ashley finished for him, lowering her voice lest the conversation carry into the nearby dining room.

*"Yeah,"* Jack said, somewhat pointedly.

"I might be," Ashley said. This was yet another thing she hadn't allowed herself to think about—until now. "I'm late. *Very* late."

He took her elbow, squired her up the stairs with more energy than he'd shown since she'd come face-to-face with him at O'Hare. "Is that unusual?"

"Yes," Ashley whispered, *"it's unusual."*

He smiled, and a light spread into his eyes that hadn't been there before. "You're not just saying this, are you? Trying to give me a reason to live or something like that?"

"If you can't come up with a reason to live, Jack Mc-Call," Ashley said, waving one arm toward the distant dining room, where his family had gathered, "you're in even sorrier shape than I thought."

He frowned. "Jack *McKenzie,*" he said, clearly thinking of something else. "I'm going by my real name now."

"Well, bully for you," Ashley said.

"'Bully for me'?" He laughed. "God, Ashley, you should have been born during the Roosevelt administration—the *Teddy* Roosevelt administration. Nobody says 'Bully for you' anymore."

Ashley folded her arms. "*I* do," she said.

His eyes danced—it was nice to know she was so entertaining—then went serious again. "Why are you here?"

She bristled. "You *know* why."

"No," Jack said, sounding honestly mystified. "I thought we agreed that I'd come back to Stone Creek after this was all over, and we'd stay apart until then."

Ashley's throat constricted as she considered the magnitude of what Jack was facing. "And *I* thought we agreed that we love each other. Whether you live or die, I want to be here."

Pain contorted his face. "Ashley—"

"I'm not going anywhere until I know what's going to happen to you," Ashley broke in. "When will you know whether the transplant worked or not?"

The change in him was downright mercurial; Jack's eyes twinkled again, and his features relaxed. He made a show of checking his watch. "I'm expecting an email from God at any minute," he teased.

"That isn't funny!"

"Not much is, these days." He took her upper arms in his hands. "Ashley, as soon as this blizzard lets up, I want you to get on an airplane and go back to Stone Creek."

"Well, here's a news flash for you: just because you *want* something doesn't mean you're going to get it."

He grinned, shook his head. "Strange that I never noticed how stubborn you can be."

"Get used to it."

He crossed the hall, opened a door.

She peeked inside, saw a comfortable-looking room with an antique four-poster bed, a matching dresser and chest of drawers, and several overstuffed chairs.

"I won't sleep," she warned.

"Neither will I," Jack responded.

Ashley turned, faced him squarely. Spoke from her heart. "Don't die, Jack," she said. "Please—whatever happens between us—don't just give up and die."

He leaned in, kissed her lightly on the mouth. "I'll do my best not to," he said. Then he turned and started back toward the stairs.

"Aren't you going to bed?" Ashley asked, feeling lonely and very far from home.

"Later," he said, winking at her. "Right now, I'm going to call drugstores until I find one that delivers during snowstorms."

Ashley's heart caught; alarm reverberated through her like the echo of a giant brass gong. "Are you running low on one of your medications?"

"No," Jack answered. "I'm going to ask them to send over one of those sticks."

"Sticks?" Ashley frowned, confused.

"The kind a woman pees on," he explained. "Plus sign if she's pregnant, minus if she's not."

"That can wait," Ashley protested. "Have you looked out a window lately?"

"I've got to know," Jack said.

"You're insane."

"Maybe. Good night, Ashley."

She swallowed. "Good night," she said. Stepping inside the guestroom, she closed the door, leaned her forehead against it, and breathed deeply and slowly until she was sure she wouldn't cry.

Her handbag and suitcase had already been brought upstairs. Sinking down onto the side of the bed, Ashley rummaged through her purse until she found the cell phone she'd bought on a wave of technological confidence, after she'd finally mastered her computer.

She dialed her own number at the bed-and-breakfast, and Melissa answered on the first ring.

"Ashley?" The twin-vibe strikes again.

"Hi, Melissa. I'm here—in Chicago, I mean—and I'm—I'm fine."

"You don't *sound* fine," Melissa argued. "How's Jack?"

"He looks terrible, and I don't think he's very happy that I'm here."

"Oh, Ash—I'm sorry. Was the bastard rude to you?"

Ashley smiled, in spite of everything. "He's not a bastard, Melissa," she said, "and no, he hasn't been rude."

"Then—?"

"I think he's given up," Ashley admitted miserably. "It's as if he's decided to die and get it over with. And he doesn't want me around to see it happen."

"Look, maybe you should just come home—"

"I can't. We're socked in by the perfect storm. I've never seen so much snow—even in Stone Creek." She paused. "And I wouldn't leave anyway. How's everything there?"

"It's fine. I've had to turn away at least five people who wanted to book rooms for Valentine's Day weekend." Melissa still sounded worried. "You do realize that you might be there a while? Do you have enough money, Ash?"

"No," Ashley said, embarrassed. "Not for a long haul."

"I can help you out if you need some," Melissa offered. "Brad, too."

Ashley gulped down her O'Ballivan pride, and it wasn't easy to swallow. "I'll let you know," she said, with what dignity she had left. "Do me a favor, will you? Call Tanner and Olivia and let them know I got here okay?"

"Sure," Melissa said.

They said their good-byes soon after that, and hung up.

As tired as she was, Ashley knew she wouldn't sleep.

She took a bath, brushed her teeth and put on her pajamas.

She watched a newscast on the guestroom TV, waited until the very end for the weather report.

More snow on the way. O'Hare was shut down, and the police were asking everyone to stay off the roads except in the most dire emergencies.

At quarter after ten, a knock sounded on Ashley's door.

"It's me," Jack called, in a loud whisper. "Can I come in?"

Before Ashley could answer, one way or the other, the door opened and he stepped inside, carrying a white bag in one hand.

"Nothing stops the post office or pharmacy delivery drivers," he said, holding out the bag.

The pregnancy test, of course.

Ashley's hand trembled as she reached out to accept it. "Come back later," she said, moving toward her bathroom door.

Jack sat down on the side of her bed. "I'll wait," he said.

# CHAPTER ELEVEN

HUDDLED IN THE MCKENZIES' guest bathroom, Ashley stared down at the plastic stick in mingled horror and delight.

A plus sign.

*She was pregnant.*

Ashley made some rapid calculations in her head; normally, if she hadn't been under stress, it would have been a no-brainer to figure out that the baby was due sometime in September. Because she was frazzled, it took longer.

"Well?" Jack called from the other side of the door. As a precaution, Ashley had turned the lock; otherwise, he might have stormed in on her, he was so anxious to learn the results.

Ashley swallowed painfully. She was bursting with the news, but if she told Jack now, she would, in effect, be trapping him. He'd feel honor-bound to marry her, whether he really wanted to or not.

And suppose he died?

That, of course, would be awful either way.

But maybe knowing about the baby would somehow heal Jack, inspire him to try harder to recover. To believe he could.

The knob jiggled. "Ashley?"

"I'm all right."

"Okay," Jack replied, "but are you *pregnant?*"

"It's inconclusive," Ashley said, too earnestly and too cheerfully.

"I read the package. You get either a plus or a minus," Jack retorted, not at all cheerful, but very earnest. "Which is it, Ashley?"

Ashley closed her eyes for a moment, offered up a silent prayer for wisdom, for strength, for courage. She simply wasn't a very good liar; Jack would see through her if she tried to deceive him. And, anyway, deception seemed wrong, however good her intentions might be. The child was as much Jack's as her own, and he had a right to know he was going to be a father.

"It's—it's a plus."

"Open the door," Jack said. Was that jubilation she heard in his voice, or irritation? Joy—or dread?

Ashley pushed the lock button in the center of the knob, and stepped back quickly to avoid being run down by a man on a mission. She was still holding the white plastic stick in one hand.

Jack took it from her, examined the little panel at one end, giving nothing away by his expression. His shoulders were tense, though, and his breathing was fast and shallow.

"My God," he said finally. "Ashley, *we made a baby.*"

"You and me," Ashley agreed, sniffling a little.

Jack raised his eyes to hers. She thought she saw a quickening there, something akin to delight, but he looked worried, too. "You weren't going to tell me?" he asked. "I wouldn't exactly describe a plus sign as 'inconclusive.'"

"I didn't know how you'd react," Ashley said. She *still* couldn't read him—was he glad or sad?

"How I'd react?" he echoed. "Ashley, this is the best thing that's ever happened to me, besides you."

Ashley stared at him, stricken to silence, stricken by joy and surprise and a wild, nearly uncontainable hope.

"You do *want* this baby, don't you?" Jack asked.

"Of course I do," Ashley blurted. "I wasn't sure *you* did, that's all."

Jack looked down at the stick again, shaking his head and grinning.

"I peed on that, you know," Ashley pointed out, reaching for the test stick, intending to throw it away.

Jack held it out of her reach. "We're keeping this. You can glue it into the kid's baby book or something."

"Jack, it's not sanitary," Ashley pointed out. Why was she talking about trivial things, when so much hung in the balance?

"Neither are wet diapers," Jack reasoned calmly. "Sanitation is all well and good, but a kid needs good old-fashioned germs, too, so he—or she—can build up all the necessary antibodies."

"You don't have to marry me if you don't want to," Ashley said, too quickly, and then wished she could bite off her tongue.

"Sure, I do," Jack said. "Call me old-fashioned, but I think a kid ought to have two legal parents."

"Sure, you *have* to marry me, or sure, you *want* to?" Ashley asked.

"Oh, I want to, all right," Jack told her, his voice hoarse, his eyes glistening. "The question is, do you want to spend the rest of your life with me? You could be a widow in six months, or even sooner. A widow with a baby to raise."

"Not if you fight to live, Jack," Ashley said.

He looked away, evidently staring into some grim scenario only he could see. "There's plenty of money," he said, as though speaking to someone else. "If nothing else, I made a good living doing what I did. You would never want for anything, and neither would our baby."

"I don't care about money," Ashley countered honestly, and a little angrily, too. *I care about you, and this baby, and our life together. Our long, long life together.* "I love you, remember?"

He set the test stick carefully aside, on the counter by the sink, and pulled Ashley out into the main part of the small suite. "I can't propose to you in a bathroom," he said.

Ashley laughed and cried.

Awkwardly, Jack dropped to one knee, still holding her hand. "I love you, Ashley O'Ballivan. Will you marry me?"

"Yes," she said.

He gave an exuberant shout, got to his feet again and pulled her into his arms, practically drowning her in a deep, hungry kiss.

The guestroom door popped open.

"Oops," Dr. McKenzie the elder said, blushing.

Jack and Ashley broke apart, Jack laughing, Ashley embarrassed and happy and not a little dazed.

Bill looked even more chagrined than before. "I heard a yell and I thought—"

"Everything's okay, Dad," Jack said, with gruff affection. "It's better than okay. I just asked Ashley to marry me, and she said yes."

"I see," Bill said, smiling, and quietly closed the door.

A jubilant "Yes!" sounded from the hallway. Ashley

pictured her future father-in-law punching the air with one fist, a heartening thought.

"I still might die," Jack reminded her.

"Welcome to the human race," Ashley replied. "From the moment any of us arrive here, we're on our way out again."

"I'd like to make love to you right now," Jack said.

"Not here," Ashley answered. "I couldn't—not in your dad's house."

Jack nodded slowly. "You're as old-fashioned as I am," he said. "As soon as this storm lets up, though, we're out of here."

They sat down, side by side, on the bed where both of them wanted to make love, and neither intended to give in to desire.

Not just yet, anyway.

"How soon can we get married?" Jack asked, taking her hand, stroking the backs of her knuckles with the pad of his thumb.

Ashley's heart, full to bursting, shoved its way up into her throat and lodged there. "Wait a second," she protested, when she finally gathered the breath to speak. The aftershocks of Jack's kiss were still banging around inside her. "There are things we have to decide first."

"Like?"

"Like where we're going to live," Ashley said, nervous now. She liked Chicago, what little she'd seen of the place, that is, but Stone Creek would always be home.

"Wherever you want," Jack told her quietly. "And I know that's the old hometown. Just remember that your family isn't exactly wild about me."

"They'll get over it," Ashley told him, with confidence. "Once they know you're going to stick around this time."

"Just *try* shaking me off your trail, lady," Jack teased. He leaned toward her, kissed her again, this time lightly, and in a way that shook her soul.

"Does that mean you won't go back to whatever it is you do for a living?" Ashley ventured.

"It means I'm going to shovel snow and carry out the trash and love you, Ashley. For as long as we both shall live."

Tears of joy stung her eyes. "That probably won't be enough to keep you busy," she fretted. "You're used to action—"

"I'm sick of action. At least, the kind that involves covert security operations. Vince can run the company, along with a few other people I trust. I can manage it from the computer in your study."

"I thought you didn't trust Vince anymore," Ashley said.

"I got a little peeved with him," Jack admitted, "but he's sound. He'd have been long gone if he wasn't."

"You wouldn't be taking off all of a sudden—on some important job that required your expertise?"

"I'm good at what I do, Ashley," Jack said. "But I'm not so good that I can't delegate. Maybe I'll hang out with Tanner sometimes, though, riding the range and all that cowboy-type stuff."

"Do you know how to ride a horse?"

Jack chuckled. "It can't be that much different from riding a camel," he grinned. "And I'd be a whole lot closer to the ground."

That last statement sobered both of them.

Jack might not be just closer to the ground, he might wind up *under* it.

"I'm going to make it, Ashley," he assured her.

She dropped her forehead against his shoulder, wrapped her arms around him, let herself cling for a few moments. "You'd better," she said. "You'd just better."

THREE DAYS LATER, the storm had finally moved on, leaving a crystalline world behind, trees etched with ice, blankets of white covering every roof.

A private jet, courtesy of Brad, skimmed down onto the tarmac at a private airfield on the fringes of the Windy City, and Jack and Ashley turned to say temporary farewells to Jack's entire family, gathered there to see them off.

The whole clan would be traveling to Stone Creek for the wedding, which would take place in two weeks. Valentine's Day would have been perfect, but with so many guests already booked to stay at the bed-and-breakfast, it was impossible, and neither Jack nor Ashley wanted to wait until the next one rolled around.

Bill McKenzie pumped his eldest son's hand, the hem of his expensive black overcoat flapping in a brisk breeze, then drew him into a bear hug.

"Better get yourselves onto that plane and out of this wind," Bill said, at last, his voice choked. He bent to kiss Ashley's cheek. "I always wanted a daughter," he added, in a whisper.

Jack nodded, then shook hands with each of his brothers. Every handshake turned into a hug. Lastly, he embraced Abigail, his stepmother.

Ashley looked away, grappling with emotions of her

own, watched as the metal stairs swung down out of the side of the jet with an electronic hum. The pilot stood in the doorway, grinning, and she recognized Vince Griffin—the man who'd held a gun on her in her own kitchen, the night Ardith and Rachel arrived.

"Better roll, boss," he called to Jack. "There's more weather headed this way, and I'd like to stay ahead of it."

Jack took Ashley's arm, steered her gently up the steps, into the sumptuous cabin of the jet. There were eight seats, each set of two facing the other across a narrow fold-down table.

"Aren't you going to ask what I'm doing here?" Vince asked Jack, blustering with manly bravado and boyishly earnest at the same time.

"No," Jack answered. "It's obvious that you wangled the job so you could be the one to take us home to Stone Creek."

*Home to Stone Creek.* That sounded so good to Ashley, especially coming from Jack.

Vince laughed. "I'm trying to get back in your good graces, boss," he said, flipping a switch to retract the stairs, then shutting and securing the cabin door. "Is it working?"

"Maybe," Jack said.

"I hate it when you say 'maybe,'" Vince replied.

"Just fly this thing," Jack told him mildly, with mischief in his eyes. "I want to stay ahead of the weather as much as you do."

Vince nodded, retreated into the cockpit, and shut the door behind him.

Solicitously, Jack helped Ashley out of her coat, sat

her down in one of the sumptuous leather seats and swiveled it to buckle her seat belt for her.

A thrill of anticipation went through her.

*Not yet,* she told herself.

Jack must have been reading her mind. "As soon as we get home," he vowed, leaning over her, bracing himself on the armrests of her seat, "we're going to do it like we've never done it before."

That remark inspired another hot shiver. "Are we, now?" she said, her voice deliberately sultry.

Jack thrust himself away from her, since the plane was already taxiing down the runway, took his own seat across from hers and fastened his belt for takeoff.

Four and a half hours later, they landed outside Stone Creek.

Brad and Meg were waiting to greet them, along with Olivia and Tanner, Carly and Sophie, and Melissa.

"*Thank God* you're back," Melissa said, close to Ashley's ear, after hugging her. "I thought I was going to have to *cook.*"

Brad stood squarely in front of Jack, Ashley noticed, out of the corner of her eye, his arms folded and his face stern.

Jack did the same thing, gazing straight into Brad's eyes.

"Uh-oh," Melissa breathed. "Testosterone overload."

Neither man moved. Or spoke.

Olivia finally nudged Brad hard in the ribs. "Behave yourself, big brother," she said. "Jack will be part of the family soon, and that means the two of you have to get along."

It didn't mean any such thing, of course, but to Ashley's profound relief, Brad softened visibly at Olivia's words. Then, after some hesitation, he put out a hand.

Jack took it.

After the shake, Brad said, "That doesn't mean you can mistreat my kid sister, hotshot."

"Wouldn't think of it," Jack said. "I love her." He curved an arm around Ashley, pulled her close against his side, looked down into her upturned face. "Always have, always will."

*Two weeks later*
*Stone Creek Presbyterian Church*

"IT'S TACKY," OLIVIA PROTESTED to Melissa, zipping herself into her bridesmaid's dress with some difficulty, since she was still a little on the pudgy side from having the twins. "Coming to a wedding with a U-Haul hitched to the back of your car!"

Melissa rolled her eyes. "I have to be in Phoenix bright and early Monday morning to start my new job," she said, yet again. The three sisters had been over the topic many times. Most of Melissa's belongings had already been moved to the fancy condo in Scottsdale; the rented trailer contained the last of them.

Initially, flushed with the success of helping Ashley steer the bed-and-breakfast through the Valentine's Day rush, Melissa had seemed to be wavering a little on the subject of moving away. After all, she liked her job at the small, local firm where she'd worked since graduating from law school, but then Dan Guthrie had suddenly eloped with Holly the Waitress. Now nothing would move Melissa to stay.

She was determined to shake the dust of Stone Creek off her feet and start a whole new life—elsewhere.

Ashley turned her back to her sisters and her mind to her wedding, smoothing the beaded skirt of her ivory-silk gown in front of the grainy full-length mirror affixed to the back of the pastor's office door. She and Melissa had scoured every bridal shop within a two-hundred-mile radius to find it, while Olivia searched the internet, and the dress was perfect.

Not so the bridesmaids' outfits, Ashley reflected, happily rueful. They were bright yellow taffeta, with square necklines, puffy sleeves, big bows at the back, and way too many ruffles.

*What was I thinking?* Ashley asked herself, stifling a giggle.

The answer, of course, was that she *hadn't* been thinking. She'd fallen wholly, completely and irrevocably in love with Jack McKenzie, dazed in the daytime, *crazed* at night, when they made love until they were both sweaty and breathless and gasping for air.

The yellow dresses must have seemed like a good idea at the time, she supposed. Olivia and Melissa had surely argued against that particular choice—but Ashley honestly had no memory of it.

"We're going to look like giant parakeets in the pictures," Olivia complained now, but her eyes were warm and moist as she came to stand behind Ashley in front of the mirror. "You look so beautiful."

Ashley turned, and she and Olivia embraced. "I'll make it up to you," Ashley said. "Having to wear those awful dresses, I mean."

Melissa looked down at her billowing skirts and shuddered. "I don't see how," she said doubtfully.

A little silence fell.

Olivia straightened Ashley's veil.

"I wish Mom and Dad and Big John could be here," Ashley admitted softly.

"I know," Olivia replied, kissing her cheek.

The church organist launched into a prelude to "Here Comes the Bride."

"Showtime," Melissa said, giving Ashley a quick squeeze. "Be happy."

Ashley nodded, blinking. She couldn't cry now. It would make her mascara run.

A rap sounded at the office door, and Brad entered at Olivia's "Come in," looking beyond handsome in his tuxedo. "Ready to be given away?" he asked solemnly, his gaze resting on Ashley in surprised bemusement, as though she'd just changed from a little girl to a woman before his very eyes. A grin crooked up a corner of his mouth. "We can always duck out the back door and make a run for it if you've changed your mind."

Ashley smiled, shook her head. Walked over to her brother.

Brad kissed her forehead, then lowered the front of the veil. "Jack McKenzie is one lucky man," he said gravely, but a genuine smile danced in his eyes. "Gonna be okay?"

Ashley took his arm. "Gonna be okay," she confirmed.

"We're supposed to go down the aisle first," Melissa said, grabbing Olivia's hand and dragging her past Brad and Ashley, through the open doorway, and into the corridor that opened at both ends of the small church.

"Is he out there?" Ashley whispered to Brad, suddenly nervous, as he escorted her over the threshold between one life and another.

"Jack?" Brad pretended not to remember. "I'm pretty sure I spotted him up front, with Tanner beside him. Guess it could have been the pastor, though." He paused for dramatic effect. "Oh, yeah. The pastor's wearing robes. The man I saw was in a tuxedo, tugging at his collar every couple of seconds."

"Stop it," Ashley said, but she was smiling. "I'm nervous enough without you giving me a hard time, big brother."

They joined Melissa and Olivia at the back of the church.

Over their heads, and through a shifting haze of veil, extreme anticipation, and almost overwhelming joy, Ashley saw Jack standing up front, his back straight, his head high with pride.

In just two weeks, he'd come a long way toward a full recovery, filling out, his color returning. He claimed it was the restorative power of good sex.

Ashley blushed, remembering some of that sex, and looking forward to a lot more of it.

The organist struck the keys with renewed vigor.

"There's our cue," Brad whispered to Ashley, bending his head slightly so she could hear.

"Go!" Melissa said to Olivia, giving her a little push.

Olivia moved slowly up the aisle, between pews jammed with McKenzies, O'Ballivans, McKettricks, and assorted friends.

Just before starting up the aisle herself, Melissa turned, found Ashley's hand under the bouquet of snow-white peonies Brad had had flown in from God-knew-where and squeezed it hard.

"Go," Brad told Melissa, with a chuckle.

She made a face at him and started resolutely up the aisle.

Once she and Olivia were both in front of the altar, opposite Jack and Tanner, the organist pounded the keys with even more vigor than before. Ashley *floated* toward the altar, gripping Brad's strong arm, her gaze fixed on Jack.

The guests rose to their feet, beaming at Ashley.

Jack smiled, encouraged her with a wink.

And then she was at his side.

She heard the minister ask, "Who giveth this woman in marriage?"

Heard Brad answer, "Her family and I."

Ashley's eyes began to smart again, and she wondered if anyone had ever died of an overdose of happiness.

Brad retreated, and after that, Ashley was only peripherally aware of her surroundings. Her entire focus was on Jack.

Somehow, she got through the vows.

She and Jack exchanged rings.

And then the minister pronounced them man and wife.

Jack raised the front of Ashley's veil to kiss her, and his eyes widened a little, in obvious appreciation, when he saw that she'd forsworn her usual French braid for a shoulder-length style that stood out around her face.

She'd spent the morning at Cora's Curl and Twirl over in Indian Rock, Cora herself doing the honors, snipping and blow-drying and phoofing endlessly.

The wedding kiss was chaste, at least in appearance.

Up close and personal, it was nearly orgasmic.

"Ladies and gentlemen," the minister said triumphantly, raising his voice to be heard at the back of the church, "may I present Mr. and Mrs. Jack McKenzie!"

Cheers erupted.

The organ thundered.

Jack and Ashley hurried down the aisle, emerging into the sunlight, and were showered with birdseed and good wishes.

The reception, held at the bed-and-breakfast, was everything a bride could hope for. Even the weather cooperated; the snow had melted, the sun was out, the sky cloudless and heartbreakingly blue.

"I ordered a sunny day just for you," Jack whispered to her, as he helped her out of the limo in front of the house.

For the next two hours, the place was crammed to the walls with wedding guests. Pictures were taken, punch and cake were served. So many congratulatory hugs, kisses and handshakes came their way that Ashley began to wish the thing would *end* already.

She and Jack would spend their wedding night right there at home, although they were leaving on their honeymoon the next day.

The sky was beginning to darken toward twilight when the guests began to leave, one by one, couple by couple, and then in groups.

Bill and Abigail McKenzie and their large extended family would occupy all the guestrooms at the bed-and-breakfast, so they lingered, somewhat at loose ends until Brad diplomatically invited them out to Stone Creek Ranch, where the party would continue.

Good-byes were said.

Except for the caterers, already cleaning up, Melissa was the last to leave.

"I may never forgive you for this wretched dress," she told Ashley, tearing up.

"Maybe you'll get back at me one of these days," Ashley answered softly, as Jack moved away to give the twins room to say their farewells. Melissa planned to drive to Scottsdale that same night. "You'll be the bride, and I'll be the one who has to look like a giant parakeet."

Melissa huffed out a breath, shook her head. "I think you're safe from that horrid fate," she said wistfully. "I plan to throw myself into my career. Before you know it, I'll be a Supreme Court Justice, just as you said." She gave a wobbly little smile that didn't quite stick. "At least my memoirs will probably be interesting."

Ashley kissed her sister's cheek. "Take care," she said.

Melissa chuckled. "As soon as I swap this dress for a pair of jeans and a sweatshirt, and the heels for sneakers, I'll be golden."

With that, Melissa headed for the downstairs powder room, where she'd stashed her getaway clothes.

When she emerged, she was dressed for the road, and the ruffly yellow gown was wadded into a bundle under her right arm.

"Will you still love me if I toss this thing into the first Dumpster I see?" she quipped, as she and Ashley stood at the front door.

"I'll still love you," Ashley said, "no matter what."

Melissa gave a brave sniffle. "See you around, Mrs. McKenzie," she said.

And then she opened the front door, dashed across the porch and down the front steps, and along the walk. She got into her little red sports car, which looked too small to pull a trailer, tossed the offending bridesmaid's dress onto the passenger seat and waved.

Jack was standing right behind Ashley when she turned from closing the door, and he kissed her briefly on the mouth. "She's an O'Ballivan," he said. "She'll be all right."

Ashley nodded. Swallowed.

"The caterers will be out of here in a few minutes," Jack told her, with a twinkle. "I promised to overtip if they'd just kick it up a notch. Wouldn't you like to get out of that dress, beautiful as it is?"

She stood on tiptoe, kissed the cleft in her husband's chin. "I might need some help," she told him sweetly. "It has about a million buttons down the back."

Jack chuckled. "I'm just the man for the job," he said.

Mrs. Wiggins came, twitchy-tailed, out of the study, where she'd probably been hiding from the hubbub of the reception, batted playfully at the lace trim on the hem of Ashley's wedding gown.

"No you don't," she told the kitten, hoisting the little creature up so they were nose to nose, she and Mrs. Wiggins. "This dress is going to be an heirloom. Someday, another bride will wear it."

"Our daughter," Jack said, musing. "If she's as beautiful as her mother, every little boy under the age of five ought to be warned."

Ashley smiled, still holding Mrs. Wiggins. "Get rid of the caterers," she said, and headed for the stairs.

Barely a minute later, she was inside the room that had been hers alone, until today—not that she and Jack hadn't shared it every night since they got back from Chicago.

The last wintry light glowed at the windows, turning the antique lace curtains to gold. White rose petals covered the bed, and someone had laid a fire on the hearth, too.

Their suitcases stood just outside the closet door, packed and ready to go. Tomorrow at this time, she and Jack would be in Hawaii, soaking up a month of sunshine.

Ashley's heart quickened. She put a hand to her throat briefly, feeling strangely like a virgin, untouched, eager to be deflowered, and a little nervous at the prospect.

The room looked the same, and yet different, now that she and Jack were married.

*Married.* Not so long ago, she'd pretty much given up on marriage—and then Jack "McCall" had arrived by ambulance, looking for a place to heal.

So much had happened since then, some of it terrifying, most of it better than good.

Mrs. Wiggins leaped up onto a slipper chair near the fireplace and curled up for a long winter's snooze.

Carefully, Ashley removed the tiara that held her veil in place and set the mound of gossamer netting aside. She stood in front of the bureau mirror and fluffed out her hair with the fingers of both hands.

Her cheeks glowed, and so did her eyes.

The door opened softly, and Jack came into the room, no tuxedo jacket in evidence, unfastening his cuff links as he walked toward Ashley. Setting the cuff links aside on the dresser top, he took her into his arms, buried his hands in her hair, and kissed her thoroughly.

Ashley's knees melted, just as they always did.

Eventually, Jack tore his mouth from hers, turned her around, and began unfastening the buttons at the back of her dress. In the process, he bent to nibble at her skin as he bared it, leaving tiny trails of fire along her shoulder blades, her spine and finally the small of her back.

The dress fell in a pool at her feet, leaving her in her petticoat, bra, panty hose and high heels.

She shivered, not with fear or cold, but with eagerness. She wanted to give herself to Jack—as his wife.

But he left her, untucking his white dress shirt as he went. Crouched in front of the fireplace to light a blaze on the hearth.

Another blaze already burned inside Ashley.

Jack straightened, unfastened his cummerbund with a grin of relief, and tossed it aside. Started removing his shirt.

His eyes smoldered as he took Ashley in, slowly, his gaze traveling from her head to her feet and then back up again.

As if hypnotized, she unhooked her bra, let her breasts spill into Jack's full view. His eyes went wide as her nipples hardened, eager for his lips and tongue.

It seemed to take forever, this shedding of clothes, garment by garment, but finally they were both naked, and the fire snapped merrily in the grate, and Jack eased Ashley down onto the bed.

Because of her pregnancy—news they had yet to share with the rest of the family, because it was too new and too precious—his lovemaking was poignantly gentle.

He parted her legs, bent her knees, ran his hands from there to her ankles.

Ashley murmured, knowing what he was going to do, needing it, needing him.

He nuzzled her, parted the curls at the juncture of

her thighs, and his sigh of contented anticipation reverberated through her entire system.

She tangled her fingers in his hair, held him close.

He chuckled against her flesh, and she moaned.

And then he took her full in his mouth, now nibbling, now suckling, and Ashley arched her back and cried out in surrender.

"Not so fast," Jack murmured, between teasing flicks of his tongue. "Let it happen slowly, Mrs. McKenzie."

"I—I don't think I—can wait—"

Jack turned his head, dragged his lips along the length of her inner thigh, nipped at her lightly as he crossed to the other side. "You can wait," he told her.

"*Please,* Jack," she half sobbed.

He slid his hands under her bare bottom, lifted her high, and partook of her with lusty appreciation.

She exploded almost instantaneously, her body flexing powerfully, once, twice, a third time.

And then she fell, sighing, back to the bed.

He was kissing her lower belly, where their baby was growing, warm and safe and sheltered.

"I love you, Jack," Ashley said, weak with the force of her releases.

He turned her to lie full length on the bed, poised himself over her, took her in a slow, even stroke.

"Always have," she added, trying to catch her breath and failing. "Always will."

# EPILOGUE

*December 24*
*Stone Creek, Arizona*

JACK MCKENZIE STOOD next to his daughter's crib, gazing down at her in wonder. Katie—named for his grandmother—was nearly three months old now, and she looked more like Ashley every day. Although the baby was too young to understand Christmas, they'd hung up a stocking for her, just the same.

The door of his and Ashley's bedroom opened quietly behind him.

"The doctor is on the phone," she said quietly.

Jack turned, took her in, marveled anew, the way he did every time he saw his wife, that it was possible to go to sleep at night loving a woman so much, and wake up loving her even more.

"Okay," he said.

She approached, held out the cell phone he'd left downstairs when he brought Katie up to bed. They'd been putting the finishing touches on the Christmas tree by the front windows, he and Ashley, and the place was decorated to the hilt, though there would be no paying guests over the holidays.

Busy with a new baby, not to mention a husband, Ashley had decided to take at least a year off from running the bed-and-breakfast. She still cooked like a French chef, which was probably why he'd gained ten pounds since they'd gotten married, and she was practically an expert on the computer.

So far, she didn't seem to miss running a business.

She'd been baking all day, since half the family would be there for a special Christmas Eve supper, after the early services at the church.

They'd stayed home, waiting for the call.

He took the cell phone, cleared his throat, said hello.

Ashley moved close to him, leaned against his side, somehow supporting him at the same time. Her head rested, fragrant, against his shoulder.

He kissed her crown, drew in the scent of her hair.

"This is Dr. Schaefer," a man said, as if Jack needed to be told. He and Ashley had been bracing themselves for this call ever since Jack's last visit to the clinic up in Flagstaff, a few days before, where they'd run the latest series of tests.

"Yes," Jack said, his voice raspy. Wrapping one arm around Ashley's waist. He felt fine, but that didn't mean he was out of danger.

And there was so very much at stake.

"All the results are normal, Mr. McKenzie," he heard Dr. Schaefer say, as though chanting the words through an underwater tunnel. "I think we can safely assume the marrow transplant was a complete success, and so were the antirejection medications."

Jack closed his eyes. "Normal," he repeated, for Ashley's benefit as well as his own.

She squeezed him hard.

"Thanks, Doctor," he said.

A smile warmed the other man's voice. "Have a

Merry Christmas," the doctor said. "Not that you need to be told."

"You, too," Jack said. "And thanks again."

He closed the phone, tucked it into the pocket of his shirt, turned to take Ashley into his arms.

"Guess what, Mrs. McKenzie," he said. "We have a future together. You and me and Katie. A long one, I expect."

She beamed up at him, her eyes wet.

Downstairs, the doorbell chimed.

Ashley squeezed Jack's hand once, crossed to the crib, and tucked Katie's blanket in around her.

"I suppose they'll let themselves in," Jack said, watching her with the same grateful amazement he always felt.

Ashley smiled, and came back to his side, and they went down the stairs together, hand in hand.

Brad and Meg, with Carly and Mac and the new baby, Eva, stood in the entryway, smiling, snow dusting the shoulders of their coats and gleaming in their hair.

Olivia and Tanner arrived only moments later, with the twins, who were walking now, and Sophie.

"Where's Melissa?" Olivia asked, looking around.

"She'll be here soon," Ashley said. "She called about an hour ago—there was a lot of traffic leaving Scottsdale."

Ashley looked up at Jack, and they silently agreed to wait until everyone had arrived before sharing the good news about his test results.

The men spent the next few minutes carrying brightly wrapped packages in from the trucks parked out front, while the women and smaller children headed for the kitchen, where a savory supper was warming in the ovens.

Ashley and Meg and Olivia carried plates and silverware into the dining room, while Carly and Sophie kept the smaller children entertained.

A horn tooted outside, in the snowy driveway, and then Melissa hurried through the back door.

"It's cold out there!" she cried, spreading her arms for the rush of small children, wanting hugs. "And I think I saw Santa Claus just as I was pulling into town."

Soon, they were all gathered in the dining room, the grand tree in the parlor in full view through the double doors.

"I have news," Melissa said, just as Jack was about to offer a toast.

Everyone waited.

"I'm coming back to Stone Creek," Melissa told them all. "I'm about to become the new county prosecutor!"

The family cheered, and when some of the noise subsided, Ashley and Jack rose from their chairs, each with an arm around the other.

"The test results?" Olivia asked, in a whisper. Then, reading Jack's and Ashley's expressions, a joyous smile broke over her face. "They were good?"

"Better than good," Ashley answered.

Supper was almost cold by the time the cheering was over, but nobody noticed.

It was Christmas Eve, after all.

And they were together, at home in Stone Creek.

*  *  *  *  *

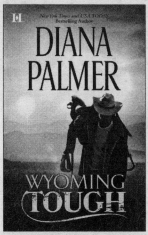

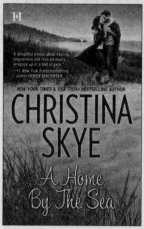

# REQUEST YOUR
# FREE BOOKS!

## 2 FREE NOVELS
## FROM THE ROMANCE COLLECTION
## PLUS 2 FREE GIFTS!

**YES!** Please send me 2 FREE novels from the Romance Collection and my 2 FREE gifts (gifts are worth about $10). After receiving them, if I don't wish to receive any more books, I can return the shipping statement marked "cancel." If I don't cancel, I will receive 4 brand-new novels every month and be billed just $5.99 per book in the U.S. or $6.49 per book in Canada. That's a saving of at least 25% off the cover price. It's quite a bargain! Shipping and handling is just 50¢ per book in the U.S. and 75¢ per book in Canada.* I understand that accepting the 2 free books and gifts places me under no obligation to buy anything. I can always return a shipment and cancel at any time. Even if I never buy another book, the two free books and gifts are mine to keep forever.

194/394 MDN FELQ

| Name | (PLEASE PRINT) | |
|---|---|---|

| Address | | Apt. # |
|---|---|---|

| City | State/Prov. | Zip/Postal Code |
|---|---|---|

Signature (if under 18, a parent or guardian must sign)

### Mail to the **Reader Service:**
**IN U.S.A.:** P.O. Box 1867, Buffalo, NY 14240-1867
**IN CANADA:** P.O. Box 609, Fort Erie, Ontario L2A 5X3

Not valid for current subscribers to the Romance Collection
or the Romance/Suspense Collection.

**Want to try two free books from another line?**
**Call 1-800-873-8635 or visit www.ReaderService.com.**

* Terms and prices subject to change without notice. Prices do not include applicable taxes. Sales tax applicable in N.Y. Canadian residents will be charged applicable taxes. Offer not valid in Quebec. This offer is limited to one order per household. All orders subject to credit approval. Credit or debit balances in a customer's account(s) may be offset by any other outstanding balance owed by or to the customer. Please allow 4 to 6 weeks for delivery. Offer available while quantities last.

**Your Privacy**—The Reader Service is committed to protecting your privacy. Our Privacy Policy is available online at www.ReaderService.com or upon request from the Reader Service.

We make a portion of our mailing list available to reputable third parties that offer products we believe may interest you. If you prefer that we not exchange your name with third parties, or if you wish to clarify or modify your communication preferences, please visit us at www.ReaderService.com/consumerschoice or write to us at Reader Service Preference Service, P.O. Box 9062, Buffalo, NY 14269. Include your complete name and address.

ROMII

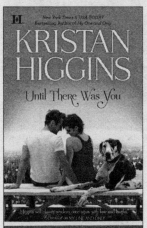

# LINDA LAEL MILLER

| | | | | |
|---|---|---|---|---|
| 77623 | THE McKETTRICK LEGEND | __ $7.99 U.S. | __ | $9.99 CAN. |
| 77600 | THE CREED LEGACY | __ $7.99 U.S. | __ | $9.99 CAN. |
| 77580 | CREED'S HONOR | __ $7.99 U.S. | __ | $9.99 CAN. |
| 77563 | McKETTRICK'S PRIDE | __ $7.99 U.S. | __ | $9.99 CAN. |
| 77562 | McKETTRICK'S LUCK | __ $7.99 U.S. | __ | $9.99 CAN. |
| 77561 | MONTANA CREEDS: LOGAN | __ $7.99 U.S. | __ | $9.99 CAN. |
| 77555 | A CREED IN STONE CREEK | __ $7.99 U.S. | __ | $9.99 CAN. |
| 77502 | THE CHRISTMAS BRIDES | __ $7.99 U.S. | __ | $9.99 CAN. |
| 77492 | McKETTRICK'S CHOICE | __ $7.99 U.S. | __ | $9.99 CAN. |
| 77446 | McKETTRICKS OF TEXAS: AUSTIN | __ $7.99 U.S. | __ | $9.99 CAN. |
| 77441 | McKETTRICKS OF TEXAS: GARRETT | __ $7.99 U.S. | __ | $9.99 CAN. |
| 77436 | McKETTRICKS OF TEXAS: TATE | __ $7.99 U.S. | __ | $9.99 CAN. |
| 77388 | THE BRIDEGROOM | __ $7.99 U.S. | __ | $8.99 CAN. |
| 77364 | MONTANA CREEDS: TYLER | __ $7.99 U.S. | __ | $7.99 CAN. |
| 77358 | MONTANA CREEDS: DYLAN | __ $7.99 U.S. | __ | $7.99 CAN. |
| 77330 | THE RUSTLER | __ $7.99 U.S. | __ | $7.99 CAN. |
| 77296 | A WANTED MAN | __ $7.99 U.S. | __ | $7.99 CAN. |
| 77200 | DEADLY GAMBLE | __ $7.99 U.S. | __ | $9.50 CAN. |
| 77198 | THE MAN FROM STONE CREEK | __ $7.99 U.S. | __ | $9.50 CAN. |
| 77194 | McKETTRICK'S HEART | __ $7.99 U.S. | __ | $9.50 CAN. |

*(limited quantities available)*

| | |
|---|---|
| TOTAL AMOUNT | $ _____ |
| POSTAGE & HANDLING | $ _____ |
| ($1.00 FOR 1 BOOK, 50¢ for each additional) | |
| APPLICABLE TAXES* | $ _____ |
| TOTAL PAYABLE | $ _____ |

*(check or money order—please do not send cash)*

To order, complete this form and send it, along with a check or money order for the total above, payable to HQN Books, to: **In the U.S.:** 3010 Walden Avenue, P.O. Box 9077, Buffalo, NY 14269-9077; **In Canada:** P.O. Box 636, Fort Erie, Ontario, L2A 5X3.

Name: _____

Address: _____ City: _____

State/Prov.: _____ Zip/Postal Code: _____

Account Number (if applicable): _____

075 CSAS

*New York residents remit applicable sales taxes.
*Canadian residents remit applicable GST and provincial taxes.

HQN™ | HARLEQUIN®
www.Harlequin.com

PHLLM1111BL